A Fire at The Exhibition

A Fire at the Exhibition

A Lady Hardcastle Mystery

T E KINSEY

THOMAS & MERCER

Published by Thomas & Mercer, Seattle

www.apub.com

Amazon, the Amazon logo, and Thomas & Mercer are trademarks of Amazon.com, Inc., or its affiliates.

ISBN-13: 9781662512940
eISBN: 9781662512933

Cover design by Tom Sanderson

Cover illustration by Jelly London

Printed in the United States of America

A Fire at the Exhibition

Chapter One

It was May Day, and Lady Hardcastle and I had walked down the lane immediately after breakfast to join the crowd that was gathering on the village green. We were all there to watch the local children dance around the maypole, which had been painstakingly wrapped in ribbons of different colours in an elaborate woven pattern. The atmosphere was friendly and festive, with an air of relaxed anticipation of the fun to come.

Sir Hector and Lady Farley-Stroud had hailed us as we arrived, and we stood with them as Miss Rossiter, the new schoolmistress, attempted to herd her charges into the correct positions around the beribboned pole.

'And did you rise early to wash your face in the May Day dew?' asked Lady Farley-Stroud.

'I rise early to wash my face in the dew every day,' I said with a smile.

Lady Farley-Stroud regarded me quizzically.

'I rather think you might be teasing me, m'dear,' she said with a smile of her own.

'Of course she is, Gertie,' said Lady Hardcastle. 'Take no notice. She's been in a giddy mood all week.'

Sir Hector let out his joyous bark of a laugh.

'I believed you, m'dear,' he said. 'Has to be somethin' to account for your youthful complexion, what?'

'Clean living, fresh air and honest labour,' I said. 'I also have a painting in the attic.'

'Like Dorian Gray?' said Lady Farley-Stroud.

'No, it's a picture of Cardiff Docks. Climbing up to the attic a couple of times a week to dust it provides healthy exercise.'

Sir Hector laughed again and Lady Farley-Stroud shook her head indulgently.

'I remember when you came to the village a timid and deferential lady's maid, young Florence,' she said. 'You wouldn't have said boo to a goose when I first met you. And now look at you.'

Lady Hardcastle snorted derisively.

'There's many a terrified goose who would argue with you there, Gertie dear,' she said. 'She's not nearly so demure as she'd have you believe.' She craned her neck for a better view of the maypole preparations. 'I believe our little treasures are in place, so I shall have to leave you for a moment.'

Lady Hardcastle had been persuaded – though, in truth, little actual persuasion had been required – to accompany the maypole dance on her newly acquired accordion.

She pushed politely through the throng and took up her place beside Miss Rossiter, where she hefted the instrument into position on her chest. Once comfortable, she squeezed the bellows to produce a jolly chord in a major key. It sounded like a fanfare.

The children, well rehearsed, each took hold of their assigned ribbon and faced in the appropriate direction, ready to unweave them as they danced.

Lady Hardcastle struck up one of the jaunty hornpipes she'd been practising for the past couple of weeks, and the children began their dance.

'I'm so glad we still have these traditions,' said Lady Farley-Stroud. 'Don't the little ones look enchanting?'

The little ones did, indeed, look enchanting, as they skipped and hopped unselfconsciously around the maypole.

'I gather your pal is to be Queen of the May,' said Sir Hector as the children danced.

I turned away from the dancing children. 'Daisy? She's rather pleased about it, too. Apparently it's her first time.'

'It is,' said Lady Farley-Stroud. 'She used to have . . . well, one doesn't like to malign the gel, but she had a reputation. We couldn't possibly make a gel like that May Queen before now.'

'She was a little flighty, I agree. But she's grown up a lot since we first met her. She'll make a fine queen.'

'D'you know what I miss?' said Sir Hector, apparently no longer interested in Daisy Spratt's regnal virtues.

'No, Sir Hector,' I said. 'What do you miss?'

'Jack o' the Green.'

'Oh, Hector,' scolded Lady Farley-Stroud impatiently. 'You favour anything that involves drunkenness and tomfoolery. We're well rid of it. Happy, dancing children and pretty Queens of the May, that's what we need.'

'If you say so, my little plum duff. If you say so.'

It took another few minutes for the children to finish their dance and completely unwrap the pole. Lady Hardcastle ended her hornpipe with another fanfare flourish, and the smiling villagers applauded. The ribbons were fastened to stakes in the ground to create something that resembled a multicoloured tree.

The children formed up in neat ranks, clutching sticks and hoops – each decorated with flowers and yet more ribbons – and joined the procession that was to lead Daisy, Queen of the May, to her coronation.

Lady Hardcastle rejoined us, her accordion still strapped to her front. It wheezed asthmatically as she walked.

'I say. Brava, m'dear,' said Lady Farley-Stroud. 'You were absolutely splendid. I'd never have believed you only took it up a few weeks ago.'

'You weren't in our drawing room night after night as she picked her way through a selection of reels, hornpipes and jigs. You'd believe it then.'

'Well, I for one admire your talent and application, m'dear. Takes hard work to master a musical instrument.'

'Oh, I admire her, too,' I said. 'Please don't misunderstand me. It's just—'

'She's quite right, Gertie dear,' said Lady Hardcastle. 'Even I reached the point where I was ready to build one of Mr Wells's time machines, so that I might travel back and distract whichever blackguard had written the Sailor's Hornpipe long enough to prevent him dreaming up the wretched tune. One can only imagine how it must have been for poor Flo as she listened to me stumbling ineptly over it time and again.'

'I *love* the Sailor's Hornpipe,' said Sir Hector, gleefully. 'You should have played that, m'dear. Diddle-um-pum-pum . . .' He danced a surprisingly agile little jig as he hummed the tune.

Lady Farley-Stroud tutted.

'I think it's time for us to make our way to the coronation. Come along, Jolly Jack Tar.'

We followed the villagers to the centre of the green, where a throne bedecked with blossoms and boughs had been set on a small dais. A dais for Daisy.

The queen herself was led to the throne by her two handmaidens – our cook, Blodwen Jones, and Cissy Slocomb from the dairy – where she was crowned with a circlet of flowers and presented with a willow sceptre bound with still more delicate blossoms. I should like to be able to supply the names of the blooms, but my horticultural knowledge still extends only to 'green leaves' and 'pretty flowers'. It shall have to suffice to know that the leaves were of a luscious and lustrous green, and that the variety and beauty of the flowers was enough to make even the most jaded and cynical soul smile in joy and wonder at the glory of Nature's splendour.

The ceremony was a short one, but the celebrations were far from over. There was food to be eaten and drink to be drunk. The May Day committee had prepared a feast for the beginning of summer, of sandwiches, pies and cold meats. Meanwhile Old Joe, landlord of the Dog and Duck, had donated several barrels of Mattick's Cider to keep the revels properly lubricated.

We caught up with the newly crowned Queen of the May as she stepped down from her throne.

I gave her a warm smile. 'Well done, Dais.'

Daisy grinned. '"Your Majesty", if you please. I'm the blinkin' queen, I am.'

'Quite right, too,' said Sir Hector. 'Congratulations, Your Majesty.'

'Thank you kindly, Sir Hector,' said Daisy with a regal inclination of the head. Her crown slipped over her eyes and she pushed it up with a tut. 'I don't know how they does it, they royals. I can't even keep a ring of flowers in place – they has to cope with gurt big 'eavy crowns.'

'They have special training, dear,' said Lady Hardcastle. 'Latin, French, small talk and crown-wearing before lunch every day. Afternoons are spent practising cutting ribbons, launching ships, and waving from a moving carriage.'

Daisy and Sir Hector chuckled. Lady Farley-Stroud tried to smile but I could see she was struggling not to appear too scandalized by Lady Hardcastle's irreverent commentary on our beloved King and his family. Time to change the subject.

'How are the preparations for the art exhibition coming along?' I asked.

'Very well indeed, thank you, m'dear,' said Lady Farley-Stroud, clearly grateful to be on less disrespectful ground. 'We have all the villagers' pieces – thank you for your lovely paintings, Emily dear – and the exhibits from the Chipping Bevington museum will be arriving on Friday.'

'Is you-know-who still willing to display the you-know-what?' asked Lady Hardcastle.

'It is to be the star exhibit,' said Lady Farley-Stroud. 'Which is just as well, really – we've already alerted the local press.'

Much had been made in the local – and, indeed, the national – press about the Littleton Cotterell Art Exhibition's main attraction: Basil Westbury's book.

Westbury himself was a genial businessman who lived nearby. He did something inexplicably complex but astonishingly lucrative in an engineering workshop in the centre of Bristol, and lived with his wife in the house just outside Chipping Bevington formerly owned by James and Ida Seddon of the shipping agents Seddon, Seddon and Seddon. The Westburys were a charming couple, and Lady Hardcastle and I had been invited to a party at their new home shortly after they moved to the area.

Unlike the previous occupants of the house, they wore their wealth lightly and were largely unostentatious in their habits, with one major exception. Mr Westbury, it turned out, was obsessed by William Shakespeare, and indulged his passion by collecting everything Shakespeare-related that he could lay his hands on. His study, which he proudly showed off to all his guests, was a veritable shrine to the Bard of Avon. The walls were lined with valuable editions of the plays and poems. There were portraits of Shakespeare, busts of Shakespeare, and novelty souvenirs of Shakespeare – some almost as old as the great man himself. There was a fragment of wood in a satin-lined box on one shelf, accompanied by a wax-sealed, formally witnessed declaration that it was from one of the beams of Shakespeare's own house in Stratford-upon-Avon.

All of which marked Mr Westbury as charmingly eccentric, but not especially worthy of further examination or comment.

Until he bought *the book*.

Two years before moving to Littleton Cotterell, Basil Westbury had commissioned Dowers-Stillwell, the world-renowned bookbinders of London, to produce a wholly remarkable, one-of-a-kind copy of the complete works of Shakespeare. The binding was set with over a thousand specially cut jewels, and was made from more than five thousand individual pieces of carefully selected leather, skilfully inlaid to depict characters and themes from the plays and poems. That alone would have made it a magnificent work of art, but it was raised to a higher level still by the one hundred square feet of gold leaf that had been painstakingly applied to the inlaid and embossed leather. Not only were the front and back covers decorated, but also the insides of the boards (known, I later learned, as 'doublures') and the book's thick spine. It was thirteen inches wide by sixteen inches tall, and its value, though not officially disclosed, had been estimated to be in excess of one thousand pounds.

Its creation had been enthusiastically reported by the press at home and abroad, and the Shakespearean devotee who had commissioned it became a minor celebrity for a time.

Lady Farley-Stroud had asked Westbury if he would be prepared to display his newly delivered book at the Littleton Cotterell Art Exhibition, and he had gleefully acceded. He could think of nothing more wonderful than showing off his new possession. So excited was he, in fact, that not only had he agreed to allow the committee to display the book, he had offered to cover the cost of the insurance himself. His insurers had insisted that a condition of the cover was that their own security guards would accompany the book while it was on display, and that this round-the-clock security would attract a substantial additional charge. Even then he hadn't demurred – he wanted as many people as possible to experience its beauty before he took it back to his Shakespeare shrine.

'I'm looking forward to the local exhibits more,' I said. 'I'm very keen to see what our talented friends can do. But I can't deny I'm fascinated to lay my humble mortal eyes upon the wonder of *the book*.'

Lady Hardcastle laughed.

'It has been rather enthusiastically over-promoted by the popular press, hasn't it? In rare moments of self-doubt, I, too, have wondered if we're deserving of having such a marvel in our midst.'

'You're both utterly beastly,' said Lady Farley-Stroud. 'Basil Westbury is a charming and generous man, and his magnificent book will draw the crowds and put our little exhibition on the map.'

'It will, dear,' said Lady Hardcastle. 'As it deserves to be.'

'Yes. Well. Thank you,' said Lady Farley-Stroud. 'But you can make up for your mockery. I wonder . . . are you both free on Friday morning? I could do with a couple of pairs of trustworthy hands to hang the more expensive exhibits.'

'Hmm,' said Lady Hardcastle. 'Friday. Well, the tea house in Chipping always has lovely cream cakes on a Friday. And there's a matinee in Bristol I've been hoping to catch . . .'

Lady Farley-Stroud looked crestfallen.

'You silly goose,' said Lady Hardcastle. 'Of course we'll help, won't we, Flo.'

'Happy to,' I said. 'I can't paint for toffee but I have a keen eye for unevenly hung pictures and skewy sculptures.'

'Thank you so very much, m'dears. Would you meet us at the village hall at ten sharp?' Lady Farley-Stroud looked around. 'I'm so sorry, must dash. Hector! Hector, where are you going?'

Sir Hector had seen his chance and had made a break for the cider, with his wife now in hot pursuit.

'Would you care for some luncheon, Your Majesty?' Lady Hardcastle asked Daisy as we watched our friends disappear across the green.

'I thought you'd never ask,' said Daisy. 'I's famished. It's 'ungry work bein' the queen, you know.'

◆ ◆ ◆

Thursday passed largely without incident. The local badgers had been rootling in the flowerbeds again, but Jed Halfpenny – our jobbing gardener – repaired the damage in no time. Once he had gone, I explained to the flowers that it was the risk they took when they accepted free board and lodging in our garden. I think they understood.

On Friday morning I was gossiping in the kitchen with Miss Jones, and our housekeeper, Edna Gibson, as I buttered some toast for Lady Hardcastle.

Edna was still resisting the job title of 'housekeeper'. She'd worked as a housekeeper before but thought it was too much trouble. She much preferred to be a housemaid, she said, but she was so much more than that and she was just going to have to lump it. Housekeeper or not, though, she absolutely refused to be known as Mrs Gibson.

'Too formal for the likes of me,' she said.

'But you call me Miss Armstrong,' I said.

'That's different, you's a lady's maid. They's always Miss.'

'Housekeepers are always Mrs. Like cooks.'

'But I'm Miss Jones,' said the cook.

'And I i'n't no housekeeper,' said the housekeeper.

'We all agreed that Mrs Jones doesn't suit you,' I said. 'And you have it your way, Edna. But you deserve more respect for the excellent work you do.'

'As long as it don't involve me bein' called Mrs Gibson, you can call my job what you likes, I s'pose.'

'Excellent,' I said. 'You can have your new visiting cards printed at once.'

'That would be summat, wouldn't it? Me with a visiting card.'

'You'd be the talk of the village.'

'As long as it didn't say "Mrs Gibson". Mrs Gibson is my Dan's mother, and she's a right one – I don't want to be mistaken for her.'

There was a shuffle of house slippers at the kitchen door.

'Good morning,' said Lady Hardcastle with a yawn.

Edna and Miss Jones both *Mornin', m'lady*-ed.

'Lovely to see you,' I said. 'I was just waiting for your coffee to brew so I could bring up your starter breakfast. I have your toast.'

I handed her the plate and she looked at it in sleepy confusion.

'Take it through to the morning room and I'll be with you in a minute,' I said.

She plodded obediently off.

'You go with her, my lover,' said Edna. 'She i'n't very good at mornin's. I'll bring the coffee through in a minute. You want any toast yourself?'

'No, I'll wait for breakfast proper, I think. Thank you, Mrs Edna.'

She laughed and flicked at me with a tea towel, but I was already out the door.

Lady Hardcastle, meanwhile, was sitting at the table in the morning room, propping up her head with her hand on her cheek. She smiled as I entered.

'Good morning, Flo dear,' she said wanly. 'As they say round these parts, 'ow bist?'

'Passing well, thank you,' I said. 'Are you sure you wouldn't rather wake up more slowly in bed?'

'Nightmare,' she said with a shake of the head. 'I woke with a start and decided I'd rather be down here among friends than risk drifting back to rejoin the horrors.'

'The usual?'

'I'm afraid so. Still, I'm up now.'

During her career as a spy, Lady Hardcastle had faced the threat of imminent death with infuriating good humour for almost all her adult life, and with no apparent ill effects. She had been hunted, attacked, imprisoned, and tortured with imaginative cruelty more times than either of us could count. But it was not until 1908, when we began our short-lived retirement in Littleton Cotterell, that she had suffered her first, real, life-threatening wound. She took a stray bullet to the stomach during the murder investigation we unexpectedly found ourselves embroiled in, and it was this accidental injury that still gave her nightmares. When we talked about it, it was the arbitrariness of it that angered her most. There had been no intention on the part of her almost-killer to do her harm – the shot, if it had been intentional at all, had been aimed at someone else. Blind chance had directed the bullet to her abdomen, and there had been nothing she could say or do to predict or prevent it. And still the events played out in her dreams as her mind continued to rage at the unfairness of it.

I never told her that the same event haunted my own dreams. It was my mistimed kick that had shifted the gun's aim, but it seemed altogether too self-indulgent to seek sympathy for my own nightmares when she had been the one who suffered the consequences.

She noticed my look of concern and frowned.

'If you're going to get maudlin, I shall reconsider my decision and head straight back to bed,' she said. 'I came down for cheery company, not sympathy and hand-holding.'

'Right you are, then,' I said. 'Pull yourself together, you miserable old bat.'

'That's more like it. Now, where's my coffee?'

'It's right here, m'lady,' said Edna as she entered carrying a tray. 'I brought you some toast anyway, Miss Armstrong. I knows how temptin' someone else's hot buttered toast can be.'

She set the tray down and left.

'Thank you, Edna,' said Lady Hardcastle and I in chorus.

Then we tucked in, and discussed our plans for the day.

◆ ◆ ◆

At 'ten sharp', exactly as ordered, Lady Hardcastle and I presented ourselves for duty at the village hall.

The hall's roof had been badly damaged by fire the previous summer, and the rebuilding work had been slow, delayed first by the unusually hot summer, then by the cold, wet winter. By mid-April, though, the repairs had been completed, inspected, and judged to be fit for the needs of the village for years to come.

Guided, as they always were, by Lady Farley-Stroud's vision, the village hall committee had decided that the grand reopening would be a celebration not just of the hall, but of the village itself. And what better way to celebrate, they had said, than by sharing the wealth of the villagers' collective artistic talents? There had been a few dissenting voices – some members of the committee had insisted that the best way to celebrate would be by having an actual celebration, preferably with abundant food and drink. But Lady Farley-Stroud's view – as Lady Farley-Stroud's view so often did – prevailed, and an art exhibition had been organized.

The bulk of the show was to be made up of villagers' own work, and we had been promised sketches, watercolours and oils, as well as photographs, collages and even sculptures. Those who felt they lacked the necessary talent to produce work of their own had been encouraged to share any paintings or objects from their homes if they thought others might appreciate them.

The museum at Chipping Bevington had offered to lend a few local pieces from its collection to augment this section of the show, and after just one additional meeting with Lady Farley-Stroud had amended the offer to 'a few *important* local pieces'.

The hall, as we entered, smelled of sawdust, plaster, putty and paint. The walls were bright, even in the wan light of the dull day that dribbled through the newly glazed windows. The air was filled with the energizing buzz of happy industry, with Lady Farley-Stroud's volunteers already hard at work arranging the villagers' pieces under her watchful eye.

'I think Mrs Bland's wonderful portrait of her dog—' said Lady Farley-Stroud.

'Hamlet, m'lady,' said Mrs Gardner, secretary of the embroidery society.

'What did I say?'

'You didn't, m'lady. I was just sayin' as how the vicar's wife's dog is called Hamlet. He's a Great Dane.'

'Quite. Well, Mrs Bland's portrait of Hamlet might look better over here, next to Mrs Stitch's sketch of her pet cat, don't you think? All pets together and all that.'

Mrs Stitch was Mrs Gardner's best friend and the treasurer of the gardening society. Apparently I was the only one who found their respective roles in any way worthy of comment.

But while Mrs Stitch's skills as a horticulturalist were beyond question, her artistic abilities were, though joyously enthusiastic, somewhat more rudimentary. This was intended to be a celebration, not an opportunity for sniggering, and I thought it would be unfair to place Mrs Stitch's cheerfully amateurish sketch next to Jagruti Bland's professional-looking oil portrait of her absurdly large dog.

'If you'd welcome a non-artist's opinion,' I said, gently, 'perhaps the cat might be better on the other side there. If we put it on the wall behind the knitting society's jumpers and scarves, it will look as though Mr Bumble is playing with the yarn.'

'Minnie's cat is called Mr Bumble,' said Mrs Gardner, helpfully.

'I surmised as much,' said Lady Farley-Stroud. 'And thank you, Florence, I think your non-artist's idea is a splendid one. It will add a touch of charm and whimsy to the knitters' work. Goodness knows it needs it.'

I smiled my acknowledgement of her thanks, and stepped aside so they could rearrange the exhibits.

'Your place in heaven is assured, dear,' said Lady Hardcastle as we strolled around the hall, admiring the nascent exhibition.

'I don't know about that,' I said. 'I harbour some terribly wicked thoughts.'

'Don't we all. Gracious me, even the most stout-hearted among us would have a fainting fit if they could see the inside of my head.'

'I can well believe it. You're a disgrace at the best of times.'

'Well, quite. But you did a good thing there, tiny servant.'

'One tries to be kind. On the outside, at least.'

Lady Farley-Stroud had noticed our aimless meandering and was heading our way at full steam.

'I'm sorry to leave you ladies unemployed,' she said. 'I had hoped the museum's delivery would be here by now.'

'That's quite all right,' said Lady Hardcastle. 'We were just admiring the display. We have a very talented village.'

'We do, don't we,' said Lady Farley-Stroud, beaming with almost maternal pride. 'And your pieces look especially wonderful. Thank you.'

Lady Hardcastle had three pictures on display. One was a watercolour, painted entirely from memory, depicting the Chinese city at Shanghai. There was another watercolour study, this time of the busy port at Calcutta, painted while we waited to board our ship home to England in 1901. And finally a picture in oils of Park Street and the cathedral in Bristol, painted a few months earlier from a photograph I had taken when we were in town one day.

'I'm glad you like them, dear,' said Lady Hardcastle. 'I do so enjoy painting. I ought to devote more time to it.'

'You have a rare gift, m'dear,' said Lady Farley-Stroud. 'But you really don't mind?'

'Mind what?'

'Having nothing to do. What with the delayed delivery and all, I worry you might think I have dragged you here under false pretences.'

'Have no fear, Gertie dear. I'm always happy to turn up for a job where there's nothing actually to do. I can indulge my natural indolence while basking in the self-satisfied glow of having conscientiously volunteered my non-existent services in the first place.'

Lady Farley-Stroud let out a bark of a laugh uncannily like her husband's. Several of the more timid volunteers looked round in alarm.

'We shall have you busy enough, Emily, don't you worry,' she said. 'Busy enough indeed.'

We were standing beside a wooden plinth.

'This is rather splendid,' I said. 'What's going here?'

It was a square column of pale, waxed wood, about three and a half feet tall and perhaps a little over a foot square, topped with a very sturdy glass-sided cabinet. The cabinet was perhaps three or four inches larger all round than the plinth upon which it stood, and a little over a foot high. The sides of the plinth had been carved with a subtle pattern of interwoven vines – enough to add interest and texture without distracting from what was obviously intended to be the main attraction: whatever was going to lie upon the angled stand in the case at the top.

'It is, isn't it. Charley Hill made it for us. He oversaw the roof repairs and made all the marvellous panelling for the walls as well. Each panel is removable, you know. Hill said it might suffer a little damage from time to time in a place like this, so he made it so individual sections can be taken out and repaired without having to dismantle the whole thing. He's an ingenious man.'

'He certainly is,' I agreed.

'But this magnificent thing he built in his spare time. I told him he could earn a handsome living as a cabinetmaker, but he insists he gets more satisfaction from his carpentry and joinery work. "I likes makin' places for people to live and work, m'lady," he said.'

'He's very skilled,' I said. 'But what . . . ?' I gestured at the empty glass case.

'Oh, sorry, m'dear, ramblin' on as usual. It's for Basil Westbury's book.'

'Ah, yes. Of course it is.'

Neither the book nor its guards had arrived – they weren't due until the following morning, just before the exhibition opened – but the plinth was ready, and it looked to me like a very suitable temporary home for one of the world's most famous books.

I was about to ask more questions about the security arrangements but Lady Farley-Stroud was distracted by the sound of grinding wheels and the clip-clopping of a heavy horse's hooves outside, as a large wagon drew up at the hall.

'That's our delivery, I'd wager,' said Lady Farley-Stroud. 'Come on, ladies, let's see what treasures they've sent us.'

At midday on Saturday, the fourth of May 1912, when the farm labourers had knocked off for the weekend and the local businesses had closed, almost the entire population of Littleton Cotterell and the surrounding villages had gathered outside the village hall.

Queen Daisy's dais had been repurposed as a bunting-bedecked platform from which Lady Farley-Stroud praised the extraordinary efforts of the villagers in raising money for the repairs to the hall, and the wonderful work of the craftsmen who had carried out those repairs. When the applause died down, the mayor of Chipping Bevington stepped up and welcomed us all to the inaugural Littleton Cotterell Art Exhibition.

I looked to Lady Hardcastle and raised an eyebrow.

'My thoughts exactly,' she said. 'Inaugural? Let's wait to see how this one goes before we commit to doing it all again.'

There was a polite and orderly stampede for the doors, and we all filed in.

The hall, of course, was horribly overcrowded. Far too little thought had been given to the possibility that if the entire village turned up to the opening ceremony, then the entire village would want to get in to see the exhibition.

Fortunately we had been able to take a good look round the day before, and were already well acquainted with *Mop and Bucket*, a still-life watercolour painted by Mrs Grove, the vicar's housekeeper. We had already seen Dr Fitzsimmons's charcoal anatomy sketches and an expressionist work in pastels by Her Majesty Queen Daisy entitled *Old Joe at the Bar*.

We had carefully hung Chipping Bevington Museum's series of oil-on-canvas landscapes depicting the Severn Valley as seen from the hill to the west of the village, and I had been personally responsible for nearly dropping a Bronze Age beaker that had been found close to a burial mound near Woodworthy. It had already been reconstructed once, so I was certain the experts could easily rebuild it a second time. I was nevertheless relieved that years of training in Chinese fighting arts had honed my reactions sufficiently that I was able to catch the prehistoric pottery before we needed to test those experts' skills once more.

As predicted, the Westbury Shakespeare proved to be the biggest draw – it's not every day that people get the chance to see a one-thousand-pound book, after all – and we were unable even to get close to it. This unevenness of crowd distribution did mean, though, that we just about had room to get to Sir Hector further back in the hall, where he was standing proudly beside his own exhibits.

'I say, Hector,' said Lady Hardcastle. 'These are magnificent. Did you do them yourself?'

Again the familiar bark of a laugh.

'No, m'dear,' he said. 'These are from m'collection. This is *The Grange from the East* by Edgar Summerhays.' He pointed to a magnificent oil painting in a gilt frame. I was sure I must have seen it before, but amid all the Victorianesque clutter at The Grange it was hard to tell. It showed the buildings as they had been in the eighteenth century, after the building of the Palladian façade, but before the addition of the neo-Gothic sections in the mid-1800s. The house looked as magnificent as ever, though oddly naked without its turrets and pointed arched windows.

'And this,' he continued, indicating an alabaster bust of a man with tousled hair who was wearing a high collar and very realistically carved cravat, 'is the late Sir Theodore Elderkin. He was a major in the 8th Dragoon Guards during the Peninsular War. Fought at Vitoria, you know. And when he came home, he bought The Grange. One of m'predecessors, you might say.'

'He's a handsome chap,' said Lady Hardcastle.

'Is he? I suppose he is, now you come to mention it.'

'They're nice pieces, Sir Hector,' I said.

'Thank you, m'dear, I'm very fond of 'em m'self. Interestin' bit of local history, what?'

'Very interesting indeed,' I agreed. 'Do you know much about Sir Theodore—'

I was interrupted by a shout from the back of the hall.

'Fire!'

There was immediate panic.

I could hear Lady Farley-Stroud appealing for calm and urging people to leave the hall in an orderly fashion, but no one was listening. It was understandable, given the building's recent history, and there was a definite desire to get out as quickly as possible.

People were pushing, barging. There were shouts and screams. There were denials.

'I can't see nothin'.'

There were immediate responses.

'I can smell it.'

'It's smoke.'

'The buildin's on fire.'

I could smell it now. I tried to look round to see if I could locate the source, but the crowd pressed on and we were dragged with them towards the doors.

Lady Hardcastle, much taller than I, was also trying to see.

'The rear of the hall,' she said. 'Near the side wall.'

Again I tried to turn, but the slight slackening of pace infuriated the man behind me. He snarled angrily and gave me a hearty shove.

'Keep movin', you dozy mare – we's all goin' to get burned to death.'

Under other circumstances I might have remonstrated with him for his rudeness – or perhaps given him a playful elbow to the solar plexus – but he had a point. Any hold-up in a panicked crowd

19

could be fatal – if anyone were to stumble they'd be trampled. I held my tongue and shuffled on.

The smell was stronger now. Foul, oily smoke.

The panic grew.

The screams increased in volume.

And then suddenly we were outside, swept through the front doors by the surging crowd and out on to the road.

Freed from the confines of the hall, the crowd spread, giving us all room to collect ourselves and evaluate the situation.

Many had followed us through the front door, but now that we were able to take a proper look around, it was apparent that many others had found their way out through the side door.

The smell of smoke was stronger than ever, but even now that the doorway was less crowded, I could still see no flames inside.

'Should we go back in?' I asked. 'People might be trapped.'

'I was thinking the same thing,' said Lady Hardcastle. 'Let's see what we can do to help.'

Slowly we fought our way back towards the entrance, against the tide of frightened villagers. It was hard going and we were roundly cursed for our efforts, but we eventually made it to the doors, where we were met by Lady Farley-Stroud.

'This is terrible,' she said. 'Terrible.'

'Where's the fire?' I asked. 'Is everybody out?'

'I think so, m'dear,' she said. 'They said the fire was in the office.'

Lady Hardcastle gave me a nod, and together we slipped past Lady Farley-Stroud and in through the doors before she could stop us.

The hall was filling with smoke, but there were still no signs of actual fire.

'Is there anyone here?' I called.

There was no answer. Nor could I hear the expected crackle of flames.

The smoke appeared to be coming from underneath the office door, exactly as Lady Farley-Stroud had said. I approached quickly, with Lady Hardcastle only a step behind.

'Hello!' she called. 'Is there anyone in here?'

Still no answer.

I put my hand against the office door and found it cool to the touch.

'Odd,' I said. 'This door's cold. If there were a fire in there—'

'It would be hot by now, yes,' said Lady Hardcastle. 'I think we're safe to take a look.'

I carefully opened the door and more thick black smoke billowed out, making us both cough. But the only sign of fire was coming from a galvanized metal bucket in the middle of the room. Lady Hardcastle grabbed one of the red fire buckets hanging on the wall outside the office and swiftly extinguished the last of the flames with the sand.

The bucket in the office had been filled with paper, wood shavings, and oily rags – enough to make a very smelly fire but not enough to cause any real harm.

'Curious,' said Lady Hardcastle.

We searched the other side rooms for frightened villagers, but the building was clear and we were able to confirm that there was no damage.

It was only as we crossed the hall on our way to tell Lady Farley-Stroud the good news that I noticed the bad news.

'Sir Hector's bust and painting,' I said. 'They're gone.'

'And so,' said Lady Hardcastle, pointing at the empty case atop the beautiful wooden plinth, its glass lid smashed, 'is the Westbury Shakespeare.'

Chapter Two

Sergeant Dobson and Constable Hancock, our trusty village police-men, were already on the scene. Their duties had kept them from enjoying the delights of the exhibition, but the commotion outside the hall had attracted their attention and they were there within minutes of the first cry of 'Fire!'

We reported our discoveries – the diversionary fire and the thefts – to the sergeant, who promptly took charge of the case. He made a careful note of our witness statements, and then instructed his young colleague to talk to the many other villagers who were still milling about.

The police station occupied two cottages beside the village green, and the two officers were responsible for much of the coun-tryside south of the market town of Chipping Bevington, including our own village and nearby Woodworthy. Officially they were part of the Gloucestershire Constabulary, but Sergeant Dobson didn't trust their detectives. Against all instructions, and in the face of repeated rebukes from his superiors, he usually found a way to refer complex cases to the Bristol force. But this time, no such referral was needed. He judged this a simple theft and one that was well within his capabilities. We agreed and left him to it.

We loitered for almost an hour, hoping to find out more as we earwigged on our fellow villagers' conversations. From what we overheard, though, no one had seen anything of either the fire or the thefts, and it soon became apparent that we were, if not exactly wasting our time, then at least not spending it profitably.

We decided to return home, and approached the sergeant so that we might make our excuses and leave. We knew we didn't need his permission, but our friendship with the genial policeman, and our four-year-old custom of helping him wherever and whenever we could, made it feel as though a cheery goodbye would be the polite thing to do.

Fortunately, he seemed to be briefly alone, taking a moment's pause from his interviews and reviewing his notebook.

'Is there any more information you need from us, Sergeant?' asked Lady Hardcastle.

'I don't think so, m'lady,' said the bearded policeman. 'Young Hancock and I have matters well in hand.'

'As always,' said Lady Hardcastle with a smile.

Sergeant Dobson looked down at his notebook briefly, then back at the pair of us. His expression didn't quite match his confident tone.

'Is there something the matter, Sergeant?' asked Lady Hardcastle.

'Well,' he said, slowly, 'I know I said as how we's got it all in hand . . . but . . . well, I don't mind tellin' you, m'lady, but I's worried about this book o' Mr Westbury's. We deals with people who's had tools stole from their sheds, or who's lost a couple of cows. I can do that. But this blessed book . . . it's worth a thousand pounds, they says. A thousand bloomin' pounds – beggin' your pardon, m'lady.'

I suppressed a smile. Like all members of the upper classes, Lady Hardcastle swore like a navvy and wasn't in the least bit bothered by the sergeant's blushing euphemisms. Still, she graciously put a hand on his forearm.

'We're all friends here, Sergeant,' she said. 'You should hear the things I say in the privacy of my own drawing room. Or perhaps you shouldn't – I'd make a docker blush sometimes, really I would. But as for the book, think of it like this: it's just a stolen item. Its value is just a number we attach to it for the purposes of commerce. Whether it's a hay knife stolen from a farmer's shed costing four shillings, or an ornate book stolen from an art exhibition costing a thousand pounds, it's still just a stolen thing. If you can find one, you can find the other.'

'You're very kind, m'lady. But we's still goin' to be a bit more worried about it than about old Jim Palmer's stolen pitchfork.'

'I understand. At least it's insured.'

'Well, there is that, m'lady,' he said with a smile.

'Speaking of which,' I said, 'where are the insurance company's guards? I thought they were supposed to be taking care of things.'

'Haven't seen hide nor hair of 'em, miss,' said Sergeant Dobson. 'By the time me and Hancock got here they'd done a bunk. Didn't want to be questioned too closely about their dereliction of duty, I'd wager. Mrs Gardner says she saw 'em leavin' in a motor car with Mr Westbury, so perhaps he's taken 'em off somewhere to give 'em a roastin' in private.'

'Perhaps,' I said.

'Someone ought to,' said Lady Hardcastle. 'I mean to say, what on earth is the point of a security guard who allows the one thing he's guarding to be stolen?'

'Some folk don't take their work as seriously as others,' said the sergeant.

'Then it's a good thing for Mr Westbury that you and Constable Hancock are on the case,' said Lady Hardcastle.

'You're very kind, m'lady.'

'I mean it, Sergeant. You'll have it all wrapped up in no time. And we'd better leave you to it. You're sure there's nothing we can do for you right now?'

'No, m'lady. Thank you, but we's fine.'

'In which case, if it's all right with you, I think we shall be off. You know how to reach us if you think of any further questions.'

'I do indeed, m'lady. Thank you.'

Our intention had been to try to talk to Sir Hector and Lady Farley-Stroud. As one of the two victims of the theft and the main organizer of the exhibition, they had both been very busy with the police at first, so we had kept out of the way. But now we wished to talk to them, we found that they had gone.

'They left about ten minutes ago,' said Mrs Gardner. 'Bert took them home in the motor car.'

We thanked her and started to walk back to our own house.

'We should potter up to The Grange,' said Lady Hardcastle. 'I think this is one of those occasions when one can drop in on close friends unannounced.'

'I think you're right,' I said. 'I remember a section of *Debrett's* devoted to the correct etiquette when a close friend has had a painting stolen from an exhibition.'

'Indeed,' she said. 'It's between "Misplacing of a Much-Loved Pen" and "Resignation of a Favourite Cook". We shall take the Rolls.'

Lady Hardcastle's Silver Ghost Roadster was a beautiful machine. She had taken delivery the previous June and it had brought us both great joy, until it broke down in Bristol in November while we were investigating the murder at the theatre. Actually, that wasn't strictly true. When the car had been returned to us by a company representative and a liveried driver, she had been informed that Rolls-Royces 'do not break down'.

'I rather think mine did,' she had said. 'It left us stranded in Bristol and unable to return home.'

'Ah, yes, madam,' the man had replied. 'We are aware of the temporary failure to proceed but the vehicle is working as expected now.'

She had signed the paperwork, and the man and his driver had purred away in the car we had been lent while the Roadster that hadn't broken down wasn't being repaired.

A subsequent investigation – both Lady Hardcastle and I were keen to learn as much as possible about motor cars – had indicated that the non-repairs had been extensive, with several important ancillary components replaced, and evidence that the engine itself had been stripped down. We had been unable to wrest any details from Rolls-Royce, who remained insistent that no repairs were needed on a motor car that had not broken down.

The newly non-repaired car had seen us through the winter and spring without further incident and we had decided not to torment the poor Rolls-Royce staff any further with questions they were obviously not allowed to answer.

The gleaming silver machine was standing on the miniature driveway outside the house as we approached. It always looked eager to me, like a dog who knows the sound of its lead being taken down and is bouncing about ready for its walk.

We hopped in and I pressed the starter button – we had an electric starter motor courtesy of Lady Hardcastle's racing-car-designing friend, Lord Riddlethorpe. The Rolls started first time and turned over with a hypnotic rumble, so that just a few moments after our arrival home it was smoothly and elegantly transporting us up the hill towards The Grange.

The architectural chaos of the local manor house was largely concealed by hedgerows on the lane that led to it. When it finally burst into view it was like an illustrated history of English architecture from 1560 to 1860, and I loved it. No thought had been given by previous owners to visual harmony, and each addition had been slapped on willy-nilly wherever there was room.

We swept in through the ever-open gates. There's another section in *Debrett's* covering the approach to country houses, and it is always necessary to sweep in through gates – any other means of entry is considered the most appalling social faux pas.

The gravel on the drive scrunched pleasingly beneath the Silver Ghost's tyres, and the sound alerted Sir Hector's spaniels – named for the three Fates of Greek mythology – who came tumbling and barking towards us from the rear of the house.

I parked neatly beside the front door and we stepped out to greet 'the gels' as they bounced excitedly around us.

'Hello, you three,' said Lady Hardcastle as she bent to scratch Atropos – or Troppo to her friends – affectionately behind the ear. 'Is your family at home?'

Jenkins, the Farley-Strouds' white-haired butler, had heard the dogs and opened the door to see who was visiting his employers. He smiled when he saw us.

'Good afternoon, Lady Hardcastle,' he said. 'And good afternoon, Miss Armstrong.'

'Good afternoon to you, too, Jenkins,' said Lady Hardcastle. 'Are they at home?'

'The master and mistress are in the drawing room. Please come in.'

'Thank you.'

We followed him along the familiar route to the drawing room, where he knocked and entered.

'Lady Hardcastle and Miss Armstrong to see you, my lady,' he said before stepping aside to allow us to enter.

'Oh, Emily,' said Lady Farley-Stroud. 'Thank you so very much for coming.'

Her eyes were red and her face puffy.

Lady Hardcastle walked swiftly across the room and embraced her.

'You poor thing,' said Lady Hardcastle. 'I'm sure it can all be sorted out.'

'How, Emily? How? Hector's painting gone. The bust gone. And poor Mr Westbury . . . his beautiful book. All stolen. All because of me.'

'All because of a thief, Gertie dear. You didn't do it. You didn't make it happen. And at least there was no damage to the village hall.'

Lady Farley-Stroud pulled gently away. She wiped her eyes on a monogrammed handkerchief.

'But I did leave the office door unlocked,' she said. 'If they hadn't been able to get in there . . .'

'Then they'd have found somewhere else to set their fire,' said Lady Hardcastle, kindly.

'You're right, of course,' said Lady Farley-Stroud with a sniff. 'Just bein' a ninny.'

'They won't get far,' I said. 'Dobson and Hancock will have them caught in no time.'

'In two shakes of an eye and the twinkling of a lamb's tail,' agreed Lady Hardcastle.

Lady Farley-Stroud managed a small laugh.

'Are you just leavin' it to the boys in blue?' asked Sir Hector.

'We were planning to, Sir Hector, yes,' I said. 'Sergeant Dobson is a very capable man.'

'Oh, yes,' said Sir Hector, 'very capable indeed. It's just . . . well, the wheels of Wally Dobson turn slowly. And sometimes even then they don't grind especially fine. I'm . . . we're . . . in a bit of a bind, d'you see?'

'Hector, no,' said Lady Farley-Stroud.

'These are our friends, Apfelstrudel, and I'm beggared if I can do this on my own any more. Ain't no shame in askin' a friend for help.'

'But—'

'He's right, Gertie,' said Lady Hardcastle. 'If there's trouble we shall do everything in our power to help. More if we can. Never, ever, be afraid to ask.'

'But—'

'Butts are for rainwater, my little Baumkuchen,' said Sir Hector. 'Emily and Florence have proven themselves more than capable of solvin' much more complicated mysteries than this. And we really don't have time to wait for Wally Dobson.'

'Why don't you tell us all about it,' said Lady Hardcastle, 'and we'll see what we can do.'

He gestured for us both to sit, and we settled ourselves on the old but comfortable sofa. He waited for his wife to sit, too, and with a defeated sigh, she eventually did.

'You've always known money was a little tight up here at The Grange,' said Sir Hector. 'We've never made a secret of it.'

'*I* have,' said Lady Farley-Stroud indignantly.

'Actually,' said Lady Hardcastle, 'it was one of the first things you ever confided in us. When the Emerald Eye was stolen, remember? You needed it back because you had a loan secured against it.'

'Ah,' said Lady Farley-Stroud. 'Yes. Well.'

'And we still do – the loan, I mean,' said Sir Hector. 'But at least we have the emerald to cover that one. But that's not the full extent of our troubles, m'dear. Not by a long chalk. We've had a couple of bad years, d'you see? Rents dryin' up. Dower House has been empty for a year – only just got a new tenant there. Still haven't got a tenant for the orchard after last summer. Havin' to survive on what the bank will lend us, d'you see? But their patience ain't infinite. Time's runnin' out. And . . . well, we got the dreaded letter

29

last week. We have just over a month – until the seventh of June, to be precise.' He paused for a moment. 'Then we lose The Grange.'

'Good heavens,' said Lady Hardcastle. 'You lose The Grange? How can that be?'

'Latest loan secured against the house, d'you see? A large one. Had to cover livin' expenses, wages – you name it. It all mounts up. Rents would have just about met the repayments . . . if we had any rents. I don't have no talents nor skills to earn a livin', and I'm too old to do proper work. Although it might come to that. Know anyone who needs a handyman?'

'They'd need to hire another handyman to mend all the things you broke while you were tryin' to fix 'em,' said Lady Farley-Stroud.

'Ha!' barked Sir Hector. 'Buy cheap, buy twice. Quite right. So, you see, we're very much on our beam ends.'

'Good heavens,' said Lady Hardcastle. 'Could you not sell the Dower House? The orchard?'

'Tried it, m'dear. No takers. Would still only have been a stop-gap, though. And would have left us with no income for the future when things pick up.'

'How awful. Is there anything we can do?'

'Get m'paintin' back,' he said bluntly. 'It's one of a pair, d'you see? Edgar Summerhays.'

'I'm afraid I don't—' I began.

'He's an early-nineteenth-century landscape artist,' said Lady Hardcastle. 'Largely ignored at the time, at least by the more snob-bish members of the art world, but he's enjoying something of a surge in popularity at the moment. One of his paintings sold at Sotheby's recently for an absolute fortune.'

'Exactly so, m'dear,' said Sir Hector. 'Which is why I had our Summerhayses valued. The pair together would pay all our debts, with enough left over to keep us goin' until things pick up. Either one on its own would raise a decent sum, but not enough to cover the debts. Once there's a pair like mine, though, the collectors go barmy.'

'In which case,' said Lady Hardcastle, 'we shall do all we possibly can to retrieve it.'

'Absolutely,' I agreed. 'Under the circumstances, I'm sure Sergeant Dobson wouldn't mind.'

'He absolutely must not know,' said Lady Farley-Stroud. 'No one must know. No one.'

'Of course, dear,' said Lady Hardcastle. 'It would be helpful to keep him on our side, though, so we'll have to tell him what we're up to. But if we share our findings with him and make sure he takes all the credit for the arrest, I agree with Flo that he almost certainly won't mind.'

'D'you really think you can find it?' asked Sir Hector. 'It would save us. It really would.'

'I can't promise,' said Lady Hardcastle. 'That would be reckless and unhelpful. But we shall do our utmost. If it's possible to find your lost Summerhays, we'll find it.'

'If anyone can do it, m'dear, it's you two,' said Sir Hector.

'I'm flattered by your confidence, Hector dear. We'll certainly do our best.'

'We shall,' I said.

Sir Hector nodded his thanks.

'What about the Westbury Shakespeare?' said Lady Farley-Stroud.

'What about it?' asked Lady Hardcastle.

'You'll be looking for that, too? I don't know how I'm going to face poor Basil Westbury. He trusted us with his beautiful book and now it's gone.'

'He had security guards, dear. I can't help but think the safety of the book was their responsibility, not yours.'

'And yet I gave the thief the opportunity to set the fire.'

'Did you see the security guards?' I said. 'Sergeant Dobson said they disappeared with Westbury soon after the fire alarm, but were they at their posts before that?'

'All present and correct, m'dear, yes,' said Lady Farley-Stroud. 'Two of 'em. Older and younger. Uniforms and all.'

'They took off pretty sharpish, according to Dobson,' I said.

'Westbury spoke to Sergeant Dobson soon after you reported the book and painting missing, but only stayed long enough to confirm that the book really had gone. He summoned the two guards and they left in his motor car.'

'I'd like to speak to them,' I said.

'I would, too,' said Lady Hardcastle. 'Do you have the details of the security company, Gertie?'

'Westbury gave us all the details when we were making the arrangements – he was very excited. I can let you have their address.'

'Thank you.'

'Please don't get sidetracked by the man's gaudy book, though, m'dear,' said Sir Hector. 'It's a shame it's gone missin', but findin' it won't save The Grange.'

'Have no fear, Hector dear,' said Lady Hardcastle. 'Your painting will remain our topmost priority, but we would be foolish to ignore the book. One presumes they're together, so when we've found one, we've found everything. If it happens that the missing Shakespeare provides us with good leads, then we shall pursue those. I'll wager we'll end up finding both the Shakespeare and the Summerhays at the same place.'

'And the bust?' I said.

'Oh, don't worry about that,' said Sir Hector. 'Interestin' piece of history, but only worth a few bob. I kept it for its links to the house, not its monetary value.'

Lady Hardcastle nodded, and we all fell silent for a few moments.

'Where on earth do you start with something like this?' asked Lady Farley-Stroud suddenly.

'We start at the scene of the crime and work our way outwards from there,' said Lady Hardcastle. 'We usually have a limited pool of suspects, but in this case it's not quite so simple. Everyone from Littleton Cotterell, Woodworthy, and all stations to Chipping Bevington was there. I think we can safely rule out a lot of familiar faces, but there were people there I'd never seen before.'

Lady Farley-Stroud looked as though she might cry again.

'Oh, but that won't deter us,' said Lady Hardcastle, hurriedly. 'It might muddy the waters at the start, but we'll soon find a way to clear things up.'

'Most grateful to you, m'dears,' said Sir Hector. 'Most grateful. Will you stay for tiffin?'

'That would be most agreeable, thank you. Somehow we managed to miss lunch, and I confess to being absolutely starving.'

◆ ◆ ◆

The Farley-Strouds' cook, Mrs Brown, was a thoroughly unpleasant bully of a woman, but she was skilled at her job and her afternoon teas were almost works of art.

As we tucked in to the delicious sandwiches and cakes, we managed to keep the conversation away from diversionary fires and stolen art works. Instead we enquired about the Farley-Strouds' daughter and son-in-law, Clarissa and Adam Whitman, and their enchanting daughter, Louisa. Little Lou-Lou, now almost two years old, was thriving at their home in France, where, thanks to her nanny, she was chattering away as easily in French as in English.

'Don't know where she gets her brains from,' said Sir Hector. 'Must be Adam,' he added with a wink.

'Hector!' said Lady Farley-Stroud.

'Oh, don't "Hector" me like that, my little Eccles cake. The whole world knows Clarissa's a puddin' head.'

'That's not at all fair, Hector,' said Lady Hardcastle. 'She's a very bright young woman.'

The first time Lady Hardcastle had met Clarissa Farley-Stroud she had described her to me as 'quite the most vacuous ninny ever to struggle into a fashionable frock', but her view had mellowed as we got to know her better.

'You're right, of course, m'dear,' said Sir Hector. 'But you didn't know her when she was a little gel. I used to look on in despair sometimes. D'you remember that time she got her hand stuck in the spokes of the perambulator when she reached through the wheel to pick somethin' up instead of reachin' round it? Or when she made lunch for her shoes?'

'All children do silly things, Hector,' said Lady Farley-Stroud.

'Or when I pointed out a wood pigeon sittin' on top of the wall and she asked me why no other birds were made of wood.'

'That's a very good question, actually,' said Lady Hardcastle. 'Why *are* no other birds made of wood? Why do red kites not have strings? Where do they keep the lids for the nightjars? Why do cranes not apply for work at the docks? Can you use a yellowhammer for carpentry?'

'Point taken, m'dear, point taken,' said Sir Hector with a chuckle. 'But I still say she was a muttonhead.'

Jenkins appeared at the drawing room door and coughed politely.

'There's a telephone call for you, sir,' he said. 'Mr Amersham.'

'Old Jimmy, eh?' said Sir Hector with evident glee. 'Wonder what he wants. Mischief and larks, I'll be bound. Excuse me, would you, ladies? Got to talk to m'pal.'

He was following Jenkins out the door before any of us could say a word.

Lady Hardcastle leaned forward in her seat.

'You know you don't have to lose The Grange, dear, don't you?' she said. 'I can lend you the money to see off your creditors. No interest. Pay me back when you can.'

Lady Farley-Stroud looked at her earnestly.

'That really is extremely generous and kind of you, m'dear,' she said. 'But I couldn't possibly. You understand, don't you?'

'Not entirely, dear, no.'

'I simply couldn't bear it. I love you as if you were my own daughter, and I know you mean it for the best . . . but the shame of it . . . I just couldn't.'

Lady Hardcastle regarded her for a moment.

'Very well,' she said at length. 'I don't want to embarrass you so I shall say nothing more. You know the money is yours if you need it, but we shall find the Summerhays in good time and you'll not need it anyway.'

Lady Farley-Stroud reached out and touched Lady Hardcastle's clasped hands by way of reply.

The silence that followed was broken by the return of a very cheerful Sir Hector.

'Goin' out to play,' was all he said as he kissed his wife goodbye. 'Jimmy has a new tricycle.'

'Just you be careful,' said Lady Farley Stroud, but he was already gone. She sighed. 'You can see where Clarissa gets her pudding-headedness.'

Chapter Three

On Monday morning we thought it might be helpful to visit the village police station. If we were to be meddling in the investigation – even if only to hasten the return of the Summerhays landscape – it seemed best that Sergeant Dobson knew what we were up to.

We made ourselves ready for the short walk into the village straight after breakfast.

I had already been into the garden to complete my regular morning exercises, so I was able to say with confidence that jackets or light coats would be required. Armed with this knowledge, we were suitably protected against the slight morning chill as we made our way down the lane towards the village green.

The skies were grey, but the hawthorn was in bloom and birds were abroad, performing their avian morning chores. There was a feeling in the air that the wet, cold winter and dreary spring might soon give way to something approaching the comforting warmth of summer.

We skirted the green, greeting shopkeepers and their early-morning customers as we passed the parade of shops which ran along its eastern side. The village baker, Septimus Holman, was pasting a notice to his window advertising his delicious lardy cake, and he offered us a friendly 'good morning'. Queen Daisy gave us a cheery wave from behind the counter in her father's butcher's shop. Hilda Pantry, the general grocer, scowled at us, then ostentatiously turned her back.

'She still doesn't like me,' said Lady Hardcastle.

'You're a toff,' I said. 'She can't abide toffs.'

'I know. But I'm enchanting.'

'Without question. But you're an enchanting *toff*. Your bourgeois title and inherited wealth make you a class enemy. You're an exploiter of the proletariat. You and your kind are responsible for propping up the capitalist system that holds back the working man – or in this case, woman – and prevents him – or her – from fully benefiting from the profits of their labour.'

'That goes without saying. The sooner the world is rid of the likes of me, the better it will be. But I'm still delightful.'

'And it's her loss that she doesn't appreciate it. But her late husband once read a pamphlet explaining the works of Messrs Marx and Engels and now she can do nothing but prepare for the coming revolution and gleefully anticipate your downfall.'

'She's right to do so, though it probably won't solve anything. But I shall persevere with our Mrs Pantry. I'll make her warm to me.'

'It doesn't help that she always thinks you're teasing her. That cheery politeness thing you do – she thinks you're making fun of her.'

'She's not entirely wrong.'

'And yet you still complain that she doesn't like you.'

'Does she like you?'

'She tolerates me,' I said. 'But grudgingly. I'm friends with a toff, but I have proletarian roots and an exploitative proletarian job, so she can't quite justify open hostility. We also settle our account promptly each month. That counts for a lot, even to a revolutionary Marxist.'

Our conversation stalled when we were distracted by a minor commotion at the police station, where a young man was talking animatedly to Constable Hancock. He seemed to be frustrated.

'. . . and when I returned just now, my bicycle was missing,' said the man. 'I park it quite safely there most days, and today it was gone.'

'But there was a bicycle there when I passed by, sir,' said Constable Hancock.

'There was a bicycle there when I went looking for mine, yes.'

'It was a black BSA Road Racer, sir.'

'Yes, it was.'

'And your bicycle is . . . ?'

'A black BSA Road Racer.'

The constable raised a single eyebrow so that it disappeared from view beneath the brim of his helmet.

'I don't see the pr—'

'It isn't mine,' said the exasperated man. 'That one was there when I arrived and is still there now. Mine, though, has gone.'

'How can you tell the difference, sir?'

'One simply knows one's bicycle, Constable. It's an extension of one's very soul.'

'I see, sir. But—'

'And mine has my initials painted in white on the head tube.'

'The what, sir?'

'The bit at the front where the handlebars go.'

'I see, sir. In that case, I'm sure we'll find it. If I could just take your name, please?'

'Nisbet,' said the man. 'Felix Ulysses Nisbet.'

Constable Hancock made a careful note.

'So we're on the lookout for a black BSA Road Racer,' he said at length, 'with the word "fun" painted on the' – he consulted his notes – 'head tube.'

'Not the word "fun", Constable. My initials: F U N.'

I knew the constable well enough to know that he was almost certainly trying to work out what the difference between the two might be.

'F U N, sir, yes,' he said.

The conversation showed no sign of ending, so Lady Hardcastle took my arm as she changed course to head, instead, for the village hall.

'I think poor Constable Hancock might be tied up there for a while,' she said. 'And if I know Sergeant Dobson he'll be hiding away from that little lot. He wouldn't welcome our drawing attention to his presence.'

'I know I wouldn't,' I said. 'I'd definitely leave that one to my underling.'

'You should have underlings, dear – you'd suit an underling.'

'Too much effort. It's hard enough trying to manage myself without having to think about everything someone else is doing.'

'You might be lucky – you might have an underling like you.'

'Can you imagine the horror of it? Two of me?'

'I often think I could do with two of you, dear. But I have to make do with just one, and I suggest that the one of you and the one of me take a look around the village hall to see if it sparks any sort of problem solving, painting finding, Grange-saving brainwave.'

'And take a look at this BSA Racing Whatnot,' I said. 'I'm keen to see if it's better than the bicycles we bought.'

'Nothing could beat our mighty iron steeds,' she said. 'Raleigh is a name to be reckoned with.'

The hall was open and the exhibition still on. We walked in through the newly decorated entrance and weaved our way amid the exhibits. We found a very different scene to the one we had witnessed on Saturday. Then, the room had been jam-packed with villagers and visitors, jostling for a look at their friends' work or a glimpse of the famous bejewelled book.

Now there were two of Lady Farley-Stroud's volunteers gossiping beside the tea table, three elderly ladies admiring the knitting exhibit . . . and two security guards stationed beside the empty display case. The smashed glass had been cleared away, leaving only the frame and the book stand sitting atop the carved plinth. The guards were chatting to each other about Gloucestershire's chances in the coming county cricket championship.

No one paid us any attention as we weaved our way through the tables and display boards to the empty space where Sir Hector's painting and bust had once stood. There was, as one might expect, nothing to see.

'Missing paintings are much less interesting to look at than present ones,' said Lady Hardcastle.

'Although it's a good idea for an exhibition,' I said. 'The Missing *Mona Lisa*, the Missing *Laughing Cavalier*. Missing *Water Lilies* for devotees of the French Impressionists. A series of Missing Portraits of the Great and Good, too, perhaps.'

'Why stop there? Missing Statues of the Roman Emperors. The Missing Complete Works of Shakespeare . . .'

'Well, quite,' I said. 'I wonder how they got it all out. Not through the front door – someone would have noticed.'

'Same with the side door,' said Lady Hardcastle. 'There were people streaming out of both.'

'There's a back door, though. I remember using it for something a couple of years ago. We'll have to take a look.'

'We shall. But first, let's have a word with those nice men in their neat uniforms.' She made her way over to the security guards. 'Good morning, gentlemen.'

'Mornin', ma'am,' said the older of the two.

'I'm Lady Hardcastle, and this is Florence Armstrong.'

'Pleasure to meet you, m'lady. I'm Don Porter and this here's Larry Templeman.'

The younger man grinned, and nodded a greeting.

'You're the security guards employed by Mr Westbury's insurers, is that correct?'

'We are, m'lady, yes,' said Porter.

'You'll have to forgive me if I sound rude,' I said, 'it's certainly not my intention . . . But why are you guarding an empty case?'

'That's what we's been paid to do, miss.'

'Surely the brief was to guard the book,' said Lady Hardcastle.

'The job was to come to the Littleton Cotterell village hall and stand guard at this plinth, m'lady. So that's what we's doin'.'

'But the point of standing guard at the plinth,' I said, 'was to protect the contents of the case.'

'Granted, miss, but the job sheet specifically mentions the case as well as the book, so even though the book's not here no more, we's still got to guard the case.'

There was something about this unwaveringly literal approach to the instructions that I found quite endearing.

'Were you on duty on Saturday?' I asked. 'Or was that someone else?'

'We was here, miss. Both of us. Wasn't we, Larry?'

The younger man grinned and nodded again, but still said nothing.

'Standin' just here, we was,' said Porter.

'We came to the exhibition, too,' said Lady Hardcastle. 'It was busy, wasn't it?'

'Very busy, m'lady, yes. Quite took us by surprise it did. I said to Larry, I said, "It's busy, i'n't it, lad?"'

'And what did Larry say?' I asked.

'Oh, he just smiled and nodded, didn't you, lad?'

The young man did exactly that.

'He don't say much,' continued Porter. 'But he's a good lad.'

'It would have been nice to have met you on Saturday,' said Lady Hardcastle. 'We were keen to see the book but it was frightfully busy in this part of the hall, wasn't it? You were so thoroughly surrounded we couldn't get so much as a glimpse. It was a shame – I was rather looking forward to it.'

'It certainly was a sight to see, m'lady.'

'One can only imagine. And then someone shouted "Fire!" and we were swept out with the crowd.'

'As were we, m'lady,' said Porter. For the first time he looked a little unsure of himself. 'We tried to stay at our posts, but . . . well, there was too many of 'em. Like bein' carried out to sea by the tide, it was. We just couldn't get back. And then . . .'

'And then it was gone,' said Lady Hardcastle.

'Smashed the glass and took the book. We never saw hide nor hair of it again.'

'You're obviously highly trained professionals,' I said. 'So did you notice anyone suspicious while you were on guard? Was there anyone who made you think, "Hello, he's a wrong 'un"?'

Porter laughed.

'No, miss,' he said. 'No one like that. It was just a friendly village crowd, like. Young and old. Men and women. Boys and girls. Everyone was happy and excited. It was a very jolly atmosphere.'

'I thought so, too,' I said. 'It's a lovely village full of lovely people.'

'It certainly seemed that way, miss. Except for one of 'em. One of 'em stole the book we was guardin'.'

'Exactly so,' said Lady Hardcastle. 'It's such a pity you're not local – it would be nice if you'd recognized anyone.'

'I'm sorry, m'lady, I doesn't know no one. Well, there's your Lady Barley-Cloud—'

'Farley-Stroud,' I said.

'Yes, her,' said Porter without any embarrassment. 'And we met Mr Westbury when we escorted him here with his book, of course.'

'Did he stay for the exhibition?'

'Couldn't say, m'lady. He went off with Lady Charley-Proud.'

'Farley-Stroud,' I said again before I could stop myself. I could see Lady Hardcastle grinning.

'I'm so sorry,' said Porter. 'You did tell me. What did I say this time?'

'Charley-Proud.'

'Did I?' he said with a laugh. 'Did I really? Well I never. Funny what the mind drags up, i'n't it? I was in the army with a bloke named Charlie Proud, see? Bravest fella I ever met, old Charlie Proud. I remember this one time—'

'Mr Westbury went off with Lady Farley-Stroud,' said Lady Hardcastle, patiently.

'That's right, m'lady. I never saw him after that. Tell the truth, we wasn't expectin' to see him again until the exhibition closed at five, when we was supposed to escort him and the book back to his house outside Chippin' Bevin'ton. Anyway, he walks off, then there was a few minutes while you was all outside listenin' to speeches. Then the doors opened and we was swallowed up in the deluge, wasn't we, Larry.'

Larry smiled and nodded as usual.

'Well, I hope they come and relieve you soon,' said Lady Hardcastle. 'It can't be fun standing here guarding nothing.'

'It's all the same to us,' said Porter. 'Standin' here, standin' there. As long as we gets our pay at the end of the week, we don't mind, do we, Larry?'

Larry did not.

'It was extremely generous of you to spare the time to talk to us,' said Lady Hardcastle. 'If we should have any further questions, how can we contact you?'

'We works for Moberley, Burgess and Vincent, m'lady.'

'That's the name of the insurance company?'

'That's right, m'lady.'

'Thank you, Porter, you've been most helpful.'

We left the guards to their guarding and walked through the exhibits once more to the large storeroom at the back of the hall. The old green doors were now painted blue, but we knew there had been no structural alterations to the building and that meant the room itself would be unchanged. And that was significant because there was another pair of similarly sized doors at the back of the room which opened out to a weed-infested patch of ground behind the hall.

The interior doors were unlocked, and we made our way between the newly tidied piles of bentwood chairs and the trestle tables stacked against the walls.

'I like Daniel Potter,' said Lady Hardcastle.

'Donald Porter,' I said, without thinking.

'That will never stop being funny,' she said with her familiar little laugh.

It had become her habit to pretend to get names wrong so that she could enjoy my exasperation as I corrected her. I'd already seen her glee when Porter himself had done it naturally, and I should have been on my guard. But she got me every time.

'I like him, too,' I said, trying to steer us away from her little victory. 'He's an odd one, though.'

'It's odd that he seems so unfazed by everything, perhaps, but that's what I like about him. As long as he gets his pay packet at the end of the week, all's right with the world. Whatever strange things everyone else gets up to in the meantime are of no concern to our dear Porter – he just seems to accept the peculiarities of the world and all the people in it. He doesn't know us from Adam, for instance, but he didn't mind us asking him questions, and he didn't bat an eyelid when I said we might have more for him later.'

'It's not a bad way to be when you put it like that,' I said. 'Perhaps we should all just accept the peculiarities of the world and all the people in it.'

'It would certainly be less frustrating,' she agreed.

'It would,' I said. 'Take this, for instance,' I continued as I tried the outside doors. 'If I were more accepting of people's failure to secure their doors, I'd find this much less frustrating.'

The doors were unlocked and we stepped out into the chaos at the rear of the village hall.

There was a heap of burnt timber from the original roof, and a stack of offcuts of fresh wood from the repairs. There were empty paint cans, old rags, and a few large piles of general builders' rubbish.

We walked to the corner of the building and looked back in the direction of the village green. The side door was hinged to open towards the rear of the hall, so that anyone coming out of the hall would be unable to see us.

'One could come out here,' said Lady Hardcastle, 'hide one's booty, and then join the crowd streaming out through the side door without any problems. One could come back later – perhaps under cover of darkness – and retrieve the loot.'

'True,' I said. 'Although with this much cover you could just hide here until the crowds had gone.'

'Or that. It's riskier – there's no guarantee the rozzers wouldn't check the back door – but certainly possible. I think we've found where the thief came out.'

'I think we probably have,' I said.

We rounded the building and found the BSA Road Racer leaning against the wall.

'I say,' said Lady Hardcastle, 'that's jolly smart.' She inspected the area around the handlebars. 'It's not FUN, though.'

'Sadly for Mr Nisbet, no, it's not,' I said. 'It looks faster than ours, though, FUN or otherwise.'

'Faster, perhaps, but ours have a ladylike elegance I enjoy. And look at that saddle. It doesn't look comfortable at all.'

She was right. The saddle seemed to have been made with lightness and streamlining in mind, rather than comfort. I winced at the thought of having to ride any distance sitting on it.

'Why would anyone voluntarily do that to themselves?' I said.

'I fear we shall never fathom the mind of the sportsman. Rather than try, shall we retire to the Dog and Duck for an early lunch and a ponder on the theft?'

'I like that idea very much,' I said.

'Then let us away . . . Oh, but who's this in the fancy little car?'

A smart green motor car drew up outside the village hall, and an elegant woman of about Lady Hardcastle's age stepped out. She took a small calfskin briefcase from the car and walked towards the front door.

We quickened our pace along the side of the building to intercept the new arrival. She spotted us and quickened her own pace to try to get to the front door before we reached her. The result was the socially awkward meeting of three slightly out-of-puff women on a grass verge in front of a village hall. It would be more correct to say two out-of-puff and one calmly relaxed woman, but I shouldn't wish to make the others appear in any way lazy or unfit.

'Good morning,' said Lady Hardcastle, cheerily. 'Lovely day, isn't it?'

The other woman made a show of looking at the overcast sky.

'Delightful,' she said. 'I don't wish to be rude, but I am rather busy. Is there something I can do for you?'

Lady Hardcastle's smile faltered briefly and I saw a familiar look cross her face. She was trying to remember something.

The smile returned brighter than ever as she said, 'Cordelia? Cordelia Harrill?'

'I'm afraid you have the advantage of me,' said the woman. 'Now, if you will excuse me, I really must—'

'It's Emily. Emily Featherstonhaugh. Well, it's Hardcastle now, but at Girton you'd have known me as Featherstonhaugh. You used to tease me about it. "Why on earth is it spelled like that if you pronounce it Fanshaw?"'

'Oh, yes. I think I recall. You had a brother at Queen's?'

'King's. That's right. Harry.'

'Well, it's delightful to meet you again after all these years, but I'm afraid I really do have to—'

'What are you up to these days?' persisted Lady Hardcastle, blithely.

'What? Oh, insurance investigation. Would you excuse me, please?'

'I say, you don't work for Moberley, Burgess and Vincent, do you? I can see you'd be terribly busy if you did.'

Cordelia stopped trying to get past, and eyed us both warily.

'What do you mean?'

'Well, Moberley, Burgess and Vincent . . . actually I'm sure they must call themselves MBV – what a mouthful. Imagine having to say the whole thing every time. Anyway, this MBV insured the Westbury Shakespeare for an extraordinarily large sum . . . it's a book, you see – an unimaginably expensive and extravagantly bound book. They insured the book, provided guards – charged the owner for them, too, I gather – and then somebody only went and pinched the blessed thing. Can you believe it? From right under their noses. Do you work for them? Is that why you're here?'

'You seem to know an awful lot about it,' said Cordelia.

'One likes to keep one's ear to the ground, but it's not necessary in this case. It's a village, Cordelia dear – everyone knows everything in a village. And your guards are perfectly enchanting. Porter and Templeman. Salt of the earth, those two.'

'You've spoken to our security guards?'

'Of course, dear. They couldn't have been more helpful.'

'I shall thank you not to speak to them again. This is a matter for MB— for Moberley, Burgess and Vincent. We don't take kindly to outside interference.'

'Duly noted,' said Lady Hardcastle, still smiling. 'If you need any help, we're in the house down the lane over there, on the other side of the green. You can't miss us. Do drop in for tea.'

Cordelia Harrill, insurance investigator and former student at Girton College, turned on her expensive heel and strode into the village hall.

'That's a turn-up for the books,' I said once she was gone. 'Fancy you knowing the insurance investigator.'

'Oh, I know her, all right,' said Lady Hardcastle as we resumed our walk to the pub. 'We didn't get on.'

'I gathered that from the way you were trying so very hard to irritate her.'

'Oh dear. Was I that obvious?'

'Only to anyone with eyes and ears. Was she really that bad, though?'

'You can only begin to imagine her awfulness. Deceitful, dishonest . . . I swear she was a thief, too, you know. Several pieces of jewellery went missing from college rooms.'

'And you think it was her?'

'We all *knew* it was her. We just couldn't prove it.'

'There's more to it than that, though,' I said. 'You'd not still bear a grudge twenty-five years later over a few pilfered trinkets.'

'Oh, there was much more. Do you know she once made advances to Roddy? At the May Ball at King's. She knew he and I were engaged. I should have tossed her in the Cam.'

'She'd have remembered you if you had.'

'Oh, she remembers me well enough. It's a shame she's on the case – we'll get no help there.'

'We shall have to get by without her help then,' I said. 'But now it's time for a cheese doorstop and a ponder.'

Our pondering at the pub was curtailed by the arrival of Jagruti Bland and Agnes Bingle, who were canvassing for ideas for the village's summer fête. Instead of discussing the art thefts we found ourselves spending a very pleasant hour trying to come up with fun ways of parting villagers from their money. Lady Hardcastle suggested a variation on the ducking stool, and sketched a design that would drop the unfortunate victim into a large pool when someone hit a target with a beanbag. Mrs Bland had some gleefully vindictive ideas for who she'd like to see on the receiving end of a dunking, but swore us to silence – vicars' wives shouldn't be talking like that. We agreed, and suggested a few names of our own.

Back at the house, Lady Hardcastle had some correspondence to catch up on while I spent the rest of the afternoon reading before making our dinner from the ingredients Miss Jones had prepared before she left for the day.

With dinner eaten, I cleaned the dishes and set a pot of post-prandial coffee brewing. A refuelled Lady Hardcastle settled in the drawing room and decided that the one thing she could absolutely no longer go without was her crime board.

The blackboard upon which she liked to record her crime-solving musings lived in the attic most of the time but was hauled out – I leave you to guess by whom – when there was a case. When a new investigation began, Sherlock Holmes would have donned his Ulster, checked that he had his pipe, and said, 'Come, Watson. The game is afoot.' Lady Hardcastle scratched her ear, brushed crumbs from her dress, and said, 'Be a poppet and fetch the crime board, would you?' We all have our own ways of going about things.

'Of course,' I said. 'It would be quicker if you helped, mind you.'

'Nonsense – I'd just get in the way. I shall pour the coffee instead.'

Almost thirty frustrating minutes later, I had set up the blackboard on its easel in its usual place in the corner of the drawing room. There had only been a small amount of swearing – some of it in Welsh – and there was only minor damage to my dress where I'd caught it on the corner of an old tea chest in the attic. Other than that it went very smoothly and I was ready for my coffee and a sit-down.

Lady Hardcastle had entirely forgotten to pour the coffee, which was cold now anyway, but she had made a start on sketches for the board. She already had a reasonable likeness of Sir Hector's painting and the bust of Sir Theodore Elderkin. We hadn't seen Basil Westbury at the opening of the exhibition but we had met him before and the sketch was a good representation. She had to guess what the Westbury Shakespeare might look like, but the affectionately amusing caricatures of the two security guards were based on life. As I sat down she was working on a much less flattering depiction of Cordelia Harrill.

'Would you like a cup of coffee?' I asked.

'I should love one, please, dear. Thank you.'

I went out to the kitchen to make a fresh pot, and by the time I returned the sketches were on the board and she was writing notes in chalk beside them.

'We know that the ceremonies began at noon,' she said as she wrote.

'"Ceremonies" is a bit grand for a couple of speeches and an "off-you-go",' I said.

'I thought "pompous pontificating" might be a bit too judgemental. If Gertie comes round she might see the board.'

'Diplomatic,' I said with a nod.

'That all took, what shall we say, three minutes? Five at the most. Then we were all in the hall by no later than a quarter past the hour.'

'Squashed up like sardines.'

'Oh, I used to hate playing sardines,' said Lady Hardcastle. 'My mother absolutely loved it, so we had to play every Christmas. Anyway, yes, there we all were, a great deal too many of us crammed into far too small a space. How long would you say we were there before the shout went up?'

'We'd had time to waddle about a bit, and then to speak to Sir Hector,' I said. 'Perhaps twenty minutes? Half an hour at the absolute outside.'

'By around a quarter to one, then, a person or persons unknown had set a small, smoky fire in the office.'

'Using builders' rubbish from outside,' I suggested.

'That seems most likely, yes. I shall assume they'd had a prowl round the place beforehand to get the lie of the land. Leaving those blessed doors unlocked was an absolute gift – Gertie really should have been more careful.'

'That could have been the builders,' I said. 'But any half-decent thief could have picked those locks. I could do it in seconds.'

'In which case, why not just break in at night? Why go to all that effort to frighten everyone out, and then run the risk of being spotted?'

'The book was only in the hall during the exhibition. Porter said they escorted it there in the morning, then they were to escort it back to Westbury's house in the evening.'

'Ah, yes, of course,' she said. 'So the thieves had to strike while everyone was there, because that was the only time the book would be present.'

'And it had to be on opening day because that's the only time they could guarantee a crowd big enough to cover their movements.'

'Exactly so.' She made a few more notes on the crime board. 'It's not a marvellous plan,' she said after a while.

'There are far too many unknowns,' I agreed. 'It relied on the crowd fleeing all at once, on no one thinking to try to put out the fire, on no one else using the back door to escape, on the guards being swept out . . . It's a dreadful plan. Utterly amateurish.'

'And yet it worked.'

'Like a charm. Unless . . .'

'Unless what, dear?' said Lady Hardcastle.

'Well, what if it wasn't a plan at all? What if the fire was just a prank and not a diversion? What if some quick-witted opportunist decided to make hay when they saw everyone running for their lives?'

'That's a possibility worthy of consideration, definitely,' she said as she made another note.

'The mechanics of it all seem fairly straightforward,' I replied, 'even if they do rely altogether too much on luck. But I'm still puzzled by something.'

'I'm puzzled by almost everything.'

'Well, yes, but look at the stolen items. There's Westbury's book, which is worth, by popular estimate, around a thousand pounds. And then there's Sir Hector's landscape, which is worth, what?'

'He didn't say, but he implied that on its own it wasn't much – certainly not enough to get him out of financial trouble.'

'Although we don't know how much that would require.'

'It must be a decently large sum – or an indecently large one,' said Lady Hardcastle. 'I see Hector's point about selling other bits of property being a poor long-term idea, but there are plenty of bits and bobs around The Grange that could be sold to keep the bank happy for a few more months.'

'He said the loan was secured against the property itself,' I said. 'What do we think The Grange is worth?'

'A whelkingly huge amount, I'm sure.'

'More than a thousand?'

'I couldn't begin to say, dear, but I'm not going to put Hector down as a suspect for the theft of the Westbury Shakespeare. He'd have no need if his Summerhayes would cover the debt.'

'Just being thorough,' I said. 'But back to the incongruity. We have those two valuable items, but then there's the alabaster bust, which he said was more of a curio than anything and would probably only get you a few bob at Pomphrey's Bric-a-Brac Emporium. So why those three? Why not just the book? Why not the book and one of the "important local pieces" from the museum?'

'Opportunism again?' suggested Lady Hardcastle. 'Sir Hector's things were more or less on the route from the book display to the storeroom, and that gilt frame made the painting look significantly more impressive than the villagers' pieces around it. Perhaps it just caught their eye and they scooped it up as they hurried by.'

'Perhaps,' I said. 'It certainly makes sense.'

'So whom do we suspect?'

'Everyone in the village except you and me. A fair number from Woodworthy and Chipping. And probably a few strangers who saw one of the many posters about the place and came along for a chance to gawp at the Westbury Shakespeare.'

'Our two security guard friends from this morning?'

'Porter doesn't strike me as the type,' I said. 'And a stiff breeze would blow Larry Templeman away. Even if there is more to him than smiling and nodding, he looks like holding his head up under the weight of his cap is a strain. I doubt he'd have the strength to make off with a big, heavy book.'

Lady Hardcastle tapped the stick of chalk pensively against her teeth.

'It's a start, at least,' she said, picking flakes of chalk from her lip. 'Backgammon or piano?'

'I beg your pardon?'

'Our evening's diversion: backgammon or piano?'

'Oh, I see. I'm rather enjoying my book, actually, so if you think you'd be sufficiently amused by your piano I should like to sit and read while you entertain me with your musical brilliance.'

'You're a shameless flatterer, Florence Armstrong, but I shall dazzle you nonetheless. If you bring the brandy and cheese through, it'll save you getting up later.'

She spent a few minutes rootling through the pile of music in her piano stool, and by the time I'd returned with the decanter, brandy glasses, and some cheese and crackers she had settled down with some Chopin Nocturnes.

Chapter Four

On Tuesday we visited The Grange, where we asked Lady Farley-Stroud if she had any record of the attendees at the art exhibition. It was a long shot – it had not been a ticketed event, after all, and we had seen no evidence of anyone keeping track of who was there – but if anyone would know, it was sure to be the committee's chairwoman.

She had no idea.

With our pool of suspects still no smaller and our minds still mulling over the puzzle of the thefts, we spent the rest of the day on our individual projects. Lady Hardcastle was working on a new animated moving picture in which a society of intelligent water voles built a submarine and discovered a rodent Atlantis at the bottom of their lake. At least I think that's what she said.

For my part, I did some much-needed training with a punching bag and then spent a relaxing afternoon with a set of spanners and a tyre pump, checking that our new bicycles were in tip-top shape.

And that was important because Wednesday was to be Bicycle Ride Day.

We had taken delivery of the new bicycles the week before, having spent much of the previous four years talking about what a thoroughly splendid idea it would be for us to own bicycles, but never actually doing anything about it. We had ridden many times over the years, but our semi-nomadic, mostly city-based, lives had not seemed conducive to ownership. And so we had indulged our bicyclian curiosity by borrowing machines from friends or, during one frantic escape from the police in Belgrade, by stealing them.

Now, though, we had two gleaming machines built by the Raleigh Bicycle Company of Nottingham. We had gigglingly ridden up and down the lane a few times shortly after taking delivery, but there had been no time to take them out into the Gloucestershire countryside and give them their head.

Until Wednesday.

As I prepared Lady Hardcastle's starter breakfast on that exciting morning, the conversation in the kitchen was not, as I had anticipated it might be, about the mechanics of bicycles, nor the potentially exhausting effort of riding them. The question uppermost on Edna's mind was far more practical.

'What you gonna wear, then?' she asked.

Although it was a perfectly sensible question, I was sufficiently surprised by it that I could only offer a confused 'What?' in response.

'Well, you i'n't gonna wear them jodhpurs again, are you? I remember the fuss you both caused in the village that first year you was here when you turned up to the circus in them ridin' jodhpurs. T'i'n't seemly.'

'We have new cycling skirts,' I said. 'Very decorous.'

'That's all right, then,' said Edna with an approving nod. 'I admires you both for everythin' else you does, but ladies didn't ought to be wearin' trousers. T'i'n't natural.'

'Duly noted,' I said with a smile. 'Skirts, blouses, and sensible boots.' I neglected to add that the cycling skirts in question were actually culottes, carefully cut and shaped to appear like skirts when we were off the bicycles and walking about.

If pressed I would have agreed that the idea of anyone encasing their legs in tubes of cloth was, in the sense that it didn't occur in nature, 'unnatural'. I briefly considered asking Edna why such a practice might be considered unnatural only for women, but I knew I would have to listen to the explanation of the moral and medical reasons without arguing – an argument would have ruined both our days for no real profit, after all. I felt that even my exasperated eye-rolling might have caused unnecessary friction, so I decided that diplomatic silence would be my best course.

I took the tray up to Lady Hardcastle and found her already sitting up in bed, studying the map she'd taken up with her when she retired for the night. She peered over the top of her reading glasses as I entered.

'Good morning, pint-sized pedaller,' she said. 'Ooh, is that my toast? Thank you.'

I set down the tray.

'You're just moments too late,' she said as she put down her map.

'Oh,' I said, slightly dismayed. 'Too late for what?'

'If you'd arrived a few seconds earlier I could have told you there's a village near Dursley called Stenchcombe, and we could have had a chuckle about how bad it must smell. In the intervening moments, I've realized I misread it and that it's actually Stinchcombe, which isn't nearly so pleasing.'

'A lost opportunity for mirth,' I agreed. 'I do apologize.'

'Heigh ho. What I've actually been doing is planning our route.'

'We're not going too far, I hope.'

'Good heavens no,' she said. 'We must start gently. But unless we have a plan we shall cycle round the village green a couple of times while we try to decide where to go, then come home because we're tired and bored. I thought a gentle ride up to Woodworthy, a light lunch at the Mock of Pommey, then an even easier ride back.'

'That's a vicious hill up to Woodworthy,' I said. 'Are you sure?'

'This is why I needed the map. If we were to take the Gloucester Road then the hill is, as you say, quite vicious. The route we usually take on the lanes past the orchard is better, but still a little steep in places. But I've found a route that will get us to Woodworthy without the challenge of any steep climbs at all. It's about a mile longer, but it will be less intense. And we can fly down the hill on our way home with our feet off the pedals and our legs stretched out before us, like a couple of wild young tearaways on an adventure.'

'Would you mind taking the role of wild young tearaway on your own?' I said. 'I'm not sure it would suit me. And one of us has to be sensible in case of accident.'

'Very well. But you must at least shout "Woo-hoo!" as we descend. It's practically the law.'

'I shall do my best. Breakfast is in a quarter of an hour.'

By half past nine, with our outfits properly approved by the not-housekeeper, we mounted up and set off down the lane.

I encouraged Lady Hardcastle to take the lead.

'Your map-reading and navigation skills are far better than mine,' I fibbed. 'You should be the one to guide the way.'

She genuinely was an excellent navigator – though not better than me, if we're being honest – but that wasn't why I wanted her setting the pace. I knew she did very little exercise and I was afraid she might struggle to keep up if I were out in front. If I shot off down the lane and left her behind, I'd never hear the end of it. And that, like an argument with Edna about trousers, would ruin everyone's day.

The weather, though miserable for picnics and garden parties, was ideal for cycling. It was bright, but overcast. It was warm enough not to feel a chill, but cool enough that once we started properly exerting ourselves, it wouldn't be uncomfortable.

Lady Hardcastle turned to look at me over her shoulder.

'I'm not sure about this plan,' she called.

'Which plan?' I called back.

'This riding-in-line-astern plan. I can't talk to you.'

'Eyes front!' I yelled, just in time to stop her crashing into the hedge.

She turned back towards me.

'You see?' she called. 'It's never going to work. I can't look at you and look where I'm going at the same time.'

'Then stop blooming well looking at me,' I muttered under my breath as I accelerated to draw level with her.

'There,' she said, 'that's better. Now we can natter as we pedal.'

We emerged from the end of the lane and started round the green. Daisy was walking from her father's butcher's shop down to her other job at the Dog and Duck. She waved, and we slowed to a stop as we reached her.

'You off anywhere nice?' she asked.

'Just testing them out, Your Majesty,' said Lady Hardcastle, patting the handlebars of her bicycle.

'A little jaunt up to Woodworthy and back,' I added.

'Lovely,' said Daisy. 'Are you enterin' the race?'

'No?' I said, as innocently as I could. 'What race?'

In truth I knew there was to be a race on Sunday, organized by the local cycling club. But I also knew that Lady Hardcastle was possibly the most competitive woman I had ever met and would have been unable to resist the challenge if she had found out about it. Any hopes I might have had of a pleasant jaunt in the countryside on Sunday would be dashed, as we slogged our way round a marked course in vain pursuit of cyclists far more capable than we could ever hope to be.

'A race?' said Lady Hardcastle. 'I say, what a lark. We should enter, shouldn't we, Flo?'

'We should,' I said, with a much less convincing air of innocence.

Daisy caught my pained expression and laughed.

'There's a race for the serious sorts and a more gentle social ride for everyone else. I'd go if I had a bike.'

'Oh, that's a shame,' said Lady Hardcastle. 'We'd love to have you with us.'

'Didn't the new landlord at the Mock of Pommey inherit two bicycles?' I said. 'Cissy still works there, doesn't she? Why don't you see if she can borrow them?'

'That would be smashin', wouldn't it,' said Daisy. 'I'd like that.'

'I'm sure they'll let her.'

If she was going to start blabbing about bicycle races like that, she could jolly well get on a bike and keep us company.

'Thank you,' she said with a cheery smile. 'But I'll have to leave you for now – time and Joe Arnold waits for no woman. Turns out that even now I's queen I still has to sweep out the bar afore openin'.'

'See you later, Dais. I mean, "Your Majesty",' I said.

We cycled on.

'Why didn't you tell me about the race?' asked Lady Hardcastle as we turned right and followed her carefully planned route up past the church. 'It sounds like exactly the sort of fun we need.'

'That was the first I'd heard about it,' I lied.

'Well, we know about it now. We shall have to tap Her Majesty, Queen Daisy, for more information upon our return.'

Despite the lack of sunshine, nature was happy with the marginally increased warmth and was going about its late-spring business as usual. Birds flittered about gathering food for their hungry offspring, trees blossomed, and bees buzzed.

A farm cat sat sentinel on a gate post, licking her paw and surveying her demesne with nonchalant superiority. A rabbit scurried across the road in front of us, startled by the sound of our approach. The cat noticed the sudden movement but decided the bunny was too big to be easy prey and resumed her paw-licking.

'This is the life, eh?' said Lady Hardcastle.

'Very pleasant,' I said.

'And a good deal less arduous than I'd envisioned.'

'We've only been going a few minutes. Wait until we have to start climbing up to Woodworthy.'

'We can stop and rest if it becomes too much,' she said. 'We shall sit by the roadside and chew contemplatively on stems of grass while we catch our breath.'

The arduousness began ten minutes later. Lady Hardcastle's route was clever and, as promised, avoided not only the terrifying hill on the Gloucester Road but also the series of lesser hills on the route we would usually take by car. As clever as it was, though, there was no magical way to get from Littleton Cotterell to Woodworthy without somehow gaining the two hundred or so feet of elevation that separated the two. Steep hills were transformed into a long, steady, but insistent incline.

I began to feel a shortness of breath and a burning in my thighs. I was beginning to wonder how Lady Hardcastle was coping when it occurred to me that she hadn't said anything for a while. I looked over and saw that she was struggling even more than I, but I knew how stubborn she was. Despite her assurances that we'd rest as soon as we felt the strain, she wouldn't allow herself to be beaten by something as mundane as a slight slope.

'Blimey, this is hard work,' I said. 'Do you mind if we stop for a few minutes? I'm puffed.'

'Of course, dear,' she panted. 'I did . . . say . . . we could . . . stop . . . any time . . . you . . . wanted.'

A tree formed a gap in the hedgerow a few yards further along, with a soft-looking grassy bank around it. We leaned our bicycles against the hedges on either side and flopped gratefully on to the grass.

We lay for a few moments, staring up at the dull, grey sky.

'How much further?' I asked after a while.

'Another couple of miles, I think,' said Lady Hardcastle. 'We could turn back. It will be downhill all the way home.'

'Only another two miles? We can do that. We could walk it in half an hour if it came to it.'

'If I ever manage to get up again,' she said. 'I might just lie here and wait for a farmer to pass by with a nice cart I can ride in.'

My heart was finally beginning to slow to a more normal pace.

'Are you still interested in the race on Sunday?' I asked, a decent part of me hoping she might have changed her mind.

'Rather,' she said, weakly. 'Though perhaps we could join the social ride with Daisy and treat it as another pleasant day out, rather than taking part in the race. Slow and steady and all that.'

I smiled at the sky and a passing crow cawed. Perhaps he saw me and wanted to share his own thoughts on the matter.

'Right you are,' I said. 'We'll bring haversacks. With sandwiches, and cake, and bottles of . . . something.'

'Beer,' she said, decisively. 'It has to be beer for a cycle ride.'

'Not cider?'

'Ooh, even better. Does Mrs Pantry stock bottled cider?'

'I can't recall,' I said. 'But we'd be taking a chance even if she does. She might slip some arsenic in it if she knows it's for you – start the revolution early.'

'That's always a risk with dear old Comrade Pantry,' said Lady Hardcastle. 'Still, I'm sure Joe could bottle some for us from his barrel.' She sighed contentedly at the thought. 'Cider, sandwiches and cake for a Sunday jaunt in the country. What could be better?'

'I'm sure it will be lovely.'

'Do you know what route they're taking?'

'I have no idea,' I said. 'As I said, the first I knew there even was a cycle race was when Daisy mentioned it just now.'

'We both know you heard about it weeks ago, dear. You've been wisely keeping it from me in case I became overly enthusiastic and committed us to some impossible challenge. Where's it going?'

The problem with having a spy for a best friend is that very little gets past them. They spot the subtlest of signs – the furtive glance, the change of tone, the slight pause before their subject answers. It's undeniably useful in the field, but utterly infuriating at home.

'Up to Berkeley Castle and back,' I said with a sigh.

'Oh, that's not too bad. I'm sure the social cyclists will be just as keen as we are to take it easy. And it will be a treat to finally see Berkeley Castle – even after all this time in the area we've still never paid a visit.'

We rested quietly for another ten minutes, then resumed our steady climb towards Woodworthy and . . .

'We're going to be far too early for lunch at the Mock of Pommey,' I said. 'It can't be eleven o'clock yet.'

Lady Hardcastle looked at her watch.

'It's almost that now. We'll be there in, what, ten minutes. Oh, yes, I see what you mean. I should have planned more carefully. Perhaps we might see if the village shop can sell us something to sustain our onward trip to Chipping Bevington. We shall lunch at the Grey Goose instead.'

We pedalled on.

By the time the Woodworthy village green hove into view, I was ready to sell the bicycles to the first person we saw and walk home. The sheep grazing the green were unfazed by our scarlet, puffing arrival, though I imagined we earned a nod of greeting from the leader. She remembered us from the previous summer, I fancied, and was curious to know why we had abandoned the smart motor car in favour of these peculiar instruments of two-wheeled torture.

I wondered if they had seen many humans riding about on such absurd machines since the former tenants of the Mock of Pommey – both keen cyclists as I remembered it – had left, but then I saw they had. Leaning against the wall of the village pub were at least a dozen bicycles. Not sturdy runabouts like our own, but sleek, purposeful racing machines. We had clearly stumbled upon a midweek meeting of a cycling club.

'Oh, I say, look there,' said Lady Hardcastle, pointing at the bicycles. 'They certainly mean business, don't they?'

'I was just thinking the same,' I said. 'Those are the sort of people we'd have been up against if we'd been foolish enough to enter the race.'

'We wouldn't stand a chance.'

At that moment, five of the cyclists came out of the pub door and started fussing with their machines. The four men were wearing shorts and close-fitting jerseys. The lone woman among them would have horrified poor Edna. She, too, was wearing a tight woollen jersey, but her legs were clad in tweed breeches.

As we approached on our way towards the road to Chipping, one of the men hailed us.

'Good morning, ladies,' he said. 'Lovely day for a ride.'

We pulled up alongside them.

'Enchanting,' said Lady Hardcastle. 'Though we're not quite at your level. What magnificent machines you all have.'

The man patted his saddle affectionately, as one might a favourite horse.

'Pride might be a deadly sin,' he said, 'but I have to admit I'm very proud of this old girl.'

'As well you might be. But where are our manners? I am Lady Hardcastle and this is Miss Armstrong.'

'Delighted to meet you,' said the man, tipping his cap. 'I'm Parslow, chairman of the Woodworthy and Littleton Cotterell Cycling Club. These other reprobates are Blackmore, Screen, and Nurse. And this delightful lady is Miss Irene Vibert.'

We had to complete a comically long round of how-do-you-dos before we were able to say anything further.

'I say,' said Parslow. 'Hardcastle . . . Hardcastle. You're from Littleton, aren't you?'

'We are, yes.'

'Splendid, splendid. Thought I'd heard the name around and about. And will you be joining us on Sunday?'

'We were just discussing that very question,' said Lady Hardcastle. 'And we probably shall, yes. We rather think we might be better suited for the social ride, though.'

'Exactly why we decided to include it,' said the man who had been introduced as Blackmore. 'The idea is to get as many people out on bicycles as possible. A race for the poor saps like us who are obsessed with the things, and a more leisurely ride for everyone else.' He patted his bicycle affectionately, just as Parslow had.

As he spoke, Blackmore focused solely on Lady Hardcastle. Like all charming and attractive people, he had the uncanny knack of making the subject of his attention feel as though they were the only person in the world.

Usually.

Lady Hardcastle – quite used to being the centre of attention – was completely oblivious. Irene Vibert noticed, though, and didn't seem in the least bit happy about it. Her expression turned to a sardonic rolling of the eyes when she realized I was looking at her, and I gave her a sympathetic shrug before turning my own attention to the cyclists' impressive machines.

There was a brand-new Vélo Bastide, a Rudge-Whitworth, an Imperial Triumph, a Coventry Eagle, and even another BSA Road Racer. All were the latest models, and all were clean, polished, and obviously very well cared for.

'Do you have any tips?' I said. 'We've ridden before, but not for a while. It's a good deal more exhausting than I remember.'

'There's no trick to it, I'm afraid,' said Irene. 'You just have to soldier on as best you can. It gets a little easier after a while.'

'And if you're heading back to Littleton,' said Blackmore, 'it's downhill all the way.'

'That's rather what we're counting on,' said Lady Hardcastle. 'Do we have to register our interest in the ride on Sunday?'

'No,' said Parslow, 'just turn up. We'll have a registration desk outside your village hall from eight o'clock, so we can keep track of numbers and make sure everyone gets back safely, but it's supposed to be a fun and informal affair. The racers will set off at nine sharp, then the leisure riders at about half past once they've all gone. We'll try to have someone there to log late arrivals until about six, but after that we'll probably all be in the pub.'

'The Dog and Duck,' I said.

'The very place. They do a nice drop of Mattick's Cider in there. Just what the doctor ordered at the end of a long day's cycling.'

'We look forward to seeing you all on Sunday, then,' said Lady Hardcastle. 'Cheerio.'

With a wave, we pressed on past the village shop and onwards towards Chipping Bevington.

We received a warm welcome at the Grey Goose in Chipping Bevington, where we had dined many times. The head waiter knew us well, and directed us to Lady Hardcastle's preferred table. He was discreet enough not to comment on our bedraggled, shiny-faced appearance, but did bring a large jug of iced water with our menus without needing to be asked.

There were better tables in the former coaching inn – I should have loved to sit at the one in the bay window from where I could watch the good people of the little market town going about their business – but Lady Hardcastle was very particular about seats in restaurants and cafés. Her early training, and subsequent years of service in the field, had taught her that she had to have her back to the wall, with a clear view of the main entrance and an easy path to an alternative exit. That a bicycling lunch in Chipping Bevington and an espionage mission in Budapest were entirely different propositions made not the slightest difference. Best practice was best practice, no matter what the circumstances.

In truth I agreed with her, and had often repositioned myself to get a better view of any secondary entrances, but that table in the window was very enticing.

The substantial lunch we ate was almost certainly a tactical error, but it was difficult to regret dining at the Grey Goose, no matter how uncomfortable the overstuffed journey home might be. We lingered for quite a while over coffee to try to give our lunch 'time to go down', as my mother always used to say, but eventually we could put it off no longer. We were going to have to get ourselves home.

As has been noted more than once already, the journey home down the Gloucester Road was downhill almost all the way, and it was this knowledge that gave us the strength to mount the bicycles once more and start pedalling. Once astride our machines, though, we were quickly made aware of one of the more serious problems with bicycling.

I was, and remain, in awe of the elegant simplicity of the design of the bicycle – the shape of the frame, the slender strength of the wire-spoked wheels, the ingenious chain and toothed wheels driven by the pedals. Where my admiration falters, though, is in the construction of the saddle. The rider's weight must be supported, but their legs must be free to move to provide propulsive power. The whole machine relies on its narrowness for its function and efficiency, and this means that it is impossible to provide a broad and supportive seat. Horse saddles are notoriously uncomfortable for the novice rider, but they are at least wide enough to spread the load. A bicycle saddle, though, is necessarily narrow, and this has serious implications for the neophyte bicyclist. We needn't dwell on the physics involved, nor on the specifics of Monsieur Pascal's pressure calculations – it shall suffice to know that the pressure exerted on the body of the rider is much greater when the seat upon which they sit is narrow than when it is broad. Next, consider precisely where that pressure is applied. Selling the bicycle was no longer a consideration – I was by now ready simply to give my machine to the very next person we met.

The Gloucester Road brought some relief. At last I could stand on the pedals and freewheel down the long hill. Lady Hardcastle, true to her word, was sitting with her legs out in front of her, whooping with delight. For a short while I was able to forget about the discomfort and simply revel in the thrill of speed, and share Lady Hardcastle's infectious joy in just being alive.

The turning to Littleton Cotterell arrived all too soon, and I was compelled once more to retake my uncomfortable seat and resume pedalling.

The road into the village passed the old Dower House – part of The Grange's estate and one of the Farley-Strouds' few remaining sources of income. Sir Hector had said there was a new tenant but we'd not yet met them, so I was intrigued as we approached to see a woman leaving the front door and wheeling yet another bicycle along the path to the gate.

Lady Hardcastle saw her, too, and slowed to say hello. Cycling, I was beginning to learn, was a most sociable form of transport.

'Good morning, dear,' said Lady Hardcastle. 'How lovely to see someone living in the Dower House again. Welcome to the village.'

'Thank you,' said the woman. She was lean and lithe, with greying hair and delicate lines forming around eyes that I imagined smiled often. Or perhaps she just squinted a lot. She certainly squinted at me as I smiled back.

'I'm Emily Hardcastle, and this is Florence Armstrong, by the way. Have you met many of the other villagers?'

'Only a couple of the shopkeepers. I moved in last week, y'see, so I've not had many opportunities. I'm still finding my way about.' She held out a hand. 'Angelina Goodacre.'

She shook both our hands. Her grip was firm and her expression warm. Her accent, I judged, was from somewhere in the North-East. Newcastle, perhaps, or Middlesbrough. It was soft, though – barely noticeable. She had travelled.

I gestured towards the bike she'd leaned against the garden wall. 'Another cyclist, I see.'

'Very much so,' said Angelina. 'For most of my life. Love the things.'

I had slipped free of the seat and was standing on the road, my feet either side of the frame.

'We're rather new to the whole thing.'

'I thought you looked a little puffed.'

'More than just a little, dear,' said Lady Hardcastle. 'I'm absolutely done in.'

'It gets better, you'll be addicted in no time.'

'I hope so,' I said. 'And talking of getting better . . . have you any tips on' – I twisted slightly so I could gesture at the Saddle of Infinite Torment – 'these things.'

She laughed. 'Ah, "those things".' She gave a nod of under-standing. 'I'd like to be able to tell you there's a secret known only to experienced cyclists that will save you from the agony of the saddle. A simple but effective trick that will make riding a bike like sitting on pillows stuffed with feathers plucked from their own bellies and cheerfully donated by magical, extra-fluffy geese.'

'But?' I said.

'But you just have to get used to it, I'm afraid. It'll take a few days but soon you won't even notice it.'

I looked suspiciously at the saddle. I couldn't imagine ever not noticing that thing.

She laughed again.

'I promise,' she said. 'And the thighs will get stronger, too.' She patted her own beneath her cycling skirt.

'I'm not entirely convinced I shall be able to walk again for a few hours,' said Lady Hardcastle, 'let alone cycle. But we shall persevere.'

'We shall,' I said with a good deal less conviction.

'Oh, but we have to,' she said. 'We're going on the ride to Berkeley on Sunday.'

'The race?' said Angelina. 'I haven't learned much about village events apart from the art exhibition and the cycle race. I'm defi-nitely going to enter that.'

'There's a leisurely ride for those of us who aren't racers,' said Lady Hardcastle.

Angelina smiled – she was spared having to say anything kind about our chances in the race.

'Then I shall see you on Sunday, if not before,' said Angelina, mounting up.

'Or drop in anytime for a cup of tea and an introduction to local gossip, if you find yourself at a loose end. We're on the lane on the other side of the village green. You can't miss us.'

'You're very kind. Ta-ta, pet.'

And with that she was off towards the Gloucester Road at a speed we could only dream of.

'Back home for cooling baths and a pot of tea, I think,' said Lady Hardcastle as she scooted her bicycle forwards to get it moving.

We pedalled wearily back to the house.

Chapter Five

By Thursday morning both Lady Hardcastle and I were barely capable of moving. I would have counted myself as one of the fitter members of our little village community, but our short cycling adventure had left me stiff and sore. Climbing the stairs was particularly unpleasant.

Lady Hardcastle was worse afflicted and was, as was her custom, entirely uninhibited about letting everyone know exactly how much discomfort she was in. Edna was sympathetic for a while, but soon decided that all the bedrooms needed a thorough clean and set off to do just that. Miss Jones listened patiently and offered tea and cake, but soon she, too, had to ask to be excused so she could get on with her work.

I was as kind and considerate as always, and this, I think, was my saviour. I listened solicitously to a particularly lengthy outburst of moaning and grumbling as we made our way slowly from Lady Hardcastle's study to the drawing room for morning coffee. As we stood by the window contemplating the view of the tidy little front garden and the lane beyond, I gave her a few 'oh, I knows' and at least one 'you poor thing'.

Suddenly, she looked at me and said, 'Oh, but listen to me going on about myself. You must be suffering, too, dear. Are you?'

'I've been better,' I said with a smile, and seized on this break in the hitherto-unending stream of complaint as a splendid opportunity to change the subject. 'Have you had any more thoughts about the art theft?'

'One or two, yes,' she said, adding a loud groan as she settled into an armchair. 'I keep coming back to the shambolic contradiction of it all. One begins by assuming it must have all been meticulously planned, but once one delves into the details it seems so chaotically improvised and lackadaisical. The fire, one presumes, absolutely had to be part of a plan. They knew they needed to clear the hall, and decided a fire alarm would do the trick. In order to pull that off, they had to find some suitably combustible materials and a fireproof bucket to put them in. They seem quite organized up to that point. Ideally, they would have decided upon the best place to set the fire – my choice would have been one of the side rooms – but the choice of the office seems to have been made by chance. Gertie lamented her failure to lock the office door, so one presumes that was how it was usually expected to be. Which means that the use of the office was just happenstance – they simply found the door unlocked and made up their minds on the spot. The ability to improvise is vital in any sort of underhand activity, but that seems like an unnecessary deviation. Why not use the meeting room next door? That's always open. And then there's the overall complexity of the scheme. There are so many moving parts, so many things that have to work just so for it all to succeed, and yet the execution is starting to look slapdash and amateurish.'

'It did work, though,' I said.

'It worked well. I'm stumped.'

'For my part,' I said after a few moments' thought, 'I'm still baffled by the fact that two professional security guards managed to allow themselves to be driven from the hall by the crowd and then made no attempt to return. We didn't see them at all after we'd been inside to check for stragglers.'

'I think "professional" might be over-egging it a bit. They're paid, certainly, and they wear uniforms, but I'd not infer any special skills or abilities based on those two facts alone. And Porter said he didn't mind where he was standing as long as he was paid to stand there, so I don't see any particular dedication to duty, either.'

'I still think there's something odd about them,' I said.

'As odd as odd can be,' she agreed. 'But do we have any aspirin? I do ache so.'

◆　◆　◆

We were feeling a little more like our old selves on Friday, and decided that if we were to enjoy our Sunday ride to Berkeley, we really ought to spend a little more time on the bicycles. A short jaunt through the local lanes before lunch was called for, we thought. Just a few miles to keep us limber and to try to get beyond 'great merciful heavens will this torment never end?' and closer to 'actually, you know, bicycle saddles aren't so bad'.

The weather was pleasingly warm, with the sun peeking through the clouds every so often to lift our spirits. Once more we cycled along the lane, skirted the village green, and headed up past St Arilda's church. The vicar gave us a wave as we passed by, but he was with Mrs Stitch – presumably in her capacity as chairwoman of the church flowers committee – and we decided to keep going.

We were still among the small thatched farmworkers' cottages which clustered round the back of the churchyard when Lady Hardcastle slowed to an unexpected stop.

'Blow this,' she said, defeated. 'I fear my optimism was entirely misplaced. I hurt in places where there didn't ought to be places and my hat has come loose from its moorings. I propose we return to the pub for a light lunch and a large glass of something reviving.'

I wasn't feeling too bad, but I was happy to forgo even a short ride if there were sandwiches and cider on offer instead. We wheeled around in the road and cycled sedately back to the Dog and Duck, where we propped our bikes against one of Old Joe's popular outdoor tables and stepped inside.

The lunchtime crowd of farmhands and other local workers was beginning to build. Daisy was behind the bar but was looking a lot less chipper than usual. The cause of her unusually harassed demeanour was easy to see, though, and came in the form of insurance investigator Cordelia Harrill.

'. . . but that's what I'm asking you, Miss Spratt,' she was saying. 'Exactly where were you standing when the shout of "Fire!" went up, you stupid girl? Are you too simple-minded to understand? It's really not a terribly complicated question.'

'And what I'm tellin' you, *Miss Harrill,* is that I doesn't remember exactly where I was stood.'

'You *don't* remember where you were *standing,*' said Cordelia, superciliously.

'*That's* what I *said,*' said Daisy with a shake of her head.

'Good afternoon, Cordelia dear,' said Lady Hardcastle. 'How lovely to see you again so soon. Have you come to our delightful village pub for a little light luncheon? I recommend the sandwiches. So generous. Or the pies made by our local baker, Mr Holman. And wash it all down with a glass of Mattick's Cider. It's a treat not to be missed.'

'I'm working,' said Cordelia through gritted teeth.

'Are you, dear? Is that what it was? Do you know, it sounded to the untrained ear for all the world as though you were just being unpardonably rude to one of my dearest friends.'

Daisy rolled her eyes and treated me to her very best cheeky grin. She was perfectly capable of standing her ground against the likes of Cordelia Harrill, but no one is ever disappointed to have an ally.

'The wretched girl won't tell me where she was stood . . . standing,' said Cordelia, now slightly flustered.

'Perhaps she doesn't remember,' said Lady Hardcastle. 'I can tell you precisely where I was stood if it helps.'

'You're on my list, don't you worry.'

'I should be dismayed were I not. What kind of investigator would ignore me? I have been arrested by the police on three continents, after all. I'd be suspicious of me from the outset.'

Cordelia regarded Lady Hardcastle closely before snorting derisively. 'Arrested? You? What for? Using the wrong fork at dinner?'

'Good lord, yes, now you mention it. I'd quite forgotten that one. There was that incident in that hotel in New York, Armstrong, do you remember? Make that four continents.'

Cordelia tutted and shook her head.

'Now,' continued Lady Hardcastle, 'I think you've had your answer from Miss Spratt, don't you? You're welcome to question me, or Miss Armstrong, or anyone else here if you wish. But if you do, I caution you to be a good deal more polite about it. Armstrong is the sweetest soul you could possibly imagine, but she won't take kindly to you if she hears you speak to anyone in the village like that again.'

'She's right,' I said. 'I'm funny about things like that.'

Cordelia sneered at me.

'And what would you do about it?' she asked.

I leaned in close and said softly, 'Why don't you try it and find out?'

She let out a dismissive *pfft*.

'And if you don't wish to ask any more questions,' said Lady Hardcastle, 'might I respectfully suggest that you either order yourself some lunch – my treat – or sling your hook. There's a good girl.'

Cordelia picked up her briefcase from the floor, slammed her notebook in it, and stomped out the door without saying another word.

'Lovely girl,' said Lady Hardcastle. 'I knew her at Girton, you know. She was always a charmer then, too.'

'I was about to wallop her one meself,' said Daisy. 'It's only my professional dedication to the Barmaid's Code as stopped me.'

'There's a Barmaid's Code?' I said.

'There is,' she said with an emphatic nod. 'But its secrets is vouchsafed only to fully admitted members of the Ancient and Most Worshipful Company of Inn Keepers, Publicans and Servin' Wenches. Alas, I am forbidden from revealin' any of the secrets of our guild, save that it is generally considered bad practice to wallop payin' customers, even if they are "right cows" as the official terminology has it.'

'You're an accomplished woman, Dais,' I said. 'And a fine serving wench.'

'I reckon I'd suit one o' they old-fashioned bodices,' she said, hitching herself up. 'What do you think?'

'You'd look delightful, dear,' said Lady Hardcastle.

'Have you really been arrested on four continents, though?' asked Daisy.

'Just the three, I'm afraid,' said Lady Hardcastle. 'Europe, Asia and Africa. The American one was a fiction to irritate Cordelia.'

'Whatever was you arrested for?'

'Mostly because we'd annoyed someone important. The Turkish charges were definitely trumped-up, but at least that was in Constantinople so I'm able to claim Asia as my third continent.'

'Whereabouts in Africa, though? I'd love to go to Africa.'

'Cairo. More trumped-up charges.'

'How do you get out of all these things?'

'Charm, mostly,' said Lady Hardcastle with a smile. 'Or some-times with help from the local British consulate or embassy.'

'And sometimes we just break out,' I said.

'Or that,' agreed Lady Hardcastle. 'Now then, Daisy dear, what do you have for lunch?'

'Much as you said, m'lady,' said Daisy. 'We gots Joe's door-stops – cheese, ham or roast beef. And we gots Holman's pies, though I's not sure what flavours. Beef again, probably. And maybe lamb and tater – our dad's just startin' to get lamb in so Holman might have been pressed into buyin' some. But, honestly, I doesn't know.'

'Your reputation as a Master Wench seems to have been exag-gerated,' I said. 'I may have to report you to the guild.'

'You can try,' said Daisy, 'but it won't get you nowhere. There's special provision in the code for pies supplied by outside contractors.'

'I shall have a mystery pie and a large glass of cider, please, dear,' said Lady Hardcastle.

'Same for me, please, Dais,' I said.

'Shall we eat outside?' asked Lady Hardcastle. 'It seems a shame to waste what little sunshine we have.'

I nodded my agreement.

'You go and find yourselves somewhere nice to sit,' said Daisy, 'and I'll bring your pies out in a bit.'

It was far from hot out on the village green, but the occasional bursts of May sunshine made it feel warmer than it was. After the previous summer's deadly heatwave, there were many who were relieved that 1912 had so far seen much cooler, damper weather, but I would have settled for a compromise. Warm but not hot, perhaps. As for the much-needed rain, I would have preferred occasionally drizzly to perpetually drenched. My daydream paradise island featured warm sunny days, cool rainy nights, and fields filled with ripening crops. And a complete absence of cattle. And a house which tidied itself as Lady Hardcastle passed through it.

The Dog and Duck's landlord, Joe Arnold, had introduced outdoor tables the year before and they had been an instant hit. It hadn't exactly turned the village pub into a Parisian pavement café, but it did at least allow people to enjoy a drink in the sunshine on a late-spring afternoon, or to watch the cricket on a summer's evening with a pint of cider in front of them.

This spring, the rickety trestle tables and folding chairs had been replaced by sturdy outdoor tables and benches. We chose one in the shade of an unidentified tree and made ourselves comfortable. Lady Hardcastle sat with her back to the pub, looking out across the green. I sat opposite her with a much less interesting view of the pub and the shops beside it. I looked up at the tree instead.

'It's a common horse chestnut,' said Lady Hardcastle, noticing my puzzled gaze at the fat hands of leaves and the pinkish-white blossom. '*Aesculus hippocastanum.*'

'Ah, conkers,' I said.

'And the same to you, dear. But yes. Conkers. You've seen them on the ground here every autumn for the past four years and yet . . .'

'You've known me for eighteen years. You know I never pay attention to plants and trees. And yet . . .'

'Point taken, dear.'

'Aeschylus I've heard of,' I said. 'I once found a translation of *The Persians* on a dusty shelf in a library somewhere in Lancashire. It didn't make much sense to me, but I was only eleven.'

'Different spelling, I'm afraid,' she said. 'You know, it's a source of constant wonder that you can converse with dentists, duchesses and dustmen on everything from Greek tragedy to the capitalist exploitation of the working man, from the latest releases at the cinema to Bradford's chances in the FA Cup—'

'I was right there.'

'You were. And yet . . . you can't retain even the most basic horticultural information.'

'It's a question of interests and priorities,' I said. 'As I've explained many times before: most plants are green, some have pretty flowers, some bear tasty fruit. What more do I need to know?'

'If you knew which plant was which, you'd know whether the fruit was safe to eat, for a start.'

'That's what greengrocers are for.'

'Your reasoning is sound, dear, of course. But this is a horse chestnut. And it will still be a horse chestnut next month when you've erased this conversation from your mighty brain and have to ask me again.'

'And for as long as I have you to ask, I have no need to retain the information myself. I can devote my mighty brain to matters that actually interest me.'

'Like the two young strangers over there on matching bicycles?'

'That is rather interesting, actually,' I said, turning to look. 'More interesting than conker trees, at any rate. And how is it that everyone is suddenly on a bicycle?'

'I wonder if bicycles have always been commonplace but that we notice them more now that we have machines of our own. I should probably write a monograph on the subject.'

'You probably should. They're coming this way.'

The young man and young woman were, indeed, heading for the Dog and Duck. They passed behind us and leaned their bikes against the pub wall before going inside. A few minutes later, Daisy emerged bearing a tray weighed down with pies and cider, followed by the two cyclists, each carrying a glass of cider of their own.

I judged them to be in their mid-twenties, though I was beginning to find it difficult to accurately assess the ages of people younger than I. I had originally thought them to be a couple, but there was such a family resemblance between them – the same slight frame, the same fair hair, the same blue eyes, the same straight nose and strong cheekbones – that I decided instead that they must be brother and sister.

Daisy set the tray on the table and turned to the newcomers.

'These is the two ladies I was tellin' you about,' she said. 'Lady Hardcastle and Miss Armstrong, these is Ezekiel and Hephzibah Freer of Yorkshire. They's treasure hunters.' She said this last phrase with awe-filled relish. Actual treasure hunters in our little village. Whatever next?

'How do you do?' said the young man, fussily pushing his spectacles up his nose with his free hand.

'How do you do, dear?' said Lady Hardcastle. 'Treasure hunters, eh? How wonderfully exciting.'

'I hopes you don't mind, m'lady,' said Daisy, 'but they's interested in The Grange and I told 'em if anyone round 'ere knows about The Grange, it'll be you two.'

'I suspect Sir Hector and Lady Farley-Stroud know a good deal more than we do,' said Lady Hardcastle, 'but we're a reasonable substitute for now. Would you care to join us, Mr and Miss Freer?'

'Zeke and Zibbie,' said Zeke.

They sat down on opposite sides of the table, one beside each of us, and set their drinks in front of them.

'You don't mind if we eat?' said Lady Hardcastle. 'I'm absolutely famished, I'm afraid.'

'No, not at all,' said Zibbie. 'We have sandwiches on the way.'

'Oh, you have a treat in store. Old Joe's sandwiches are legendary in these parts.'

'We know,' said Zeke with a warm smile. 'We arrived here yesterday and they was the first thing we tried.'

We took our plates from the tray – Daisy's failure to perform that simple service for us was further evidence of substandard wenching, I felt – and tucked in gratefully. My pie was lamb and potato. Lady Hardcastle's was beef and mushroom.

Thankfully, Daisy reappeared before our decision to eat without waiting for our new companions became awkward, and as soon as they had their enormous sandwiches I felt comfortable giving voice to my curiosity.

'So then, Zeke and Zibbie,' I said, 'what exactly does a treasure hunter do? I presume you don't have maps leading to Captain Flint's treasure where X marks the spot?'

They both laughed politely.

'We don't, I'm afraid,' said Zeke. 'It's all a fair sight more mundane than that. We spend most of us time in libraries and local archives, looking through long-forgotten books and files. Collections of correspondence, council documents, plans – anything that might lead us to what we seek.'

'And how do you know what it is that you seek?' asked Lady Hardcastle. 'Where does that first clue come from?'

'Could come from anywhere,' said Zibbie. 'A reference in a tattered book, some story the old folk tell . . . anything, really.'

'And what story led you to our little village?' I said. 'And to The Grange in particular?'

'It were somethin' we read in an old account of the Peninsular War,' said Zeke. 'Wars are always a good source of treasure. The siege is broken, the battle won, and the victorious troops ransack the town, takin' whatever catches their eye. Spoils of war.'

'Looting,' I said.

'Looting implies it's illicit in some way,' said Zibbie, 'but this was almost encouraged. Generals tended to turn a blind eye and let their men take what they wanted. It was a reward.'

'So we came across a story about a huge trove of gold and jewels,' said Zeke. 'Portable stuff. It had been . . . "collected" by a French colonel as Napoleon's armies made their way through northern Spain and into Portugal. Then it was seized from him by a British officer as Wellington chased the French back to France.'

'All we knew was it were a cavalry major as took it,' said Zibbie, 'but none of the accounts told us where it happened or who was involved.'

'We've been chasing up and down the country,' said Zeke, 'following trail after dead-end trail, trying to find out who this cavalry major was. We thought we'd tracked him down to an old place just outside Dursley, but the fella who'd lived there never served in Iberia – he were at home living off his spoils from the war in Austria by then.'

'But the family as lives there let us look through their library,' said Zibbie, 'and that was where we came across a history of the 8th Dragoon Guards we'd never seen before. The fella's an amateur army historian, y'see? And it talks about their heroism at the Battle of Vitoria, and how one of their majors distinguished himself with his bravery and gallantry before losing his arm trying to save his men when they were surrounded by French hussars.'

'The French were routed at Vitoria and fled,' said Zeke, 'leaving their baggage behind. And that were when the British troops fell on the baggage train and helped themselves to whatever they could get their hands on.'

'This time,' said Zibbie, 'Wellington wasn't best pleased and called his men "the scum of the earth". But the baggage contained almost all the French loot from the campaign and at least one officer managed to secure several chests of gold and jewels for himself before his men could get their hands on it. He retired back to England "with his fortune" and moved to Gloucestershire, so when we read that we knew we were finally in the right part of the country. There were another reference later on to Major Teddy Elderkin and his one arm meeting some of his old comrades in Chipping Bevington.'

'So we come down to Chipping Bevington—' began Zeke.

'They have a marvellous library in Chipping,' said Lady Hardcastle.

'They do,' he said. 'That were the first place we went.'

'I hope they were helpful. If not, have a word with Miss Francis and mention my name. We found her most accommodating.'

'Small woman in her sixties?' asked Zibbie.

'That's her. Fauna Francis. She has a sister called Flora, a fact that restores my faith in English parents.'

'We met her,' said Zeke. 'And she were as helpful as you say. She pointed us towards the local history section, where we learned about Major Sir Theodore Elderkin, late of the 8th Dragoon Guards, who retired to Littleton Cotterell with his beautiful wife and his army pension in 1814. He bought The Grange, an old Elizabethan manor house which had been recently extended by its owners to incorporate a modern Palladian façade, and they lived out their days there. No one ever heard from him again.'

'And you think he bought the place with his looted – sorry, *liberated* treasure?' I asked.

'It all fits together,' said Zibbie. 'So, yes, we do.'

'And you think some treasure remains?' I said. 'How do you know he didn't blow what was left after buying The Grange on gambling and loose living?'

'The archives at the Chipping Bevington library show how much he paid for The Grange,' said Zeke. 'And the story of the treasure gave an estimate of how much it was worth. With what he had left he could have raised merry hell for decades.'

'But no one heard of him or his treasure again,' said Zibbie. 'He lived modestly as far as we can tell, well within the means of a retired cavalry major with a pension and rents from his tenants. That treasure is still at The Grange somewhere.'

'I shouldn't like to be the one to pour cold water on your dreams,' said Lady Hardcastle, 'but we know the present owners very well. If there were treasure at The Grange, they'd know about it and so would we.'

'Ah, but that's the point, d'you see?' said Zeke. 'No one knows about it. Elderkin brought it home, bought his home with it, then hid it away for a rainy day. He doesn't seem ever to have mentioned it, and nor does anyone else. The couple died childless within a few months of each other in 1851. The house was sold on to a tobacco merchant from Bristol who added a new wing in the Gothic Revival style, then the Farley-Strouds bought it when they returned from India for good in 1876.'

'There's no mention in any local histories of Sir Theodore's enormous wealth,' said Zibbie. 'Nothing in the archives about generous acts of philanthropy. No scandals of debt or dishonour. Just an old war hero living a quiet life as a country squire.'

'Assuming he had the treasure in the first place,' I said.

'We always has to make some assumptions,' agreed Zeke. 'But never outlandish ones. There were treasure after Vitoria, and some of it came home with a cavalry major. And in Sir Theodore Elderkin we have a cavalry major with enough money to buy a manor house and set himself up for a comfortable retirement. His family was well-to-do, but not enough to buy their middle son a big house in the country. That money came from somewhere and we reckon it were the treasure.'

'And if no one's seen it since 1814,' said Zibbie, 'then it's still at The Grange.'

'Well I never,' said Lady Hardcastle. 'What a fascinating development.'

'You say you know them well?' said Zeke.

'Firm friends, dear.'

'So you could introduce us?' asked Zibbie. 'We'd love to explore the house and grounds.'

'We can certainly tell them your story. As for whether they wish to allow you to explore their home . . . we shall have to see. I shall plead your case as well I can, but the final decision must be theirs.'

'We understand,' said Zeke.

'Can't say fairer than that,' agreed Zibbie.

'Splendid. We shall try to see them this evening. You're staying here at the Dog and Duck?'

'We are,' they said together.

'Then we shall send word here as soon as we have it. Now then, how are your sandwiches? Would anyone like more cider?'

Lady Hardcastle telephoned Sir Hector as soon as we returned from the pub, and said that while we were no nearer finding his lost painting, we did have intriguing new information. It would be better shared in person, she said, and wondered if they were at home to callers later that evening. Sir Hector, ever the generous host even in straitened circumstances, invited us to dine with them.

We arrived at The Grange at half past seven, dressed for dinner.

Jenkins showed us through to the drawing room, where Lady Farley-Stroud was reading a magazine while Sir Hector, his bow tie endearingly askew, fussed over the preparation of pre-prandial gin and tonics.

'Ah, good evenin', ladies,' he said. 'Just in time. I say, you're both lookin' lovely. Special occasion?'

'Dining with you is always a special occasion, Hector dear,' said Lady Hardcastle.

'You're too kind, Em'ly, too kind. Get yourselves outside these.'

He handed us each a glass.

I raised mine in salute and took a sip. As usual he had been rather more generous with the gin than the tonic, but you got used to these things when you spent time with the Farley-Strouds.

Lady Farley-Stroud held up the magazine and gave it a triumphant two-handed wave.

'Another piece by Clarissa,' she said, proudly. 'Summer fashions from Paris.'

Before her marriage to Adam Whitman, Clarissa had worked in London as a fashion and society writer for a small magazine. She and Adam now lived just outside Bordeaux, which made her, in the eyes of English editors, extremely well placed to write about the latest Paris fashions. That Paris was further from Bordeaux than it was from London seemed not to trouble them – they had a correspondent in France and that was what mattered.

'How wonderful,' said Lady Hardcastle. 'I'm so pleased she's doing well.'

'Very well indeed,' beamed Lady Farley-Stroud. 'And soon to be a mother again.'

'Oh, I say, congratulations. When?'

'Early September,' said Lady Farley-Stroud.

'Only just found out,' said Sir Hector. 'After the fiasco with little Lou-Lou she decided to withhold the announcement until she had triple-checked the dates.'

Clarissa had managed to tell her parents entirely the wrong due date for her first child, and was clearly wary of making the same mistake again.

'Oh, shush, Hector,' said Lady Farley-Stroud. 'She couldn't help it.'

'Couldn't help havin' a head stuffed with fluff, y'mean? No, I suppose not.'

'Well, if she does, she gets it from her father.'

'Touché, my little pineapple upside-down cake. Touché. Left m'self open for that one, what?'

'Will you be visiting them?' I asked.

'If we can afford the trip, dear, yes,' said Lady Farley-Stroud.

'Might have to move in with 'em if the bank takes The Grange,' said Sir Hector.

Lady Farley-Stroud looked crestfallen for a moment, but then made a very obvious effort to brighten the mood.

'Hector tells me you have news,' she said. 'Do say it's something diverting and fun.'

'It's to do with The Grange, actually,' said Lady Hardcastle. 'And, yes, I suppose it is quite fun.'

And for the next few minutes we told them about our meeting with Zeke and Zibbie Freer, and recounted, as best we could remember it, the story of the Treasure of The Grange.

'Well I never,' said Sir Hector when we had finished. 'Are they certain there's treasure here, this Zeke and Zibbie?'

'What kind of names are those?' asked Lady Farley-Stroud. 'Not sure we can trust people who call themselves Zeke and Zibbie.'

'Their full names are Ezekiel and Hephzibah,' I said. 'To be honest, if I'd been saddled with a moniker like either of those, I'd find a suitable nickname as soon as I could.'

'I suppose so,' she said.

'But, yes, Hector,' said Lady Hardcastle. 'Dubious hypocorisms aside, they do seem to be in earnest.'

'And can we trust 'em?'

'Can we trust anyone, dear? That's the thing. They're extremely keen to meet you, we know that, and I would guess they'll press you for carte blanche to poke about the house and grounds once they do. If you're thinking about letting them, I'd keep close tabs on them. And make very certain you all agree on what share they get of the spoils if they happen to find anything.'

'Never mind this fabled treasure, they'll be tryin' to pinch the family silver,' said Lady Farley-Stroud.

'They'll be disappointed,' said Sir Hector. 'Family silver went years ago.'

'Well, it's up to you, dear,' said Lady Hardcastle. 'If you want to meet them I'd be happy to make the introductions.'

'Can't see it would hurt,' said Sir Hector after a few moments' thought. 'There's precious little left to steal now the Summerhays has gone. And it's not as though they'll find anythin'. We've been here, what, thirty-six years? I've been over every inch of the place one way or another. Never seen so much as a stray Napoleonic franc. Then again, I wasn't lookin' for lost treasure, so if they know where to look, I'd be happy to give 'em a cut. If they're right about what Elderkin brought back, there'll be more than enough for everyone.'

'What fun. I was going to offer to bring them to you, but the Rolls isn't built for four. Or even three, come to that.'

'No matter, m'dear, just send 'em up. We'll know who they are. Not many Zekes and Zibbies in the world.'

'They can easily make their own way,' I said. 'They have bicycles. Everyone seems to have a bicycle all of a sudden.'

'Everyone?' said Lady Farley-Stroud. 'Are you sure? I'm certain I've not seen a bicycle for years.'

'You'll see them everywhere now, dear,' said Lady Hardcastle. 'Just you wait.'

Lady Farley-Stroud frowned in puzzlement, but before she could ask anything further, Jenkins sounded the dinner gong and we obediently made our way to the dining room.

Chapter Six

We managed to catch the Freers at the pub on Saturday morning, and passed on Sir Hector's message. They expressed their delight and gratitude and we spent the rest of the day trying to get on with our regular obligations. Lady Hardcastle shut herself away to catch up with some correspondence while I checked the household accounts, mended a dress, and wrote to my sister.

Sunday morning came all too soon. I was never a lover of Sundays, but this one, with its prospect of painful, perspiration-soaked pedalling – and many other things beginning with 'p' apart from pleasure and plum pie (it was too early in the year for plums) – filled me with a particular dread.

Nevertheless, we had made our promises to ourselves and others, and a commitment is a commitment, no matter how exhausting. So I was up early putting together a picnic while Miss Jones got on with preparing a fortifying breakfast.

She had asked if she could leave early so that she could spend the day with her new beau, a postman from Chipping Bevington. He was a keen cyclist – postmen often are – and she wanted to see him off on the race. A topsy-turvy dispute had ensued which would have bewildered the heads of households throughout the land.

Lady Hardcastle had tried to insist that she should take the whole day off, and that she should henceforth take two days off every week for the same pay. It was only fair, she had said. Everyone else had at least one and a half days off every week, and some had two. Why should Miss Jones not be able to enjoy the same?

Miss Jones had countered that she only worked half-days as it was, and that anyway she enjoyed her work and would miss coming to the house every day to see us.

The argument had become bizarrely heated and Lady Hardcastle had only backed down when she realized that Miss Jones had begun to cry. Miss Jones explained through her sniffles that she was bewildered and distressed that her loyalty was being rebuffed, and said she thought she was being pushed out. Lady Hardcastle for her part said she was bewildered and distressed that what she had thought of as an act of generosity and kindness was being so staunchly rejected.

I had sighed, tutted, and made them both a cup of tea.

Apologies were offered all round, the status quo was restored, and the original request – leaving early on Sunday to watch the race – had been granted.

As the bacon and sausages sizzled, I was packing the picnic into a couple of old haversacks.

'Are you going to be slinging them over your shoulders?' said Miss Jones.

'It's the only thing I can think of,' I said. 'We might be more comfortable with rucksacks, but this is all we have.'

'You should have a nice wicker basket on the front. Old Mrs Gardner has one. She brings sewing things round to my mother in it.'

'If you mention it to Herself, don't say that *Old* Mrs Gardner has one. Dear Lady Hardcastle is almost entirely free of vanity and usually doesn't care what people think of her, but she never wants to be thought of as "old". She's happy to age. She faces the prospect of greying hair and the other physical imprints of the passage of time with cheerful equanimity. But she never wishes to be "old".'

'Who doesn't, dear?' said Lady Hardcastle from behind me.

'You,' I said, without turning round.

'My word, no. Ageing is absolutely fine. I'm perfectly at ease with the knowledge that my appearance will change, my youthful vigour diminish. A wrinkle here, an impertinently sprouting hair there, a creaking knee and a stiff back – they'll all be perfectly wonderful. I shall wear them as badges of honour; medals in recognition of my valour in the daily battle against random death. Although, now I come to think about it, I might prevail upon Flo to pluck the wayward chin hairs now and then. But being thought of as old? Ghastly. "Here comes old Emily with her old ways and her old ideas." Ugh.'

'And how would you feel about having a wicker basket on your handlebars?' I said.

'Is that something old ladies do? It sounds jolly practical.'

'Mrs Gardner has one.'

'Oh, but she's "old" in so many other ways. I'm not certain a bicycle-mounted wicker basket is a reliable indicator of an elderly attitude on its own. I shall keep my eyes open for them and if my first thought is "gracious, it's an old lady on a bicycle", I shall know. For now, though, my mind is open. When's breakfast?'

'It's imminent,' I said. 'Sit down and we'll be through in a minute.'

◆ ◆ ◆

Breakfasts eaten, skirts brushed, hats fastened and boots buttoned, we cycled along the lane and onwards to the registration table on the village green. Or, at least, to the end of the queue that had formed at the registration table.

We joined the queue behind Zeke and Zibbie Freer.

'Good morning, dears,' said Lady Hardcastle. 'How goes the treasure hunting?'

They both looked round, furtively.

'Very well indeed,' said Zeke, quietly. 'Thank you for the introduction.'

'You've been to The Grange then?' said Lady Hardcastle in a slightly-louder-than-normal voice.

Once again the urgent glances at the queue.

'Yes,' said Zibbie in a stage whisper.

Lady Hardcastle was well aware of the need for circumspection when talking about delicate matters, but she was also able to assess her situation at a glance. She knew the assembled cyclists, absorbed as they were in their own conversations about the ride ahead, weren't even aware that others were talking, let alone that they might be openly discussing enticing secrets. I could see from the girlish twinkle in her eye, though, that she was enjoying teasing the treasure hunters.

'I'm so pleased,' she said, just as loudly as before. 'Was Sir Hector excited? I bet he was. Treasure at The Grange? Who wouldn't be?'

The agitation on their youthful faces was a joy to behold, and I had to concentrate hard on not laughing.

'Lady Hardcastle, please,' hissed Zeke.

'What's the matter, dear?' she said.

'It is unwise to discuss . . . such matters so carelessly,' whispered Zibbie. 'We must always be mindful of who might overhear us.'

Lady Hardcastle looked around, as though noticing her surroundings for the first time.

'Oh,' she said, slowly, as realization apparently dawned. She continued in an exaggerated whisper of her own. 'Sorry. Mum's the word, eh?' She tapped the side of her nose.

Further teasing was forestalled by the arrival of the gaggle of competitive cyclists we'd met outside the Mock of Pommey on Wednesday. They had been walking along the line, greeting people in the queue and engaging in some cheerful and encouraging banter. They were moving as a group, and the first of them, Blackmore, bypassed the Freers to stop beside Lady Hardcastle and me with his companions behind him, each of them talking to someone new.

'Good morning, ladies,' he said. 'We met the other day. Russell Blackmore.'

'A pleasure to see you again, Mr Blackmore,' said Lady Hardcastle.

'I'm glad you were able to make it after all,' he said. 'You didn't look as though you were enjoying yourselves on Wednesday and I thought . . . well, I thought you might decide against it.'

'I've had more fun, certainly,' I said. 'And we may yet back out before we reach the front of the queue. It looks like we have plenty of time.'

'Yes, I'm sorry about that – that's rather why we're doing this.' He indicated his friends, who had each begun similar conversations with our fellow queuers. 'We hadn't reckoned on the popularity of the event, you see? We thought we could have everybody registered in no time, but it's proving a good deal slower than we anticipated. And we rather underestimated the sudden rush once the morning service had finished over at the church.'

The vicar, himself a keen cyclist, had persuaded many of his parishioners to join him on a healthy Sunday ride. Relaxed chatter with departing worshippers at the church door had been curtailed for one week only, while they all hurried off to collect their bicycles and register for the event. They, it seemed, were responsible for the longer-than-expected queue.

'It's fine, dear,' said Lady Hardcastle. 'As Flo says, it gives us time to decide whether we really do want to go through with it or whether we'd rather sit outside the Dog and Duck with a nice glass of cider and wait for you all to come back.'

'Well, I hope you don't,' said Blackmore. He lifted his light cotton cap and brushed back his thick, dark hair as he spoke to her. His smile was a good deal warmer than the smile of a committee member apologizing for a delay really needed to be.

'We were admiring your bicycle outside the pub on Wednesday,' I said. 'The BSA Road Racer, wasn't it?'

'What? Oh, yes,' he said, reluctantly turning his attention away from Lady Hardcastle. 'Yes, it is. You know your bicycles, Miss Armstrong.'

'I'd like to be able to pretend I do,' I said. 'But I only recognized it because we saw one just like it earlier in the week outside the village hall. It's quite distinctive.'

'That was probably mine, actually. I came over to the art exhibition last weekend and ended up leaving it there for a couple of days. Not the sort of thing I'd usually do, to be honest. Quite fussy about the old girl. But I was with some pals, and when we were driven out of the hall by the fire we sort of ended up at the pub and . . . well, you know, what with one thing and another I didn't get a chance to pick it up until Monday afternoon.'

The queue shuffled forwards and he shuffled with us.

'I don't suppose you saw anything out of the ordinary that day?' asked Lady Hardcastle.

'The day of the fire?' he said, his head whipping keenly back towards her. 'Not unless you count dozens of people stampeding for the village pub, no. Why?'

'The thefts,' she said. 'Some artwork went missing.'

'Really?' He laughed. 'Who would ever want . . . ? Oh, I'm so sorry. Did you have anything on display?'

'Nothing worth stealing, I'm afraid. Mr Westbury's book was taken, though, along with an oil painting and a bust, both belonging to the Farley-Strouds.'

'Oh, I say. How terrible. I ought to pay more attention. I saw the book. A bit gaudy for my taste, but the papers say it's worth a packet.'

'About a thousand pounds,' I said.

'So I heard,' he replied, absently. He didn't even pretend to look my way.

'You coming, Blackmore?' said a voice I recognized as belonging to club chairman, Parslow.

'On my way,' said Blackmore, still without looking away from Lady Hardcastle.

'We're assembling the racers,' said Parslow, slightly less patiently.

'I'm sorry,' said Blackmore. 'I have to go. Perhaps I'll see you later?'

'If we make it back from Berkeley in one piece,' said Lady Hardcastle.

'I look forward to it,' he said, and reluctantly wrenched himself away.

'Someone's got a pash on you,' I said with a grin.

'What?' said Lady Hardcastle. 'Oh, don't be so silly.'

'You really didn't notice?'

'Notice what?'

'Never mind,' I said, shaking my head. 'Last chance to back out. Are we going to Berkeley or sitting under the—'

'Horse chestnut tree,' she said with a weary sigh.

'—sitting under the conker tree with a cider and waiting for your new admirer to come home victorious.'

'We ride,' she said, decisively. 'To glory. Or to Berkeley and back, whichever is the easier.'

We shuffled on towards the registration table.

◆ ◆ ◆

By the time the racers were finally assembled it was almost a quarter past nine. They would be setting off a good fifteen minutes later than advertised, but would do so with no less excitement or sense of occasion.

There was a palpable air of anticipation and excitement as Parslow climbed to the top of a stepladder holding a tin megaphone. He held the comically conical instrument to his mouth.

'Welcome, one and all,' he trumpeted, 'to the inaugural Woodworthy and Littleton Cotterell Cycling Club's Annual Race and Convivial Ride.'

'They're going to need a catchier title if they're going to try to do this every year,' muttered Lady Hardcastle.

There were titters from those around us.

'You convivial riders will be free to set off soon,' continued Parslow, 'but the main event of the day will be the two laps of the twenty-two-mile course to Berkeley Castle and back. The winner of this forty-four-mile race will receive this magnificent trophy' – he reached down to take hold of the large silver cup that was being passed to him by one of the other committee members – 'generously donated by Parslow Engineering.' He held the trophy aloft.

'I'm not certain it's quite the done thing to praise one's own generosity,' muttered Lady Hardcastle, to more titters.

Parslow passed the trophy back to his assistant and was handed a starting pistol in its place.

'Our volunteer marshals have been working hard to make sure the route is properly signposted, and will be available to offer assistance at key points along the way.'

This elicited a polite ripple of applause for the volunteer marshals.

'And now,' shouted Parslow. 'Racers, make ready.' There was a rustle of clothing and a chatter of metallic clicks as the riders steadied themselves. 'Take your marks. Get set . . . Go!'

There was a loud bang and a plume of grey smoke as he fired the starting pistol.

I could almost feel the collective heave as more than twenty energetic racing cyclists set off, accompanied by a rousing cheer from we 'convivial riders'. Among the committee members and a few complete strangers, I managed to catch sight of Angelina Goodacre, the new Dower House resident, in sporting breeches and a loose blouse, and wearing a lightweight cotton cap.

Such was the congestion as they funnelled into the lane leading up beside the church that Parslow was able to get down from the ladder and mount his own racing machine before the last of them had gone.

His place on the stepladder was taken by a lady of middle years I recognized from our own village. She was holding the club's megaphone but seemed a good deal less comfortable than Parslow with having to use it.

'Um . . .' she began, apologetically. 'Well, then, um . . . "convivial riders". I mean, what an awful phrase.' She seemed to have forgotten that the speaking trumpet was amplifying her voice. 'We – that is to say, the committee – would like to allow the racers a clear fifteen minutes to get themselves on the way to Berkeley before we – that is to say, we convivial riders – set off. It is intended that this should be a relaxed and sociable ride. Please take your time, and do take the opportunity to chat to your neighbours as you go. We – that is to say, the committee – anticipate that some of us – that is to say, we convivial riders – will be passed by some, if not all, of the racers on their second lap of the course before we return home. Please give them room to pass and don't be shy about offering a hearty "hurrah" as they go.'

She began to climb down from the stepladder but was stopped by one of her committee colleagues.

She stepped up again and still had the megaphone to her mouth as she said, 'What? Why? . . . No dear, I don't want to fire the blessed thing . . . Well, you do it, then.' She looked out at the amused crowd of convivial riders. 'My colleague Mrs Bennett will be firing the starting pistol when it is time for us to leave. Enjoy your ride.'

She climbed down and we lost sight of her in the small crowd.

'Are we all set, then, dear?' asked Lady Hardcastle as we wheeled our bicycles on to the road with the others.

'Raring to go,' I said. 'If nothing else we can enjoy a convivial lunch and a convivial bottle of cider when we convivially reach the convivial halfway point of our convivial ride at convivial Berkeley.'

'It's odd, isn't it, how words can suddenly sound entirely alien when one repeats them like that. I saw a reference to it in a journal a few years ago.'

'It's a shame,' I said. 'I was rather fond of "convivial" until just then.'

'A most agreeable word. Shall we be trying to keep up with the herd, or shall we just potter at our own speed?'

'I think our chances of keeping up with anyone are slim at best. Even the older ladies from the gardening and sewing clubs look like they're more at home on bicycles than we are.'

Mrs Gardner and Mrs Stitch were surrounded by the embroiderers and dibblers of their respective societies, and they definitely did appear more comfortable than we did. Grey hair, a little stoutness, and a few wrinkles belied their ages, but they were far from 'old'.

'Our own pace, then,' said Lady Hardcastle. 'But if we find ourselves among . . . congenial company on the way, so much the better.'

We waited for the wholly unnecessary sound of the starting pistol.

◆ ◆ ◆

Somewhere ahead of us in the crowd of bicycles on the road out of the village, a watch chimed the half hour. Seconds later, the crack of the starting pistol told us it was finally time to go.

Lady Hardcastle and I laboriously set off.

We managed to keep pace with the dibblers and embroiderers for a while, engaging in light conversation about the pleasant weather and expressing our collective hope that we would all make it to Berkeley and back in one piece.

At one point I inadvertently found myself in conversation with one of the gardeners, while Lady Hardcastle was trapped with a stitcher. To the delighted amusement of the other two ladies we managed to shuffle our positions on the road so that we could each have conversations we actually understood. Until that point I had been utterly unable to comment on the best place to plant clematis, while Lady Hardcastle was ill-equipped to discuss the relative merits of different brands of silk embroidery thread. Once we'd swapped over, though, our temporary travelling companions had a knowledgeable conversation partner for another mile or so.

Conversation ebbed and flowed as the Gloucestershire countryside drifted lazily by, and I began to wonder what we'd been making such a fuss about. If you approached it in the right frame of mind, I decided, this cycling lark could be rather fun.

We passed the neatly painted halfway sign shortly before half past ten, and then caught sight of Daisy Spratt and Cissy Slocomb leaning against a gate at the side of the road, their borrowed bicycles dropped carelessly on the grassy bank beside them. As we slowed to speak to them, our group carried on and I was struck by the sudden tranquillity of an English Sunday in spring. Insects buzzed, birds chirruped, and somewhere in the distance a cow lowed terrifyingly.

'All right, Flo. Lady H,' said Daisy as we dismounted. 'Enjoyin' yourselves?'

'I'm having a wonderful time, certainly,' said Lady Hardcastle.

'Me too,' I said. 'Very convivial.'

'I'n't it, though?' said Cissy. 'I a'n't never been so convivial in me life.'

'What are you looking at?' I said, joining them at the gate.

'Well, that's the thing, see?' said Daisy. 'We a'n't got no idea. We was just sayin' how good it would be if you two was to turn up. If anyone knows what they is, we said, it'd be Lady H and Flo.'

She indicated the creatures in the field. There were about a dozen of them, perhaps a yard high at the shoulder, luxuriantly fleeced in colours from soft white to dark black by way of tans and browns. They had the faces of long-eared sheep . . . and absurdly long necks. They looked like furry, miniature, humpless camels.

'Alpaca,' said Lady Hardcastle and I together.

'You'll pack a what?' said Cissy.

'No,' I said. 'They're alpaca. They're from Peru. They keep them for their wool and their meat.'

'You've been to Peru?' said Daisy.

'Sadly not,' said Lady Hardcastle. 'We saw them at the zoo in Washington.'

'You've been to Washington?' said Cissy. 'In America?' Our travels were now clearly more interesting than the charming creatures in the field.

'We have,' I said. 'Where we saw these sweet little South American creatures. They're quite friendly. More inquisitive and less skittish than sheep.'

'What they got 'em here for, I wonder?' said Daisy. 'Our dad a'n't never been offered no alpaca meat.'

'For their wool, then, I expect,' said Lady Hardcastle. 'It's very soft. It makes the most wonderful fabric.'

'I'll take your word for it,' said Cissy. 'They's adorable, though, innum?'

'They are indeed,' I said.

'Better press on, though, I suppose,' said Daisy. 'What have you two got in your bags?'

'Lunch,' I said, proudly. 'For when we get to Berkeley.'

Daisy laughed.

'Lunch?' she said. 'T'i'n't gonna take you much more than another half hour to get to Berkeley. Early elevenses more like. The whole idea is to be back at the village for lunch. Old Joe's doin' a big roast. Got loads of meat from our dad special, like.'

'One can never be too prepared,' said Lady Hardcastle. 'But if there's a big lunch waiting for us at the Dog and Duck, perhaps we should share our fortifying snack with you two ladies. We shouldn't want to be so full we can't eat Old Joe's special roast.'

'A very generous offer, m'lady,' said Cissy. 'Can we ride with you?'

We set off again. We were moving no quicker with the youngsters, neither of whom were overly familiar with the mysteries of cycling, but the journey passed just as pleasantly in their cheerful company.

◆ ◆ ◆

The marshal's post at the convivial turning point – a trestle table and folding chair with a cardboard sign on a wooden post beside it – was just outside the town of Berkeley, within sight of the castle. We gave our names to the marshal – a nice old gentleman from one of the little hamlets between Littleton Cotterell and Woodworthy – and turned round to find somewhere to eat our sandwiches.

A grassy bank by the side of the road gave us a comfortable place to sit, complete with a view of the ancient castle, and of our fellow cyclists as they approached the marshal's post. At least, we would have been able to see them had we not been the last of the convivial riders to arrive.

We took our time over a leisurely break, soaking up the warmth of the watery sun and enjoying Cissy and Daisy's seemingly endless supply of village gossip. During a lull in the conversation, following a particularly salacious story about one of the church bell ringers and a widow from Charfield, Daisy looked wistfully up at the castle.

'I always wanted to go in there,' she said.

'Into the castle?' I asked.

'Yes. I remember seein' it years ago when I come up with our dad for somethin' in the town. It's like a fairy tale.'

'I suppose it is a bit,' I said.

'I bet you's been in loads of castles, a'n't you?'

'A fair few. European ones. Now those are *proper* fairy-tale castles.'

'I'm sure I met the baroness once,' said Lady Hardcastle.

'Which one?' asked Daisy.

'This one. Baroness Berkeley. It was at some sort of tiresome society function in London, I imagine. Unless she's secretly employed by Harry's lot and I met her at work, in which case I probably shouldn't have mentioned it. It's unlikely, though.'

'It was last year, at the coronation,' I said.

'Oh, Flo, you're a marvel. So it was. Anyway, she's a charming woman and I'm sure I could invite myself and a few friends round for tea if you're keen to go inside.'

'I wouldn't know what to do with myself,' said Daisy.

'Oh, nonsense. Just be Daisy Spratt, butcher's daughter and barmaid. She'll love you. You too, Cissy. You're both thoroughly charming company.'

'I don't think I could, m'lady,' said Cissy.

'As you wish,' said Lady Hardcastle. 'But if either of you changes your mind, just say the word and we'll have you inside the castle before you can say "Edward the Second and the red-hot poker".'

While we were talking I'd been tidying up the detritus of our elevenses, packing the leftovers in one bag and the rubbish in the other.

'Shall we set off for home soon?' I asked.

'I'm ready,' said Lady Hardcastle. 'What about you, ladies?'

'I been ready for ages,' said Daisy. 'I thought you looked like you needed a rest, though, so I didn't say nothin'.'

We were mounting our bicycles as the first of the racers shot past us. It was Angelina Goodacre, and she disappeared up the street to complete a short loop around the town before beginning the return leg of her second lap.

'We might want to give it a few minutes,' I said. 'Where there's one, there's bound to be—'

With that, half a dozen more flushed and perspiring riders hurtled through.

'We might get stuck here a while,' said Lady Hardcastle. 'I suggest we set off and just try to obey old Mrs What's-her-frock's exhortation to keep out of their way as best we can.'

'Don't forget the hearty hurrah,' said Daisy.

'Heaven forfend,' said Lady Hardcastle. 'Hearty hurrahs all round. Come, ladies, we ride once more.'

◆　◆　◆

By the time we eventually returned to the safe haven of our little village, the entire field of racers had passed us. We signed ourselves back in at the registration desk, and retired to the Dog and Duck for a refreshing cider and a nice sit-down.

We were sufficiently frazzled-looking that a group of young men gave us their seats beneath the conker tree, and one of them even offered to fetch drinks for us. We gratefully accepted, and Lady Hardcastle treated them all to a round of their own. We sat quietly for a moment. Twenty-two miles on a bicycle is no distance at all if you're used to it, but the four of us were decidedly unused to anything even remotely like it.

The quiet of our repose was broken by a familiar voice.

'Good afternoon, ladies,' said Dinah Caudle. 'Have you had the most possible fun? You certainly look like you have.' She sat down and put her glass of cordial on the table. 'No drinks? Would you like me to—'

At that moment the kind young man arrived with a tray of four ciders, which he set down next to Miss Caudle's cordial.

'There you goes, ladies,' he said. 'I gots your change and a message.' He put some coins on the table with the drinks.

'A message?' said Lady Hardcastle. 'How intriguing.'

'It's not for you, I'm afraid, m'lady. It's for Daisy. Old Joe says . . . now let me get this right . . . would I "tell Her Majesty, Queen Daisy, to get her lazy behind back in the bar at her earliest convenience". He said it with a smile, mind, but I think he's sufferin' in there a bit. It i'n't 'alf busy.'

'Are you going back inside?' asked Daisy, wearily.

'I am.'

'Tell him I'll be there as soon as I'm able to stand upright again.'

'Right you are.'

The young man left.

'It's all go, isn't it?' said Miss Caudle.

106

'It never stops round here, let me tell you,' said Lady Hardcastle. 'One hardly has a minute's peace.'

I rolled my eyes.

'To what do we owe the pleasure of your delightful company this afternoon?' I asked.

'I'm doing a piece about the cycle race for the *Bristol News*,' said Miss Caudle. 'Not my usual thing, you understand, but I thought it would be fun to come out and see you. Two birds, one stone and all that. Imagine my surprise when I found the birds had flown. Then imagine my utter, goggling astonishment when Edna told me the reason you weren't at home was because you'd gone on the ride yourselves. I didn't even know you owned bicycles.'

'We got them a short while ago,' said Lady Hardcastle. 'We'd been threatening to for ages.'

'Oh, you had. But I thought them idle threats. You know, like, "We really must invite you and Simeon round for dinner some time." I didn't expect you to actually buy them.'

'We really must, though. When are you free?'

'I shall consult my diary – and the good Dr Gosling – and telephone you. But I'm delighted you were in the race. Would you mind if I interview you?'

'Not at all, dear. Though we weren't in the race.'

'Ah, you were "convivial riders"? Even better. I'm sure our readers would warm more to a group of lively convivial riders than a shower of Eager Edgars in tweed breeches with oil on their socks.'

The young man returned to the table.

'Sorry to interrupt,' he said diffidently, 'but Old Joe is in a right state in there. Could you . . . ?'

'Course,' said Daisy. 'Sorry, ladies, duty calls.'

She stood up, taking her cider with her.

'I'll give you a hand,' said Cissy, and she grabbed her own cider before following Daisy inside.

'I'll be in later to talk to you,' called Miss Caudle. 'Don't think you've got away that easily.'

Cissy gave a casual wave of acknowledgement as she disappeared through the door.

As best we could, trying our hardest not to sound like the world's least capable cyclists, we described the events of the morning while Miss Caudle took notes in her expensive notebook with her expensive pen.

When we were done, she said, 'Thank you, that's just what I need. I'll get a few words from Cissy and Daisy and it'll make a lovely little piece.'

'You'll get more than just a few words from those two,' I said.

'I know. Even better. There's absolutely nothing more tiresome than a monosyllabic interviewee. But now that's out of the way' – she leaned forwards – 'what do you know about the stolen book?'

'You probably know more than we do on that one, dear. It's been quite the story in the *Bristol News.*'

'It has, but I've not been covering it. I'm sure you know more than you're letting on, though. Tell Aunt Dinah all.'

'Honestly, dear, you really do know everything there is to know about the book,' said Lady Hardcastle. 'Two security guards, beautiful display case, fire, glass smashed, book gone. That's it.'

'Poor old Westbury. Such a nice chap.'

'We've met him,' I said.

'Of course you have, darling, you've met everyone. He's an engineer, isn't he? Didn't he design the reciprocating flange nurdler or the diesel-powered sprocket crumper?'

'Something like that,' I said. 'Made a fortune at it.'

'And then wasted it on Shakespearean tat and gaudy books. Such a shrewd businessman in every other regard, and then he goes and plunges a packet on binding a book. A book he had specially printed, too. Not even a valuable First Folio.'

'We all have our fancies and foibles, dear,' said Lady Hardcastle.

'I suppose so. Weren't some other pieces stolen, too?'

'Oh, actually,' I said, 'there might be something you don't know there. At least, it's not been mentioned in the reports I've read. The other missing pieces belonged to Sir Hector Farley-Stroud.'

'Did they really?' said Miss Caudle. 'Well, that is interesting. To me, at least – I know the Farley-Strouds, after all. I suppose our dear editor thought it wasn't worth mentioning them, though. When a book worth a cow goes missing, that's the main story. What were the pieces?'

'A landscape painting of The Grange by Edgar Summerhays, and a small bust of one of the former owners.'

'Summerhays? I'm surprised we didn't mention that. It must be worth a few bob. Didn't someone sell one of his at Sotheby's recently? Enough to buy themselves most of Leicestershire?'

'Quite a few bob,' said Lady Hardcastle. 'But it's one of a pair and much less valuable on its own. And that's rather why we're more interested in the painting than the book. We want to get it back for them.'

'A much more noble pursuit than retrieving dear Basil's vanity piece. How far have you got?'

'Nowhere at all,' I said. 'We allowed ourselves to be distracted by bicycles.'

'We've been cogitating,' said Lady Hardcastle. 'Sometimes these things have to slosh around in the brain for a while before they make sense.'

'Is there anything I can do?' asked Miss Caudle.

'Actually, there might be. Do you have contacts among the local art dealers and auction houses? Perhaps they might have heard something?'

'I shall make discreet enquiries.'

'That renewed interest in Summerhays should work to our advantage,' said Lady Hardcastle. 'If something of his is newly on the market it might make waves.'

'I shall keep my ear to the ground.'

'Thank you, dear.'

The conversation among the cycle club committee at a nearby table became suddenly animated and we stopped talking to listen.

'And I'm telling you he's not back,' said one.

'Are you sure it's not just a mistake in the register?' said another.

'Are you saying I don't know how to keep a register?' said the first.

'Gentlemen, please,' said Parslow. 'I'm sure it's just an oversight. He probably forgot to report himself home.' He clambered up and stood on the table. 'Ladies and gentlemen,' he called, 'has anyone seen Russell Blackmore?'

Murmurs and head-shaking followed, but no news of Blackmore.

'Anyone? Was anyone riding with him?'

More head-shaking.

'Thank you,' said Parslow. 'If anyone sees him, could they tell him to let the committee know he's safe.'

Parslow climbed inelegantly down from the table and resumed his seat.

'That's odd,' I said.

'Probably found a quieter pub somewhere and stopped for a pint,' said Miss Caudle. 'I know I'd have been tempted.'

'No,' I said. 'Not him. We met him – he was serious about the race. And he was keen to get back here.'

'Whatever for?'

I nodded towards Lady Hardcastle.

'An admirer, eh?' said Miss Caudle. 'Well, I'm hardly surprised. I mean, look at you there with your face all red and your hair askew. You're a catch.'

'Oh, do shush, the pair of you,' said Lady Hardcastle. 'But Flo's right – he should definitely be here by now. We ought to offer to help. Flo, be a poppet and fetch the Rolls, would you? I'll tell the committee we'll make a tour of the route. The poor chap might be lying in a ditch somewhere.'

◆ ◆ ◆

An hour later, we returned to the village green. I had driven slowly round the entire route from Littleton Cotterell to Berkeley and back, with Lady Hardcastle kneeling on the passenger seat looking forwards and Miss Caudle perched on the luggage rack looking to the rear. We had seen a couple of farmers, a dispiriting number of cows, and a courting couple. But of Russell Blackmore there had been no sign.

We reported back to the cycling club committee and returned home.

Miss Caudle joined us for afternoon tea but had to get back to Bristol to see her fiancé, Dr Gosling, so she was unable to stay for dinner.

Lady Hardcastle and I tried to play backgammon after dinner, but we were both so exhausted that we retired early, in hopes that, rested and rejuvenated, we might be able to make some progress in the case of the stolen painting in the morning.

Blackmore should have reappeared by then, too.

Chapter Seven

Monday was spent, once more, on prosaic domestic matters, but we did find time over morning coffee in the drawing room to discuss our lack of progress in finding Sir Hector's stolen painting. Time was not on our side – the bank would foreclose on the loan on the seventh of June and it was already the thirteenth of May. We had less than four weeks to save The Grange, and so far we had nothing.

'They won't have to leave, though, will they?' I said once we'd run through what we knew – or, more properly, didn't know. 'You'll lend them the money, won't you?'

'I would do it without a moment's hesitation,' said Lady Hardcastle. 'There'd be a delay of a few days while my solicitors in London arranged for the liquidation of certain assets and the raiding of one or two rainy-day accounts, but the money would be theirs. The problem is, they won't take it. Gertie is adamant, as you know, so I buttonholed Hector the other evening after dinner to try to talk some sense into him. He won't budge, either. If they won't accept the money, there's nothing we can do. It's not as though I can trot along to their bank and make a deposit on their behalf.'

'I suppose so,' I said, sadly.

We returned to pensively sipping our coffee and staring at the crime board. A few moments later, Edna bustled in, apparently on the hunt for a lost duster.

'Sorry to interrupt,' she said, 'but you a'n't seen my long feather duster, have you?'

'You're not interrupting at all,' said Lady Hardcastle. 'We're just lamenting our ongoing failure to track down poor Hector's lost landscape.'

'I has every faith in you,' said Edna. 'You always comes through in the end.'

'In the end, dear, yes. But this time we can't drift on in our usual haphazard fashion and hope for the best. They need that painting back soonest.'

'Rumour is they's got money troubles,' said Edna with a sage nod.

'One forgets how effective the village rumour network can be,' said Lady Hardcastle. 'Obviously one ought neither to confirm nor deny, but . . . well . . . yes. And having a pair of Summerhayses will dig them out of their hole.'

'Then they's lucky to have you helpin' 'em.'

'I hope we can live up to your faith in us, dear, I really do. I don't suppose you have any insights that might help us?'

'Help you find a missin' paintin', m'lady? I can't even find a missin' feather duster.'

'It's in the dining room,' I said. 'Propped up against the sideboard. You can't see it from the door.'

'Oh, my word, you're right,' said Edna. 'I put it down yesterday while I was cleanin' that lovely Chinese figurine. She looks so beautiful, that lady, sittin' there with that bird on her finger. I loves that one. I got a bit lost in it, I don't mind sayin' – imaginin' her life, wonderin' what she's thinkin', imaginin' your lives, for that matter, wonderin' about all your adventures. After all that, I completely forgot my duster. Thank you, Miss Armstrong.'

'My pleasure,' I said. 'But are you sure you can't think of anything that might help the Farley-Strouds? You know everything and everyone.'

'And them as I don't know, I probably knows their mothers,' she said with another nod.

'So who are the local ne'er-do-wells and good-for-noughts?' asked Lady Hardcastle. 'If something goes missing in the village, what's the first name on everyone's lips when they're looking for the culprit?'

'Mickey Yawn,' said Edna without a moment's hesitation.

'He's a bad lot, is he?'

'Ah, now, I never said that. You asked who everyone points the finger at, and it's definitely Mickey. But as for him bein' a wrong 'un . . . Well, he's no angel, that's for sure. He was lovely when 'e was a little 'un, but 'e was a bit of a terror as a young lad – always in some sort of bother. He's been caught more than once with things that wasn't his. But he's been accused more often than he's been guilty. Once you gets a reputation like that, it's hard to shake off, i'n't it?'

'It is,' agreed Lady Hardcastle. 'But he might be acquainted with the sort of people who could have committed the theft.'

'He might,' conceded Edna. 'His girlfriend's a right one, for a start. Olive Churches, her name is. Her dad . . . well, now her dad's a proper villain. Nasty piece of work.'

'Might he have had something to do with it?'

'Bill Churches wouldn't know a valuable paintin' from a copper pie tin. He's more the sort to wallop you over the 'ead and nick your purse. No, it wouldn't be him.'

'But if Yawn knows him, he might know other local criminals, too,' I said.

'True,' said Edna. 'But this i'n't the beatin' heart of the criminal underworld out here, mind. I doubts any of 'em knows any proper thieves. Not like the sort you's lookin' for.'

'That's the thing, though,' I said. 'From everything we've seen so far, this wasn't the work of "proper" thieves. It looks like the work of bumbling chancers who got away with it more by good luck than good judgement.'

'Well, Mickey Yawn's what you'd call a bumblin' chancer, that's for sure. And I reckon his mates are, an' all.'

'And that's why he might know what's going on and who's doing what,' said Lady Hardcastle. 'If our experience over the years has taught us anything, it's that petty criminals like to boast to each other about their latest coups.'

'You might be right there,' said Edna. 'He's always boastin' about this and that. A right braggart, he is. Or a puckfist, as our grandpa would have called him.'

'Oh, I say, what a splendid word. Where was he from, your grandfather?'

'Dudley.'

'Really? We once pursued a Prussian spy to a boarding house in Dudley. Is it a local word, do you know?'

'Couldn't say, m'lady. But it fits little Mickey Yawn to a tee.'

'If we wanted to speak to him, where might we find him?' I asked.

'Funnily enough,' said Edna, 'I knows his mother. She was tellin' me t'other day 'e's doin' some labourin' for a builder over Tortworth way. I can get you the address if you likes.'

'That would be most helpful, dear, thank you,' said Lady Hardcastle.

'Happy to help,' said Edna. 'Now, if you'll excuse me, I'll get my duster from the dinin' room and get on with my cleanin'.'

With that, she bustled off.

'I doubt that young Michael Yawn, rapscallion of this parish, will have had anything to do with it,' said Lady Hardcastle as we resumed our coffee-drinking and pondering, 'but I should like to speak to him nonetheless.'

◆ ◆ ◆

True to her word as always, Edna had spoken to Mrs Yawn later that day under the pretence that she and her husband, Dan, might have need of a builder. The ruse might have come undone when Mrs Yawn started asking questions about exactly what sort of work they needed doing and wondering why the landlord wasn't taking care of it, but Edna's improvisation skills were more than up to the challenge. She managed to ascertain the address where Mickey was working, and passed it on to us when she arrived for work on Tuesday morning.

We would never have bumped into the little cottage without her help, it being hidden down a lane which led, as far as we could tell, only to the cottage itself and a disused barn beyond. But Edna's directions were accurate, if a little eccentric – 'there's an old ash tree on the left that looks like a bear with a hat on' – and we reached our destination in no time.

There was a builder's cart in the lane beside the cottage's low garden wall, its wheels scotched with wooden wedges. The horse was in the field opposite and was taking a break from cropping the grass to look over the gate and contemplate the eternal mysteries of the universe. Or she might just have been staring vacantly into the middle distance – it's difficult to tell with horses.

A long ladder leaned against the ivy-covered wall of the cottage, and there were buckets and tools nearby. Of Mickey Yawn there was no sign.

Lady Hardcastle parked behind the cart and we climbed out on to the road. I said a cheerful good morning to the builder's horse but she ignored me, so I carried on towards the gate. It opened noiselessly – a trick our own gate had never mastered, no matter how frequently Jed oiled it for us – and I stepped inside.

A sudden movement among the hollyhocks (obviously I didn't know what they were at the time – Lady Hardcastle told me later) caught my eye, and I turned to see a young man and a younger woman scrambling out from behind the plants, hastily rearranging their clothes. The young man wore a shirt but no collar and had his cap tilted towards the back of his head. The girl – she couldn't have been more than eighteen or nineteen years old – wore a plain dress with the sleeves rolled up to reveal slender, sunburnt arms.

They seemed momentarily nonplussed by our presence, but quickly regained their composure.

'What do you want?' said the man truculently.

Lady Hardcastle smiled warmly.

'What a lovely place to be working,' she said, indicating the cottage.

'Gaffer will be down later,' said the man. 'You can see 'im then. He had things to deal with in the village so I come down in the cart.'

'And you brought a helper for the gardening,' I said.

'We a'n't been doin' no gardenin',' said the girl with a leery grin.

Lady Hardcastle smiled and turned her attention back to the young man.

'It's actually you we wanted to see,' she said with her customary calmness. 'Not your gaffer.'

'Me?' he said, still bristling with cocksure belligerence. 'What do you want with me?'

'You're Mr Michael Yawn, aren't you?' said Lady Hardcastle.

'So what if I am? I a'n't done nothin' wrong. What you come lookin' for me for?'

'Your mother said we might find you here. We're making some enquiries on behalf of a friend. Some items went missing from the Littleton Cotterell Art Exhibition a couple of weekends ago, and we're trying to form a picture of what exactly happened that morning.'

'So you come lookin' for me. I didn't steal no paintin's. Nor no fancy book, neither. We weren't even there, were we, Livvie?'

'We weren't,' said the girl, who must have been Olive Churches if Edna's intelligence was up to date. 'We was up the Mock all mornin'.'

'The Mock of Pommey at Woodworthy?'

'Yes,' said Olive, as though Lady Hardcastle were the stupidest woman in the world. 'You's all the same, you toffs. Somethin' goes missin', blame Mickey or the Churches.'

'I'm so terribly sorry,' said Lady Hardcastle, 'I didn't mean to suggest we thought you were involved, it's that we're hoping to be able to talk to as many people as possible who might have an idea of what happened that morning.'

'There was a fire, everyone ran out, some stuff got nicked,' said Olive.

'Well, that's it in a nutshell,' said Lady Hardcastle. 'But we were hoping to find more details.'

'Like I said,' said Mickey, 'we weren't there.'

'And yet . . .'

'We knows what happened,' said Olive. 'We didn't have to be there – it was in the papers.'

'It was,' agreed Lady Hardcastle. 'And I expect everyone's been talking about it, too.'

'They has,' agreed Olive. 'Non-stop.'

'And does anyone know who did it?'

'We i'n't narks,' said Mickey.

'No, but you know the police will come knocking on your door sooner or later. Yours, too, Miss Churches.'

'How d'you know my . . . ?'

Lady Hardcastle simply cocked an eyebrow.

'But you have a reputation, Mr Yawn,' she continued. 'And we understand that the Churches are known to the police, too, so it's only a matter of time before the rozzers turn their steely gaze upon you both. Surely it's in your best interests to tell us what you know so as to keep them off your backs. It's one thing to cop it for something you actually did, quite another to be harassed by the forces of law and order for something you didn't.'

The two young people looked at each other and seemed to have an entire conversation without saying a word out loud, in that way that lovers have. Finally they nodded in unison and turned back to face us.

'Our dad reckons it's a gang from Bristol,' said Olive. 'He says they's the only ones with the know-how to pull off a job like that.'

'I see,' I said. 'I don't suppose . . . ?'

'Oh, he knows who it was, but 'e i'n't no nark, neither. He i'n't never gonna tell no one which gang it was,' said Olive. 'But your copper mates'll know whose doors to kick in. And you knows how much they loves kickin' in doors.'

'They do seem to have a fondness for it,' said Lady Hardcastle. 'Well, thank you very much, Mr Yawn, Miss Churches, you've been most helpful. Unless anyone asks us, of course, in which case we shall tell them you said nothing at all.'

'You'd better,' said Mickey with comical menace, 'or it'll be the worse for you.'

He took a threatening step towards us with his fists drawn, and seemed most put out that we didn't flinch.

'Duly noted, dear,' said Lady Hardcastle.

'I means it,' he said, though with somewhat less conviction.

'I don't doubt it. But if we are to trust you, and take you at your word when you say you're not involved, then you are honour-bound to trust us when we say we won't drop you in it with your associates.'

'Yeah, well,' he said. 'Just you watch it, that's all.'

'Consider it watched, dear,' said Lady Hardcastle with a smile. 'Now, I feel we've taken up far too much of your working day with our idle chatter, so we shall leave you to your labours.' She looked at Olive and made a show of brushing her own hip. 'You've got a little dirt on your dress, dear,' she said. 'Just there.'

Olive looked down and flicked at the dusty spot with delicate fingers.

'That's it. Good day to you both.'

We turned and left through the annoyingly silent gate.

Our route back to the village took us once more past the Dower House, where Angelina Goodacre was pottering in the front garden. She was dressed in engineer's overalls – something I knew would endear her to Lady Hardcastle, who spent a great deal of her time in overalls when she was working on her moving pictures in the orangery. She had the handle of a wicker trug over one arm and a pair of secateurs in her other hand.

She recognized us as we rounded the corner, and waved, gesturing for us to stop. Lady Hardcastle applied the brakes with a wholly unwarranted ferocity and we skidded to a halt a few yards before the gate. I tried not to sigh as I got out between the Rolls and the garden wall.

'I'm glad I caught you,' said Angelina as we walked towards the gate. 'I've been meaning to take you up on your invitation but . . . well . . .' She indicated the unruly mess of the front garden, which clearly hadn't been tended to for a long while. 'I found myself rather busier than I'd hoped.'

'Hector hasn't been able to find a tenant for a while,' said Lady Hardcastle. 'We know a chap if you'd prefer someone to take care of it all for you. He's very reasonable.'

'From the village? I haven't been able to find a gardener in the village.'

'No, he lives in the woods. A charming little caravan. He's not overly fond of company, but he's honest and hard-working.'

'If you could ask him for me, that would be grand, thank you. I'm no gardener. I'm just hacking at things and trying to tidy up a bit. Probably doing more harm than good.'

'Jed will see you right,' said Lady Hardcastle.

'Will you come in for some tea? I need a break.'

'That would be lovely, thank you.'

'Door's open. Kitchen's out the back where you'd expect it to be. Make yourselves comfortable and I'll get rid of this lot.' She joggled the trug full of clippings and weeds.

The Dower House, like The Grange itself, had seen better days. It was clean and tidy, but it could have done with a lick of paint, and the furniture – which had been the latest thing about fifty years ago – was slightly battered and definitely in need of the ministrations of a good upholsterer.

The kitchen, as Angelina had suggested, was easy to find, and I took the liberty of putting the kettle on. Lady Hardcastle took three cups and saucers from the dresser and between us we set about making a pot of tea.

Angelina arrived, wiping her hands on her overalls, just as the kettle boiled.

'Oh, you've shown me up as a rotten hostess,' she said. 'I really was going to make the tea, I promise.'

She washed her hands in the sink and then wiped them on her overalls again. I noticed oil stains among the garden grime.

'At least let me cut you some cake,' she said. 'I got it from . . . Hulbert's?'

'Holman's,' I said.

'Yes, that's him. Nice chap. Makes a lovely lardy cake.'

At her invitation, we sat down together at the large oak table.

'How are you settling in?' asked Lady Hardcastle as Angelina poured the tea.

'I still need to get the house squared away,' said Angelina, 'but other than that, things couldn't be better. I've had a chance to explore the village a little more since we last spoke, and it seems like I made a good choice. The people are friendly and kind, the shops are convenient and well stocked, and the pub seems lively and fun.'

'Glad to hear it. There are a number of clubs and societies beyond the cyclists if you have any other interests.'

'I shall keep my eyes and ears open. Did you enjoy the ride on Sunday?'

'We did, thank you. Most convivial.'

'I saw you setting off,' I said. 'How did you get on in the race?'

'Ah, I might have caused some upset there,' said Angelina. 'I . . . well, I won.'

'I say, well done, you,' said Lady Hardcastle.

'Thank you. They put on a show of being gracious about it, but the only one who was genuinely pleased was a young woman called Irene.'

'Irene Vibert,' I said. 'We met her the other day up at Woodworthy, when we were out for a ride.'

'That's the girl. Only woman on the committee. I think the men are perfectly happy for women to ride bicycles as long as we don't beat them in races.'

'It does seem to make them unhappy,' said Lady Hardcastle. 'But I'm pleased you're finding us acceptable company aside from that.'

'More than merely acceptable,' said Angelina. 'As I said, everyone has been friendly and kind.'

'Excellent. And you really must come round for dinner one evening. We owe some friends from Bristol a dinner, perhaps we could make an evening of it – introduce you to some people from beyond the village, too. It can be a dreadful bore moving to a new place and not knowing anyone.'

'Thank you, that would be lovely. Although I actually think I do know you, Flo.'

'Me?' I said, somewhat surprised.

'I think so. Is your father Joe Armstrong?'

'He was,' I said.

'The Great Coltello?'

'Yes, that was him.'

'I used to do a trick cycling act,' said Angelina.

'Oh my goodness,' I said as realization dawned. 'You're the Angel of the Velocipede?'

She laughed.

'Well, I was,' she said. 'It's been years since I was called that, though. You and your sister . . . ?'

'Gwen,' I said.

'Gwen and Flossie, that was it. You two used to pester me to teach you tricks.'

'You didn't tell me you could do tricks, Flo,' said Lady Hardcastle. 'You've been carrying on as though you're as unfamiliar with the bicycular arts as I am.'

'I don't like to show off,' I said.

'She likes nothing better than to show off,' said Lady Hardcastle to Angelina. 'Most especially if it shows me up at the same time. I'm utterly delighted to meet someone from Flo's past.'

'And I'm delighted to meet you both, too,' said Angelina. She turned to me. 'I thought I recognized you the other day, but I knew I'd not met you recently, and you're too young for it to have been more than a few years ago. Then it struck me who you reminded me of: Meg Armstrong. She and I were great pals in the old days. How is she?'

'She passed away in ninety-nine,' I said. 'Shortly after my father.'

'Oh, I'm so sorry. That must have been terrible. They were lovely people.'

'Thank you. They were. But I was away at the time, so I didn't find out until we got back a couple of years later.'

'Good heavens, how awful for you. Where were you?'

'China, at first, then Burma, then India.'

'Quite the traveller,' said Angelina.

'I've been very lucky,' I said, with a nod towards Lady Hardcastle. 'I work for an adventurous lady.'

'You do? I thought you were just pals.'

'Oh, we're definitely pals,' I said. 'But officially, I'm her lady's maid.'

'Well I never,' said Angelina.

'I keep trying to promote her to "companion",' said Lady Hardcastle, 'but she won't have it.'

'It's just a job title,' I said. 'And it's one that would sometimes put me in an uncomfortable position. I'm happy as lady's maid.'

'Our housemaid's the same,' said Lady Hardcastle. 'I keep trying to promote her, too. She's definitely the housekeeper, but she's having none of it, either.'

'I think I've made a breakthrough there, actually,' I said. 'But we're absolutely not to call her Mrs Gibson.'

'I shall do my best to remember.'

'Is she married to Dan Gibson?' asked Angelina.

'That's right,' I said.

'I've met them at the Dog and Duck. Life and soul, the pair of them.'

'They're wonderful,' said Lady Hardcastle. 'And I don't know what we'd do without her about the house. Tell me, dear, are you still trick-cycling?'

'Sadly not,' said Angelina. 'There's not much call for it any more. I did some work for a moving picture company last year, but I think the days of crowds of circus-goers ooh-ing and ahh-ing at a woman on a bicycle are long gone. There's an added element of jeopardy when it's a woman in her fifties' – she gestured to herself – 'but only in that she might have a heart attack and peg out in the middle of the act.'

'You don't look as though there's any danger of that,' I said. 'You still look fit as a flea.'

She really did look as strong and vital as I remembered her. To a small child every adult looks ancient, of course, so the difference in my mind was just between an ancient woman with red hair on a bicycle and an ancient woman with white hair at a kitchen table. But she was still lithe and lissom, and I couldn't imagine her heart giving up any time soon.

'You're very kind,' she said. 'But it would be a young woman's game, even if the game still existed. I get by, though.'

Lady Hardcastle, I knew, was desperate to ask exactly how Angelina was getting by, but there's a peculiar English taboo against such enquiries. People may volunteer the information themselves – though that can still be regarded as something of a faux pas – but it's absolutely not at all the done thing to ask a new acquaintance what they do for a living. Lady Hardcastle had been skating on thin social ice with her 'are you still . . . ?' but it would be a serious gaffe to press the matter. I decided to steer us to less frustrating topics.

'We've never been in the Dower House before,' I said. 'It's much nicer than I expected. There's a back garden and an outbuilding, too, isn't there?'

'There is,' said Angelina. 'The back garden is even more of a wilderness than the front, though. I think the only digging it's seen over the last few years has been the local badgers. They get in through a hole at the bottom of the gate, I think.'

'There's a large sett in the woods,' I said. 'They roam far and wide in their search for food, and we're definitely on their route.'

'I love them. And if they want to dig up the garden searching for earthworms, then good luck to them.'

We chatted on, and the teapot was filled at least once more, but eventually we had to make our excuses and go. Lady Hardcastle repeated her invitation to dine with us and said she'd be in touch as soon as we had a date from Dinah Caudle and Dr Gosling.

Angelina saw us out and we drove off into the village, leaving her with her trug, her secateurs, and her Herculean labour.

As we approached the green I noticed that Cordelia Harrill's car was parked outside the village hall again.

'Your mate's back,' I said, pointing.

'Ooh, so she is,' said Lady Hardcastle. 'Let's go and see what she's up to.'

She parked the Rolls reasonably neatly behind Cordelia's brand-new Wolseley. We alighted, straightened ourselves out, and strode into the hall.

Cordelia was standing next to the now empty display plinth, deep in conversation with the book's owner, Basil Westbury.

Mr Westbury had his back to us but I could see Cordelia's smiling face as she reassured him that she had every confidence the book would be recovered soon, and that it wouldn't actually prove necessary to settle the insurance claim he had just made. Her warm expression changed to cold hostility when she caught sight of us.

'What do you want?'

Lady Hardcastle smiled. 'Good afternoon to you, too, Cordelia dear. And to you, Mr Westbury. How lovely to see you again.'

Mr Westbury turned round and his own face lit up with a welcoming smile.

'Why, Lady Hardcastle,' he said. 'It's wonderful to see you, too. And Miss Armstrong. The circumstances could definitely be better, but it's always a pleasure to see you both.'

Cordelia was still glaring. 'This is a private meeting.'

'A private meeting in a public place, dear,' said Lady Hardcastle. 'We'll not be in the way. We just wanted to take a look around the hall again while the exhibits are still here, in case it inspires any new insights into the crime.'

'Oh, I say,' said Mr Westbury. 'Are you investigating, too? How exciting. Lady Farley-Stroud was extolling your virtues as expert crime-solvers only the other day.'

'They are most definitely *not* investigating anything,' said Cordelia. 'I absolutely forbid it.'

'Yes, Mr Westbury,' said Lady Hardcastle, completely ignoring this oafish outburst. 'As a matter of fact, we are. Hector lost a couple of pieces, too, and we've offered our help to try to retrieve them for him.'

'I will not have amateurs getting in the way of an official insurance investigation,' said Cordelia. 'I shall take legal steps to stop you if I have to.'

'Obviously we're still in the early stages,' continued Lady Hardcastle, 'but we've had a certain amount of luck with this sort of thing in the past, so we're a long way from giving up hope. Our assumption is that your book was the principal target, while Hector's pieces were swept up opportunistically, as it were, as the thieves made their exit. The museum's expensive pieces are over there, beyond those display boards' – she pointed to the other side of the hall – 'so Hector's landscape and bust were the only other objects of value between your book and their means of escape. We think they grabbed your book and made for the exit. On the way they saw an expensive-looking frame and a Regency alabaster bust and thought, "Hello, what's this? In for a penny and all that," and legged it out the back with all three.'

'Legged it out the back?' said Cordelia. 'How on earth can you possibly know that?'

Lady Hardcastle finally paid attention to the increasingly irritated insurance investigator.

'We don't *know*, dear, but it's a safe assumption. The crowd was streaming out through the front and side doors so they'd have been tumbled at once if they'd gone that way. Even the most inattentive visitor would have noticed someone carrying a hulking great book, with a painting under the other arm and a bust of Sir Theodore Elderkin peeking out of their coat pocket.'

'You seem to know a lot about the layout of the building,' said Cordelia. 'How do you even know there *is* another door.'

'We live here, dear. Do try to keep up. But please don't let us interrupt any further. We'll have our little poke about and be on our way. Just carry on as though we weren't here.'

The exhibition was still officially open, though with the star exhibit gone and with the initial romantic attraction of the scene of the crime having already worn off, visitor numbers had dwindled to just a handful each day, and the organizing committee had decided that just one volunteer was required to supervise them. She was sitting beside the tea table, concentrating on her knitting. Lady Hardcastle and I had doubled the visitor numbers just by turning up.

We wandered the room, taking our time over not really looking at anything, presumably merely to irritate Cordelia. It was fun for a while but eventually, having extracted all the childish pleasure we could from our little game, we added one last dig by leaving through the storeroom and the back door.

'Well, that was fun,' said Lady Hardcastle as we returned to the Rolls.

'Most entertaining,' I said. 'But we didn't really learn anything.'

'Au contraire, my little croquembouche—'

'Must you?'

'My apologies, dear. Been spendin' too much time with Hector, what? But we learned two interesting things: Mr Westbury has made a claim against his insurance policy, and Moberley, Burgess and Vincent are not at all keen to pay out.'

'And how does that help us?'

'I have no idea. Lunch at the Dog and Duck?'

'I don't mind if I do,' I said.

We left the motor car where it was and walked across the green to the pub.

The pub was as lively as ever, with the usual crowd making the usual amount of cheerful noise over the usual pies and sandwiches and the usual pints of beer and cider. I noticed the Freers in the snug and suggested we join them.

'That's a wonderful idea,' said Lady Hardcastle. 'I find their oddness strangely endearing, and they might have some news of the fabled treasure. Pie and a pint?'

'Go on, then,' I said. 'No, better make it a half – a pint will just make me sleepy. I'm only little.'

'I'll put the order in with our gracious queen, then. You go and sit with the intrepid Freers.'

The intrepid Freers were deep in conversation, but they looked up as I entered and invited me to sit with them.

'Is Lady Hardcastle with you?' asked Zibbie.

'She is,' I said. 'She's just ordering some lunch. She'll be here in a moment.'

'That's good,' said Zeke. 'We were just talking about the' – he looked around to make sure we weren't overheard, then mouthed the word – '. . . treasure.'

'How exciting,' I said. 'How are you getting on? Have you found anything new?'

'We've found nothing new,' said Zibbie. 'We visited the Farley-Strouds again but our latest information seems to have led us astray.'

Lady Hardcastle arrived carrying two glasses of cider and joined us at the table.

'Good afternoon, Freers all,' she said. 'How goes the treasure hunting?'

'Fine, thank you,' said Zeke, quietly.

I smiled. 'They were just about to tell me all about it.'

'Oh, splendid,' said Lady Hardcastle, sitting down. 'Does that mean you've made some progress?'

'Some,' said Zibbie. 'We found another reference to the . . . hidden items, in another book at the library.'

'My goodness. How very exciting.'

'It confirmed the other stories we'd heard about the French colonel – Munier – and his plunder,' said Zeke. 'Treasure from northern Spain and Portugal, some of it looted from the Americas. There was mention of Incan gold, Mayan opal, silver from Brazil. There's yet another mention of Major Teddy Elderkin and his sudden wealth.'

'And then,' said Zibbie, 'almost as a side note, there's an account of a grand ball at The Grange in 1815 to celebrate the British victory at the Battle of Waterloo. It said that "treasures of the New World and the Old, captured from the French" were on display. And then . . . nothing else.'

'Either the trail has gone cold,' said Zeke.

'Or it ends at The Grange,' said Zibbie.

'We have certain . . . clues as to where the treasure might be hidden,' said Zeke.

'But when we visited The Grange,' said Zibbie, 'there was nothing there.'

'Oh, how frightfully disappointing,' said Lady Hardcastle. 'Do tell me you're not giving up, though.'

'We most definitely are not,' said Zibbie. 'But we might need your help.'

'Our help? I'm sure we'd love to, but what help could we possibly be? We know nothing of' – she made an exaggerated show of looking around and then lowered her voice – 'secret, hidden valuables.'

'Ah, but you do know Sir Hector and Lady Farley-Stroud,' said Zeke. 'We thought perhaps you might be able to have a word with them, find out what else they might know about the history of the house.'

'But you can ask them yourself, dear. They're really frightfully friendly. You'll have a job stopping dear old Hector telling you everything there is to know if you give him but half an excuse.'

'I'm not sure he took to us,' said Zibbie. 'And Lady Farley-Stroud was quite frosty.'

'Well, I can't promise anything,' said Lady Hardcastle, 'but I'll have a quiet word. If they say they're no longer interested, then that shall have to be the end of it. But if I can talk them round, I shall.'

'Thank you, Lady Hardcastle,' said Zeke.

'Yes, thank you,' said Zibbie.

At that moment there was a commotion in the public bar. The door clattered open and a man's voice called out breathlessly, 'It's Russ Blackmore. They found him in the woods. He's dead.'

Voices erupted around the pub, expressing shock and disbelief, and clamouring for more details.

Lady Hardcastle and I rose together and went through to the other bar. I couldn't tell whether our appearance was in some way reassuring, or perhaps merely surprising, but the effect was to silence the uproar. The owner of the voice was one of the committee members we'd met in Woodworthy, but I couldn't remember his name.

'Have the police been informed?' asked Lady Hardcastle.

'They have, my lady. A couple of young lads found the body when they were playin' in the woods. They raced to the village and told Sergeant Dobson. Blackmore's head was smashed in, they said. Then Dobson telephoned the CID in Bristol and they're sending up an inspector and a police surgeon. They're meeting Dobson at the police station.'

'Thank you, dear,' said Lady Hardcastle. 'Come on, Flo, I think we'd better go and speak to dear Sergeant Dobson.'

As we swept out I could hear someone in the bar say, 'What they goin' for?'

Another voice replied, 'Don't you know nothin'? They's experts at this sort of thing. Solved many a murder round here, they have.'

The door closed behind us and we marched swiftly across the green to the village police station.

Chapter Eight

Sergeant Dobson was sitting behind the desk in the little police station eating a pork pie. He leapt to his feet as we entered, then brushed pastry crumbs from his tunic. He hurriedly swallowed the last of his pie and swigged a mouthful of tea from a tin mug to wash it down.

'Afternoon, ladies,' he said, wiping tea and yet more crumbs from his beard. 'What can I do for you?'

'The word in the pub is that you've found Russell Blackmore's body,' said Lady Hardcastle.

'News travels fast round 'ere, m'lady. Some young lads found 'im in a copse out towards Oldbury.'

'No wonder we didn't see him when we went out looking,' I said. 'Was he on the route of the cycle race?'

'No, miss, a lane just off it. Up by Wood Acre Farm.'

'Oh, I know where you mean. By the blasted tree.'

'That's it, miss.'

'I wonder what he was doing there,' said Lady Hardcastle. 'A dalliance, perhaps?'

'That don't make no sense to me, m'lady. I talked to all the cyclin' committee when they was arrangin' the race. I was police liaison, see?' He said this with enormous pride. 'Russell Blackmore was keenest of the lot. He wouldn't have allowed no distractions, not even for a lady. Though he was definitely one for the ladies.'

'It's a terrible shame he's gone,' I said. 'I rather liked him.'

'He was a decent fella,' said the sergeant with a nod.

'The cycling chappie in the pub said you'd telephoned the Bristol CID and they were sending an inspector. I don't suppose . . . ?'

'Inspector Sunderland, m'lady, yes. Always my first call, Inspector Sunderland. You knows what I thinks of Gloucester CID. It'll be a chilly day in Hades afore I ever calls them idiots first.'

Lady Hardcastle smiled. Other than Sergeant Dobson and Constable Hancock, we had seldom had any dealings with the Gloucestershire force, and the others we had met always seemed at least averagely competent. I couldn't imagine that the CID could possibly be as bad as Sergeant Dobson claimed, but for reasons of his own, he had taken very strongly against them.

'It will be lovely to see the inspector,' said Lady Hardcastle. 'Is he coming right away?'

'He is, m'lady. I called 'im almost an hour since, so he should be here soon.'

'News doesn't travel that fast, then,' I said. 'The Dog and Duck only just found out.'

'Reasonably fast, though, miss. I telephoned Mr Blackmore's employer, Mr Parslow, after I spoke to the inspector. Then he must have told the rest of the committee. They none of 'em 'as telephones – he was the only one as I could talk to when we was plannin' the route – so he must have sent messages out. Or telegrams. Either way, 't'i'n't bad goin' to get news to the Dog and Duck in less than an hour.'

'I suppose not, when you put it like that,' I said.

'Who was it as told you?'

'It was either Screen or Nurse – we weren't introduced properly when we met them. Tall, gangly, dark hair, spectacles.'

'That'll be John Nurse,' said the sergeant. 'He works up the road at the coal merchants. I 'spect Parslow sent a lad over there – he runs the timber yard out on the way to Chippin'. Gordon Screen's a stocky little fella, works for Parslow as a bookkeeper.'

Sergeant Dobson was, as always, very well informed about the goings-on in the area, and I was about to ask for more information about the cycling club committee, but we were interrupted by the sound of a motor car drawing up outside. Moments later, Inspector Sunderland walked in, closely followed by Dinah Caudle's fiancé, the police surgeon Dr Simeon Gosling.

'Good afternoon, Sergeant,' said the inspector as he strode in. 'Oh, and ladies. What an unexpected delight. Please don't let us interrupt, though. We're happy to wait while you complete your business.'

'Don't be silly, Inspector dear. *You* are our business. We heard what had happened and came over to the station to see if we could find out more. Were we cats, we should be long dead.'

Dr Gosling had grinned and waved as he entered but was now frowning in confusion. Inspector Sunderland caught sight of his expression.

'Curiosity and its consequences, Gosling,' said the inspector.

Dr Gosling was still frowning.

'It killed the cat,' said the inspector with a sigh.

'Ohh,' said Dr Gosling as realization slowly dawned. 'Of course it did. With you now. Do carry on.'

With only occasional interruptions from Lady Hardcastle, Sergeant Dobson recounted the pertinent details of the bicycle race and its attendant convivial ride, of Blackmore's failure to return, of the search of the route – this prompted an entire description from Lady Hardcastle of our own efforts on Sunday – and of the discovery by two boys earlier that day of the unfortunate cyclist's body.

'Why were the boys not at school?' asked the inspector when the sergeant had finished.

'Hoppin' the wag, sir,' said Sergeant Dobson. 'I went easy on 'em over it on account of how they'd reported the body instead of pretendin' they 'adn't seen nothin'.'

'And the body is still in situ?'

'I sent Hancock up there to keep watch, sir.'

'Right you are, Sergeant. Thank you very much. If you'd be good enough to give us directions, Dr Gosling and I will go up and look for ourselves.'

'We know the way,' said Lady Hardcastle. 'We can navigate.'

'Assuming I allow you to tag along, my lady,' said the inspector with a smile.

'Oh, now you're being silly again, Inspector dear. We both know you delight in our company.'

'Come along, then,' he said with mock weariness. 'Lead the way.' He turned back to Sergeant Dobson. 'Thank you for the information, Sergeant. I alerted the mortuary before we left so they should be here soon. Please give *them* directions.'

'Of course, sir. If they's not there afore you needs to leave, just tell Hancock to wait for 'em.'

'Thank you. We'll call in before we return to town, to bring you up to date on our findings.'

'Very good, sir.'

The inspector turned on his heel and made to leave, only hindered briefly by Dr Gosling's clumsy attempt to get out of his way.

Lady Hardcastle made to follow them but then turned back.

'One more thing, Sergeant. We had a word with Mr Michael Yawn and his delightful paramour, Miss Olive Churches. They say they couldn't possibly have been involved in the theft from the art exhibition because they were drinking at the Mock of Pommey in Woodworthy at the time.'

'Thank you, m'lady. I'll check with Will Morgan.'

'The new landlord?'

'Yes, m'lady. Nice fella. Keeps an orderly house.'

'Splendid. Miss Churches also intimated that her father knew who was responsible. She was keen to impress upon us that neither she nor anyone she's connected with is a nark, you understand, but she did suggest that there are only a few gangs in Bristol capable of carrying out such a daring theft. She won't give names, but she says that the coppers will know whose doors to kick in.'

'We do love kickin' in doors, m'lady,' said the sergeant with a chuckle. 'I'll 'ave a word with the inspector when you all gets back from the woods.'

'Thank you, Sergeant. Now, though, we need to dash. Poor Inspector Sunderland will be waiting for his navigators.'

We left the sergeant making notes in his daybook and went to join the inspector and Dr Gosling.

With the inspector driving and me navigating, the journey to the woods was a swift one. Lady Hardcastle sat gossiping in the back with her old friend Dr Gosling, and we found the left turn on to the lane by the lightning-struck tree at Wood Acre Farm without any difficulty.

Constable Hancock was standing with his hands clasped behind his back when we arrived, though I surmised from the dirt and dust on his trousers and tunic when he turned round that he had been sitting on the grass until he heard the sound of the approaching motor car.

'Good afternoon, Constable,' said the inspector. 'Thank you for standing guard for us.'

'Just doin' my duty, sir,' said Constable Hancock, though his face beamed with pride.

'Lead the way, would you?'

'Certainly, sir. He's through here.'

The constable took us a few yards into the trees to a small clearing. Blackmore's body lay beside his bicycle, still dressed in the linen shirt and tweed breeches we had seen him wearing on Sunday morning. One of his shoes was missing and his socks were rumpled. His cap was a few feet away.

Dr Gosling knelt and quickly examined him.

'As always, I'll not give you an official cause of death until I have him on the slab,' he said, 'but I doubt I'll find it to be anything other than this blow to the head.' He indicated a large wound on the back of Blackmore's skull. 'He was hit with something with a right-angled edge,' he continued, 'and there are some splinters of wood in there. A rough-cut wooden post, perhaps? But not too hefty. No bigger than two-by-two, I should say. From the state of the poor chap I'd say he's been here a couple of days.'

'Killed on the day of the race, then,' said Lady Hardcastle.

Now that she was face-to-face with Blackmore's body, I could see she was a good deal more upset by his death than she'd been letting on.

'I should say so, yes,' agreed Dr Gosling.

As he continued his preliminary examination of the body, I looked around the small clearing. I could see Blackmore's missing shoe a little way away and immediately noticed something else.

'He was dragged here,' I said, and pointed to the tracks in the soft dirt. Two lines led from the lane to the body, but one became fainter after the point where his shoe had come off.

'Thank you, Miss Armstrong,' said the inspector, making a note.

I continued my static examination of the scene, and lit next upon the BSA Road Racer.

'The saddle's missing from the bicycle,' I said.

Lady Hardcastle knelt to look more closely at the seat tube. If we had been given notice of our trip to a murder scene, she would have brought paper and pencils and would be sketching the body and its surroundings. Without this absorbing task to occupy her mind, she seemed in want of something to do.

'It was carefully removed rather than ripped off,' she said. 'The bolt is almost completely undone.'

'Are they especially valuable?' asked Dr Gosling as he continued his own work. 'Bicycle saddles, I mean. It seems odd to steal a saddle and leave such a handsome machine behind.'

'There's always a market for spare parts,' said Inspector Sunderland. 'But you're right, it does seem an odd thing to take.'

'I remember seeing the bicycle outside the village hall last week,' I said. 'The saddle was certainly . . . sporty. Handmade leather rather than pressed out in a factory somewhere, I'd say. I imagine they're highly sought-after.'

'I shall ask around,' said the inspector. 'One of the lads at the Bridewell is a keen cyclist – he's bound to know.'

When Dr Gosling had finished making his notes, the four of us carefully searched the clearing. Then we followed the path of the tracks in the dirt back to the lane and Constable Hancock, but we found nothing else of any particular interest. There were traces of boot prints in the soft ground, but they had been largely obliterated by the smaller prints of the two boys who had found the body, and we were unable to learn anything helpful from them.

Inspector Sunderland asked the young constable to wait for the mortuary men, and then drove us back to the village.

Inspector Sunderland and Dr Gosling went into the police station to brief Sergeant Dobson on their findings, and we stood for a few moments outside on the grass.

'What next, then?' I asked.

'I've been wondering that myself,' said Lady Hardcastle. 'Were the situation different, I'd suggest we head home and set up the crime board as we usually do, and try to fathom poor Blackmore's murder. But as much as I'd like to see his killer brought to justice, we've pledged our help to Gertie and Hector. The treasure hunters might yet save the day, but unless and until they do, the lost painting ought to be our priority. The murder seems somehow incidental. I didn't even have my drawing things to make a sketch of the scene of the crime. I find myself somewhat at sea.'

'Then we should leave the murder to Inspector Sunderland for now and concentrate on the stolen painting. Why don't we have another go at recreating the theft? The exhibition hasn't been doing the briskest business, so it will be quiet in the hall again – let's walk it through one more time.'

'Let's do that,' she said. 'Perhaps another look will inspire us.'

It was a quarter past five, and the village hall was deserted apart from the lone exhibition committee member on duty to oversee the show.

'We're closing at half past,' she said officiously as we entered.

'Right you are, dear,' said Lady Hardcastle, breezily. 'We just want a quick look round, then we'll be out of your way.'

'I'll be lockin' up on the dot, mind,' said the committee member. 'I gots me 'usband's tea to get.'

'Don't worry, dear, we shan't hold you up.'

She was already back to her knitting as I led the way to the back of the hall and out through the storeroom to the builders' rubbish behind the building, and I don't think she noticed us at all.

'I'm completely in your hands here, dear,' said Lady Hardcastle once we were outside. 'You've done this before, after all. You're the queen of re-enactments. How do we proceed?'

'We imagine ourselves as the thieves,' I said. 'It's the opening day of the exhibition and we're lurking out here, unseen.'

'How many of us are there?'

'At least two, I should say. I don't think anyone could do it alone. Well, one of *us*, perhaps, but not mere mortals.'

Lady Hardcastle smiled.

'Now,' I continued, 'I know you and I aren't convinced it was an expertly planned job, but they must have had *some* sort of plan. They must at the very least have had *some* idea how they were going to steal the most expensive book in the country.'

'Agreed.'

'In which case, our first task would be to find wood shavings and oily rags, and a galvanized bucket to put them in.'

'That's a very specific shopping list,' said Lady Hardcastle. 'Wouldn't we be better bringing that sort of thing with us?'

'Perhaps we sourced it beforehand and stashed it here?' I suggested.

'That seems to be crediting us with a little too much forethought, but all right. If we're a gang from Bristol we might at least have planned that much. So, perhaps we brought the bucket, but were confident we could cast about out here among the detritus of the arcane builders' arts for the rest.'

'Seems reasonable,' I said, looking around.

To be fair to the workmen, though they had generated a good deal of mess, they had stacked it neatly, ready for later disposal. As we had noted before, there was burnt timber in one pile, fresh offcuts in another. There were empty tins of paint and oil of turpentine. There was a pile of rags. And a pile of general rubbish.

I began with this last pile, where I quickly found several hessian sacks full of wood shavings.

'The combustible material is easy to find,' I said, pulling one of the sacks free of the pile. 'With this and some of those old rags, we could replicate the fire we found. All we'd need would be a bucket, and we might have brought our own.'

'We might,' said Lady Hardcastle distractedly. 'What's that under there?'

'Where?' I asked, turning back to the rubbish pile.

'Under that sack. Something shiny.'

I put down my wood shavings and hefted out the sack she had indicated.

'Well, well, well,' she said. 'That's a turn-up.'

Lying on the dusty ground beneath the sacks of general waste was a broken gilt picture frame. The four sides had been smashed apart at the joints, but I recognized the carving. This was the frame that had once held Sir Hector's Summerhays.

A little more searching revealed two sizeable chunks of alabaster which were clearly recognizable as parts of the bust of Sir Theodore Elderkin.

It took us quite a few minutes to gather up as many pieces of shattered frame and figurine as we could find. By the time we had placed them all carefully in a pile and I had gone back into the hall to try to find something clean to put them in, the volunteer had gone home and the front door was closed, presumably locked.

I managed to find an old tea chest in the storeroom, which I took out to Lady Hardcastle and the pile of bits.

'That cheery committee lady has gone,' I said.

'Mrs Palmer,' said Lady Hardcastle.

'Look at you and your name-remembering skills.'

'I served on a village committee with her at some point. I can't remember which one, I'm afraid. How do you know she's gone?'

'She wasn't there.'

'That's usually the first sign. Had she locked up?'

'The front door,' I said. 'As far as I could tell, at least. I didn't actually check.'

'But not this one. It all adds to the idea that very little forward planning was needed. It's an opportunist's paradise.'

'It is. What are we going to do with this little lot?' I indicated the pile of pieces we were placing carefully in the tea chest.

'I thought we might take them to their owner,' she said. 'It's not quite the heartening news I should prefer to take him, but it does at least indicate that we haven't forgotten him.'

'Right you are,' I said. 'Now?'

'It's as good a time as any. Would you be a pet and fetch the Rolls for me? I'll wait here and guard our treasure.'

With the tea chest loaded on to the luggage rack on the back of the Silver Ghost, I drove us up to The Grange, where we were greeted, as we so often were, by the three boisterous springer spaniels.

'Hello, ladies,' said Lady Hardcastle as she stepped out of the motor car. 'How are my favourite girls?'

The dogs wagged their greetings and pushed and shoved for their turn at receiving attention as she crouched to scratch their ears.

'Are your people at home? Are they? I'm sure they are. They wouldn't leave three wonderful girls like you behind, would they? No, they wouldn't. Shall we go and find them? Shall we?'

She stood, and the three Fates in canine form continued to bounce energetically around her. As she started towards the front door of the house, they formed an honour guard and the four of them marched together in stately procession.

I unstrapped the tea chest and lifted it free.

'It's all right,' I said. 'Don't worry about the box. I'll bring it.'

'Thank you, dear,' said Lady Hardcastle without turning round.

The tea chest wasn't especially big. On the other hand, though, neither am I – holding it in front of myself in both arms, I was unable properly to see where I was going. Given Lady Hardcastle's insouciant dismissal of my efforts, I was less than properly concerned when my unsightedness caused me to bump into her as she stood on the doorstep ringing the bell.

'Oops-a-daisy,' she said. 'Are you all right back there?'

'Quite all right, thank you,' I said.

Jenkins answered the door and the three dogs disappeared at speed from my limited line of sight, presumably having bolted into the house. He greeted us warmly and led the way to the drawing room, where he announced us and left. I was mildly irked that he hadn't offered to relieve me of my light but cumbersome burden, but I said nothing.

Lady Farley-Stroud gave us a friendly 'Hello, m'dears' from her armchair but didn't get up.

Sir Hector, though, bounded to his feet.

'Hello, gels,' he said jovially. 'What do we have here?'

'Some bad news, I'm afraid,' said Lady Hardcastle. She finally took the tea chest from me and put it on the floor at Sir Hector's feet. 'And perhaps a little good news.'

He peered into the wooden box.

'That looks like m'picture frame,' he said, sadly. 'And, oh . . . is that the last earthly remains of Sir Theodore Elderkin?'

'We rather fear it might be,' said Lady Hardcastle. 'It took a fair amount of rootling about, but I think we have all of him. He broke into fairly large pieces so it should be possible for a competent restorer to repair him.'

Sir Hector bent down and did some rootling of his own. Eventually, he gathered all the pieces of the broken bust and laid them on a side table.

'Where's his base?' asked Lady Farley-Stroud.

'His what, dear?' said Lady Hardcastle.

'He was on an alabaster base. It's missing.'

Lady Hardcastle indicated some of the more finely smashed pieces.

'Are they not it?' she said.

Lady Farley-Stroud rose from her chair and poked at the shards.

'These are some sort of biscuit ware,' she said. 'Probably from somethin' else. The base was solid alabaster. They've taken the base and left the bust. In bits.'

'Sorry, dear,' said Lady Hardcastle. 'This was all we could find. But that does lead on to the good news. We might not have the painting yet, but at least we know it hasn't just been wantonly destroyed like the bust. It was taken very carefully from its frame, so it's still out there somewhere.'

'With Westbury's blasted book,' said Sir Hector with uncharacteristic venom. 'If that wretched parvenu hadn't been so insistent on showin' off his tawdry book, none of this would have happened. I'd still have m'Summerhays and we'd still have a home.'

'We'll find it, Hector,' said Lady Hardcastle. 'It's early days yet. Sergeant Dobson is going to arrange for some likely suspects to be interviewed in Bristol. Our friend Dinah Caudle of the *Bristol News* is keeping a lookout for sale notices at the auction houses. I'll ask Inspector Sunderland if he knows of any fences in Bristol who might be able to handle such things.'

'Fences?' said Lady Farley-Stroud.

'Receivers of stolen goods, my lady,' I said.

'Just so,' said Lady Hardcastle. 'And, of course, we'll keep digging. We spoke to some local ne'er-do-wells this morning and they claim to have had nothing to do with it, but I'm sure they know more than they're letting on.'

'Get young Florence to beat it out of 'em,' said Sir Hector with a weak smile.

'If it comes to it, you know I would,' I said.

'Don't go gettin' yourself in trouble on our account, m'dear,' he said. 'But we appreciate the sentiment.'

'And the treasure hunters might yet save the day,' said Lady Hardcastle. 'We spoke to them earlier and they seem absolutely convinced that the treasure of Teddy Elderkin is real. I'm sure they'll find it.'

'Are you, m'dear?' said Lady Farley-Stroud. 'Are you really? They came up here the other day, you know. They scuttled about the place with their notebook, muttering to each other like little goblins, then came and muttered to Hector about . . . about what, exactly, dear?'

'Nothin' of any substance,' said Sir Hector. 'Some stuff I already knew about a French colonel, a story about a ball here at The Grange – already knew that one, too – and some wild specu-lation about a secret vault in the grounds.'

'A secret vault?' I said. 'They didn't mention that to us.'

'Probably because they knew you'd laugh your heads off,' said Lady Farley-Stroud. 'Secret vault, indeed.'

'Got to say I agree with the memsahib,' said Sir Hector. 'We've been here thirty-six years and I ain't ever found a secret vault. Went all over the place with builders, engineers and architects in the early days – whole thing always looked to me as though it'd fall down any minute, d'you see? Had to get the experts in. But none of us ever found anythin' even remotely like a secret vault. Not sure your treasure hunters are on the right track, m'dear.'

'A couple of useless articles if you ask me,' said Lady Farley-Stroud.

'They do seem a little peculiar,' agreed Lady Hardcastle. 'But I find them rather charming.'

'You certainly enjoy teasing them,' I said.

'Oh, definitely. They adopt the most serious and mysterious manner whenever they mention *the treasure*. They're quite delightful. But they asked us to pump you for more tales of Teddy Elderkin's hoard and its possible resting place. I told them to ask you themselves but they don't think you like them very much.'

'I certainly don't,' said Lady Farley-Stroud. '"They makes I shudder," as Cook would say. Talking of Cook, will you stay for dinner?'

'Thank you, dear, but no. Our own wonderful cook was preparing something delicious for us and we have one or two matters to attend to at home. Another night, perhaps.'

'You're always welcome, m'dear,' said Sir Hector. 'While we still have a home, that is.'

'Oh, shush, Hector,' said Lady Farley-Stroud. 'You know how that sort of talk distresses me.'

'Sorry, my little Victoria sponge.'

'Is there anything we can tell them, though?' said Lady Hardcastle. 'The treasure hunters, I mean.'

'Oh, tell 'em they can come back and speak to me,' said Sir Hector. 'I can't lose anythin' by it. And talk of this fanciful treasure is a pleasant daydream, if nothin' else. Distracts a fella from his troubles, what?'

'We shall pass it on, dear, thank you,' said Lady Hardcastle. 'And now we had better leave you to your dinner. We shall press on with our investigation of the art exhibition theft and keep you fully apprised of our progress.'

'Thank you, m'dears,' said Sir Hector. 'Come along, then – I'll show you out.'

◆ ◆ ◆

After devouring the splendid meal left for us by Miss Jones, we retired to the drawing room with the brandy decanter, paper and pencils. Lady Hardcastle sketched with her pad balanced on the arm of the chair as we talked.

'Where the devil are we?' she asked.

'Up a gum tree without a paddle,' I said. 'That's where we are.'

'I rather fear you may be right.'

Further despondency would surely have followed had not the doorbell rung at that moment.

'Who the devil can that be?' said Lady Hardcastle, looking towards the window. It was eight o'clock in the evening and although the sun had not long ago set, it was dull enough outside that I had already lit the lamps. She would have seen nothing but the room reflected back at her against the dim outline of the trees across the lane.

'I know a way to find out,' I said, putting down my brandy balloon and standing up.

'Send them away with a flea in their impertinent ear,' she said. 'Calling on a lady at this hour. I mean, really.'

I opened the door, braced for trouble. Well, you never know – the countryside can be as dangerous as the city at night-time.

I needn't have worried. It was Dinah Caudle.

'Miss Caudle,' I said with a smile. 'Hello.'

'You're never going to call me Dinah, are you, Flo dear?'

'I never am.'

'Corders?' she said with an encouraging shrug. 'Oh, I know. The girls at school used to call me Brontë. How about that?'

'Why on earth . . . ?'

'It started out as Dinosaur – you know, from Dinah. Then it went to Brontosaurus because I have a long neck. And then just Brontë.'

'And did you like that?'

'Not at all. Ghastly.'

'Then why . . . ?'

'Just anything other than Miss Caudle. We're best pals. Have been for ages. I can't have my pal calling me Miss Caudle.'

I shrugged apologetically.

'Not to worry, dear thing,' she said. 'Look, I'm sorry to call on you so late—'

'Shockingly late,' I said. 'I have strict instructions to send you away with a flea in your ear for your impertinence.'

'Quite right, too. I should come back tomorrow.'

'You should,' I said, standing aside. 'But since you've come all this way, you'd better come on in. There's cognac and a mad old lady in the drawing room. I'll fetch another glass. Or would you like something other than cognac? Something to eat, too, perhaps? I can't do anything about the mad old lady, I'm afraid – she's part of the fixtures and fittings.'

'I don't suppose you have any cheese? And a little port?'

'Coming up,' I said. 'I'll join you both in a moment.'

I put together a tray – cheese, crackers, port, a jug of water, yet more glasses – and by the time I returned to the drawing room, Miss Caudle and Lady Hardcastle were standing at the crime board.

'. . . smashed to pieces,' Lady Hardcastle was saying as I entered. 'Oh, hello, dear. I was just telling Dinah about our finds behind the village hall.'

'I wish I'd been there instead of at dinner with the Chipping Bevington Chamber of Commerce,' said Miss Caudle.

'What a glamorous life you lead,' I said, setting the tray down.

'It was a splendid dinner – at the Grey Goose on the High Street – but my goodness they're a boring lot. Thank goodness for Hubert Pomphrey. Have you met him? Runs a junk shop.'

'Pomphrey's Bric-a-Brac Emporium,' I said.

'Flo's favourite Chipping Bevington shop after Boxwell's Books,' said Lady Hardcastle.

'Well, he's a thoroughly endearing chap,' said Miss Caudle. 'But even with his company to jolly up the proceedings, I should still have preferred to be with you two scoundrels.'

'On our less-than-glamorous exploration of the builders' rubbish behind the village hall,' I said.

'It would have been fun. What have you learned?'

'So far, we believe the thieves—'

'More than one?'

'We think so, yes,' I said.

'Do you have any suspects?'

'Not really.'

'Oh, that's disappointing. I thought you'd have at least one or two by now.'

'Well,' I said, slowly, as I marshalled my thoughts. 'There are the two security guards employed by the insurance company. Though we doubt them capable of the planning and it would have been difficult for them to set the diversionary fire without help.'

'There's the insurance investigator,' said Lady Hardcastle. 'Cordelia Harrill.'

'But mostly because Herself doesn't like her,' I added.

'Can't abide the woman,' agreed Lady Hardcastle.

'Local rapscallions Mickey Yawn and Olive Churches have to be considered,' I said. 'Though they might have alibis.'

'Is she one of the infamous Churches . . . es?' asked Miss Caudle. 'Churcheses. I say, that doesn't sound at all right, does it? Churches.'

'She is,' I said. 'They're both belligerently defensive, but I think I would be if people accused me every time something went missing.'

'If anything goes missing, though, her family usually has it. Or ends up with it. Or knows where it went.'

'Which is the principal reason we spoke to them,' said Lady Hardcastle.

'Both of them together?'

'Yes,' I said. 'He's labouring for a builder out near Tortworth.'

'And what was she doing?'

'Lending moral support.'

'I don't suppose they were pleased to see you.'

'Not entirely, no,' I said. 'We interrupted them.'

'Oh, ah,' said Miss Caudle with a grin. 'What were they up to?'

'They were in the . . . rhododendrons?' I said as I looked to Lady Hardcastle for confirmation.

'Hollyhocks, dear,' said Lady Hardcastle.

Miss Caudle's grin widened.

'Were they any help?' she asked.

'Sort of,' I said. 'They snarled at us a bit while fiercely protesting their innocence. Then suggested it was probably a Bristol gang. We thanked them for their help, they offered us some half-hearted threats, and we left them to it.'

'To what?' asked Miss Caudle with a grin.

'To exactly what you suppose,' said Lady Hardcastle. 'Ah, to be young and in love.'

'Other than that lot, though, and everyone else who was at the exhibition, we've no ideas,' I said.

'Hmm,' said Miss Caudle. 'But I interrupted. You believe that the thieves . . . what?'

I ran through our supposed sequence of events, starting with the discovery that the rear door of the hall was seldom locked, on to starting a fire with builders' rubbish, and then stealing the book, the painting and the bust. 'Then they slipped out through the back door, removed the painting from the frame, smashed up the bust, and mingled with the crowd before slipping away.'

'Why would they do all the business with the painting and the bust, though? That would have taken time.'

'They had plenty of time,' said Lady Hardcastle. 'That wasn't the problem. The problem, I believe, was that the painting and bust weren't part of the original plan. We never managed to see the book, but it's a big blighter by all accounts—'

'Huge,' said Miss Caudle with a nod.

'So they say,' said Lady Hardcastle. 'If we assume that was the target, then they'd already have devised a means of spiriting it away. If they were dressed as builders they might wrap it in sacking and wheel it out on a porter's truck. There's been so much work going on there that no one would pay any attention to a couple of builders moving heavy things about, even on exhibition day.'

'If they were dressed more smartly, they might put it in a perambulator,' I suggested.

'I've never seen a man pushing a perambulator,' said Miss Caudle. 'Oh, I know. They were father and uncle and they dressed the book as a small child and swung it by its arms as though on a Saturday afternoon walk.'

'All excellent suggestions,' said Lady Hardcastle. 'But with the addition of the painting and bust, their best-laid plans had gang agley. That frame was a good deal bigger than the book – judging by the size of the display case, at least. So they got the painting free and smashed up the frame, concealing it in the rubbish pile.'

'Why smash the bust?' asked Miss Caudle.

'It wasn't an especially impressive piece,' I said. 'At first glance, and because it was with a very nice painting, they might have thought it worth picking up, but once they were outside in the daylight . . . I imagine they thought it was more trouble to conceal it and get it away than it was worth. They were already in the mood for smashing things up, so a few quick blows with something heavy and they could hide it with the broken frame. No one would be any the wiser.'

'That all makes sense,' said Miss Caudle. 'Then off to a waiting builders' wagon and on to Bristol and the sale rooms.'

'Any luck there?' asked Lady Hardcastle.

'Not a peep, sadly. I wouldn't expect the book to turn up – it's far too famous for open sale – but I'm hopeful the painting might appear at some point. It'll be reframed, of course, but an unknown Summerhays wouldn't attract the same attention as the most famous book in the country. On the other hand, our thieves might not know it's a Summerhays so it could just disappear into the general stolen-goods market for much less than it's worth.'

'I've already promised Hector and Gertie that we'll ask Inspector Sunderland to lean on some fences.'

I quickly dismissed the image of Inspector Sunderland leaning on his garden fence as he chatted with his neighbour about stolen artwork.

'Who are these two?' asked Miss Caudle, pointing at the newest sketches.

'They are the aforementioned Mickey Yawn and his beloved, Olive Churches,' I said.

'Ah, of course.'

'You said you know the Churches?'

'Know *of* them. They make regular appearances in the Crown Court reports at the *Bristol News*. But you said you were only talking to them because of what they might know.'

'Well, we were,' said Lady Hardcastle. 'But . . . he's a spiky chap, you see – in appearance and manner. As I said, it was his reputation for taking things that aren't necessarily his that prompted us to talk to him . . . but I don't know. He and Miss Churches certainly appeared to know more about what was going on than they were prepared to tell us.'

'I think they're worth putting on the board,' said Miss Caudle. 'They look like wrong 'uns.'

'Perhaps I've just drawn them that way. But we suggested to Sergeant Dobson that it might be worth his while asking Bristol CID to have a word with the Churches.'

'Have you heard about Russell Blackmore?' I asked, changing the subject.

'The missing cyclist from the race on Sunday?' said Miss Caudle.

'Yes,' said Lady Hardcastle. 'Found dead this afternoon. Murdered.'

'Good heavens,' said Miss Caudle, rummaging in her bag for her notebook and expensive pen. 'Details, please.'

We recounted our visit to the scene, including Dr Gosling's presumption of murder.

'Who on earth would want to do such a thing?' asked Miss Caudle when we were finished.

'Who indeed?' said Lady Hardcastle.

'I wonder if he might have been a philanderer,' I said. 'So it might perhaps have been a jealous husband.'

'What are you basing that on?' asked Miss Caudle. 'Rumours? Gossip?'

'She is fixated upon the idea that he was flirting with me in the registration queue,' said Lady Hardcastle.

'He couldn't have made it more obvious without getting down on one knee and proposing marriage there and then,' I said.

'Pish and fiddlesticks,' said Lady Hardcastle with an added *pfft*.

'Pish and fiddlesticks notwithstanding,' I said, 'it's possible that our dear friend Lady Hardcastle was not the only woman in the area at whom the late Mr Blackmore had set his cap. If other targets of his amorous attentions were less gormless – and more receptive – he might have upset any number of husbands and suitors.'

'It's more than possible,' said Miss Caudle. 'And this is very much my area of expertise. I shall make discreet enquiries.'

Conversation turned then to less criminal matters, as we munched our way through the cheese and sipped delicately at our drinks. By eleven, Miss Caudle was still there, and now in no fit state to drive herself home, so we put her up for the night in one of the guest rooms.

Chapter Nine

The next morning, Miss Caudle made use of the telephone to dictate a story about Blackmore's murder for the Friday edition of the *Bristol News*. Feeling pleased with herself at having filed an important story before most of the city had even arrived at work, she rejoined us in the morning room and tucked hungrily into one of Miss Jones's breakfasts.

'Well done, dear,' said Lady Hardcastle. 'It seems as though your day's work is already done. Shall we all go shopping in town to celebrate?'

'Sadly not, I'm afraid,' said Miss Caudle. 'I had expected some words of thanks from my editor for being on the spot for an important murder story but, alas, it was not to be. His first order of business was to express his dismay that my report of the latest vacuous utterances of the Chipping Bevington Chamber of Commerce has been delayed. It wouldn't do to praise me too much, after all. He was grudgingly pleased, in his own way, but a celebratory day off is out of the question. The Chamber of Dullness story has to be written, and then I have to beard Simeon in his vile-smelling lair and ask him to give me some juicy quotes about the more gruesome details of the killing. Our readers do love a gruesome detail.'

'That's a shame. Another time, perhaps?'

'Absolutely. But you two are busy anyway.'

'We are?' I said. This was news to me.

'Of course you are, silly,' said Miss Caudle. 'You've an art theft to solve and a pal's home to save.'

'Oh, that,' I said. 'We're at the "leaving it to ferment and see what ideas brew up" stage. A day's shopping would have been fun. I need some new summer shoes.'

'We're doing a lot of that at the moment, I'm afraid,' said Lady Hardcastle.

'Shopping for summer shoes?' said Miss Caudle.

'You're as bad as Flo. No, dear, fermenting rather than solving. As we said last night, other than Cordelia, the security guards, and Yawn and Churches, we've no decent suspects. And we only suspect the youngsters because of their reputation for being wrong 'uns.'

'It's a well-deserved reputation,' I said.

'Granted. But prejudice isn't proof.'

'Ollie is going to speak to Pa Churches, though?' said Miss Caudle. She was the only one among us who ever referred to Inspector Oliver Sunderland by his given name.

'Or one of his Bristol-based colleagues, yes,' said Lady Hardcastle.

I didn't catch Miss Caudle's response because I was already in the hall on my way to answer the doorbell, which neither of them, apparently, had heard.

It was Inspector Sunderland.

'Ah, Inspector,' I said. 'Do come in. We were just talking about you.'

I took his hat and hung it on the hatstand beside the door.

'Nothing good, I hope,' he said.

'Never,' I said. 'You know us.'

'I do indeed.'

I led him through to the morning room, where Lady Hardcastle and Miss Caudle were still discussing the local petty villains.

'Ollie, darling,' said Miss Caudle. 'What an extraordinary coincidence. We were just—'

'Talking about me,' said Inspector Sunderland. 'So I gather. Good morning, Dinah – you're out early.'

'Or out late. It's a matter of perspective. I found myself slightly squiffy last night – you know how generous Emily can be with the bottle – so I stayed the night.'

'Well, it's a pleasure to see you, whatever disgraceful excesses led to our meeting. Good morning, my lady – I didn't mean to neglect you.'

'Not at all, Inspector dear,' said Lady Hardcastle. 'Have you news?'

'I'm afraid I'm newsless, but I do have an invitation. I gather from Sergeant Dobson that you've met the members of the Littleton Cotterell and Woodworthy Cycling Club committee.'

'Woodworthy and Littleton Cotterell.'

'Yes. What did I say?'

'You got them the other way round. It's dismayingly important to people round these parts, I'm afraid. Village rivalry and all that.'

'I shall endeavour to get it right when I meet them. But you are acquainted?'

'I think "acquainted" is pushing it a little, but the sergeant is correct – we have met them, at least.'

'That's good enough for me,' said the inspector. 'I wondered if you might like to accompany me this morning while I interview them. I've asked to meet at their club headquarters.'

'I should love to, thank you. Flo?'

'Always,' I said. 'I love a good interview. Where's their headquarters?'

'They share the scout hut at Woodworthy,' said the inspector.

'Scout hut?' I said.

'Where the Boy Scouts meet. They have a two-room shed on the outskirts of the village and they rent it out to other organizations from time to time.'

'Ah, I see. Our local troop meets at the village hall.'

'They don't have a fancy village hall in Woodworthy,' he said. 'I'm afraid I can't invite you, Dinah. I'm pushing my luck taking these two civilians without inviting the press as well.'

'I quite understand,' said Miss Caudle. 'As it happens, I have to get back to town. I've been trying to find ways of putting it off, but I really do have to write my Chamber of Commerce piece.'

'We'll make sure you get all the gossip,' said Lady Hardcastle.

'I'll pretend I didn't hear that,' said the inspector. 'Do at least pretend to take my job seriously. At least while I'm actually in the room.'

'Nuff said,' said Lady Hardcastle, putting her finger on her lips. 'Discretion shall be our watchword.'

It took us nearly half an hour to get ready, but we left the inspector with tea, toast, and whatever else was left of breakfast, and he seemed perfectly content.

The Woodworthy scout hut stood at the end of a short track off the lane that led from the village to the Gloucester Road. We arrived just before ten o'clock and Inspector Sunderland parked his police-issue motor car on the gravelled area in front of the small wooden hut. With its whitewashed perimeter stones and its freshly painted flagpole, the gravelled patch resembled a miniature parade ground.

We approached the hut in line abreast, with Inspector Sunderland in the middle. We looked every inch the team of professional investigators, ready to find the truth and see justice done.

We stood up just a little straighter as the inspector knocked loudly and confidently on the door.

There was no answer.

He tried the doorknob.

The door was locked.

'Well, that's somewhat anticlimactic,' I said. 'I expected to sweep in with an "'Allo, 'allo, 'allo. What's all this 'ere, then? You're nicked, me old beauty." Instead there's a wooden hut with a locked door.'

'To be fair, we're only here to interview them,' said Inspector Sunderland. 'Arrests may follow, of course, but questions and proof first.'

'Spoilsport. Can't a girl daydream? I haven't so much as threatened someone for months, let alone got involved in a decent scrap.'

'You threatened Cordelia only the other day, dear,' said Lady Hardcastle.

'Technically, *you* threatened her,' I said. 'I merely backed up your threat with a little snarling menace.'

'You do it so well. You're my little Welsh terrier.'

Somehow I was always some sort of dog. I could have been a lion. Or a tiger. Or a fearsome bear. But no. Bloodhounds and terriers were my lot.

'Do I know this Cordelia?' asked the inspector.

'An insurance investigator,' said Lady Hardcastle. 'She works for Moberley, Burgess and Vincent.'

'Oh, how I loathe insurance investigators.'

'It's not like you to take against people like that,' I said.

'I do try to treat everyone fairly and equally, but insurance investigators get my goat. They're always so . . . so officious. They treat us as though we're all stupid, and then when we solve the case for them they collect their fat fee and claim all the credit.'

'You'd especially despise this one,' said Lady Hardcastle. 'We were at Girton . . . I was going to say "together", but let's settle on "at the same time". We didn't get on. We still don't, as it turns out.'

'What's her surname? So I know to ignore the case if she complains about being beaten up by a small, well-dressed woman, you understand.'

'Harrill,' said Lady Hardcastle. 'Cordelia Christiana Harrill. She went by "CC" for a time. Or tried to. It didn't catch on.'

'Harrill . . . Harrill . . . I think I've seen her name in the day book. Some jewellery went missing from a house in Sneyd Park, I think. Or maybe a painting? I can't remember the details but I vaguely recall a Harrill.'

'If she's working in the Bristol area, you're lucky that you've managed to avoid her, that's all I'll say.'

The inspector was about to respond, but we were suddenly distracted by the scrunch of narrow tyres on the fine gravel of the tiny parade square. Four cyclists had arrived.

The leader, Parslow, hailed us.

'Good morning, Inspector,' he said. 'And Lady Hardcastle and Miss . . . Miss . . . don't tell me . . . Miss Arbuthnot.'

'Close enough,' I said.

'I didn't expect to see you two here. Do you work for the police?'

'Miss Armstrong and I are acting as consultants,' said Lady Hardcastle.

'I see,' said Parslow with a slight frown. 'I'm sorry we're late, Inspector. Screen got a puncture out on the main road. Luckily we always carry spare inner tubes and tools, but it's a frightful palaver.'

'I've often wondered if it might be possible to repair a perforated inner tube in the field,' said Lady Hardcastle. 'A small rubber patch coated on one side with some sort of rubber fixative . . . one wonders why no one has come up with a solution. It would need to set reasonably swiftly without too much complicated additional fiddle-faddle, though. Perhaps that's why.'

'Perhaps,' said Parslow, now even more puzzled by this strange lady. 'Shall we go inside?'

He unlocked the scout hut door and ushered us all in.

Although it was, apparently, its official designation, it would perhaps be doing the building a disservice to describe it as a 'hut'. The main room was, I estimated, about twenty-five feet wide and thirty feet long, with windows on two sides. It was like a scaled-down version of our own village hall.

'The scoutmaster's office is over there,' said Parslow, pointing to a door at the far end of the room.

So far, none of the other three cyclists had said anything. Thanks to the helpful details Sergeant Dobson had given us the day before, I now knew the tall man with the dark hair and spectacles to be John Nurse, while the shorter, stockier one with the fair hair was Gordon Screen. The woman was easy to remember, even without the sergeant's help – she was, as Angelina Goodacre had told us, the only woman on the committee. She was Irene Vibert.

They filed in, still silent, and stood expectantly, waiting to be told what to do. These were not people, I judged, who were used to being interviewed by the police. I wondered how they'd all managed to get time off work and why the inspector had allowed them to come together. Perhaps he didn't suspect them, after all.

Parslow unlocked the office door and ushered Lady Hardcastle, the inspector and me into the cluttered scoutmaster's office. It had a desk with a battered leather chair, with just enough room amid the boxes and books for a folding visitor's chair on the other side.

'We weren't expecting such a large police contingent, I'm afraid,' said Parslow. 'There are some more folding chairs in the storeroom, but I'm not entirely certain where we'd put them.' He gestured at the tiny remaining floor space.

'Lady Hardcastle can have the chair,' said the inspector. 'I'll perch on the desk. Miss Armstrong? I don't wish to appear too ungentlemanly, but would you mind standing?'

'Not at all,' I said. 'There's just about enough room in that corner behind Lady Hardcastle.'

'You're very kind,' he said. 'In which case, Mr Parslow, I think this will do splendidly. I'd like to speak to you one at a time, if I may. Does anyone need to get away urgently?'

'Screen and Miss Vibert both work for me,' Parslow said, 'so I think I can get them the time off.' Grinning, he paused for the laugh that never came. 'But, er, Nurse has been given time off from his job at the coal merchant's under sufferance, so perhaps he's the one we shouldn't detain.'

'Thank you,' said Inspector Sunderland. 'Would you send him in, please?'

Parslow left us briefly alone.

'I'm going to find it a little difficult to take notes sitting here,' said the inspector, indicating the battle-scarred desk. 'Would you mind helping me out by keeping a record of the conversations, please, my lady?'

'Not at all, Inspector dear. I'll do you proud – mine were the lecture notes the other girls wanted to copy, you know.'

'I'm sure they were. Miss Armstrong, you're sure you'll be comfortable back there?'

'If I had a ha'penny for every time I've stood in the corner listening to the conversations of my elders and betters, I'd be able to employ Herself as *my* servant, instead of the other way round.' I gestured towards the already seated Lady Hardcastle.

'Never your "betters", dear,' she said. 'Never say that. Never even think it. You're the best of us.'

'Hear, hear,' said the inspector.

Blushing, I took my station and awaited the arrival of our first interviewee.

◆　◆　◆

John Nurse had seemed bold and confident as he announced Blackmore's murder at the Dog and Duck, but here in the cluttered scoutmaster's office he seemed much less sure of himself. He was tall, but in the presence of a police inspector and two strangers from a neighbouring village he seemed somehow diminished.

'Mr Nurse,' said the inspector, warmly. 'Please take a seat. I'm sure Mr Parslow has already told you, but I'm Inspector Sunderland of the Bristol CID and I'm investigating the death of Mr Russell Blackmore at the request of the Gloucestershire force.'

'Yes,' said Nurse. 'He did say.' His voice was quiet, his manner unsure.

'Excellent. And my friends here are Lady Hardcastle and Miss Armstrong of Littleton Cotterell. They've assisted me in many cases in the past and I find their help invaluable.'

Nurse nodded to us both in turn.

'Now, then,' continued the inspector. 'You're the clerk at Leighton's Coal Merchants, I believe.'

'I am,' said Nurse.

'And you're a member of the committee of . . . the Woodworthy and Littleton Cotterell Cycling Club, is that correct?'

Lady Hardcastle had her back to me so I couldn't tell for sure, but I'd have been willing to bet she was smiling at the care the inspector took to get the village names in the right order.

'That's correct,' said Nurse. 'I'm the club secretary.'

'And Mr Blackmore was on the committee, too?'

'Social secretary.'

'Did he work with you at Leighton's?'

'No, he worked in town. He was an engineer.'

The inspector nodded. I was sure he knew all this already, but it never hurts to make a witness comfortable with some easy initial questions.

'Thank you. And did you know Mr Blackmore well?'

'Very well. We weren't what you might call pals, but we got along fine. I liked him. I believe "charming" is the word people most often used to describe him.'

'I see,' said the inspector. He paused for a moment and it took me only slightly less than the length of his pause to work out that he was making sure that Lady Hardcastle had time to make her notes. 'Tell me about the cycle race on the twelfth.'

'We had been making the arrangements for weeks,' began Nurse.

'You and Mr Blackmore?'

'No, I meant the committee. Blackmore was involved, of course, but he worked in the city so he was unable to get to all our meetings. He took care of peripheral things – making sure the village pub knew how many to expect, publicity, flyers. Things he could get on with without needing to attend endless meetings.'

'I see,' said the inspector. 'Thank you.'

'We advised the police of the proposed route,' continued Nurse, 'briefed volunteer marshals, made signs . . . we thought of everything. It was perfect. We set off a few minutes late because of delays at the registration desk.' He looked at Lady Hardcastle and me. 'You were there. You saw how popular it was.'

'It was very busy,' I said, to save Lady Hardcastle looking up from her note-taking. 'I was surprised.'

'So were we, honestly,' he said. 'But the race got underway at just after a quarter past nine by my watch.' He patted his waistcoat pocket. 'The pack stayed together for about a mile, but then we began to string out a little.'

'Where was Blackmore?'

'He was with my group for a time as we began to spread. He stayed with us for quite a while but he was much fitter than the rest of us and was trying to cajole us into upping the pace a little. No one was keen, so he started to pull away shortly before we passed the castle for the first time.'

'He was alone from then on?'

'Unless he caught the lead group, then yes.'

'Is that likely?'

'It's certainly possible. It would have taken quite a sprint to catch them quickly. He would still have had to maintain a very quick pace even to catch them slowly over a lap and a half, though, so my guess is that he probably was alone, yes.'

'He was found at . . .' The inspector turned to look at me.

'The lane by the blasted tree near Wood Acre Farm,' I said.

'Thank you, Miss Armstrong,' said the inspector. 'Do you know the lane, Mr Nurse?'

'I do,' said Nurse. 'It's a distinctive landmark, that tree.'

'Do you remember passing it that Sunday morning? Did you see anything unusual?'

'I do remember, yes. As I say, it's a distinctive landmark. And it was a sign that we weren't too far from home, so I definitely remember. But no, there was nothing untoward there on either of the two times we passed it.'

'And no one noticed that Mr Blackmore didn't come back?'

'We did notice, but not until we checked the register after the last stragglers from the leisurely ride.'

At least he hadn't said 'convivial'. I was beginning to hate that word.

'But weren't you all keen to see the timesheet to find out where you'd finished? This was a competition, wasn't it?'

'It was, but it was all done behind closed doors. Metaphorically speaking. Of the racers, only Irene was allowed to see the timesheet. She's part of the racing subcommittee and they wanted to make a big announcement of the results once all the marshals' reports had come in. It was common knowledge that the woman Goodacre had arrived home first, but she couldn't be crowned the official winner until the scrutineers had verified everything.'

The inspector asked him a few more questions but we didn't learn anything new, and he was soon thanked and sent on his way.

Next to be sent in was Irene Vibert. She was a good deal more confident than Nurse, or at least she appeared to be. Her manner was almost defiant as she walked in and took her seat, but that could just as easily have been bravado rather than actual confidence.

The introductions done, Inspector Sunderland opened the questioning in much the same way as he had with Nurse.

'You're employed at Parslow's Timber Yard?' he said.

'I am,' she said calmly.

'In what capacity?'

'I'm Mr Parslow's secretary.'

'And you serve on the cycling club committee as part of the racing subcommittee as I understand it.'

'You understand correctly.'

He asked her about the day of the race and she told a very similar story to Nurse's. The field had spread out and she was in the lead group. No, Blackmore hadn't caught up with them. No, she hadn't seen anything unusual – she stressed 'different' – on either of the times they had passed the blasted tree.

'So there was nothing different,' said the inspector, 'but was there anything unusual?'

'It's an unusual place,' said Irene. 'That lightning tree gives me the creeps.'

'I see. When we asked Nurse why no one noticed that Blackmore hadn't returned, he said it was because the scrutineers hadn't completed their work. No one outside the race subcommittee was allowed to see the register or the timesheet.'

'That's also correct. We wanted to add a little drama to the announcement of the results. A little theatre, you might say. The truth is that the results of a small club's inaugural race are of little consequence and most people couldn't give a fig. We thought that by adding a period of secret scrutiny and wise head-scratching, we might make it a bit more interesting. It also allowed the committee time to try to come up with a reason for not naming Angelina Goodacre as the winner.'

'Why would they not want to do that?'

'An incomer winning the race was bad enough, but an incomer who happens to be female? It was surely a sign of the apocalypse.'

'Did they manage to disqualify her?'

'Not on your life. I got nowhere with my argument that women had just as much right to compete as men, but I managed to persuade them how bad it would make them look if everyone thought the race result had been fixed to make sure a committee member won. Gordon Screen was second, you see.'

'And when did this discussion take place? When did you see the timesheet?'

'I had a quick look at the register when I saw what I thought were the back markers of the race coming home, then we took possession of the register and the timesheet when the last of the convivial riders arrived. That was you, Lady Hardcastle, and your friends. We reasoned that all the racers must be back if the slowest of the convivial riders were home.'

'We were a little on the sluggish side, I'm afraid,' said Lady Hardcastle without looking up. 'But we did have a lovely picnic at Berkeley.'

'So you knew then that Blackmore hadn't returned,' said the inspector.

'There was no finishing time recorded, certainly,' said Irene.

'That didn't cause any concern?'

'Russ was something of a free spirit. He was a fine cyclist, and a reasonably keen competitor, but it wasn't his life. Not like some people.' She flicked her head towards the office door and the other committee members in the meeting room beyond. 'It didn't seem odd to me that he might have been distracted by something or someone. If he got bored of the race and wandered off to find something more engaging it wouldn't have surprised many people.'

'What would you say was "his life", then?'

'He was a man of simple tastes,' said Irene. 'He liked women, art, money, and fine cognac.'

'In that order?' said Lady Hardcastle.

'Perhaps we should put money first. With plenty of that, he had more access to the other three.'

'Did you ever walk out together?' I asked.

'I beg your pardon? What business is that of yours?'

'We're trying to get as complete a picture of the man as we can,' I said. 'I saw a . . . *look* on your face when he was making eyes at Lady Hardcastle when we first met you all outside the pub in Woodworthy.'

She regarded me carefully.

'Yes,' she said after a few moments, 'we walked out together for a few months at the end of last year. But that's when I learned that although he could spell the word "fidelity" – he was a highly educated man – he didn't have the first idea what it meant.'

'He had an eye for the ladies, then?' said the inspector.

'He did,' said Irene. 'My only consolation was that he had discerning taste – all the women who attracted his wandering eye were extremely fetching. I clung to the idea that he must have thought me attractive. He gave me the comfort of satisfying my vanity, at least.'

I didn't know quite what to make of this. He had met the two of us outside the pub, and again on the green, and it was Lady Hardcastle who had caught his attention both times. To save myself from feeling too much like an old trout, I decided to change the subject.

'He told us he went to the opening day of the Littleton Cotterell Art Exhibition,' I said. 'Did he talk about it?'

'Ceaselessly. It was his idea of heaven. He couldn't wait to go. Money, art, and all the young local women, all in the same place at the same time. But it was that gaudy book that really obsessed him.'

'In what way "obsessed"?' I asked.

'He talked about how much it had cost, how much it would be worth in the future, how much he wished he had something like that. For all his professed dedication to beauty, it was the price of the thing that really lit his fuse.'

'What did he say about the theft?'

'He never mentioned it.'

Lady Hardcastle looked up.

'Not at all?' she said.

'Not a word,' said Irene. 'He came to a committee meeting and complained about having to go back to Littleton Cotterell to fetch his bicycle, but that was the closest he came.'

Lady Hardcastle returned to her note-taking.

Irene had little else to offer us, despite a few minutes' more conversation. Inspector Sunderland thanked her for her help and asked her to send in Gordon Screen.

Screen didn't look like a typical athlete, but perhaps cyclists aren't typical. At the risk of exposing a terrible, terrible prejudice, though, he did seem like a typical accountant. He was tedious, pedantic, and irritatingly humourless. He also had nothing useful to tell us. Nothing new, at least. His version of events corroborated those given to us by Nurse and Irene, as did Parslow's when we spoke to him.

With another round of thanks, the cyclists were dismissed and Inspector Sunderland drove us back to Littleton Cotterell.

◆　◆　◆

We arrived back at the house to find a familiar green motor car parked in the lane beside the front gate.

'You have a visitor,' said Inspector Sunderland.

'Not an especially welcome one,' said Lady Hardcastle. 'If you wish to meet Miss Cordelia Harrill, you've arrived at an opportune moment.'

'I'm curious, certainly. Would you mind if I came in?'

'Not at all, Inspector dear. Will you stay for lunch?'

'If it's no trouble,' said the inspector. 'I'm sorry, did that sound too eager? I shouldn't want you to think I only come here to scrounge your food.'

'Not at all, not at all. We delight in your company.'

I led the way through the front door and we de-hatted in the hall. Edna had heard us come in and bustled out to intercept us.

'You's got a visitor, m'lady,' she said in theatrically hushed tones. 'Miss Harrow, I think she called 'erself. I said you wasn't expectin' no one and that I didn't know when you'd be back, but she insisted on waitin'. And not politely, neither. I put her in the drawin' room and give her a cup of tea, but it didn't change her mood much.'

'Thank you, Edna dear, we saw her car so we knew she was here. Might I prevail upon you for three more cups of tea, please? And would you tell Miss Jones that we'll be at least three for lunch. I shall invite Miss Harrill, but I doubt very much she'll stay.'

Lady Hardcastle took the lead and we entered the drawing room behind her.

Cordelia was sitting in my armchair, reading *The Times*.

'Good morning, Cordelia dear,' said Lady Hardcastle. 'How lovely of you to drop in. Would you care for some more tea?'

Cordelia flicked down the newspaper as though noticing us for the first time.

'It's not a social call,' she said. 'I have a bone to pick with you.'

'Pick away, dear thing.'

'I'm given to understand that you have spoken to Michael Yawn.'

'You've been given the truth. We spoke to him and his beautiful girlfriend yesterday morning. Lovely couple. A little aggressive in their manner, but one usually puts that down to a lack of self-confidence.'

'I specifically forbad you from interfering in my case. You had no right to speak to him.'

'Oh dear, are we still on about that? You knew we were going to ignore you – why do you let it upset you?'

'Because—'

The inspector cleared his throat.

'And who the blistering blue blazes are you?' snapped Cordelia. 'Another interfering busybody?'

'In a manner of speaking, miss. Inspector Sunderland of Bristol CID.' He held up his warrant card.

'Oh. Well. I—'

'Lady Hardcastle and Miss Armstrong are helping me with a murder investigation, and I'm helping them in their attempts to recover their friends' lost painting. I shall be following up a lead given to them by Miss Churches as soon as I have a free moment.'

'It's my case,' said Cordelia. 'Mine. My bonus is at stake here.'

Sunderland smiled. 'I'm sure you'll get what's due to you, Miss Harrill, don't worry.'

Cordelia folded the newspaper with a snap and stood up.

'Yes, well,' she said. 'You see that I do. Good day to you.'

She made to leave.

'You won't stop for lunch, dear?' said Lady Hardcastle. 'It would be lovely to have you.'

'I'll see myself out,' said Cordelia, and did just that.

'I see what you mean,' said the inspector as the front door slammed.

'Do we put *her* aggression down to a lack of self-confidence?' I asked.

'Quite possibly,' said Lady Hardcastle. 'She's always acted as though she has something to prove. More interesting for the moment, though, is how you knew we were looking for Hector's painting.'

'I'm a policeman, my lady,' said Inspector Sunderland. 'It's my job to know things.'

'Well, yes, but . . .'

'Dobson told me,' he said with a smile. 'You know what a gossip he is.'

Edna entered with the tea.

'A pot of tea for you and the inspector, m'lady,' she said. 'I understand from the slammin' door that Miss Harrow declined your kind invitation.'

'Regretfully she had an appointment elsewhere,' said Lady Hardcastle. 'We shall be three for lunch after all.'

◆ ◆ ◆

Inspector Sunderland left soon after lunch, having eaten with such enthusiasm that Lady Hardcastle had teased him, suggesting that he wasn't eating properly at home.

'Dolly is a fine cook,' he said, 'as you well know. But I did miss dinner last night. I was watching one of the new tobacco bond warehouses down at the Cumberland Basin. We had a tip that a gang had a man working inside and were going to help themselves to a recently arrived cargo.'

'I say,' said Lady Hardcastle. 'How exciting. Did you catch them?'

'Red-handed,' he said, with uncharacteristic pride.

'Good for you. More pie?'

Once he had gone, I tidied up and went to check with Miss Jones what she had prepared for me to cook for dinner. I took coffee to the drawing room, having successfully predicted that that's where Lady Hardcastle would be.

'Ah, thank you, dear,' she said, left hand on hip, right hand tapping a stick of chalk against her teeth. She was staring contemplatively at the crime board.

'Do you think Blackmore was involved in the art theft?' she said.

'I was certainly thinking it while Irene Vibert was talking, yes,' I replied, setting down the coffee tray and joining her at the board. 'Especially when she told us about how interested he'd been in the Westbury Shakespeare. When we spoke to him in the registration queue for the race, he acted as if he was only vaguely aware of its existence.'

'That made my antennae twitch, too.'

'Though he was rather concentrating on impressing an attractive widow at the time. Perhaps he thought you might find his obsession unappealing.'

She treated me to a dismissive *pfft*.

'So,' she said after a thought-filled pause, 'he pinched the book, nabbed Hector's painting and sloped off with them. That's why he had to leave his bicycle behind. And then . . . what? A falling-out with his accomplice, who smashed his head in on the cycle race? A rival gang?'

'It's not implausible,' I said. 'But who would his accomplice be? And how does it help us find the Summerhays?'

'Valid questions, both.'

'What did Nurse say he did for a living?'

'He's a clerk at Leighton's Coal Merchants,' she said. I could see the twinkle in her eye and the hint of a nascent grin.

I sighed.

'Very good,' I said. 'And Blackmore?'

'Blackmore never said where he worked.'

'They'll never find your body, you know.'

'Nurse said that Blackmore was an engineer, but he didn't say where.'

'You don't suppose . . . ?'

'He worked for Westbury? It would sit well with his obsession with the book, certainly. One imagines Westbury's staff would know all about it. We shall have to ask the inspector the next time we speak to him. He'll know.'

Chapter Ten

On Thursday morning I volunteered to pop into the village to get some chops for lunch. Miss Jones said she was happy to go herself, but I fancied the walk so I went instead.

Spratt's was quiet, with Fred painstakingly placing little paper frills on the exposed bones of a rack of lamb while his wife, Eunice, totted up the columns in the sales book. The tinkle of the bell as I opened the door, and the scuffing of my boots on the sawdust on the floor as I entered, made them both look up.

'Good mornin', m'dear,' said Mr Spratt. ''Ow bist?'

'I'm very well, thank you,' I said. 'And you?'

'Can't complain,' he said with a smile.

''E don't do nothin' but complain,' said Eunice. 'Mornin', noon and night. This is wrong, that's wrong, they're wrong, I'm wrong. I'n't nothin' right in Fred's world.'

Fred Spratt dealt with his wife's affectionate, but ceaseless, criticism by feigning deafness. He smiled at me again and winked.

'What can we do for you this fine day?' he said.

I resisted the urge to turn and point at the seemingly perpetual greyness of the sky – there were more things to a fine day than cheerful weather, after all.

'I have a craving for chops,' I said instead.

'Then you's come to the right place, m'dear. I gots some lovely lamb in.'

'So Daisy told me. That's what made me think of it.'

'How many do you want? A dozen?'

I laughed.

'Two will be fine,' I said. 'No, make it four. Let's go mad.'

As he trimmed and wrapped the meat, I turned to Eunice, who was already making a note of the purchase against Lady Hardcastle's account.

'And how are you, Mrs Spratt?' I said.

'I'm very well indeed, m'dear,' she said, looking up. 'I 'ad a bit of trouble with me feet. I does suffer with my feet. Always has. Fallen arches, bunions, ingrown toenails – you name it, I's 'ad it. I'm a martyr to me feet. But Dr Fitzsimmons sorted I out. He's wonderful, old Dr Fitzsimmons. Do you know, I once 'ad a ganglion on my foot? Right there on the top, it was.' She lifted her left leg behind the counter and pointed to the top of her foot. 'And do you know what he did?'

'No, Eunice, I have no idea.'

'He said, "Take off your stockin', Mrs Spratt." And I said, "I reckon you ought to at least buy I a drink first." He did laugh. So I took off me stockin' and he said, "Put your foot up on this stool for a minute while I looks somethin' up." So I did as I was told and 'e picked up this big medical book from 'is shelf. And 'e comes over towards I and . . . Wallop! He slams that big ol' book down right on the top of my foot. So I yells out. Called 'im a few choice names an' all. But 'e just smiles and points to me foot. And do you know what? The cyst had gone. He burst it with 'is book. He's a clever man, ol' Dr Fitzsimmons.'

'He certainly is,' I said with another laugh. 'Is the family well?'

'Grand, thank you. Our Sammy sent a letter from Singapore, if you can believe it. Imagine a Spratt seein' the world?'

Sammy Spratt, their eldest, served in the merchant navy.

'He's enjoying himself, I take it?' I said.

'I reckon so. His letters always make it seem as though he is. So he's all right. And our Daisy . . . Well, you knows how our Daisy is.'

'I do indeed. I'm glad to hear you're all doing well.'

'She did say somethin' about wantin' to see you, mind.'

'She did?'

'Somethin' about the new woman in the Dower House.'

'Did she say what?'

'No. She's a funny one, though, I'll tell you that.'

'Daisy?' I said, innocently. Lady Hardcastle was a bad influence. Eunice laughed.

'No, you silly goose,' she said. 'That new woman up the Dower House. She'd never 'ad faggots. Can you believe it? She looks at least fifty and she a'n't never 'ad faggots.'

I suppressed a smile.

'She's from the North-East,' I said. 'I couldn't say for certain whether they have faggots up there.'

'A life without faggots and gravy,' said Eunice, sadly. 'The poor buggers.'

Fred, still smiling, shook his head as he handed me the neatly tied package of chops.

'Enjoy your lamb, m'dear,' he said.

I thanked them both and stepped outside.

I stood for a moment on the path outside the butcher's. I felt as though I ought to go straight home with my precious cargo of lamb chops, but there was nothing urgent for me to do there other than hand the meat over to Miss Jones. I knew that if Daisy wasn't helping her family in the shop, she would already be hard at work in the Dog and Duck, so I decided to pay her a visit.

The pub door was shut and bolted, so I knocked.

No answer.

I knocked again. Louder this time.

'We's closed,' called Daisy from inside.

'It's me,' I said. I've never been entirely certain why any of us ever think that's a helpful thing to say, but it remains the standard answer nonetheless.

'Flo?'

'Well, yes,' I said. 'Obviously.'

I could hear the sound of many bolts being thrown and a key being turned in the lock. After what seemed an age, the door opened to reveal Queen Daisy in a dirty apron, a broom in her hand.

''S not obvious at all, you duffer. You could be anyone.'

'I couldn't be Constable Hancock. He's much taller.'

'And his voice is deeper, an' all. But that i'n't the point, is it? Do you want me or Joe?'

'You,' I said. 'Can I come in?'

'Always nice to be wanted,' she said, stepping aside to allow me to enter.

'I've just been speaking to your mother,' I said once I was in the bar.

'Did she tell you about her feet?' she asked, resuming her sweeping.

'There was a certain amount of foot-related discourse, yes.'

'She's a martyr to 'er feet, our ma.'

'So she tells me. She also tells me you wanted to see me.'

'Oh, my word, so I did. It's about that Angelina Goodacre, from up the Dower House.'

'She told me that, too.'

'I's very suspicious of 'er. She's up to no good, I reckon.'

'What makes you say that?'

'You know as how Felix Nisbet 'ad 'is bike nicked from outside the village hall?'

'Yes, the FUN fellow.'

'I never thought he was much fun, to tell the truth.'

'They're his initials. He's Felix Ulysses Nisbet, and he has FUN painted on the head tube of his bicycle. But yes, I know it was stolen. We saw him while he was complaining about it to Constable Hancock.'

'Ah, right,' said Daisy. 'Well, I seen that Angelina on a bike just like it.'

'Half the population of Gloucestershire has a bike just like it,' I said. 'It's a very popular model.'

'That's as maybe, but I still think there's somethin' up. There's comin's and goin's up at the Dower House. It's just round the corner from ours, and I seen a van arrivin' one evenin'.'

'Probably just a delivery.'

'That's what I thought at first. Then I saw it again a couple of nights later. Same van. Same time of the evenin'. And that's when I thought, "I'n't no one does deliveries in the evenin's." There's somethin' goin' on. I reckon she's goin' round the district nickin' bikes for a gang of bike thieves and they's sellin' 'em on.'

'There's a black market for bicycles?'

'There's a black market for everythin'. You ought to know that better 'n anyone, the sort of people you hangs about with.'

'True, true,' I said. 'Have you told Hancock?'

'I did, an' 'e told me not to be so daft.'

'Hmm,' I said. 'That won't do. I shall tell Herself, and perhaps we can pass it on to Inspector Sunderland. He'll know what to do.'

'I knew I could count on you.'

'Always. Any other gossip?'

'Cissy's got some new stockin's.'

'Nice, but not up to your usual high standards.'

'It's all I got, I'm afraid.'

'Then I shall leave you to your mighty labours.' I held up the packet of chops. 'I have to get these back to Blodwen so she can work her magic on them for our lunch.'

'I'll see you about, then,' said Daisy with a smile. 'Mind 'ow you goes.'

I left the pub and walked home.

◆ ◆ ◆

I went straight to the kitchen and gave the chops to Miss Jones, who opened the packet at once and nodded appreciatively.

'He does get some lovely meat, does Fred,' she said.

We briefly discussed my preferred method of preparation, and favoured accompaniments, but we decided to keep it simple.

'Good idea,' said Miss Jones. 'Let the meat speak for itself.'

I was glad Lady Hardcastle wasn't there – or her brother Harry for that matter. We would surely have had to smile politely while they made themselves giggle about what a poor butcher Fred Spratt would be if his meat were still talking.

Lady Hardcastle was nowhere to be seen, but Edna told me that she had said something about 'makin' an early start on 'er voles'.

I went out to her studio in the orangery, where I found her painstakingly dressing the Vole Atlantis set in preparation for the next scene of her new moving picture.

'Florence Armstrong, as I live and breathe,' she said as I entered. 'What a delight to see you. What brings you to my artificially watery lair?'

'I bring news from the village,' I said.

She put down a tiny plaster statue of a heroic water vole that was apparently intended for the Atlantean town square, and looked up at me properly.

'News, you say? I am all ears,' she said.

I passed on Daisy's account of Angelina Goodacre's recent activities and her speculation about a stolen bicycle racket.

'Do you think there's anything in it?' asked Lady Hardcastle when I had finished.

'I never knew anyone at the circus who wasn't making a few bob on the side with some sort of scheme or other,' I said. 'Even as a small girl I suspected that not all those schemes were strictly above board.'

'Well, yes, but there's a good stretch of clear water between "not strictly above board" and "downright illegal". One accepts that people in all walks of life will have a little sideline, a parergon, an *agitation latérale*... an avocation if you will—'

'If I must.'

'You absolutely must, I insist upon it. But not everyone's avocation is illicit. Could Miss Goodacre be a criminal?'

'Anyone could be a criminal...'

'You're really not helping.'

'Very well,' I said with a sigh. 'From what I remember of Angelina – bearing in mind that I was about six or seven years old when I first met her – I have absolutely no idea whether she's capable of stealing bicycles and selling them on for profit. But it's easily possible that she might be.'

'Thank you,' said Lady Hardcastle. 'What about clonking people over the back of the head with a lump of wood? Would she do that?'

'Blackmore's bicycle wasn't stolen – how is that related?'

'His bicycle wasn't stolen, but it looks like his saddle was.'

'It's my turn to ask something, then,' I said. 'Do you imagine Angelina is the sort of person who would murder a man in cold blood for the sake of a bicycle saddle?'

'In which case it's my turn to say, "Anyone could murder a man in cold blood." If the circumstances are right, we any of us could be capable of murder. But she needn't have intended to kill him. She looks fit and strong, but she's small. Blackmore was a vigorous man. She almost certainly doesn't have your fighting skills to fall back on, so if things cut up rough she might grab a nearby lump of wood to even things up a little. Thus armed, it's all too easy to kill a man by accident. And having killed him, she might have decided that being caught in possession of the bicycle would be too much of a risk, whereas a saddle might still fetch a shilling or two. It would be less easily traced back to the manslaughter and would add a small sliver of profit to an otherwise unsuccessful venture.'

'That's . . . actually, that's surprisingly plausible. Oh, and Daisy said Goodacre has the same make and model of bicycle as Blackmore. If Blackmore's saddle were of some special, sporty design, it might increase the value of her own without her having to steal the whole thing.'

'Another possibility,' said Lady Hardcastle.

'How about this, though,' I said. 'She and Blackmore were the art thieves. They met in the woods to discuss their next move, but had a falling-out over the division of the spoils. A fight ensued, she grabbed a handy lump of wood . . .'

'Except,' she said, sadly, 'we didn't see a lump of wood. It all falls down there, somewhat.'

'She might have taken it and disposed of it somewhere else. I certainly would have. There's another problem, though: if she stopped to argue with Blackmore so close to home, how did she still win the race?'

'She couldn't have . . . unless all this happened on the first lap. We've assumed – well, I've assumed, at least – that he was killed on the second lap, but that's not necessarily the case. If she killed him on the first lap, she might still have had plenty of time to catch the leaders, overhaul them, and win.'

'So we need to find out more about her,' I said. 'And more about exactly how the race played out.'

'Perhaps,' said Lady Hardcastle. 'At the very least, we need to tell the inspector. I said I'd telephone him to ask where Blackmore worked, so I shall let him know of our Goodacre suspicions while I'm at it.' She paused to indicate her model. 'But I should like to finish the agora before I do.'

'An agora, no less. And here's me thinking it was a town square.'

'They are the descendants of Ancient Greek water voles, lost forever beneath an English lake. They have an agora, not a common-or-garden town square.'

'But why are they Greek?' I said. 'Surely—'

'I have imagined a race of underwater water voles, living for centuries beneath an English lake. They have built a city. They have a complex political structure, and a rich and vibrant culture. They have written poems and erected statues. They wear clothes. Their land-dwelling cousins have invented – and constructed – an iron submarine in which they shall journey to the lacustrine depths in search of this lost civilization. All of this is perfectly acceptable to you, but you draw the line at their being Greek?'

'Well, if you put it like that . . .' I said. 'Tea?'

'Coffee, please. I shall be with you in just a few moments.'

I left her to her unaccountably Hellenic water voles.

◆　◆　◆

After coffee, Lady Hardcastle telephoned Inspector Sunderland at the Bridewell in Bristol. With our heads together and the earpiece between us so we could both join in, she passed on our question about Blackmore's employer and our thoughts about Angelina Goodacre.

'I can tell you about Blackmore straight away,' he said. 'He was a draughtsman at Westbury Engineering in Bristol.'

'Well, now there's a thing,' said Lady Hardcastle.

'Is it?' he said. 'What sort of thing?'

'The sort of thing that makes one wonder if he was in some way connected with *our* case. You remember Irene Vibert saying he was obsessed with the Westbury Shakespeare? Well, his place of employment is another connection for you.'

'One I was aware of, yes. I'm already looking into it on Sergeant Dobson's behalf.'

'Oh,' said Lady Hardcastle, somewhat dejectedly.

'Cheer up, my lady,' said his distorted, distant voice. 'It was a good idea, and one worthy of pursuit. And I shall make some enquiries about Miss Goodacre for you. She sounds like quite the character.'

'We circus folk are all characters,' I said.

'Almost all the ones I've ever met have been thoroughly delightful,' he said. 'Do you have anything else?'

'No, Inspector dear,' said Lady Hardcastle. 'That's everything for now.'

'Then I shall leave you to enjoy the rest of your day,' he said. 'Thank you for calling.'

With the earpiece back on its hook we were making our way back to the drawing room when the telephone started to ring.

'Get that, would you, dear?' said Lady Hardcastle, continuing across the hall without so much as breaking stride.

I turned back and picked up the earpiece once more.

'Ahoy,' I said.

There was a pause. Then a familiar laugh.

'That you, Florence, m'dear?' said Sir Hector.

'It is, Sir Hector,' I said. 'Good morning.'

'Mornin', mornin'. You runnin' away to sea?'

'To see what?' I really was spending too much time with Lady Hardcastle.

'Ha!' came the bark of a laugh again. 'Very clever, m'dear, very clever. No, I meant sailin' the briny. It was your nautical greetin' set me off, d'you see?'

'Ah, of course. I read an article about Mr Bell the other day and I learned that when he invented the telephone it was his preferred greeting. I thought I'd try it out. Would you like to speak to Lady Hardcastle?'

'No, m'dear, you'll do . . .' There was a pause. 'I say, that sounded a bit rude, didn't it? I didn't mean you were a lesser substitute for the real thing. I just meant—'

'What can I do for you, Sir Hector?' I said, brightly.

'Wanted to invite you both for lunch, that was all. You free?'

'Today?'

'Unless you're busy today, yes. Thought it might be fun. Weather's a bit brighter so we might be out on the terrace. Good to have some company. Save me havin' to make small talk with the memsahib, what?' I could just about make out the sound of Lady Farley-Stroud's voice in the background, but I couldn't hear what she was saying. 'Nonsense, my little figgy puddin',' said Sir Hector, slightly away from the mouthpiece. 'I always enjoy your company. You're the very light of my life.' His voice returned to normal as he addressed me once more. 'Foot in it there, old thing. Didn't realize she was behind me. Can you come?'

'I shall need to check,' I said, 'but I know there's nothing in the diary. How about I agree that yes, we'd love to come, and if Lady

Hardcastle has a pressing engagement she's not told me about I shall call you back with an alternative suggestion.'

'Sounds splendid, m'dear. See you at noon unless I hear otherwise.'

'Aye-aye, sir,' I said.

'Ha!' came the bark, then the line went dead.

At The Grange we were escorted to the terrace, to my continuing delight, by the spaniels. Sir Hector was on the lawn poking at a patch of dug-up grass with a stick. Lady Farley-Stroud was sitting at the table, reading a magazine, her spectacles perched on the end of her nose. She looked up at the sound of the dogs' claws clattering on the flagstones, and regarded us in confusion. Peering over her reading glasses, she appeared quite forbidding, and I felt suddenly guilty, as though we were trespassing.

Her bewildered frown turned into a smile when she realized it was us, and my anxiety turned to relief. How absurd that I should feel like an interloper in this place I had visited so often. Brains are stupid.

'Emily, m'dear,' said Lady Farley-Stroud. 'Florence. How wonderful to see you. I'd completely forgotten you were coming.'

'Ahoy there!' called Sir Hector from the grass. He waved his stick in greeting. 'Badgers,' he said by way of explanation as he poked the ground again. 'Diggin' up m'lawn, what?'

'They dug up our buddleia, dear,' said Lady Hardcastle. 'They're handsome little fellows, but they're no respecters of garden shrubs.'

So that purple thing was a buddleia, I thought. I followed up quickly with: *You're kidding yourself, Flossie – you'll never remember that.*

Sir Hector, meanwhile, had returned to the terrace and was stamping his feet to remove the loose earth from his shoes.

'Must you do that here, Hector?' said Lady Farley-Stroud. 'We've a perfectly good boot scraper by the side door.'

'Therein lies the flaw in your scheme, my little apple crumble,' said Sir Hector. 'The side door's all the way over there.' He waved his stick in the general direction of the side of the house. 'Whereas I find m'self standin' here, greetin' our guests. Hello, m'dears. Thank you for comin'.'

'We wouldn't miss it for the world, dear,' said Lady Hardcastle. 'But you really must come to us once in a while. Miss Jones would love to cook for you.'

'Might have to hold you to that when the place is repossessed,' said Sir Hector. 'But for now, allow an old fella the chance to play the genial host as lord of the manor.'

'A role you were born to.'

'Ha! Hardly. But sit ye down. Take the weight off, what? A chota peg before lunch?'

'It's a little early to start drinking, Hector,' said Lady Farley-Stroud.

'Nonsense, m'dear. Not suggestin' we get sloshed. Just a little livener.'

Lady Farley-Stroud tutted and rolled her eyes as she closed her magazine.

'I'll keep you company, Hector,' said Lady Hardcastle. 'Can you make mine brandy rather than whisky, though, please?'

'Certainly, m'dear. Florence?'

'Same for me, please,' I said.

Sir Hector bustled off through the French doors into the house. He never asked Jenkins to make drinks, preferring to see to this important task in person.

At Lady Farley-Stroud's invitation, we joined her at the table.

'While he's gone,' she said, leaning forward conspiratorially, 'tell me honestly what chance you think you have of gettin' the Summerhays back.'

'Honestly-honestly?' said Lady Hardcastle.

'Brutally frank, with no sugar coatin',' said Lady Farley-Stroud with an emphatic nod. 'And without that old buffer interruptin'. He bolts back and forth between mindless pessimism and equally mindless optimism, like a startled horse. I can't have a sensible conversation with him about it.'

Lady Hardcastle thought for a moment.

'Very well,' she said at length. 'At the moment, the chances appear slim. We have no "leads", as the detectives say, merely a couple of fanciful notions that may yet take us nowhere. That said, though, Inspector Sunderland is helping dear Sergeant Dobson by making enquiries in the city, so things haven't stalled completely. Then there's the insurance investigation into the Westbury Shakespeare. I don't hold the investigator in particularly high esteem – ghastly woman – but she might discover something by sheer blind luck. And never forget that our customary modus operandi is to go from having no idea whatsoever what's going on, only to solve everything in a flash at the last moment. So I would say you should prepare for disappointment, but not give up hope entirely.'

Lady Farley-Stroud smiled.

'Exactly the sort of equivocal response I'd expect from a diplomat's widow, m'dear,' she said, 'but I appreciate your candour. Thank you.'

'It's the best I can do, I'm afraid,' said Lady Hardcastle. 'As far as we can fathom it at the moment, your painting wasn't the target of the theft – it seems more likely that was the Westbury Shakespeare. But the thieves' escape route took them past the Summerhays and it seems it was too tempting for them to pass it by.'

'You say Sunderland is asking questions in the city.'

'Yes, we spoke to Mickey Yawn—'

'Such a pity about that one,' said Lady Farley-Stroud, sadly. 'He was such a charming little boy. His mother used to bring him along to village events. She was always helping with this and that. She still does. Little Mickey was a mischievous little scamp, but there was no malice in him. I wonder where he took a wrong turn.'

'We may never know,' said Lady Hardcastle. 'We haven't quite ruled him out, but the information he gave us seems more promising. His girlfriend—'

'His girlfriend is that dreadful Olive Churches,' said Lady Farley-Stroud. 'Well, I say she's dreadful. To be honest, I've not said more than a dozen words to her – though seven of them were "Put that back at once, young lady!" – but her family . . . my goodness. Such villains.'

'So we're given to understand. Miss Churches was vehement in her denials of any involvement in the theft, but she did intimate that her father—'

'Her villainous father,' Lady Farley-Stroud interrupted again.

'Her gang-leading, villainous father, yes. She hinted that he knew who was behind it, and that's what Inspector Sunderland is pursuing.'

'Do you believe her?'

'It would be foolish, I think, to ignore her,' said Lady Hardcastle, 'but equally foolish to take her entirely at her word. There was a fair amount of bravado on display from both the youngsters when we spoke to them, so it's likely she was merely showing off.'

'And what do you think, Florence?' asked Lady Farley-Stroud, turning to me.

'I agree,' I said. 'It could well be a gang from the city, but there's an amateurishness about the whole endeavour that speaks against the involvement of professional crooks. The plan was clever – start a fire, pinch the book in the confusion, then disappear into the milling crowd – but none of it was foolproof. A lot was left to chance and would only work perfectly if things played out exactly as the thieves imagined they would. If even a single element of the plan had failed to work, the whole enterprise would have come crashing to the ground. And there's the theft of your own pieces – it just doesn't seem like something an experienced gang would allow themselves to be distracted by. They'd have been in, grabbed the Shakespeare, and hoofed it. No shilly-shallying, no eyes lingering on other shiny things. Grab the book and get out the back door.'

'And so whom do you suspect, m'dear?'

'I can't escape from the thought that the late Russell Blackmore is tangled up in it somehow. He worked for Basil Westbury, and he was – at least according to one of his cycling friends – obsessed by the Shakespeare book. He has something to do with it all, I'm sure.'

We could hear Sir Hector's footsteps as he crossed the ballroom on his way back to the French doors.

'Hush now, gels,' said Lady Farley-Stroud. 'We're talkin' about Clarissa and her happy news.'

Sir Hector arrived at the table and set down the tray of drinks.

'I brought you one, Sachertorte. Didn't want you to feel left out, whar?'

Lady Farley-Stroud rolled her eyes, but took the proffered whisky nevertheless.

'So, what have I missed?' he said. 'What have you ladies been talkin' about?'

'Babies,' said Lady Farley-Stroud.

'Ha! Leave a group of women alone for five minutes and they'll always talk about babies. Or overthrowin' the government and introducin' a parliament of women. One of the two.'

'It would be a mighty improvement if we did,' said Lady Farley-Stroud.

'Can't gainsay you on that one, my little tarte Tatin. We chaps have made a proper hash of it. Good health.' He raised his glass in salute, then took a sip and smacked his lips in appreciation. 'Ah, that's the stuff.'

We returned his toast and sipped our own small drinks.

'Luncheon is on its way,' he said as he set his glass down. 'It'll be a few minutes yet, though, says Jenkins.'

'Lovely,' said Lady Hardcastle. 'Have you heard anything more from the Freers?'

'As a matter of fact, I have. That's rather why I wanted to talk to you. Get your opinion on things. Spoke to them yesterday, d'you see? Showed me all sorts of documentation – stories, journals and whatnot. They're not givin' up. They told me about a key that Sir Theodore mentions in his diary, and speculated about it openin' this secret door they've been on about. Makes all kinds of sense.'

'And are they any closer to finding the treasure?' I asked.

'Not an inch closer, m'dear. Not an inch,' he said. 'Full of ideas, mind you. And enthusiasm. Enthusiasts always manage to draw me in. And their latest wheeze is to do a full survey of the outside of the buildin', concentratin' on the east side. That's where they think the door will be. Me and the memsahib have to go up to Gloucester tomorrow – a meetin' of one of m'charities – so we said they could come over and do it then. We won't be in the way, and they won't get on Gertie's nerves if she can't see 'em, what?'

'It sounds intriguing,' I said.

'Don't it, though?' said Sir Hector. 'But what do you both think? Are they on to somethin'? Or are they just stringin' a chap on?'

'It does sound like they might be on to something, yes,' said Lady Hardcastle. 'But—'

'"But", m'dear?' said Sir Hector.

'But I'm not sure about leaving them alone. It's not that I mistrust them, you understand . . . but then again I can't be certain

I entirely trust them, either. We know nothing about them, after all. What if they're right, and the treasure of Sir Theodore Elderkin really is buried here at The Grange? If they uncover it while you're not here, what's to stop them packing it up in their haversacks and spiriting it away? "No, Sir Hector, we found nothing. Looks as though it was just another fanciful legend after all. We get a lot of those in our line of work."'

'Well . . . when you put it like that . . .'

'What say Flo and I potter up and casually bump into them? "We're just visiting our pals," we'll say. "Not here? Oh, what a shame. We should have telephoned. What are you up to? Something fun?" And then we could join them on their exploration and keep an eye on things for you.'

'I say,' said Sir Hector. 'That's not a bad idea at all.'

'It would make me a good deal more comfortable,' said Lady Farley-Stroud.

'Splendid,' said Lady Hardcastle. 'What time did they say they'd be here?'

'Ten o'clock,' said Sir Hector. 'I said I'd make sure the staff were expectin' them and to give them the run of the grounds.'

'Then we shall be here at ten. Stout boots and tweeds, as though expecting a walk around the grounds with our dear friends. We shall invite ourselves to join them and entirely refuse to be put off should they object.'

'Thank you, m'dear,' said Sir Hector. 'Is the plan acceptable to you, young Florence?'

'It is, Sir Hector,' I said. 'Though I look dreadful in tweed.'

'Nonsense,' said Lady Farley-Stroud, one of the county's foremost tweed-wearers. 'Everyone looks marvellous in tweed. And it's the great leveller. Farmers, clergymen, doctors, workmen, land-owners – put 'em in tweeds and they all look like they belong to the countryside. Can't beat a bit of tweed.'

I smiled, still unconvinced, but I felt it would be insulting to argue.

Conversation was temporarily halted at that moment by the arrival of Jenkins, the butler, and Dewi, the footman, bearing trays heaped with Mrs Brown's excellent cooking.

It was time for lunch.

Chapter Eleven

Getting to The Grange by ten o'clock on Friday morning shouldn't have required a Herculean effort. People throughout the land make it to work at dawn. Even in the towns and cities, people are washed, dressed and breakfasted in plenty of time to allow them to travel to their places of employment and arrive by eight or nine o'clock. And yet, even with professional help from her thoroughly excellent lady's maid, getting Lady Hardcastle anywhere before eleven was always a struggle.

Somehow, though, we managed to leave the house on time, and were both suitably clothed in outdoor togs. I couldn't bring myself to wear the dreaded tweed and settled on a skirt of heavy cotton in a shade of brown I hoped would make the inevitable mud and dirt more difficult to see, even if it didn't conceal it completely. The white blouse was a risk, but the fawn tailored jacket should help protect it, I thought. My boots, though, were entirely appropriate for outdoor trudging.

Lady Hardcastle, in confirmation of Lady Farley-Stroud's confident assertion, looked marvellous in her tweeds. But she somehow managed to look marvellous in an engineer's overalls, so it didn't come as much of a surprise.

We saw the Freers on the steep hill that led to The Grange. They were on their bicycles and we gave them a cheerful wave as we passed them, as though we had no idea we were all going to the same place.

Jenkins had been briefed on our intentions before we left the previous day, and played his part perfectly. Even though there was no one there to hear him, he explained that the Farley-Strouds were out for the day and weren't expected home until late afternoon. And even though there was no one there to hear *us*, we apologized for interrupting his work, and asked if he would tell them we had called.

We returned to the Rolls and he shut the front door behind us, just as the Freers cycled on to the drive. We waved again and waited for them to reach us, something that took a little longer than anticipated as they wobbled tentatively along the gravel.

'Good morning, dears,' said Lady Hardcastle when they finally drew to a halt and hopped off their bicycles.

'Good morning, Lady Hardcastle,' said Zeke.

'Good morning, Miss Armstrong,' said Zibbie.

'Good morning,' I said with a smile. 'I'm afraid the Farley-Strouds aren't at home.'

'We thought we might join them for a walk around the grounds and a spot of elevenses,' said Lady Hardcastle. 'Sadly, we find that they are at Gloucester for the day. It seems we should have telephoned after all.'

'It's all right,' said Zeke, 'we know they're not here.'

'Sir Hector invited us to explore the grounds while they were out,' said Zibbie.

'Oh, I say,' said Lady Hardcastle. 'More treasure hunting? How exciting.'

'We wish to examine the eastern aspect of the house in some detail,' said Zeke.

'Our researches have led us to believe that the entrance to Sir Theodore's treasure vault is somewhere on that side,' said Zibbie. 'Perhaps where the Elizabethan and Regency sections join.'

'That sounds fascinating,' I said. 'I don't suppose we could join you?'

'Oh, what a splendid idea,' said Lady Hardcastle. 'Would you mind awfully? It would be wonderful to see you at work. We shan't get in the way.'

The Freers regarded us for a while, but said nothing. After a few moments they leaned in close to each other and conducted a rapid, whispered conversation. Another few moments passed while they discussed our request. I found it impossible to hear what they were saying, but to judge from the deadly serious expressions on their pale-skinned faces, it was not an uncomplicated matter. Then again, I couldn't recall seeing either of them with an expression other than one of deadly seriousness. I wondered if they ever told jokes.

'Very well,' said Zeke eventually.

'We'd welcome the company,' said Zibbie.

'And your insights,' said Zeke.

'You've known The Grange for some while,' said Zibbie.

'So you might be able to guide us to things we'd not notice for ourselves,' said Zeke.

'Marvellous,' said Lady Hardcastle, whose head had been swivelling back and forth between the treasure-hunting siblings as though she were at a tennis match. 'Lead on, dears. We shall follow, and offer help whenever we can.'

Lady Hardcastle and I leaned on the bonnet of the Silver Ghost while we waited for the Freers to do . . . whatever on earth it was they were doing. There was a lot of rummaging in rucksacks, and a good deal more heads-together whispering, but very little apparent progress towards setting off. I began to wonder if we would ever manage to explore the grounds at all.

'Do you remember when we first came to The Grange?' asked Lady Hardcastle as they continued to fribble about with their notebooks, pencils and diagrams. A compass was consulted, distant landmarks pointed at, and marks made on a map.

'I do,' I said. 'Although we didn't come up together at first. You came to a welcome-to-the-village dinner, and then I was sent up on my own a couple of weeks later to help with Clarissa's engagement party. We didn't come here together until after that, when Lady Farley-Stroud asked you to help find her missing emerald.'

'Ah, yes, that's right. I've always loved it here. And I've always loved Gertie and Hector.'

'It took Lady Farley-Stroud a little while to warm to me, but I love them, too. It would be a shame to see them lose The Grange. I'm sure they'd be fine, but they go with this place like crumpets and butter. Crumpets are lovely things. Butter is a splendid invention. But fresh butter on a hot, toasted crumpet has a magical wonderfulness that neither component can manage on its own. And I'd miss visiting this place, too. It's a shabby, chaotic shambles, but it's so warm and welcoming.'

'I would, too. We'll not let them lose it. We'll find a way.'

The fiddle-faddling seemed to be over – or at least easing off a little – and the Freers appeared at last to be ready.

'Shall we begin?' asked Zeke in a tone that suggested Lady Hardcastle and I had somehow been the cause of the delay.

'But of course, dear,' said Lady Hardcastle. 'Ready when you are.'

We pushed ourselves up from the bonnet of the Rolls and followed them to the eastern aspect of The Grange.

They set off with great purpose, striding here, pointing there, poking this, prodding that, and all with the conspiratorial muttering that had characterized their behaviour since their arrival.

We explored every inch of the wall, paying special attention to the sections where the early nineteenth-century construction and the original Tudor building met the Victorian additions.

Zibbie was no draughtswoman but she had nevertheless been nominated as graphical note-taker. She was making sketches as they made their way round the building, and the look of concentration on her pretty face was thoroughly endearing. The results of her efforts, though, were far from impressive. Her frowning, her lip-biting, and her painstaking drawing had produced little, as far as I could tell, that was of any use.

It might be that I was maligning her. We had recently been made aware of an exciting new Spanish artist – Pablo Picasso – and it was possible that Zibbie was a follower of the Cubist school. Whatever the truth, it was going to take a good deal of patient interpretation to make sense of her scrawls.

We watched the creation of the sketches with growing fascination as the Freers progressed around The Grange.

Although, perhaps 'progressed' is the wrong word to choose. It carries connotations of success and achievement alongside the more mundane notion of merely moving forward through a task. As we watched, it slowly became apparent that success and achievement were in short supply and that the Freers were growing increasingly frustrated at expending so much painstaking effort for so little reward.

Lady Hardcastle and I managed to be fascinated in the process at first, and both asked what I considered to be perfectly reasonable questions. We wanted to know more about their research and their methods. We asked about treasure in general and The Grange in particular. At first their responses were polite, if a little vague, but as time passed, the politeness turned to impatience and the vagueness to terse evasion. Things, I surmised, were not proceeding according to plan. Or at least not according to hopes and expectations.

There was a brief moment of excitement and enthusiasm when Zeke hauled on a large stone planter to tip it slightly so that Zibbie might look underneath. I wondered what they might be expecting to find. A spare key, perhaps? My grandmother's neighbours in Cwmdare seldom locked their doors, but when they felt the need to do so, they always made sure there was a spare key concealed outside, usually under a flowerpot on the windowsill. Or perhaps it wasn't a spare, perhaps it was the key that Sir Hector had mentioned – the key to the secret vault.

As it turned out, it was merely providing dark, damp shelter for half a dozen now panicking woodlice, who scurried back into the gaps between the flagstones as the unexpected daylight and unwanted attention hit their armoured backs. Zeke lowered the planter, shaped like a giant's goblet, back into position with a good deal less care than it deserved.

After almost two hours of diligent but wholly unrewarding examination of the external fabric of The Grange, the Freers declared themselves finished, and with curt goodbyes stalked back to their bicycles. By the time we had strolled back to the Rolls, they had gone, with only narrow tyre tracks in the gravel to show that they had ever been there at all.

We arrived back at the house just as Edna was putting on her coat to go home, having previously asked if she could leave at noon to tend to her husband's latest injury. Lady Hardcastle had, of course, agreed.

Dan Gibson's continual misfortunes were famous throughout the county, and a constant source of frustration for poor Edna. There was much debate in village circles as to whether Dan was the unluckiest man in Gloucestershire, or the clumsiest, and opinion was more or less equally divided between the two possibilities. Either way, he seemed to be permanently on the crocked list and spent much of his time with his arm in a sling, a patch on one eye, or hobbling on crutches. The time he fled from a flock of angry jackdaws and ran into a tree, breaking his nose, was a particular favourite among the regulars in the Dog and Duck.

Lady Hardcastle brushed off Edna's offer to stay to serve lunch, and we sent her on her way with our good wishes for Dan's speedy recovery.

'Thank you, m'lady,' said Edna. 'Though if you can think of a way of stoppin' the silly old duffer from hurtin' hisself in the first place, I'll gladly pay you for it.'

I checked that all was well in the kitchen and told Miss Jones to let me know if there was anything I could do to help, before joining Lady Hardcastle in the drawing room. I found her once more contemplating the crime board, which was becoming very cluttered as we tried to keep track of three completely separate matters: the art theft, Blackmore's murder, and the treasure.

'I'd been hoping to add something useful to the "treasure" section following our trip this morning,' said Lady Hardcastle. 'But as it turns out, it was a morning well and truly wasted.'

'I was so bored I started to count the bricks in the garden wall at one point,' I said.

'How many were there?'

'More than six. I'd say they could easily number in the dozens.'

'That many? You missed your calling, dear – you should have been a quantity surveyor.'

'I would have preferred any occupation to being snapped at all morning by a couple of irritable children—'

'They're in their twenties,' said Lady Hardcastle with a laugh.

'Children,' I repeated. 'And supercilious ones at that.'

'They mean well. At least, I hope they do. I'm prepared to put up with a little rudeness if it means they find the lost treasure of Sir Teddy Whatnot and save The Grange.'

'That's it, though, isn't it? I'm increasingly of the opinion that Sir Teddy Whatnot and his Napoleonic treasure are a myth. Like El Dorado. Or Atlantis. We're more likely to discover your Greek voles living at the bottom of the lake than treasure concealed in a secret room at The Grange.'

'You may be right,' said Lady Hardcastle. 'Get that, would you, dear – I'll just make a couple of notes here before I forget.'

She had said this in response to the ringing of the doorbell, as though under any other circumstances she might have answered it herself.

It was Inspector Sunderland, and I conducted him back to the drawing room.

'Good afternoon, Inspector dear,' said Lady Hardcastle as he and I entered. 'What an unexpected delight. And just in time for lunch.'

'Good afternoon to you, too, my lady,' said the inspector. 'But I'm really not here for lunch.'

'Of course not. It's just a coincidence. Flo, dear, can you see if Miss Jones can manage one more for lunch?'

'No, really,' said the inspector without a huge amount of conviction.

'Nonsense. We'd be delighted to have you join us.'

I glided out, consulted Miss Jones, and glided back again.

'Lunch will be in about a quarter of an hour,' I said.

'Splendid, splendid,' said Lady Hardcastle. 'Just enough time for us to find out the *real* purpose of the inspector's visit.' She winked.

'Honestly,' said the inspector, 'it's really not like that. I—'

'Take no notice of her,' I said.

'But, really—' he tried to continue.

'How long have you known her?'

'I've known you both since the summer of . . . 1908, I think. Four years now.'

'And you've not noticed her fondness for mischief? Her tendency to tease people?'

'Well, yes, but—'

'So don't rise to it. She'll grow tired of it soon enough, then she'll move on to something else and leave you alone.'

'You really are the most rotten spoilsport, Florence Armstrong,' said Lady Hardcastle. 'I could have had him squirming all the way to pudding. Which he would have eaten with gusto while still protesting his innocence, by the way.'

'Someone needs to keep you in check,' I said. I turned to the inspector. 'So, tell us: apart from a free luncheon, what *is* the "real" purpose of your visit?'

This earned me a Sir Hector-style 'Ha!' from Lady Hardcastle and an exasperated shrug from Inspector Sunderland.

'Actually, I'd quite like your help,' he said. 'I'm getting absolutely nowhere with the Blackmore case. Talking to the committee was of only marginal help, and my enquiries into everyone's backgrounds gave me just as little. But you two always manage to cut through to the heart of things in the end, so I thought I might ask if you wouldn't mind coming with me as I take another look at the scene of the murder. But since I'm apparently just here for free food, perhaps you'd prefer not to bother.'

'Investigative nose-pokery?' said Lady Hardcastle. 'Count me in. I apologize unreservedly for my reprehensible teasing. You absolutely do not call on us mumping for free food, and the fact that you always appear at mealtimes is entirely coincidental.'

'You'd like to come, then?'

'Rather. Would you like some free food?'

'It's the purpose of my visit.'

◆ ◆ ◆

I had to agree with Irene Vibert – the lightning tree was definitely unnerving. As we pulled up beside it in Inspector Sunderland's motor car, I imagined what it might look like silhouetted against a moonlit sky and had to suppress a shudder.

We turned into the side lane and clambered inelegantly out of the inspector's vehicle. Well, I was inelegant about it, at least. Inspector Sunderland always seemed to flow everywhere as though his suit were filled not with a policeman but with smoke, while Lady Hardcastle had a grace about her that belied the impression of clumsiness she so carefully cultivated most of the time. Of the three of us, I was the only one who ever did any actual exercise, who had ever studied the intricate, controlled movements of the Chinese fighting arts, and I always fell out of motor cars as though I had been tipped out of a sack.

'Are you all right there, dear?' asked Lady Hardcastle as I stumbled into a patch of cow parsley.

'Quite all right, thank you,' I said, straightening my dress. 'I just can't seem to get the hang of it. Do they give you lessons, or something?'

'One of my governesses tried to teach me how to alight elegantly from a carriage when I was little, but I horsed about so much, and for so long, that I made her cry. She never attempted it again. Some of it must have stuck, though.'

'Well, perhaps you can teach me one day. I've got green stains on my skirt, look.'

'Poor dear. I have a girl who cleans that sort of thing up for me.'

The inspector, meanwhile, had taken his perpetually unlit pipe from his jacket pocket and was sucking pensively on it as he considered our surroundings.

'It's quite a substantial lane, isn't it?' he said. 'Do you think he simply took a wrong turn?'

'It's possible,' I said. 'From what Nurse told us in the scout hut, he hadn't been involved in the planning of the route so he might have made a mistake. Then again, the route was clearly marked – they'd put signposts out at all the spots where they expected us to turn off from the obvious road.'

'Actually, yes, I remember reading that in Dobson's report now you mention it,' he said. 'You met Blackmore – did he seem like the sort of fellow who would get confused and take a wrong turn?'

'He seemed like quite an alert chap,' said Lady Hardcastle. 'Very with it. Not at all the vague and distant sort we so often meet.'

'So he came down here deliberately, then, we think?' said the inspector. 'But why? Was he lured? Or was it a prearranged meeting?'

'We speculated that he might have been involved in the art theft and that he met his accomplice here,' I said.

'Because he worked for Westbury and coveted the book?'

'Exactly so,' said Lady Hardcastle.

'And in this speculative scenario, who was his accomplice?' asked the inspector. 'Not your bicycle thief, Miss Goodacre?'

'She's definitely a possibility,' said Lady Hardcastle.

'Large numbers of people are possibilities, my lady. But how would he know her? She's new to the area.'

'She was a circus performer, don't forget,' I said. 'She's been everywhere. She could have met him at any time.'

'You were a circus child, and you don't know everyone,' he said.

'I was a little girl, though, not an attractive young trick cyclist. I barely met anyone other than the other people in the circus, but she'd have drawn the attention of the young men of every town we visited. She'd have met all sorts of people.'

'True, true,' he said. He walked a few steps and stopped at the beginning of the track leading to the clearing where Blackmore's body had been found. 'So he came along the lane and stopped about here. He might have dismounted, but we can't be certain.'

'We know he didn't get far along the track before he was attacked,' I said. 'The drag marks begin quite close to the road.'

'Which rather argues against a secret meeting,' said Lady Hardcastle. 'If he and his confederate wished to keep their dealings on the QT, they would have retired immediately to the seclusion of the copse.'

'Unless,' said Inspector Sunderland, 'they had their clandestine meeting there, fell out over the distribution of the spoils, and then Miss Goodacre – or whoever it was – struck him from behind as they walked back towards the lane.'

'You're right,' I said. 'Sorry. Despite everything we've said I'd still been assuming that murder was the main intention.'

'No apologies necessary. It's by talking things over like this that we refine our thinking and arrive at a solution.' He gestured towards the track with his pipe-free hand. 'Shall we?'

We stepped from the lane and walked towards the copse, pointing out the last vestiges of Blackmore's heel marks as we went. We stopped at the clearing to take stock.

'Whether before or after the meeting—' began the inspector.

'If, indeed, there was a meeting,' said Lady Hardcastle.

'Just so. But whenever his murder occurred in the unknown sequence of events, Blackmore was killed at or near the lane and then dragged here to where we found him. The killer also had the presence of mind to move his bicycle away from the lane and bring it back here with his body.'

'Having first stolen the saddle,' I said.

'The saddle, yes. A standard piece of factory-fitted equipment, says my colleague, though he agreed with you that competitive cyclists are known to fit more expensive, handmade saddles.'

'And then what?' asked Lady Hardcastle.

'And then the killer fled the scene,' said Inspector Sunderland.

'Taking the murder weapon with them,' I said.

'The murder weapon, yes . . .' he said, pensively. 'Gosling's post-mortem confirmed his original assessment. Death was caused by a subdural haematoma following a blow to the back of the head. Blackmore was probably merely unconscious when he was dragged back here, but he would have died soon afterwards, probably without knowing anything further about it.'

'A small mercy,' said Lady Hardcastle. 'It reminds me of the murder at Clarissa's engagement party. Didn't the same thing happen there?'

'It did,' said the inspector, 'and it might be used in this case in mitigation, to spare the killer the noose. It speaks against an intention to kill if the assailant thought they had merely rendered Blackmore unconscious, even though by leaving him here they abandoned him to die. Gosling also confirmed his original speculation about the murder weapon. Rough-sawn soft wood, he says. Possibly pine, to judge from the splinters in the wound, and definitely cut square. It was held vertically like a club, and struck Blackmore with some force. Gosling is presuming a long piece of thinner timber – perhaps two-by-two – or a shorter, heavier piece – four-by-two, or four-by-four, say. His thinking is that the longer piece wouldn't need to be as thick to do the same amount of damage. I believe the phrase "moment of inertia" was used but the science is beyond me, I'm afraid. More than that, though, is impossible to say from the evidence he has.'

'If it's a piece of prepared timber, though,' said Lady Hardcastle, 'it's not something the killer found in the copse. It's not a fallen branch, for instance.'

'No, Gosling is firm on that. It's definitely cut and shaped.'

'A signpost?' I said.

'From the race, you mean?' said the inspector.

'Yes. We already know there were dozens of them.'

'But not down here,' he said. 'It's a strange choice of weapon if it's something you have to bring with you.'

'We might have a better idea where it came from if we can fathom out what happened to it afterwards,' said Lady Hardcastle. 'No one is going to risk walking around with a bloodstained wooden post. It must have been dumped somewhere. And probably somewhere nearby.'

'Shall we split up?' I said. 'Let's start by assuming it's not near the track – we'd have seen it by now if it were. Let's further assume it's not more than ten yards from here – the killer would have wanted to ditch it quickly before they were seen with it. So it's somewhere in a ten-yard circle centred on the track.'

'An oval, then,' said Lady Hardcastle. 'With the track as its long axis.'

'And is that more helpful than what I said?'

'It's more accurate.'

'Will it assist us in finding the discarded murder weapon?'

'I concede the point, dear,' she said. 'Carry on.'

'Thank you.'

'But it's still an oval.'

I sighed.

'If we ignore the section nearest the track and each take one of the remaining quadrants of the *oval*,' I said, 'we can cover the ground in no time.'

'Bags I this section,' said Lady Hardcastle, her arms out to indicate the area she wished to search. She set off without waiting for us to agree.

'Which section would you prefer?' said the inspector.

'I honestly don't mind,' I said.

'In that case, why don't I go this way, and you go that?'

'A splendid idea.'

'We can meet back here when we're done.'

He walked off, eyes down, scanning the ground ahead of him.

I did the same, but in the opposite direction. For a few yards I saw little but leaf litter and creepy-crawlies. There were some twigs, and some animal droppings I couldn't identify, but no murder weapon. I walked in what I imagined was a purposeful zigzag, intending to cover the full extent of my assigned section of the circle – it was as good as a circle, no matter what Lady Finicky-Drawers said.

Time passed without my noticing as I concentrated on my task. With my eyes darting everywhere, I covered the ground thoroughly, noticing everything out of the ordinary, from unusually mossy stones to a patch of bare earth in the shape of Ireland. Or an owl. Or possibly both – Ireland is most definitely shaped like an owl.

I had almost reached the end of my self-appointed search area when I saw it. The killer had gone to a reasonable amount of effort to conceal it, brushing it over with leaves and dirt, but a flash of the unnatural whiteness of a large piece of card gave it away. I had found a bicycle race signpost.

With my fingers in my mouth I gave out a loud, piercing whistle, and in just a few moments, Inspector Sunderland was by my side.

'That was quick,' I said.

'It's one of those pieces of police training that never leaves you,' he said. 'You hear a whistle and you come running. I know it wasn't a police whistle, but it's almost an instinctive reaction nevertheless.'

I pointed to my discovery, still exactly as I had found it.

'I thought I'd leave it there so we could uncover it together,' I said. 'When you're in the witness box you need to be able to say you saw it for yourself.'

'You're rather good at this,' he said. 'I once had a defence brief try to claim a piece of damning evidence had been fabricated because I didn't see it until it had been removed from its hiding place and brought to me by a member of the public. We called the person who had found it to the stand, but without a corroborating witness it did no good.'

'I have my moments,' I said.

'You certainly do. Would you like to do the honours?'

'In a moment,' I said. 'But we ought to wait for Herself. She'll be most put out if we discover an important piece of evidence without her.'

'I wouldn't want to make things awkward for you,' he said with a smile.

'Oh, it's not like that really,' I said. 'Actually, I want to share the moment with her. We do these things together.'

He smiled again, and nodded. He knew us well enough to understand that it was true.

Two minutes later, though, I was regretting my choice. There was still no sign of Lady Hardcastle and I was growing impatient to examine what I had found. With a nod of warning to the inspector, I put my fingers in my mouth and whistled again.

'Oh, do be patient,' said Lady Hardcastle as she emerged from behind a tree. 'I heard you the first time.'

'That was ages ago,' I said. 'I feared you'd been carried off by wolves.'

'There haven't been wolves in England for quite a while, dear. Were you thinking of badgers?'

'I often think of badgers – they're adorable. But you did take your time.'

'I'm sorry,' she said, 'I was distracted by this.' She held up a bicycle saddle in her gloved hand.

'Blackmore's?' asked Inspector Sunderland.

'It looks very much like it from what I can remember,' said Lady Hardcastle.

'It rather rains on the hypothesis that Angelina Goodacre killed him to steal his saddle,' I said.

'It does,' she agreed. 'But we were none of us particularly convinced by that one, anyway.'

'True. Do you think you might be able to get fingerprints from it, Inspector?'

'I might, but I can't promise anything if it's been out here all this time. If you'd be good enough to keep hold of it just like that, my lady, that should maximize our chances of finding any unsmudged prints.'

'Of course,' she said, dropping the saddle by her side with her finger still looped through its metal frame. 'But why all the whis tling? What have you found?'

'This,' I said as I pointed to the almost concealed signpost.

'Oh, I say. Well done, both.'

'It was all Miss Armstrong's doing,' said Inspector Sunderland. 'I merely answered her whistle.'

'Well, now I feel doubly bad. Not only am I dilatory in my whistle-answering, but I've given credit to the wrong person. Can you ever forgive me, dearest Flo?'

'Do shut up,' I said. 'There's a good girl.'

'Shutting up now, dear,' she said. 'My lips are sealed. Not another word shall I utter. Silence shall be my watchword. Though my watchword shall never be so much as breathed, of course, for to speak its name aloud would be—'

'Have you finished?'

'Quite finished, thank you. Do proceed.'

I crouched beside what we believed to be a piece of white card, and began carefully to sweep away the leaves and dirt. Slowly I uncovered more of the stout card, and then the piece of two-inch pine post to which it was attached. Moving now away from the card, I revealed more of the post until, finally, about five feet from where I had started, I reached the end. It was stained brown with dried blood.

Chapter Twelve

Back at the house I'd hoped to be able to watch Inspector Sunderland at work with his fingerprint powder, but despite an extensive search of the boot of his car, it seemed he had neglected to bring it. Instead I carefully wrapped the saddle in greaseproof paper so that he could take it back to the Bridewell and examine it properly.

I made a pot of tea and took it to the drawing room, where Lady Hardcastle and the inspector were examining the bicycle race sign.

'I'm no expert in forensic science,' said Lady Hardcastle, 'and I bow to your own experience if you think differently on this, but I'm prepared to go out on a limb and say that this post is almost certainly the murder weapon.'

'I'm happy to agree with you,' said the inspector. 'Gosling should be able to ascertain the blood type from what's left here. It won't confirm it conclusively, but if it doesn't match Blackmore's at least we could rule it out.'

I picked up the sign and hefted it. It seemed an unwieldy and eminently dodgeable weapon for a face-to-face fight, but it would serve well enough for a surprise attack from behind. I swung it experimentally before examining the sign itself.

Painted in large black letters were the words 'CYCLE RACE', with an arrow underneath, pointing to the right.

'It seems identical to the signs we saw around the course,' I said. 'We should check with the race committee to see where this one was placed. You'd imagine they had a record of where they put them all so they could collect them up afterwards. They might have noted which one was missing.'

'They might, indeed,' said the inspector. 'Thank you. I presume it was placed on the left-hand side of the road to indicate that riders should just continue straight on.'

'It would,' said Lady Hardcastle. 'But turning it through ninety degrees would instruct them to turn right.'

'You're suggesting it might have been used to divert Blackmore up the lane?'

'It's a possibility, don't you think? We know Blackmore was riding on his own, so his killer might have sent him off course and then followed him, taking the sign with them. Any riders coming along behind would have carried on along the correct route.'

'Thinking about it,' I said, 'it's an odd place to put a "keep going" sign. It's not as though anyone might have been in a quandary about whether to go up the lane – it's not the sort of road the rest of the course ran on. We might find that all the committee's signs are accounted for, after all.'

'And this one is a fake made by the killer?' said Lady Hardcastle.

'Yes,' I said.

'You see?' said the inspector as he made a note in his notebook. 'This is precisely why I call upon you two for assistance. I'd have thought of that later today, I'm sure, but here you both are, putting things together at once.'

'You flatter us,' said Lady Hardcastle. 'But we're not quite as brilliant as all that. We're getting nowhere with the art theft, after all.'

'Ah, yes,' said the inspector, flipping through pages in his notebook. 'The art exhibition. I knew there was something I wanted to tell you. Now, where is it . . . ? Let me see . . . Ah, here we are. I had one of the lads look through the records and make some enquiries of other forces about your Cordelia Harrill. You knew her at university, you say, my lady?'

'That's right,' said Lady Hardcastle. 'She and I were up at Girton together.'

'But she wasn't studying the sciences with you?'

'Good lord, no. She was one of the arts crowd. They looked down on us science gels.'

'And do you know what she did after she left?'

'Not at all, no. We weren't friends, as you know.'

'She put her education to very good use,' said the inspector. 'As an art thief. She offered her services to special clients who were hoping to acquire valuable pieces without paying the market rate for them. Thanks to her education in such things, she was able to promise that she knew a Rembrandt from a Rousseau and could get them exactly the sort of thing they were after. She was ingenious and inventive in her methods. But she suffered one fatal flaw, common to many experts in their fields.'

'Which was?' I said.

'Arrogance. She imagined herself so clever that she could never be caught. And that made her complacent. She took to bragging about her exploits, but she bragged once too often. The wrong people heard, and sold the information to the French police, who nabbed her as she broke into a minor gallery in Paris. They couldn't charge her with anything much – she hadn't actually managed to steal anything on that occasion, and mere breaking and entering was a minor offence – but they told Scotland Yard they had her and she was whisked back home to face a string of charges relating to some very high-value thefts. She spent five years in Holloway, where she was a model prisoner, teaching the other inmates to read, running art appreciation classes – that sort of thing. And upon her release she managed to find employment as an insurance investigator.'

'Poacher turned gamekeeper,' said Lady Hardcastle. 'It takes a thief to catch a thief and all that.'

'That seems to have been the rationale, yes.'

'Well, well, well. Naughty old Cordelia. It rather puts her out of the frame, doesn't it?'

'Or squarely back into it,' I said. 'A leopard can't change its socks.'

'Indeed,' she said. 'No thumbs. But it would seem foolish to jeopardize her new career.'

'She didn't exhibit especially sound judgement in her first choice of career. There are many worthy things she might have done with her knowledge. And one thousand pounds' worth of book is a mighty temptation, even for a reformed thief. She'd certainly have the right contacts when it came time to sell it on and realize her profit.'

'I've been thinking along the same lines,' said Inspector Sunderland. 'I'll make sure Dobson knows, and I'll get someone to keep an eye on her movements.' He flipped another few pages in his notebook. 'Next is some bad news, of a sort. Constable Hancock went up to the Mock of Pommey at Woodworthy and spoke to the new landlord there. He confirmed Yawn and Churches' alibis – they were both there till early evening on the day the art exhibition opened. He remembers them distinctly because they had a set-to with a farmhand and his girl. The other two started it and were sent on their way, but it did mean our two were well and truly noticed.'

'It's a shame in a way,' I said. 'It would have been nice to have stumbled on the two culprits without really making an effort. But

I'm also glad. For all their bluster, and Mickey's reputation as a bad lot, I rather liked them.'

'I did, too,' said Lady Hardcastle. 'I wonder if that's why Cordelia was so irritated to learn that we'd spoken to them.'

'How so, my lady?' said the inspector.

'Well, let's imagine for a moment that she really did steal the book and the painting. A local ne'er-do-well and his popsy would make an ideal lightning rod to draw attention away from her. By speaking to them we might eliminate them as possible suspects before she'd had a chance to imply their guilt and muddy the waters.'

'Convoluted but possible,' he said.

'Convoluted and barely possible is all we have at the moment, Inspector dear. Our only other avenue of investigation remains erstwhile trick cyclist Angelina Goodacre.'

'I don't want it to be her,' I said. 'She was nice to Gwen and me when we were little. But if Daisy is to be believed, she's definitely up to something over at the Dower House. I think some surveillance is called for.'

'If it's going to involve breaking and entering, I don't want to know anything about it,' said the inspector. 'Not unless you actually find something. And even then I'll need something more than "my friend Miss Armstrong broke into her house and found something incriminating" if I wish to persuade a magistrate to grant me a search warrant.'

'I am the very soul of stealth and discretion,' I said. 'You can rely on me.'

◆ ◆ ◆

The sun set around eight. By half past it wasn't quite dark, but it was gloomy enough that I thought I might risk setting off on my snooping mission.

Dressed in my loose Chinese exercise outfit of black tunic and trousers, and armed with a battery-powered flashlight, I slipped silently along the lane towards the village. I skirted the edge of the green, keeping to the shadows to avoid being spotted, and made my way via a convoluted route through the backstreets to the Dower House.

I had to melt into an alleyway between two blocks of cottages when I saw Fred and Eunice Spratt on their way to the pub. It wasn't that they would have minded what I was up to – I knew from conversations we'd had with them over the years that they would have heartily approved – I just didn't want to be standing out in the street having a conversation about it when I could be getting on with the job at hand. There would be time for thrilling anecdotes when it was all over.

Fortunately, they were the only people I saw, and I was soon concealed by the bushes that grew between the road and the Dower House's garden wall.

The wall's bricks were old, and had been deliciously rounded by a couple of centuries of Gloucestershire weather. More importantly, age had shrunk the equally worn mortar, providing such an abundance of foot- and handholds that it was more like a ladder than a garden wall.

I was up and over in seconds, and crouched for a moment in the shelter of a leafy garden shrub while I got my bearings. It was a substantial garden, still wild and overgrown despite Angelina's recent efforts at tidying it up. The house was about twenty yards to my left, while a substantial outbuilding stood around ten yards to my right. I could just about make out what appeared to be a decent-sized gateway in the garden wall close to it. A large building with such easy access to the road would be a perfect place to store stolen bicycles or bike parts.

I picked my way carefully around the edge of the garden, sticking to the overgrown border to avoid disturbing the long grass. It would be obvious to even the most dull-witted observer that someone had been sneaking about in the garden if the grass had been trampled.

The outbuilding was sturdily built from the local grey stone, and the enormous doors and similarly broad gateway meant it had probably originally been a coach house. The main doors were only secured with a padlock, but I judged that opening them would be too noisy, and too easily seen from the house, so I searched for a side door. I soon found it, and its simple lock quickly yielded to my trusty picklocks. I was inside in less time than it would have taken Angelina to find her key and let herself in the legitimate way.

I closed the door behind me and scanned the walls for windows that might betray me, before switching on my flashlight. The dim beam seemed brighter after muddling along in the gloom, and I found myself in a well-organized workshop, absolutely heaving with bicycles, bicycle parts, and tools. There were complete bikes, empty frames, wheels with and without tyres, saddles, chains, and an assortment of other components whose names and purposes I could only guess at. Some of the fully built machines were makes and models I recognized from our many research trips to the bicycle shops of Bristol and the surrounding areas. But there were others that were not at all familiar – well-made machines painted in attractive shades of blue rather than the ubiquitous black.

The tool bench was well appointed, with what looked like welding equipment at one end.

This was the lair of an expert bicycle thief, where machines could be stripped for spares or refurbished and disguised for onward sale. I was so busy admiring the set-up that I almost didn't hear the sound of someone outside, unlocking the padlock on the main doors.

I scanned the substantial room and spotted a pile of sacking in the far corner. As quickly and quietly as I could, I extinguished my flashlight and made myself a nest among the sacks, hoping that I'd managed to properly conceal myself.

Someone came in and bustled about. I assumed it was Angelina, but obviously I couldn't tell simply from the sound of the bustling. Whoever it was seemed to be rearranging the bicycles and I hoped she wasn't the sort of person who was fond of late-night tidying. If she was, she would certainly want to do something about the lumpy pile of sacks in the corner of the workshop.

The bumping and clanking seemed to go on for ever.

I was tired. And bored. And suddenly terrified that I might fall asleep. A dozy shuffle or, worse, a snore would give me away and I'd have to explain to my old circus friend why I was curled up asleep in her workshop dressed in a Chinese jacket and trousers.

Time passed slowly and there seemed to be no end in sight.

I began to doze.

I had no idea how long I'd been asleep, but I was jolted heart-poundingly awake by the clatter of a motor van's engine outside the gates. Daisy was right: vans did come to the Dower House after dark.

I heard Angelina throw open the workshop doors and then the slightly more distant sound of the gates being unlocked.

I risked a peep from my hessian hiding place. The workshop was now illuminated by two large oil lamps, by whose light I was able to see that a number of the fully assembled bicycles had been lined up near the doors – famous makes on one side, blue-painted anonymous machines on the other. I could hear Angelina outside in the road talking jovially to the van driver. Now would be a perfect time to slip stealthily back out through the side door and disappear into the night.

I unpacked myself from the sacks and hastily rearranged them in an approximation of their former chaotic state before tiptoeing to the side door. I checked that my flashlight was still in my pocket – it would be terribly embarrassing to survive this long without being detected, only to leave an incriminating object like that behind. It wasn't as though it had my name on it, and I couldn't imagine anyone ever tracing it to me, but it was a matter of professional pride to leave behind no trace of my presence.

I was out the door long before Angelina returned from the van, and had plenty of time to relock it. I was about to try to find a suitable spot to clamber back over the wall and return home, but curiosity got the better of me. I had assumed that the bicycles arranged by the open workshop doors were about to be loaded on to the van and carted away to goodness knows where, but I knew what Lady Hardcastle would have to say about unproven assumptions. I decided to stay and find out for certain what was going on.

It was a cloudy night, and it had become very dark while I'd been hiding inside. I found a spot where I judged I wouldn't be illuminated by a lantern held by either Angelina or her chatty van driver, and settled once more to wait.

I was at once pleased and disappointed that my assumption proved to be at least partly correct. Pleased because everyone likes being right, disappointed because no one likes crouching in an unidentified bush in someone else's garden at night while something they had accurately predicted went on nearby. Well, perhaps some do, but I'm not certain how much I'd enjoy their company if I were to meet them.

But while I was almost certainly right that the bicycles were simply destined to be loaded on to the van for transport to parts unknown, there was something I hadn't banked on. And I was suddenly rather glad I'd decided to stay put and watch.

The van driver appeared at the gate and Angelina greeted him warmly. They seemed like old friends, but that was how she treated most people – she was a naturally gregarious soul, with a kindness and curiosity that always seemed to put people at their ease. She had welcomed Lady Hardcastle and me into her home, for example, even before she had confirmed our past association.

There was the sound of one of the van's doors opening and closing, and a third person strolled cockily into the light cast by the lanterns in the coach house. Mickey Yawn.

Angelina greeted him with equal warmth, but this time it was obvious that their association went beyond mere acquaintanceship. She instructed him to load the 'new ones' first, and without any of the truculence I would have expected of the lad, he all but scampered into the coach house and emerged wheeling two of the blue-painted bicycles. She hadn't explained which bikes were which, nor even pointed – he already knew.

One by one the bicycles were wheeled from the workshop and loaded on to the van. The chatter between Angelina and the driver continued without so much as a pause for breath. It was entertaining, but uninformative. At least, it didn't inform me on matters that might have helped. I learned that the driver's eldest boy had a new job at the docks, that his wife had made a lovely fish pie the night before, and that his skittles team were now second in the league. But I still didn't know what the arrangement was between the two, nor where the bicycles were bound.

Mickey chimed in cheerily from time to time. He was cheeky and funny while remaining deferential and polite – not at all the churlish boy we'd met earlier in the week. He appeared to be knowledgeable about the bicycles, too, and answered several of the driver's questions about them as they wheeled them to the van.

At last the loading was done, and good wishes were exchanged. Angelina said she would see Mickey in the morning, and van doors were slammed. I caught a glimpse of the side of the van in the lamplight as it manoeuvred in the tiny lane at the side of the Dower House, then the gates were closed and the workshop locked up. Angelina, humming an old music hall tune, walked back to the house, carrying her lanterns.

I waited until I heard the back door close, then began to edge towards the garden wall. When I was sure that the lantern light had gone from the kitchen and that Angelina had settled in the front parlour for the evening, I slithered over the wall and back out into the dark Littleton Cotterell streets.

◆ ◆ ◆

Lady Hardcastle was reading in the drawing room when I returned.

'Welcome back, tiny servant,' she said as she put down her book. 'I poured you a brandy.'

I sat in my chair and took a sip as she fussed with her reading glasses and hunted for her bookmark. The cognac was smooth and delicious – Lady Hardcastle never compromised on the quality of food and drink.

It took her an absolute age to sort herself out. She had only a book and a pair of reading glasses to deal with, but somehow this seemed to make things more complicated for her. Eventually the book was on the side table with her spectacles atop it, her brandy balloon was in her hand, and her attention was entirely mine.

'How did it go, dear?' she said.

I gave her an almost full account of my evening, skipping over the part where I dozed off, but including details of the workshop's contents and the mysterious late-night loading of the bicycles.

News of Mickey Yawn's appearance on the scene prompted a raised eyebrow.

'Your conclusions?' she asked when I had finished.

'She's refurbishing and selling bicycles,' I said. 'I'm happy to speculate that they could well be stolen, but the evidence supports any number of other possibilities. It could just as easily be a legitimate business, but moving the goods in the dead of night – or after dark, at least – is always suggestive of criminality.'

'As is the presence of the village rogue. Let's assume for the moment that it is a criminal enterprise – what would you hypothesize?'

'Perhaps she's a fence?' I suggested. 'Local thieves bring her the stolen bikes and she sells them on, having added value by repairing them.'

'And if one is already handling stolen bicycles, why not other stolen goods, too?'

'Like paintings, you mean?'

'Like paintings. Did you see signs of anything like that?'

'Not out in the open,' I said. 'It was very much a bicycle repair shop. But the Dower House is large enough that she could safely store other things indoors without running any risk that they might be seen by visitors.'

'Another possibility is that she might not be a fence at all. She must have contacts in the cycling world – it could be entirely her operation.'

'A two-wheeled Fagin, you mean? It's a possibility, I grant you. And in Mickey Yawn she may well have found her very own Artful Dodger. But what about this: she had a fencing operation in place and had lots of potential buyers for whatever came her way before she moved to Littleton Cotterell. She saw that the Westbury Shakespeare would be on display in her local village hall, with only Tweedledum and Tweedledee to guard it. She improvised a plan to steal it, without being unduly concerned about whether it would work – if it came off, then it was a cash bonus; if it didn't, no one would care. She got the book and the painting – now free of its frame – back to the Dower House somehow. She noticed the posh bicycles as she made her getaway and came back at some later point to steal them. That was when she made off with Nisbet's BSA. And then . . . well, that's where I'm stumped, honestly. I don't understand why she needed to kill Blackmore.'

'Either he saw something,' suggested Lady Hardcastle, 'or he's involved in the stolen bicycle operation somehow and they had a falling-out.'

'It's all a bit flimsy and cobbled together, though,' I said.

'Rather like the theft itself,' she said. 'And that worked despite its amateurishness.'

'I think we should let this one swirl about a bit and see how it settles overnight. Do you fancy some cheese? Sneaking about always makes me hungry.'

'I'd love some. Thank you. I shall find something suitable to play. Music to aid pondering, contemplation, and general cogitation.'

I heaved myself from the armchair and ambled to the kitchen.

Chapter Thirteen

I took Lady Hardcastle's starter breakfast up at eight the next morning, and found her sitting up in bed with her notebook on her lap.

'Good morning,' I said. 'Are you all right?'

'All right, dear?' she said, looking at me over her reading glasses. 'Oh, I see – once more you find me awake before being bullied into it. Yes, thank you, I'm quite well. I just wanted to organize my thoughts a little before the distractions of the day.'

'And how did that go?'

'Despite my efforts, my thoughts remain chaotic, jumbled, and thoroughly unhelpful. We've raised so many possibilities, and all of them make their own haphazard sense. And that was before I remembered what the inspector had told us about Cordelia and the possibility of her being involved in the theft. And then I wondered if she might also have some reason to do away with Blackmore, too. She has henchmen in the form of Porter and Templeman, after all – she might have ordered them to do him in.'

'I'd forgotten about her,' I said. 'Daisy's assessment of her is spot-on, I think.'

'A "right cow"? Yes, she's definitely that. But it's the former-thief thing that gives me pause.'

'Me too. Though "poacher turned gamekeeper who turns out to have been a poacher all along" still isn't terribly convincing.'

'I'm not sure real life has to be like the detective stories,' she said. 'Sometimes messy and unconvincing is the best reality can muster. But it's still displeasing, so I abandoned all that and turned my attention to Gertie, Hector and The Grange. And then to Ziggy and Zaggy, the Treasure Hunters from Another World.'

'Another world?'

'They can't be from ours, surely. They're so . . . well, I'm not sure what they are, but they're not like we mere mortals. There's all that incomprehensible muttering, for a start. I'm not entirely convinced they communicate with each other in English.'

'And have you noticed how they take it in turns to talk?'

'I have. I thought it endearing at first, but lately I've begun to find it peculiar and unnerving.'

'Do you think they really do know anything about the treasure?'

'I'm coming to doubt it. I'm no longer sure there's any treasure at all. I may have to intervene, and chastise them for cruelly giving Hector false hope.'

'I favour giving them a little more time, but it's up to you,' I said. 'I have to get back downstairs now, though. Breakfast is at half past.'

I left her to her musings.

Lady Hardcastle arrived at the breakfast table with a new resolve and sense of purpose. She looked like a woman on a mission as she sat down to her sausages and eggs.

'What's got into you?' I asked.

'A dislike of wallowing and self-pity,' she said. 'I spent far too long this morning complaining to myself about how much we don't know, so I decided to concentrate on what we actually do know.'

'And what do we know?'

'We know that your old circus pal Angelina Goodacre is up to something, and that Mickey Yawn is somehow involved. I'm not certain whether it's something honest or underhand, but she's up to something and I know a way to find out.'

'Which is . . . ?'

'Ask her.'

'How often does that work? "Are you breaking the law?" "Why, yes, I am. I see now the error of my ways. I shall stop at once. How can I ever repay you for setting me back on the path of righteousness?"'

'Well, I'm going to speak to her anyway. You're right that a too-direct approach never works, so I shall be circumspect. But speak I shall. And we might learn more from her silence than her answers, so it shan't be time wasted. Are you coming?'

'I wouldn't miss it for the world.'

'Splendid,' she said. 'Would you be a dear and butter me a slice of toast?'

'Can you not do it for yourself?'

'Of course I can. I just thought how much nicer it might taste if you did it.'

'Sadly, you'll never find out. I'm happy to clean mysterious stains from your skirts. I'll mend assorted rips, tears and snags in your clothes, and never wonder out loud how on earth you managed to cause them. I'll fix your hair and find your spectacles. I'll lace your corsets and button your boots. I'll do all that and more without a murmur of complaint. But getting me to butter your toast? That's just idle.'

'I'll give you a shiny shilling.'

'No.'

'Two bob.'

'Still no.'

'Half a crown. That's as high as I'll go.'

I sighed.

'Give it here,' I said. 'And you can put the two and six in Joe's charity box at the Dog and Duck. He's trying to raise enough to pay for a trip to the seaside for the village children this summer.'

I buttered her toast.

◆ ◆ ◆

There was no answer when Lady Hardcastle rang the Dower House doorbell. Her friendly – but loud – rat-a-tat on the lion's-head door knocker produced a similar lack of response. We peered in through the drawing room windows. The curtains and shutters were open, but there was no one in sight.

'Well, that's disappointing,' said Lady Hardcastle.

'She might be trying to tame that jungle of a garden,' I said. 'Or carrying on her nefarious bicycle business in her workshop.'

'She might at that. Let's be friendly country neighbours and intrude – it's the sort of thing one does out here.'

'Oh, really? Won't that be awkward? I shall trail behind you like a reluctant but obedient servant.'

'You're silly. Of the two of us, it's you she knows best. And even if she didn't, the trick to dealing with almost any potentially awkward social situation is to behave as though what one is doing is perfectly acceptable. If one exudes an air of confidence, one can get away with anything. Unsure how to eat an oyster? Who cares? Eat it confidently enough and any way is the right way. The same goes for wandering into someone's garden when one doesn't get an answer at the front door. Do it timidly and you're an impertinent intruder. Do it confidently and you're a welcome guest.'

'You've explained all this to me many times,' I said. 'But it doesn't make it any easier.'

'We'll be fine,' she said with a reassuring smile. 'Come. Let us find our new neighbour.'

She strode off around the outside of the Dower House and tried to open the gate that led through the wall into the garden. It had a fiddly latch and I smiled at the thought that it had been easier to scale the wall the previous evening than it was to enter through the gate.

Eventually, she figured out the latch's eccentricity and opened the gate to reveal the wild and untamed garden.

It looked even messier by the light of day, but it was not sufficiently overgrown as to be able to conceal a fully grown, retired trick cyclist. Angelina was not, I surmised, in the garden.

Undaunted, Lady Hardcastle picked her way along the weed-strewn path towards the stone coach house.

'Hello,' she called, cheerily. 'Miss Goodacre? Are you at home, dear?'

As we moved deeper into the garden we got a better view of the coach house and were eventually able to see that the big double doors were open. Closer still, and we were able to hear the sounds of industry within.

'Excellent,' said Lady Hardcastle. 'She's in there.' She called another cheery hello.

The noise from the coach house stopped abruptly, and Angelina appeared at the doors a few moments later, wiping her hands on a rag. She was dressed in engineer's overalls and I was struck by how similar she and Lady Hardcastle were. Both were capable, independent women, unconcerned by the social conventions that attempted to tell them how to behave, or how to dress, and perfectly at home in grimy overalls. I hoped she wasn't a crook – I was certain we might all become friends if she didn't end up in gaol.

'Good morning, Miss Goodacre,' said Lady Hardcastle. 'I do hope we're not intruding.'

'Oh, do call me Angie, please. Being Miss Goodacre at my age makes me sound like the frumpiest old spinster.'

Lady Hardcastle laughed.

'Then I ought to be Emily,' she said. 'Being Lady Hardcastle at my age makes me sound like . . . Actually, it creates quite the impression and comes in jolly handy. But do call me Emily anyway.'

'I can imagine,' said Angelina. 'And no, you're not intruding – I was just doing a little work in my shed.'

'It's a rather grand shed.'

'It suits my purposes, certainly.'

'I imagine it would suit most purposes. Other than building aeroplanes – that requires a much bigger shed.'

It was Angelina's turn to laugh.

'I should imagine it does,' she said. 'Though I've never seen an aeroplane up close, much less a shed where someone might build one.'

'Oh, you absolutely must, dear. They're quite the most exciting things. There's a factory on the road to Bristol.'

'Is there, indeed? I shall have to cycle down there one day and take a look.'

'You won't regret it.'

'I'm sure. But to what do I owe the unexpected pleasure of your visit?'

'Nothing in particular, dear,' said Lady Hardcastle. 'We were out for a walk and decided to call in on our new neighbour.'

'I'm very glad you did. Thank you. Would you care for some tea?'

'That's very kind, but no, thank you. We shouldn't want to stop you from . . .' Lady Hardcastle held out her hand to indicate the coach house and its open doors.

'From pottering in my shed? No, honestly, you're not interrupting.'

'It's nice of you to say so, dear. But we really did just come to say hello. And . . . well, I have to confess to a certain amount of nosiness. I've long been curious what lay behind these walls, you see. Walled gardens always seem so intriguing, don't you think? We walk or drive past every week and I've often thought, "I wonder what delights are contained within those old, red-brick walls. What goes on there?" Now that we know the tenant I thought it might be a perfect opportunity to have a look.'

'Are you horribly disappointed?' asked Angelina. 'It's still in a shocking state.'

'I'll not lie – it's probably seen better days. But as I said last time: the next time we see our man Jed, I'll ask if he wouldn't mind calling on you. He's terribly good with this sort of thing. The garden at the house had been neglected for a year or two before we moved in, and then for a year or two afterwards, as well. I enjoy a garden but I found the initial work more than a little daunting. But Jed has turned it into a tiny Eden in just a couple of summers.'

'I'd appreciate that, thank you.'

'I had no idea there was such a lovely coach house here, though. I should have expected it, I suppose – how would well-to-do coun-tryfolk get about without a horse and carriage? And where would they keep them but a beautiful coach house? Is it in decent condi-tion inside?'

'It's in reasonably good repair, yes. Spacious, too.'

'Plenty of room for all your gubbins.'

'A decent amount of space for storage, and still room to work,' said Angelina with a smile.

She clearly understood what Lady Hardcastle was very Englishly not asking her directly, and was equally obviously taking a good deal of pleasure in very Englishly not telling her. Despite Lady Hardcastle's optimism, I wasn't convinced we were learning anything especially interesting from her silence, so I decided to be the un-English one and ask a direct question. I am half Welsh, after all. We do things differently in Wales.

'Bicycle?' I said.

'Bicycle?' said Angelina.

'In the coach house. Are you working on your bicycle?'

'Ah, I see,' she said with a smile. 'My bicycle requires very little maintenance. Just a little tweak now and again.'

'Then what . . . ?'

'Just pottering about, you know? Got to keep the old hands busy or they'll seize up.' She flexed her fingers to demonstrate their enduring suppleness.

'Well,' said Lady Hardcastle, conceding defeat, 'we ought to leave you to your pottering. Are you free for dinner next week? How does Wednesday suit? Or Thursday? Anytime in the latter half of the week, honestly. I threatened to invite some of our friends up from Bristol, didn't I? It'll be fun.'

'I have engagements in the evenings for much of next week. How about Friday? I think that's free.'

'Friday it is, then. I shall telephone Dinah. She'll bring Simeon, of course. And Oliver Sunderland and his wife, Dolly. We'll make an evening of it.'

'I look forward to it,' said Angelina. 'Can you find your own way out? I need to get back to my . . .' She waved in the general direction of the coach house.

'Of course, dear. I'm sure we shall see you again before Friday next. Do drop in for tea whenever the mood takes you.'

'I shall. Thank you. Good day.'

'Cheerio, dear.'

We left the Dower House garden and set off to walk home. As we reached the end of the lane we bumped into Mickey Yawn. Quite literally. He bowled round the corner, cap on the back of his head, whistling a jaunty tune, and walked smack into Lady Hardcastle.

Poor Mickey came off worst in the collision. He appeared fit and able, and I had supposed that he could handle himself in a scrap, but there wasn't a great deal of him. He was wiry and slight. Lady Hardcastle was also fit and able, and carried herself with grace and an easy – almost athletic – balance. She was, though, altogether more substantial than young Mr Yawn, and gave out only a quiet and surprised 'Oof!' as he bounced off her and landed on his backside on the footpath before us.

'Why don't you bleedin' well look where I'm goin'?' he said from the ground.

Lady Hardcastle reached out a hand to help him up.

'Good morning, Mickey dear,' she said, cheerfully. 'Ups-a-daisy.'

He grudgingly took her hand and allowed her to haul him back to his feet.

'Oh, it's you,' he said as he brushed himself down.

'It is indeed,' said Lady Hardcastle. 'Are you all right there? You took a nasty tumble.'

'Fine, thanks,' he said, before checking that his cap was still at exactly the right nonchalant angle and continuing on his way.

We paused at the corner to watch his progress. If challenged I'm sure we would have said we were checking that he was all right after his tumble. In reality I, for one, was curious to see where he was going.

Without a backward glance he breezed up to the front gate of the Dower House and let himself in.

◆ ◆ ◆

'That was a rousing success, then,' I said as I put the elevenses tray on the drawing room table.

'Not my finest hour,' said Lady Hardcastle. 'It's much easier to get information out of people when one doesn't care if they'll still be one's friend afterwards.'

'It didn't help that she knew what you were fishing for and was having so much fun not telling you,' I said. 'I don't blame her, but it doesn't do a great deal to ease my suspicions of her. If what she's doing in there with all those bikes and all those tools is perfectly innocent, why not just tell us?'

'Because, as you say, it was more fun not to. She's a woman after my own heart in that respect – it's exactly the sort of thing I'd have done in her position, just for the sport of it.'

'That's true, actually, you very much would.'

'I very much would. With a big grin on my beautiful face.'

She grinned and pointed at her face in case I might not be able to imagine it for myself.

I rolled my eyes. I may have tutted.

'And what's little Michael Yawn up to, I wonder?' I said. 'First turning up with the van driver to help load the bicycles, then strolling calmly into the Dower House as though he were calling on an old friend.'

'Perhaps he was,' she said. 'I know we're trying not to allow his past to prejudice our thinking about Mickey Y, but he is, by all accounts, a wrong 'un. And if Angelina is consorting with wrong 'uns, it makes it a good deal harder to think well of her, too.'

'Which would also explain her refusal to respond to your fishing. I like the idea of her just having fun with us, but we can't rule out the idea that she genuinely is up to no good.'

'Indeed we can't. So now we have to find another angle of attack. If she won't simply tell us what she's up to, what else might we do to find out?'

'We could keep watch on the Dower House and follow the van if it calls again,' I suggested.

'*If* it calls again, we might. But if that was its last visit we might waste several evenings sitting in the Rolls in the dark. We need to know where *that* van went. If we can find that out, we needn't worry about any future vans. Did you get a good look at it?'

'I caught a glimpse as it was leaving. It was quite dark by then, and I could only see it by lantern light.'

'What did it look like?'

'It looked like a medium-sized motor van. Possibly black, certainly a very dark colour if not. White lettering on the side.'

'Saying . . . ?'

'I couldn't see – it was too dark and the van was too far away.' I sat for a moment with my eyes closed, trying to re-visualize the scene. 'They said their goodbyes,' I said, my eyes still closed. 'She hoped his son got on well with his new job at the docks. He thanked her. He slammed the rear doors of the van and he and Mickey got in the front. She banged the side of the van. Twice. Bang-bang. The van pulled out and started wiggling about in the narrow lane so it could face the right way to leave. She walked back towards the gates and lifted the first drop bolt so she could close it. The van finished its manoeuvring and started off down the lane. I could see the side. White lettering with gold outlines. Two lines of text . . . and a golden pigeon in between.'

'A pigeon?'

'A golden one. The top line might have been a name with initials – it was that sort of shape.'

'I say, well done you,' said Lady Hardcastle. 'So we're looking for a company called X. Y. Somebody's Something Ltd. that has a pigeon as its emblem. A light haulage company, I should expect.'

'Why light haulage?'

'Because it was hauling light things. And because of the carrier pigeon on the sign.'

'It sounds reasonable. How do we find this company?'

'We shall have to ask around. I shall make some telephone calls and you can go into the village to ask Daisy.'

'I love Daisy dearly,' I said. 'But does she really represent my best chance of tracking down a mysterious van?'

'Darling Daisy has two jobs, both in establishments that receive shipments of goods from outside suppliers. Her father's shop will take regular deliveries of meat, sawdust, ice, razor-sharp knives . . . you get the picture. Similarly, Joe will get beer, cider, spirits, replacement glasses, sawdust, new skittles, outdoor tables and the like. One of their suppliers might well make use of a specialist delivery company like Sir Reginald Pigeon – Hauliers to the Gentry. Daisy might recognize the emblem.'

'When you put it like that, she might indeed. And she does know everything and everyone. You're right. Sorry.'

'For my part, I shall start with the Bristol Chamber of Commerce and see where I end up from there.'

'Inspector Sunderland might know.'

'He might, but I worry about bothering him with it. We're supposed to be helping him, not giving him more work.'

◆ ◆ ◆

I arrived at the pub just as Daisy was sweeping the pub's front step.

'You're too early, Flo,' she said when she saw me approaching. 'Bad mornin', is it?'

'It's been a peculiar morning,' I said. 'After an even more peculiar evening. Can we go inside a minute?'

She finished her sweeping and we entered the bar.

'Another night on the brandy?' she asked. 'Startin' to see pink elephants?'

'The brandy came after the peculiarity,' I said. 'And we usually see teal giraffes – we're too classy for common-or-garden elephants, pink or otherwise. But the oddness began when I went up to the Dower House.'

'There's somethin' goin' on up there, i'n't there? I told you.'

'You did. And there is.'

I recounted my evening's adventures again, this time leaving in the part where I briefly fell asleep – I thought it would amuse her – but omitting mention of Mickey. It was bad enough us thinking ill of him based solely on supposition and prejudice, without spreading it to the rest of the village.

'See?' she said when I had finished. 'Vans comin' and goin' in the night. Bikes on the move. Can't be legal.'

'It might be, though,' I said. 'And that's why I've come to see you.'

'Me? I don't know nothin' about what's legal and what's not. That's your territory, that is.'

'Ah, but we thought you might know about vans.'

'I don't know nothin' about them, neither. I reckon you's made one of your rare mistakes, there, Flo m'dear.'

I ran her through Lady Hardcastle's delivery-based logic and Daisy smiled.

'When you puts it like that, I suppose I do see a lot of vans,' she said.

'And you said you'd seen the one that called at the Dower House. Do you remember anything about it?'

'Not really. It was a van.'

'The one I saw was black,' I said. 'Or dark blue, perhaps.'

'Same as the one I saw.'

'And it had white lettering on the side. Outlined in gold.'

'That's it.'

'And the writing said . . . ?'

Daisy thought for a moment, her face screwed up delightfully in concentration.

'P. J. Culver,' she said at length. 'Deliveries. And a drawin' of an eagle or somethin'.'

'It would be a pigeon if his name's Culver,' I said.

'How's that?'

'It's an old word for a pigeon. You know more about vans than you think, Your Majesty.'

'I still say I don't know nothin' about vans – I just knows how to read.'

'You read more than I managed to,' I said. 'Even if you can't tell a pigeon from an eagle. Thanks, Dais.'

I turned to leave.

'You off, then?' she said. 'Not time for a quick one and a natter afore we open? Joe won't mind, and it'll be nice and quiet – won't be nobody here for another hour.'

'No time, I'm afraid,' I said from the door. 'Places to go, people to see.'

I gave her a wave and headed for home.

Lady Hardcastle was in the drawing room with a cup of tea when I returned.

'Hard at work, I see,' I said as I helped myself from the pot on the table.

'I'm waiting for a nice young man at the Bristol Chamber of Commerce to telephone me,' she said. 'He was an absolute poppet and, I think, more than a little bored. He volunteered to scour their membership records to see if he could find anyone with a pigeon in their company sign.'

'Aha,' I said. 'You should have had more faith in your other idea. When he calls you back he's going to tell you that it's P. J. Culver. It turns out Daisy saw more than I did.'

'Oh, brava, Daisy Spratt. I shall telephone my new contact at the Chamber of Commerce and tell him he can stop looking for the emblem, and ask for an address and telephone number instead. If we're lucky they might be open this afternoon and we can pay them a visit.'

◆ ◆ ◆

As it turned out, we were very lucky indeed. Mr Culver had no telephone, but his yard just outside Westbury-on-Trym was very easy to find from the directions given to Lady Hardcastle by her new friend at the Chamber of Commerce. As we drew up in the Rolls I pointed out the dark blue motor van parked outside the open garage.

'That's definitely the one I saw last night,' I said. 'Or one very like it. Good old Daisy.'

'We should make more use of her,' said Lady Hardcastle. 'She's a very observant young lady.'

'We're building up quite the pool of potential agents.'

'We are? Who else is there?'

'Dinah Caudle is desperate to get involved. Don't you remember? That night in the apple orchard – it was all she could talk about.'

'Ah, yes, of course. And with Edna on hand for local intelligence—'

'I knows 'is mother,' I said in my best Edna voice.

'Quite,' she said with a laugh. 'Come on, though. Let's see if Mr Culver or one of his minions is prepared to be indiscreet enough to tell us about one of his clients.'

We got out of the motor car and approached what I assumed to be the office beside the garage.

Lady Hardcastle knocked on the door, opened it, and walked in.

A bald man in a neat and well-made suit sat behind a large, tidy desk. He looked up as we entered and his smile lit up his round face. He stood.

'Welcome, ladies,' he said warmly. 'What can we move for you today?'

'Good afternoon, Mr . . . Culver, is it?'

'P. J. Culver,' he said, leaning across his vast desk and offering her his hand.

'I'm Lady Hardcastle and this is Miss Armstrong.'

He stopped mid-lean. His smile, already broad, threatened to split his face in two as he heard our names.

'Lady Hardcastle,' he said in a tone of disbelief. 'The wonderful crime-solving amateur detective from Littleton Cotterell? And Miss Florence Armstrong, her remarkable lady's maid, confidante, and right-hand woman?'

'Oh,' said Lady Hardcastle. 'Well, I'm not entirely certain I would have described us in quite such glowing terms, but that definitely sounds like us, yes.'

'It's a pleasure and an honour to meet you both. Please' – he indicated the two visitors' chairs on our side of the desk 'take a seat. How may I help you? Are you on a case? Do you need to move important evidence?'

Our names had appeared in the press as a result of our sleuthing, of course, and Miss Caudle's flattering accounts of our exploits in particular had meant that we often saw a flicker of recognition whenever Lady Hardcastle introduced us. But Culver's reaction went far beyond mere recognition.

I'd encountered admirers in the circus – my father always called them 'I-loves' because they invariably introduced themselves by saying 'I love your act' – but I'd never met any since.

Until now. Culver, it seemed, was an I-love.

'We come in search of information, actually,' said Lady Hardcastle.

'For an investigation?' he said, eagerly.

'An investigation of sorts. It's more by way of filling in some gaps in our knowledge regarding events peripheral to our current investigation. The person in question isn't, as far as we know, involved in the case, but it would help us to know what their business entails.'

'How very exciting. It would be an honour to assist you, my lady. In any way at all. You can entirely count on my discretion, of course.'

'Thank you. How many vans do you have?'

'Three, my lady.'

'And do they all look like the one in your yard?' She gestured towards the door and the yard beyond.

'Yes – all identical in every respect. I bought them together last year.'

'Splendid,' said Lady Hardcastle. 'One of them was in Littleton Cotterell last evening, I believe.'

'It was,' he said, opening a large diary. 'Treadway's Bicycles and Rollerskates booked it to pick up a delivery from the Goodacre Bicycle Company of Dower House, Littleton Cotterell.'

'Ah, I see. Thank you. Is it a regular job?'

He turned a couple of pages.

'I'd not say "regular", but there have been a few deliveries and collections over the past few weeks, yes. You don't suspect my driver of anything, do you? It's usually George Brown on that run. He's a good man.'

'No, no, it's nothing like that,' she reassured him. 'You say there have been deliveries as well as collections?'

He looked through the diary again.

'Yes,' he said. 'Though I couldn't tell you exactly what. Treadway books the van for a particular day and then decides for himself what George carries.'

'Interesting,' said Lady Hardcastle. 'Where might we find Treadway's Bicycles and Rollerskates? Is it in Bristol?'

'No, my lady – right here in the village. Up on Westbury Hill, opposite the Methodist church.' He stood and pointed to the large map on the wall behind his desk. 'We're here, look,' he said. 'And that's Treadway's, there.'

We thanked him and made ready-to-leave noises, but found ourselves trapped by our own politeness. Culver's excitement at meeting us was such that we spent the next ten minutes in conversation while he talked animatedly about our past cases. He asked us about Spencer Carradine's murder at the Hayrick, about Nolan Cheetham and the moving picture show, and had one or two additional observations about the murder of the reporter Christian Brookfield during the 1910 General Election. To my complete astonishment he also knew a great deal about the murder at Lord Riddlethorpe's estate in Rutland – something I didn't think had been covered in any detail in the Bristol newspapers.

It was utterly charming to find myself held in such high regard by a total stranger, but it was also somewhat overwhelming. I didn't quite know how to react to it all, though it was obvious from her smiles and eager responses that Lady Hardcastle was in her element.

Fortunately, Culver had sufficient self-awareness to realize that his enthusiasm was keeping us from our business and, with great reluctance, he brought his questioning to a close.

We thanked him again and set off to find Treadway's.

Chapter Fourteen

The bicycle shop was as easy to find as Culver had promised, and we were parked outside in no time. It was Saturday afternoon and the shops along the street were busy, including Treadway's. If asked, I might have guessed that a bicycle shop would be a little quieter than, say, a greengrocer's – people need fruit and vegetables every week, whereas they might own just one or two bicycles during their entire lifetime. If they owned a bike at all. But the people of Westbury and its surrounds were keen to prove me wrong.

The shopkeeper was busy taking a customer's money at the till as the tinkling bell announced our entrance, but he gave us a welcoming smile and assured us that he would be with us in just a moment.

As I looked around the shop I noticed a display of the blue bicycles I had seen in Angelina's workshop. By the light of day it was obvious that they were extremely well-made machines, fitted with quality components and finished to a very high standard. I pointed them out to Lady Hardcastle.

'These are very much like the ones I saw last night,' I said quietly. 'I thought they were just old bikes that had been given a lick of paint, but now I see them in the daylight I'm not so sure.'

Lady Hardcastle was about to reply, but the shopkeeper had concluded his business with the other customer and was approaching us.

'I see you're admiring the new Goodacres,' he said. 'Fine machines. Very fine machines.'

'I've not heard of the make before,' I said.

'No, you won't have. Treadway's is the exclusive agent.' He said this rather proudly as he patted one of the saddles in the same way Parslow had done when we first met him outside the Mock of Pommey. Some cyclists treated their machines like beloved pets, it seemed. 'They're handmade by a local expert – someone who has used their vast experience of cycling to create an almost perfect machine. Lightweight, strong, perfectly balanced, and very well suited to lady riders . . .' He paused and looked around to make sure the shop was empty. 'As a matter of fact, the builder is a woman. A former circus rider. I usually have to keep that under my hat – you know how people can be about such things – but under the circumstances . . .' He gestured to us both, as though our wearing dresses explained everything.

'How wonderful,' I said. 'They do look rather splendid.'

'They are. They really are. Miss Goodacre has been a marvellous find.'

I made a show of examining the Goodacre bicycles while Lady Hardcastle turned her attention to a brand-new BSA Road Racer.

'Another excellent choice, madam,' said the shopkeeper. 'A very popular machine, especially for racing, but a little . . . shall we say "ubiquitous"?'

'I've certainly seen a good many of them about,' said Lady Hardcastle.

'Well, quite. Sometimes it can be advantageous to blend into the crowd a little, and if you want something that looks a little more conventional, this is a remarkably good bicycle. For a small additional fee, though, Miss Goodacre can make specialist adjustments so that even a factory-made bicycle can be turned into a one-of-a-kind bespoke machine.'

'It's well worth considering,' she said. 'We each have a Raleigh at the moment, but we have recently become interested in racing and we've been wondering . . .'

'Raleigh's ladies' bicycles are splendid,' said the shopkeeper, 'but not at all suited to racing. If you're serious about racing I strongly recommend one of the Goodacres. As I say, they're very much designed with the lady racer in mind. We offer a two-year guarantee against manufacturing faults, and Miss Goodacre will service and maintain the machine free of charge during that period. She does repairs for us, too, should the worst happen and you take a tumble.'

'I see,' said Lady Hardcastle. 'We're only looking at the moment, but you've given us a lot to think about. Thank you, Mr . . . ?'

'Treadway,' said the man. 'Ezra Treadway at your service.'

'Thank you, Mr Treadway, we shall give the Goodacres some serious consideration.'

'I can arrange for you to take one out for a trial run if you like.'

'Some other time, perhaps,' said Lady Hardcastle.

He caught me eyeing a display of roller skates.

'We offer a free course of lessons with those,' said Treadway.

'I'm not sure I'd ever have the opportunity to use them,' I said. 'But it's tempting.'

'Well, you know where we are if you change your mind.'

'We do indeed,' said Lady Hardcastle. 'Good day to you, Mr Treadway, and thank you for your time.'

'I look forward to seeing you both again,' he said.

We returned to the Rolls.

◆ ◆ ◆

We set off at once for home, fully intending to go straight to the crime board to organize our thoughts. But as Lady Hardcastle drove us back towards Littleton Cotterell, she announced a change of plan.

'I think we ought to go and visit Angelina,' she said.

'You do?' I said. 'Why?'

'It just feels like the sort of thing we ought to do. At the very least we should apologize for thinking ill of her.'

'Does she know we think ill of her?'

'If she doesn't, she's a great deal more dull-witted than I've been giving her credit for. I could only have made it more obvious if I'd said, "Are there stolen bicycles and artworks in your giant shed, dear?" She knew exactly what we were angling at.'

'I suppose so,' I said. 'In that case, we should definitely call on her.'

And so we did.

Unlike our earlier visit, Angelina answered the doorbell almost at once, and warmly invited us in.

'You absolutely must join me in a cup of tea this time,' she said. She grinned as she added, 'It'll be a squash, obviously, but we're all pals. You can find the drawing room.'

She disappeared off to the kitchen.

The drawing room was easy to find, especially since we had looked in through the windows and seen it earlier that morning. We settled on mismatched but comfortable chairs that looked as though they had once been at The Grange – probably because that's exactly where they had come from. There were few personal items in the room, but I was delighted to see a framed photograph of Angelina from her circus days.

I stood and went to look more closely, and found my eyes misting over with tears as I realized that I knew the others in the group. I struggled to recall any of their names, but their sternly unsmiling photograph faces brought back a flood of memories.

The Angel of the Velocipede stood proudly in the centre, looking young and beautiful. She was leaning on her bicycle, and was flanked by several other performers. There was the strongman. The acrobats. The two clowns who may have been called Bright and Breezy.

What caused the sudden tears and the tightening of my throat, though, was the man at the end of the line. With three knives fanned in his left hand, his right resting on the shoulder of the trapeze artist next to him, was the Great Coltello – my father. I had seen him only occasionally after Gwen and I had returned to Aberdare, but this was exactly how I remembered him.

It couldn't have been long after that photograph had been taken that our grandmother had become sufficiently frail that our mother had taken her two youngest girls home to take care of her. Our father had visited as often as he was able, but it wasn't long before I left home myself to work in Cardiff, and I had seen very little of any of them after that.

The man in the photograph was dark-haired and handsome. His moustache was neatly trimmed, and styled to make him appear more Italian than Northumbrian for the circus audiences. Despite the Victorian fashion for serious faces in photographs, there was a hint of a mischievous smile on his lips. I remembered how he was always the one encouraging Gwen and me to misbehave, and our mother's exasperation as we gigglingly followed his lead.

Angelina entered with the tea and set it down on the wobbly table.

'Fond memories, there,' she said, indicating the photograph. 'Good times and wonderful people. I miss them all.'

I didn't trust myself to be able to speak quite yet, so I just nodded and retook my seat.

Angelina poured the tea and we exchanged minor pleasantries about the weather.

Once we were all settled, Lady Hardcastle took a sip of her tea, and said, 'We've come to apologize, dear.'

'Apologize?' said Angelina. 'Whatever for?'

'For this morning,' said Lady Hardcastle. 'And for thinking you might be up to something nefarious.'

Angelina laughed.

'Wherever I've been, people have thought I was up to something nefarious,' she said. 'A single woman in possession of a profitable business must be in want of locking up.'

'Which is precisely why my conclusion-jumping has caused me such self-reproach – I should have known better. On the other hand, though . . .'

'On the other hand?'

'Well, you could simply have told us about Goodacre Bicycles. You knew we were curious.'

Angelina laughed again – exactly the sort of mischievous laugh I knew well from years of working with Lady Hardcastle.

'And where would be the fun in that?' she said. 'In the first place you have to remember that it's absolutely none of your business. And in the second, watching you tiptoe gingerly around the subject, desperate to ask what was in my workshop but too English to say it out loud, was just far too funny. Bringing a premature end to my entertainment by simply telling you would have been unthinkable.'

'You make an excellent point, dear,' said Lady Hardcastle, saluting her with her teacup.

'And you make an excellent bicycle,' I said. 'They look wonderful.'

'You've seen them?' said Angelina.

'We paid a visit to Treadway's,' I said.

'Good heavens, you have been busy. I wondered if you might have resorted to breaking into the workshop and taking a look for yourself.'

'That would be very unneighbourly,' I said. 'Though not beyond my capabilities.'

'So I've been hearing,' said Angelina. 'The word around the village is that the little girl who played pranks on people with her twin sister and begged to be taught bicycle tricks has grown up to be a spy and an amateur sleuth, masquerading as a lady's maid.'

'I like to think I'm at least a satisfactory lady's maid,' I said.

'More than satisfactory,' said Lady Hardcastle. 'There's no masquerading about it. But the other things are . . .' She paused for a moment, as though weighing up Angelina's trustworthiness. '. . . true,' she said, eventually.

'Are they, indeed?' said Angelina. 'I thought they were just village gossip.'

'They're certainly that,' I said. 'But they're not *just* gossip.'

'Well I never. No wonder you thought me up to no good – my little business must seem terribly suspicious to someone whose own business is suspecting people.'

'That's rather the way our thoughts run most of the time,' said Lady Hardcastle.

'And what was I up to in your suspicious imaginings?' said Angelina. 'Stealing bicycles and murdering rival cyclists? Oh, and had I stolen the book and the painting, too?'

'I'm afraid so,' I said. 'We had quite an elaborate scenario worked out.'

Once more, the naughty-girl laugh.

'And why are you telling me this?' she said. 'How do you know it's not true?'

'We don't,' said Lady Hardcastle.

'And this might be a cunning ruse on our part to lower your guard and trick you into inadvertently revealing your guilt,' I said. 'You can never tell with lady spies and their pretend maids.'

'I shall be on my mettle,' said Angelina. 'What made you suspicious in the first place?'

'A chap called Nisbet had his bike stolen from outside the village hall, and Daisy from the Dog and Duck saw you on a BSA Road Racer just like it.'

'Nisbet got it back. It just turned up at the village hall the next day. He came to me asking if I'd take a look at it, but it was undamaged. The saddle was a bit wonky, but it had come to no harm on its adventures.'

'Well, that's good news for Nisbet, I suppose. But Daisy also saw a Culver's van calling on you late one evening. That's how we traced your bicycles to Treadway's and found out about your business.'

'Nothing's a secret in a small village, I suppose,' said Angelina. 'I thought I could keep things on the QT by moving stock at night, but that clearly just made me more interesting.'

'I'm afraid it did, dear,' said Lady Hardcastle. 'But we understand now.'

She was about to say something else but we were all distracted by the loud slamming of the back door. She and I exchanged puzzled glances.

'You there, Ange?' called a familiar young voice. 'I gots the bottom bracket off like you said.' The voice was getting louder as its owner approached. 'Bearin's completely 'ad it.'

This diagnosis was delivered by a slightly oily Mickey Yawn, who was now standing in the drawing room doorway, wiping his hands on a rag.

'Oh, sorry,' he said. 'I didn't know you 'ad company.'

'Don't worry, Mickey,' said Angelina. 'Just some friends from the village. Lady Hardcastle and Flo Armstrong.'

Lady Hardcastle and I smiled greetings.

'We've met,' said Mickey. 'I'd better be gettin' back to it, though – I'd like to get it all done afore I goes tonight. I just thought you'd want to know you was right.'

'Thank you,' said Angelina. 'Always good to be proved right. I'll come out and give you a hand in a while.'

Without another word, Mickey was gone.

'You've met my new apprentice, then?' said Angelina.

'We have,' I said. 'Though the last we heard he was a builder's labourer.'

'He was. He's been working for his old gaffer this week on a job out near Tortworth, but his real passion is machines. He's a fine mechanic. He seems to understand how things work without having to be told twice. I don't suppose I'll keep him long before he gets snapped up by a motor car garage somewhere, but for now he's helping me with repairs and so on.'

'How very splendid,' said Lady Hardcastle. 'It's nice to know he's not the rascal everyone thinks he is.'

'Oh, he's an absolute rogue,' said Angelina with a chuckle. 'But he's good at his work and he does as he's told.'

'I hoped there might be good in him,' said Lady Hardcastle. 'But back to less pleasant matters. I don't suppose you have any insights into the murder or the theft? We're still rather stumped.'

'I'm afraid I can't help you. Blackmore was behind me during the race and I know nothing about the art world. Sorry.'

'Not to worry,' said Lady Hardcastle. 'It's our problem, not yours.'

Angelina looked at me as though contemplating something, then put down her teacup and stood.

'Would you just excuse me for a moment?' she said, and left the room.

Lady Hardcastle gave me a 'what's all that about?' look, and I just shrugged.

Angelina returned a couple of minutes later holding another framed photograph. She handed it to me.

'I'd like you to have this,' she said. 'We took a few photographs that day – for publicity, you know? – and this was always one of my favourites. Such a lovely picture of your fatha.' Her Geordie accent came through very strongly on this last word.

I looked at the photograph. It was the same group, in slightly different poses, and my father wasn't even pretending to try not to smile.

I couldn't stop the tears this time.

We decided to end our busy Saturday with a trip to The Grange. It was about six in the evening so we were cutting it fine if we wanted to catch the Farley-Strouds before dinner, but we knew they wouldn't mind. We had no news, but Lady Hardcastle felt we ought to keep them apprised, even if it was simply to say that we knew nothing more.

Jenkins let us in, the Fates being nowhere in sight, and led us through to the drawing room, where Sir Hector was already at work at the drinks cabinet mixing gin and tonics for himself and Lady Farley-Stroud.

'Just in time, what?' he said as Jenkins announced us. 'What'll you have?'

'One of your famous sundowners would go down a treat,' said Lady Hardcastle, indicating the drinks he had already mixed, 'even though we're still a couple of hours from sundown.'

'Sun would be setting if we were in India, m'dear. Goes down about six this time of year. Florence?'

'Looks as though I'll be driving us home,' I said. 'Just the Indian tonic water for me, please.'

'As you wish, m'dear. Sit yourselves down. Make yourselves at home.'

We did as we were asked.

'Good evening, Gertie dear,' said Lady Hardcastle. 'You're very quiet.'

'Hello, m'dear,' said Lady Farley-Stroud, cheerfully. 'No use interruptin' the old duffer when he's makin' drinks. Best just to wait till the storm passes.'

'Best plan, my little pastel de nata. Should never distract a master craftsman while he's busy at his work.'

'Will you join us for dinner?' asked Lady Farley-Stroud.

'Not tonight, dear, I'm afraid. We have plans.' We had no plans as far as I knew, but my guess was that she was trying to avoid adding unnecessarily to their food bill while times were hard. 'Perhaps you could join us for lunch tomorrow instead.'

'I've nothin' in the diary,' said Lady Farley-Stroud. 'Hector?'

'I'm seein' Jimmy Amersham in the evenin',' he said. 'But nothin' other than that.'

'Then we should love to,' said Lady Farley-Stroud. 'Your Miss Jones does a wonderful Sunday roast.'

I wondered briefly at the rashness of this invitation. *I* knew Miss Jones had a large joint of beef that would serve four comfortably with a good deal left over for sandwiches, but did Lady Hardcastle know that? After less than a second's thought I realized that yes, of course she did. She pretended to pay no attention to household matters, preferring to let Edna and Miss Jones feel as though they were trusted to run things without her interference. The truth, though, was that she knew to the farthing what was being spent, and exactly what it was being spent on. She knew there was beef aplenty.

'We usually dine at one on a Sunday,' said Lady Hardcastle. 'Do come along any time from twelve and we can have a little livener beforehand. If the weather is fine perhaps we might sit in the garden for a while.'

'What a splendid idea,' said Lady Farley-Stroud. 'I do love your little garden. Your man has worked wonders with it.'

'He has, hasn't he?' agreed Lady Hardcastle.

'Any news on m'paintin'?' asked Sir Hector as he finally joined us.

'None at all, dear, I'm afraid. We thought we might have found a likely suspect, but it turns out her business is entirely legitimate.'

'Goodacre down at the Dower House?' he said. 'You suspected her?'

'Yes,' said Lady Hardcastle, 'we did.'

'Gel's runnin' a bicycle company. Manufacture and repair.'

'You knew?' I asked.

'Of course,' he said, as though it were obvious. 'She asked me if it would be all right to run a business from there when she rented the place.'

'If only we'd known,' I said. 'We spent all morning chasing around trying to find that out.'

'Not to mention poor Flo spending a couple of hours last evening sneaking about in her garden.'

'Sorry, m'dears,' said Sir Hector. 'Never thought she might be under suspicion. Lovely woman. Very enterprisin', too. She has somethin' about her. An air of . . . can't quite put m'finger on it, but she reminds me of you two.'

'We definitely have an air of something about us,' said Lady Hardcastle. 'Usually desperation.'

'Got a touch of that m'self at the moment,' he said, taking a large swig of his drink.

'What happened when those peculiar treasure people came to The Grange yesterday?' asked Lady Farley-Stroud. 'Did they find anything?'

'They found nothing,' said Lady Hardcastle.

'They did it very thoroughly, though,' I said. 'They failed to find anything at great, tedious length.'

'Borin' work, is it, treasure huntin'?' said Sir Hector.

'It is the way they do it,' said Lady Hardcastle.

'Zibbie does have some eccentrically abstract drawings of the eastern aspect of your home, though,' I said. 'You could frame them and put them with your Summerhays.'

'Might be a nice addition if we had both the paintin's,' said Sir Hector. 'Missin' one's a view from the east, t'other one's a view from the west. That's why they need to be together as a pair. Both views of the house as it was before the new wings were added, d'you see?'

'Ah, yes, I understand,' said Lady Hardcastle. 'To be honest, I don't remember ever seeing them.'

'Keep 'em in the study.'

'Ah, that would be why. I think we've only been in there once, when Gertie was asking for help with the missing emerald in '08.'

'And to be truthful, unless you knew they were paintin's of The Grange, you probably wouldn't notice 'em anyway. Even when you know, it's difficult to interpret 'em – the place looked so different then.'

'Which makes it all the more important that we get it back for you. We've allowed ourselves to become distracted by Inspector Sunderland's murder case, but we shall redouble our efforts to track down the painting and save The Grange.'

'We'll do everything in our power,' I said.

'What would we do without friends like you?' asked Lady Farley-Stroud.

I didn't voice the reply that popped immediately into my head: *You'd be in exactly the same position – we're utterly useless and we've achieved nothing.*

Instead I raised my glass in salute and we drank to friendship.

◆ ◆ ◆

It was a nice evening, so I took us home by the roundabout route. The road I chose skirted the Grange estate, and we hadn't gone far before we spotted Zeke and Zibbie, with their compasses, maps, and what looked like a military pace stick. They were measuring distances in the field and making more notes.

Lady Hardcastle asked me to stop, so I pulled up beside a gate and we got out. The Freers paid us no attention as we approached them across the Farley-Strouds' land. They huddled together as they usually did, and didn't even look up from their maps and notebooks.

'We have the landowner's permission to be here,' said Zeke, still without looking up.

'You can ask at The Grange,' said Zibbie.

'We've just come from there, dear,' said Lady Hardcastle. 'How are you getting on?'

'Oh, it's you, Lady Hardcastle,' said Zeke. 'Good evening.'

'And Miss Armstrong,' said Zibbie. 'Good evening.'

'Good evening,' I said, trying not to laugh.

'We had a flash of inspiration,' said Zeke.

'There's a poem in one of the journals we've been reading,' said Zibbie. 'It mentions an elm tree, and talks about the pace of life. There's a line about "my heart is yours to the setting of the sun".'

'It doesn't sound like a classic of literature,' said Lady Hardcastle.

'No, it's tosh,' said Zeke. 'Which is why we thought it had to be a clue. No one would have gone to all the trouble of writing it down otherwise.'

'And how is it a clue?' I said.

'The elm tree is obviously the starting point,' said Zibbie, pointing to a tree near the boundary hedge. 'And his "heart" – or his treasure – is buried to the west, in the direction of the setting sun.'

'But how far to the west?' asked Lady Hardcastle.

'Seventy paces,' said Zeke.

'Because . . . ?' I said.

'Because the traditional span of a man's life is three score years and ten,' said Zibbie. 'The *pace* of *life*.'

'And how do you know how long his paces were?' I asked.

Zeke proudly held up the military pace stick.

'We borrowed this from the museum in Chipping Bevington,' he said. 'Sir Theodore was a military man, and this gives us a standard military pace.'

I couldn't fault their logic, though I had serious doubts about their assumptions.

'Very clever,' I said. 'So where would it be?'

'This is what's puzzling us at the moment,' said Zibbie. 'We've made all the measurements and it should be there.'

She pointed, and for the first time I noticed a mound of freshly dug earth.

'We went down quite a few feet at precisely the correct spot,' said Zeke. 'But there was nothing there.'

'If it was buried,' I said, 'might it not be six feet down? You know, where you might bury a body?'

'That's a thought,' said Zibbie. 'We should dig down a little further before we give up.'

Zeke's shoulders sagged. It was clear that 'we should dig' actually meant 'Zeke will have to dig'.

'There's another consideration,' said Lady Hardcastle. 'I presume you've come due west from the elm tree?'

'We have,' said Zeke.

'Which is fine in general terms, but the sun doesn't actually set in the west. Depending on the time of year it might set anywhere between south-westish and north-westish.' She held her arms out to indicate a surprisingly wide arc of the horizon. 'If the poet were being precise and literal, you might have to know exactly when in the year it was written. Are there other clues? The date of the journal entry, perhaps?'

'The poem is on a loose sheet,' said Zibbie. 'Tucked inside the back cover.'

'We'll have to reread it carefully to see if we can discern a time of year,' said Zeke.

'After we've dug down to six feet,' said Zibbie, pointedly.

'After that, yes,' said Zeke, wearily.

'I do hope you find something,' said Lady Hardcastle. 'It would mean a lot to the Farley-Strouds if you found their treasure.'

The Freers looked at us sharply.

'*Their* treasure?' they said together.

'Actually,' said Lady Hardcastle, 'you're right. It might belong to the Crown. But I'm sure they could come to an arrangement given that it's on their land.'

'If the coroner declares it to be "treasure trove",' said Zibbie.

'Meaning that treasure was buried with the intention of retrieving it later,' explained Zeke.

'Then it's up to the Crown what happens to it,' said Zibbie. 'Unless it has some archaeological or historical significance, though, the Crown often passes it back to the *finder*, not the landowner, just as they would if it wasn't declared "treasure trove".'

'And you would keep it all?' said Lady Hardcastle.

'We would have found it,' said Zeke.

'On the Farley-Strouds' land,' I said. 'It's treasure belonging to the former owner of the land.'

'And,' said Lady Hardcastle, 'arguably part of the estate as purchased by subsequent owners.'

'And they've helped you find it,' I said.

'Well . . .' said Zibbie.

'Not exactly "helped",' said Zeke.

'They've cooperated with you,' I said.

'And answered your questions,' said Lady Hardcastle.

'They were perfectly within their rights to tell you both to sling your hooks,' I said.

'But they welcomed you, and gave you every encouragement and assistance,' said Lady Hardcastle.

'You would certainly deserve a finder's fee,' I said, 'but almost anyone would consider the treasure to be rightfully theirs.'

'Almost anyone,' said Zibbie.

'But not us,' said Zeke.

'Then you ought to refill that hole and leave,' said Lady Hardcastle. 'Once Sir Hector finds out about your attitude, I'm sure all permissions to be on his land will be rescinded. If you don't want to be sued for trespass, you really had better sling your hooks.'

'You have no power to tell us what to do,' said Zibbie.

'Only the landowner can do that,' said Zeke.

'The landowners are dear friends of ours,' I said, taking a step towards them. 'Do you want to find out how hard I'm prepared to fight for my friends?'

They glared at us, but seemed – for now at least – in no further mood to argue. They sloped off towards the pile of earth and Zeke sullenly picked up his shovel.

We waited until we were sure he was properly refilling the hole and then returned to the Rolls.

The Farley-Strouds would be eating by now so we decided not to interrupt. Instead, Lady Hardcastle telephoned them later that evening. Sir Hector was furious and assured her that his staff would have instructions to shoot the Freers on sight if they ever reappeared on Grange land. Lady Hardcastle persuaded him that shooting them might be a step too far, but that granting them further access was definitely a bad idea. Sir Hector reluctantly agreed. His estate manager – Ambrose Mogg – had a shotgun, though, he said. Terrible accidents could happen.

Lady Hardcastle hoped most sincerely that no accidents occurred and wished him goodnight.

We spent the rest of the evening playing cards. I even allowed her to win a few hands.

Chapter Fifteen

I was up early on Sunday morning, and had done my exercises beneath the apple tree in the garden before Edna and Miss Jones arrived for work. Chen Ping Bo – the former monk who had been our guide, and my teacher, on our long trek through China in the nineties – had been very keen on the idea of performing our t'ai chi exercises among trees. I understood his philosophical explanations, but I didn't really need them. The truth was that I found trees, even though I could name very few of them, immensely calming, and exercising beneath our apple tree always seemed somehow right.

I felt good by the time I returned to the kitchen. Not only was I invigorated by the exercise, but I had managed to focus the nebulous niggles that had woken me into a single, manageable thought: we needed to find the stolen painting.

I wished Edna and Miss Jones a good morning before going upstairs to change into something more appropriate, and by the time I returned the coffee was brewing and the toast was under the grill.

At least once a week Miss Jones and I shared our wish that electricity would come to the village. She wanted it so she could have an electric toaster. I wanted decent light to read by in the evening. Edna sometimes chimed in with a desire for one of Mr Hoover's electric vacuum cleaners from America. None of us seemed likely to get what we wanted for a few years yet, so Miss Jones kept an eye on the grill, I squinted at night by the light of an oil lamp, and Edna swept the floors with her trusty broom and beat rugs in the garden with a carpet beater we had bought in Chipping Bevington.

I took Lady Hardcastle's starter breakfast up a little earlier than usual. I thought I might be able to get away with it if I was enthusiastic enough about the day ahead, and vague enough about just how early it was. Seven in the morning was not her favourite time of day.

The sun had risen more than two hours ago, and the day was already bright, so that helped. I threw open the curtains, flooding the bedroom with golden light, and wished her a cheery good morning.

For reasons she had never adequately explained, Lady Hardcastle slept with her head completely under the covers, and the croaky response to my greeting came from beneath the crisp, white sheet. Hands appeared and flicked the sheet clear of her face. Her hair – which she refused to tie up at night – was fanned about her head like a dark halo.

'Is it eight already?' she said.

'Almost,' I replied. *Keep it vague, Flossie, keep it vague.*

'How "almost"?' she said, suspiciously.

'Oh, you know. Almost.'

'Is it more or less than half an hour before eight o'clock?'

'A little more.'

She groaned and flipped the sheet back over her face.

'You've been sitting up in bed and planning the day when there was something you wanted to do,' I said. 'I thought that since there was something I wanted to do, you might not mind an early start.'

The sheet flipped down again.

'And what is it that you want to do?' she asked.

'We spent the past two days chasing our tails—'

'Chasing Angelina Goodacre.'

'Yes,' I said. 'Two days on a wild Goodacre chase. And we spent most of the three days before that on Inspector Sunderland's murder case. We haven't done any work explicitly and exclusively on the art theft since Tuesday, and that was an unproductive chat with two local youngsters with unfortunate reputations as wrong 'uns.'

'Not wholly unwarranted reputations,' said Lady Hardcastle, 'but I agree it's not entirely fair that everyone suspects them every time something goes missing. Although Mickey's presence at Angelina's the other night raises a warning flag.'

'And so I thought that today we might actually apply ourselves more directly to the problem of the stolen art.'

'I wholeheartedly agree,' she said, heaving herself upright. 'What shall we do?'

I set the tray on the bed and perched beside her, helping myself to a piece of her toast.

'I thought we might throw away everything we think we know and start again from scratch,' I said. 'We should go back to the village hall and walk through what we actually know, ignoring all our clever suppositions and oh-so-plausible explanations.'

'Fresh eyes,' she said, slapping my hand away to stop me taking more toast. 'You could bring some for yourself, you know. You're the one who cooks it and carries it.'

'It wouldn't taste as nice,' I said. 'But fresh eyes and no preconceptions, yes. As though we had never so much as thought about any of it before.'

'I like your thinking, tiny one. Do you want to start straight away?'

'I do, actually, but there's no point. The hall will be locked until after the morning service, so we have plenty of time for a proper breakfast and for me to sort out that mare's nest.' I indicated her tangled hair.

'What would I do without you?'

'You'd start plaiting it before you went to bed,' I said. 'I thought we might have breakfast soon, though, unless you object.'

'Give me half an hour, please.'

'Right you are,' I said. 'Breakfast at half past seven.'

'You mean it's only seven o'clock?' she said, and I dodged out of the door to avoid the flying pillow.

◆ ◆ ◆

After a leisurely breakfast we made sure Miss Jones was happy to feed the Farley-Strouds at lunchtime, and then strolled into the village. The sun was out for a change, and things were starting to look a little brighter. It was two weeks since the art theft, and a week since the cycle race and Blackmore's unfathomable murder. Village life continued much as always, apparently undisturbed by these two shocking events. I wondered whether it was testament to the resilience of the human spirit, or a dismaying consequence of the extraordinarily high rate of crime in this otherwise sleepy part of Gloucestershire. Murder wasn't nearly so rare around Littleton Cotterell as it ought to be, and perhaps everyone just took it in their stride.

We walked around the green and past the shuttered village shops.

Sunday morning service had just ended, and villagers were coming out of St Arilda's church in dribs and drabs, stopping to thank Reverend Bland before making their way home. I noticed two of Lady Farley-Stroud's volunteers bustling towards the village hall. A few of the villagers were making their way at a more leisurely pace behind them.

'Is today the last day of the art exhibition?' I asked.

'No, it has another week to run,' said Lady Hardcastle. 'With a grand closing ceremony and prize-giving next Saturday afternoon.'

'It's a shame it hasn't been well attended.'

'It is, isn't it. Or, rather, it's a shame it hasn't been consistently well attended. Everyone from miles around came on that first day, but then it all just fizzled out.'

'I suspect they were all here to see the Westbury Shakespeare,' I said. 'Once that was gone, it was just a rather charming display of local art.'

'Some of it rather good, it must be said.'

'Surprisingly so,' I said. 'Who would ever have guessed that the people of Littleton Cotterell possessed so much talent?'

'There's talent everywhere – we just don't give people the chance to express it. Think of all the wonderful acts at the show last year. We have musicians and performers in our midst as well as all these marvellous hidden artists. I often wonder how rich our cultural life might be if we weren't forced to toil all day to make a wealthy employer wealthier still.'

'You ought to be careful,' I said. 'That sort of utopian talk will get you locked up round here. They don't trust that sort of thing. And you've never done a day's toil in your life, by the way.'

'One doesn't have to toil to be enraged by the system that requires it of others. Unfairness and injustice affect us all.'

'When we get the vote you should consider going into politics.'

'So should you, dear. You'd make a wonderful MP.'

'I'll stick to looking after a wonderful MP, thank you. You do all the scary stuff and I'll make sure your hat's on straight.'

She laughed.

'Can you imagine it? "Mr Speaker, the Right Honourable gentleman is neither right, nor honourable, nor, as far as any on this side of the house have been able to ascertain, a gentleman."'

'You'd certainly make a name for yourself. Even if it was just for breaking the record for the shortest speech before being asked to leave the chamber.'

We had almost reached the village hall when a smart new motor car driven by Mr Basil Westbury drew up beside us. We stopped to greet him.

'Good morning, Mr Westbury,' said Lady Hardcastle. 'What a lovely day for a drive.'

He didn't seem especially pleased to see us, but his innate politeness took over.

'Good morning to you, too, Lady Hardcastle. And Miss Armstrong. Yes, my good lady wife was busy with some correspondence for one of her charities, so I thought I might take the Crossley out for a spin. I just sort of ended up here.'

'How wonderful that you did. We're going in to have another look at the art exhibition.'

He looked at the village hall and at the now half a dozen or so villagers who were making their way inside.

'It looks like a popular place to go on a Sunday morning,' he said. 'If you'd asked me I would have guessed it would be much quieter.'

'It's rather pleasing, isn't it? We were just saying we wished it had been busier over the past two weeks. Are you free to join us?'

'Well . . . ahh . . . actually, I . . . ahh . . .'

'Not to worry,' said Lady Hardcastle, 'we quite understand. You're out for a quiet drive. You carry on. It was lovely to see you.'

'Thank you,' he said. 'Good day to you.'

We walked on.

'I like him,' I said. 'He has just the right amount of awkwardness. Rich men are so much easier to bear if they're not too self-assured.'

'I find his Shakespeare obsession quite endearing, too,' said Lady Hardcastle. 'Perhaps we should invite the Westburys to our dinner party for Angelina.'

'Would she not find it a little overwhelming?'

'She's a circus performer, dear. How could a large, eager audience be overwhelming?'

◆ ◆ ◆

As we neared the door to the village hall, I touched Lady Hardcastle's arm to stop her going in.

'Let's start from the back,' I said, veering away from the front door, 'as though we were the thieves.'

'I thought we were casting all our previous assumptions aside,' she said.

'I did say that, but we've always made those assumptions from inside the hall looking out. I thought we might approach from the back door and see how it looks from there. We started it once before but we were distracted by finding the picture frame.'

'I remember . . . but . . . clean slate and all that.'

'Clean slate,' I said. 'But I really do think that the thieves coming in through the open back door is one of our more reasonable assumptions.'

'I suspect you're right, actually. It would have been much easier – and much less conspicuous, come to think of it – for them to have started the fire after slipping in through the storeroom.'

'Thank you,' I said. 'So, it's Saturday morning, and Lady Farley-Stroud has given her speech. The crowds are pressing to get in through the front door . . .'

'Many, many happy people, all desperate for a glimpse of the thousand-pound book.'

'Just so,' I said. By now we had reached the rear of the hall. 'Can we be seen from here?'

We turned to look towards the green. The angle of the building did slightly obscure us, but we would have been in plain view to anyone standing in the queue. I pointed this out.

'Ah, but don't forget the platform where Gertie made her welcome speech,' said Lady Hardcastle. 'It was right there.' She pointed. 'You can still see the dents in the ground where it stood. It would at least have partially hidden us. And the fact that it was there at all would have discouraged people from bothering to look in the first place. I think we're in the clear.'

We carried on to the builders' rubbish piles.

'We stop here,' I said, 'and collect our bucket of smelly flammables.'

'That's always seemed reasonable to me,' said Lady Hardcastle. 'Bringing it with us would be too risky.'

'I know you've always been sceptical about the hope-for-the-best approach we think the thieves took, but a little bit of scouting about the day before would have confirmed that there was sufficient material here for a fire.'

'There'd be no guarantee it wouldn't have been tidied away before the grand opening,' she said, 'but, yes, let's assume we come here, confident we'll find what we need.'

I opened the rear door – still no one had troubled to lock it – and we entered the dark storeroom.

'From here,' I said, 'I think we would split up. One of us would slip discreetly out to check that the coast was clear.'

We carefully negotiated our way among the tables and chairs to the inner door and I adopted the role of lookout.

Peering out, I found the view subtly different from what I had imagined it would be when we had looked towards the storeroom from the other side of the hall on our previous visits. I could hear the voices of villagers, but they were hidden from view by the complex arrangement of display boards and tables. Even on the busy opening day, this corner of the hall would have been comparatively quiet, especially if most of the traffic was centred on the Westbury Shakespeare.

'I doubt there'd have been anyone looking this way,' I said. 'It would be easy to get to the office unnoticed.'

Lady Hardcastle joined me and we looked around. From where we stood, we had a clear run to the office and a good view of the stand where Sir Hector's painting and bust had once been displayed.

'It's not possible to see the Westbury book from here,' said Lady Hardcastle. 'And it would be worse if there were a crowd.'

We crossed to the office as though preparing to set our smelly fire. From the office door we looked back across the hall once more.

'Still no good view of the book,' said Lady Hardcastle.

'But an even better view of Sir Hector's stand,' I noted.

'Yes,' she said thoughtfully. 'Yes, indeed. So one or both of us set the fire—'

'One inside lighting it, one outside keeping watch,' I said.

'That would certainly be how you and I would do it, but I'm still not convinced of the thieves' ability to think that sort of thing through.'

'Either way, we set everything burning and wait at the back of the hall here, until there's enough smoke coming out for one of us to be able to convincingly shout "Fire!"'

'At which point, everyone rushes for the main and side doors,' said Lady Hardcastle.

We returned to the storeroom doors.

'There's our problem,' said Lady Hardcastle, pointing to the side door.

I looked at the door, and then at the room, wondering what she meant.

'Oh,' I said, finally realizing. 'The side exit is between us and the book. If we started from here we'd have to fight our way against the tide to get to the Westbury, and we couldn't see if the coast was clear until we were almost upon it. I'd been imagining us hanging back and being the last to approach it before turning round and returning to the storeroom and escaping. But there would still have been people coming in this direction to get to the side door. We'd never make it. This is a stupid plan.'

'It's a stupid plan for stealing the book,' said Lady Hardcastle, 'but it's a surprisingly good plan for stealing the Summerhays and bust from Hector's stand.'

I looked to where she was now pointing. The flow of escaping visitors would have passed nowhere near Sir Hector's pieces – no one would have been looking that way at all. They'd be unobserved and ripe for the taking.

'So they were the target all along?' I said.

'It's not an unreasonable assumption,' said Lady Hardcastle. 'I rather think we've had it wrong all this time. It's starting to look as though we ought to be considering two completely separate thefts.'

'It just doubles the problem, though,' I said. 'We might have an idea what happened to the painting, but how was the Westbury Shakespeare stolen?'

'I have no idea. And, to be honest, I really don't care – that's Cordelia Harrill's problem. I know one shouldn't be a snob, but the much-talked-about Westbury Shakespeare sounds absolutely ghastly. I like Westbury, I really do, but that sort of gaudy, arriviste frippery doesn't show him in a good light at all.'

I laughed.

'Don't hold back, my lady,' I said. 'Imagine how you might have felt if you'd actually seen it.'

'Well. I mean. Really. All that gold leaf and those inlaid jewels? It doesn't bear thinking about.'

I laughed again.

'All right, then,' I said. 'From here, we can safely revert to our original thoughts. We grab the painting and bust while everyone is looking the other way, and hoof it out the back door.'

We slipped out, still unseen by the exhibition's few Sunday visitors, and stood once more beside the familiar rubbish piles.

'Once we're safely out here, away from any prying eyes,' said Lady Hardcastle, 'we break the painting out of its frame, smash the bust—'

'Why?' I asked. 'Why go to the trouble of taking the bust if we're just going to smash it up outside?'

'You have me there, I'm afraid. An attempt to confuse matters? To make it look more like a crime of opportunity than a planned theft?'

'Perhaps,' I said. 'Or perhaps they simply dropped and broke it in their haste, then smashed it up completely to make the pieces easier to conceal. Either way we've destroyed the frame and the bust.' I started poking about in the rubbish piles again, near where we'd found the broken frame. 'Now, do we leave the painting on its stretcher, or cut it out?'

'Ah, good thinking. Is that what you're looking for?' she asked.

'It is,' I said.

'Free it from the stretcher, I'd say – not much point in getting rid of the frame and then still leaving it difficult to carry about.'

I rummaged for a few minutes and eventually found four lengths of softwood with canvas tacked to them. They'd be easy to overlook as general builders' scraps if I hadn't been looking specifically for them. The painting had been cut away very cleanly, leaving nothing of the actual picture behind. If we ever did find it, an expert restorer would be able to reframe it without any problems.

Lady Hardcastle took a look, and her satisfied nod seemed to indicate that she agreed with my positive assessment.

'So now we have a loose canvas,' I said, 'and for some reason we've smashed up the bust. Without the cumbersome book, and with the canvas rolled up and concealed under a jacket, getting away is even easier than we'd originally supposed. No need for handcarts or perambulators. We just walk off into the crowd without any difficulty.'

'There might be some minor difficulty,' she said. 'It's not a small painting, after all. But it wouldn't be anywhere near as hard as moving that ridiculous book.'

'You've really taken against the book, haven't you?' I said with a chuckle.

'I have. I've wasted hours of cogitative effort on that ghastly thing, thinking it was the key to finding Hector's Summerhays, and it was completely irrelevant. Cordelia's welcome to it.'

'We need to get back to the crime board and think things through again,' I said.

'We do. And then change for lunch before Gertie and Hector arrive.'

We walked home, discussing our new version of events.

Lunch with the Farley-Strouds was extremely enjoyable. Sir Hector was as wonderful a guest as he was a host, and kept us all amused with tales of their life in India – which delighted Lady Farley-Stroud, who joined in the reminiscences, adding colour and correcting details. The stories of his exploits back in England with his friend Jimmy Amersham pleased his wife slightly less, but even then she regarded him with a fond indulgence.

We finally said our goodbyes at around six o'clock, having telephoned The Grange to get their chauffeur, Bert, to come and collect them.

'What now?' said Lady Hardcastle as we closed the door. 'I'm not ready for the fun to end just yet.'

'I ought to do some tidying up,' I said.

'Hang the tidying up – Edna will take care of it in the morning. If you're still feeling puritanical about it, you can help her then. For now, though, I want to carry on the jolly mood. If we were in London we could drop in on some of our more disreputable friends and laugh the night away.'

'We could go to the pub,' I suggested. 'We have plenty of friends there.'

'We do, don't we. Hats, coats and outdoor shoes, then. Last one ready is a lady's maid.'

This was the sort of truism against which it was impossible to compete.

◆　◆　◆

The Dog and Duck was still quiet when we arrived, it being quite early. There were a few villagers in the public bar, and one or two nodded greetings as we entered. I looked into the snug, where I saw the Freers huddled over their notebooks, glasses of cordial on the table in front of them. I silently pointed them out to Lady Hardcastle.

'Let's stay in the public tonight, then,' she said.

Daisy was behind the bar, doing whatever it was she did when she wasn't pouring drinks. Polishing glasses was her main distraction activity. She smiled broadly when she saw us.

'Well, good evenin',' she said. 'What brings two fine ladies like you to our disreputable establishment?'

'We heard this was the place to come for fine wines and scintillating conversation,' said Lady Hardcastle.

'I can do you passable cider and a bit of gossip?' said Daisy.

'Even better. Two small ones, please.'

'Coming up.'

She began her barmaidly bustling, taking down two glasses and walking to the cider barrel.

'And what do you have by way of gossip, young Daisy?' I asked.

'That's "Your Majesty" to you, commoner,' she said without looking round.

'I was a fine lady a few moments ago.'

'That was afore you showed me such disrespect. But I gots very little to report, I'm afraid. I'n't no one doin' anythin' very much worth talkin' about. What have you been up to?'

'We've done nothing especially interesting,' I said. 'Oh, but we did have some ideas about Sir Hector's stolen painting this morning.'

'I heard a little bit about that. Mostly people's been talkin' about that book. Did you see it? Gorgeous, it was. Gold, jewels – the lot. It was like all the treasures in the world on one beautiful book. I loved it.'

'Ah,' I said. 'Well, Sir Hector lost a painting at the same time. An incredibly valuable landscape by Edgar Summerhays. He's dev astated to have lost it.'

'Moderately valuable,' corrected Lady Hardcastle. 'It would only be incredibly valuable with its companion piece. Summerhays painted a pair, you see. Two views of The Grange in the early 1800s, one from the east and one from the west. It's the eastern view that's been stolen. It's worth a few bob on its own, but with its partner . . . well . . . judging from recent sales of Summerhayses in London, the sky's the limit.'

'I never knew. All people has mentioned was that he lost a paintin' and a statue. I thought they was just some of the old stuff they has hangin' about up at The Grange. You knows what these old houses is like – all portraits of dogs and horses, and slightly ugly women in uncomfortable frocks.'

'That's usually the case,' said Lady Hardcastle, 'but this time it's a much-sought-after work of art.'

'And you're tryin' to get it back?'

'We are,' I said.

'I thought you was tryin' to find the book,' said Daisy.

'Not any more,' I said.

'We're leaving that to Cordelia Harrill,' said Lady Hardcastle.

'Or tryin' to find out who killed Russell Blackmore,' said Daisy.

'Inspector Sunderland's case,' I said.

'Ably assisted by Sergeant Dobson,' added Lady Hardcastle.

'We are putting all our efforts into finding our friend's valuable painting,' I said.

Daisy put the drinks on the bar.

'That's all you got, though?' she said.

'Sorry,' I said.

'I mean, I could have told you Nellie Ellens from up Woodworthy is in the family way, but I didn't think it was interestin' enough. If I'd known how weak the competition was, I'd have led with that one.'

'Do I know Nellie Ellens?' said Lady Hardcastle.

'I doubts it. Her dad farms a few cattle and some pigs.'

'She's not married, I take it? Hence the gossipworthiness of the news.'

'Not only that, she i'n't even sure whose it is. I senses a juicy scandal brewin'.'

'That's fine gossip indeed,' said Lady Hardcastle. 'I knew we'd come to the right place.'

We spent most of the evening at the pub, chatting to village friends, and by the time we left at nine o'clock we were feeling, as always, very pleased to be part of such a lively and welcoming community.

Back at the house, Lady Hardcastle played some Schumann while I prepared a light supper of cold beef sandwiches.

She was in a showing-off mood and didn't break to eat, instead carrying on playing with one hand while inelegantly scoffing her sandwich from the other. She would then swap hands to play the other part while she took another mouthful.

Suddenly, she stopped.

'Oh,' she said. 'We've overlooked a terribly important possibility.'

'About the Summerhays?' I asked.

'No, the Westbury Shakespeare.'

'I thought we didn't care about the Westbury Shakespeare.'

'We don't.'

'But you've been thinking about it anyway?'

'Not actively. It just came to me all of a sudden.'

'You're not going to tell me, are you.'

'Of course not, dear. Where would be the fun in that? Is there any fruitcake? And I'd murder for a cup of cocoa.'

I got up to take the sandwich plates back to the kitchen.

'Put some brandy in mine, dear,' she called as I crossed the hall.

Chapter Sixteen

On Monday morning we went to the village hall straight after breakfast. We decided not to let ourselves in through the back door – it seemed rude – and had to wait a few minutes for Lady Farley-Stroud's volunteer to arrive.

'You're early,' said Mrs Stitch as she bustled up. 'I'm glad we're still getting visitors, though. Doubly glad it's you, my lady. Would you be able to keep an eye on things for a quarter of an hour or so? I have to see Mrs Gardner about something but I'm not allowed to leave the place unattended.'

'Of course we would, Mrs Stitch,' said Lady Hardcastle. 'It will be our pleasure.'

'Thank you so much, my lady. I shan't be long.'

She fussed with the keys and fumbled with the lock. It was extremely frustrating to watch, not only because the back door was open and it was only politeness that had prevented us from already being inside, but because both of us knew we could have picked the lock in less time than it took her to find the right key.

Eventually the door was open and she ushered us inside, before bustling off to her important meeting with Mrs Gardner.

The hall was quiet, but looked exactly the same as always. I had no idea what we were doing there, so I just waited for Lady Hardcastle to get on with her performance.

She led the way into the hall, and stood where she could properly see the plinth.

'We should have thought of this two weeks ago,' she said.

'I wish we had,' I said. 'What should we have thought of, exactly?'

'The book is carefully displayed in the centre of the hall. Gertie must have been paying attention all those times you tried to explain how to draw visitors into a show. It's impossible to see this plinth without walking past other exhibits, no matter which direction you approach from.'

'No matter from which direction you approach,' I said.

'Silly linguistic superstition, dear. Lots of dull men in the seventeenth century trying to make English behave like Latin.'

I knew this – an Englishwoman's right to end sentences with prepositions was one of her favourite rants. She might have enjoyed teasing me by pretending to misremember names, but I played games of my own from time to time. I briefly considered provoking a lecture on the utter stupidity of avoiding split infinitives, but I decided we probably had better things to do. I did inadvertently grin at the thought, though.

'Oh, touché, tiny servant,' she said. 'But I'll get you back, don't you worry. Just as soon as we've solved the mystery of the missing Westbury Shakespeare.'

'You're going to have to try harder than that, though,' I said.

We were interrupted by the sound of the door opening.

'That'll probably be Mrs Stitch,' said Lady Hardcastle. 'I was hoping she might take a little longer. I have something I'd like to do and I'd prefer we were alone. Heigh ho.'

The footsteps on the hall's parquet floor were not those of a middle-aged lady, though – they were the solid, resonant clicks of a man's shoes.

We turned to see Mr Westbury rounding a pottery display.

'Oh,' he said. 'Good morning again, ladies.' He passed us and stood next to the empty plinth where his book had once lain. 'We have to stop meeting like this.' He gave a small, unconvincing laugh.

'We were just contemplating your stolen book,' said Lady Hardcastle.

'I've thought of nothing else,' said Westbury.

'I imagine it's been much on your mind.'

She took a few small steps as she spoke, and Westbury matched her movements, keeping himself between her and the plinth.

'It has. I just wish I knew what had happened to it. I love that book.'

She stepped again, and again he tried to block her, though not quite as well as before. I quickly worked out what she was trying to do.

'We began by wondering,' I said as I moved in the opposite direction to Lady Hardcastle, 'why someone who had managed to grab your valuable – and very heavy – book would stop on the way out to steal Sir Hector's painting and bust as well.'

He stood his ground, and I assumed he was hoping he could cover us both from where he was. I tested my assumption by moving again, but this time he moved to cover me, even though this left the plinth open to Lady Hardcastle.

'It certainly seems like a strange decision,' said Westbury. 'Much better to make good their escape with the Shakespeare and leave the tat behind.'

'Oh, it wasn't tat,' I said. 'It was an Edgar Summerhays.'

'Was it?' he said. 'Was it really?'

I made a sudden lunge towards the plinth and he moved immediately to tackle me – two mistakes in one. On his part, anyway. Not only had he left the plinth unprotected from the real attack by

Lady Hardcastle, but he ended up flat on his back with me gripping his hand and wrist in a very painful hold.

'Then we realized,' said Lady Hardcastle as she triumphantly opened the concealed door in the base of the plinth, 'that the book hadn't gone anywhere at all . . . Oh.'

This last disappointed 'Oh' came in response to the discovery that the plinth, though fitted with a shelf that seemed very much to have been designed with a big, expensive book in mind, was empty.

'Well, that's disappointing,' said Lady Hardcastle.

'You're mad, the pair of you,' said Westbury from the floor. 'Let me up. Let me up at once.'

I replayed the sequence of events in my mind. Lady Hardcastle moved . . . he moved . . . she moved again . . . I moved . . . he stayed where he was . . . I moved . . . he stopped me . . . I retraced the angles, reviewed the sight lines. I got it.

'The panelling,' I said.

Lady Hardcastle looked round at me.

'What about it?' she said.

'He wasn't trying to stop us getting to the plinth, he was trying to stop us getting to the panelling. That section over there, I'd say.' I pointed to the part of the newly panelled wall that I now thought he had been protecting.

Westbury struggled to get up but I gave his wrist a twist, making him yelp in pain.

'Would you mind just staying there for a moment, please, Mr Westbury?' I said. 'At least until Lady Hardcastle has had a look behind that panel.'

He gave me a mouthful of very colourful abuse, but I ignored him and watched Lady Hardcastle instead.

Carpenter Charlie Hill had done a magnificent job with the panelling, making our humble village hall look more like the meeting room of some exclusive club. With his typical forethought, he had made the individual panels easy to replace in the event of accidental damage – something that was very likely in a room used by so many different groups of people for so many different activities.

Lady Hardcastle approached the section I had pointed at and began pulling at the joins between the sections.

'The door on the plinth had a latch,' I said. 'Try pressing.'

She changed her approach, and for a few frustrating moments, still nothing happened. But then, with a satisfying and surprisingly loud click, the panel unlatched and came away from its supporting batons. There was something large in the gap, wrapped in a tweed jacket.

Lady Hardcastle took it out and carefully removed the jacket to reveal, in all its magnificence, the Westbury Shakespeare.

'I think we've found your book,' said Lady Hardcastle.

'I . . . I, ahh . . . I can explain,' stammered Westbury from the floor.

'I'm sure you can, dear, but I really don't care – I find insurance fraud so terribly grubby and boring. Look after him for me, would you, Flo? I'll fetch Sergeant Dobson.'

She walked out, leaving me to guard the now very subdued Westbury. I smiled down at him. He sighed and just lay there, the fight completely gone.

Sergeant Dobson had been reluctant to arrest such a well-liked local businessman, but had respectfully invited Westbury to remain at the small village police station as his guest while he made some further enquiries.

Dobson had then telephoned the offices of Moberley, Burgess and Vincent at Chipping Bevington to tell them the book had been recovered safe and sound. Within half an hour Cordelia Harrill had arrived in her shiny green motor car with the security guards, Porter and Templeman, sitting in the back like visiting dignitaries.

We saw her arrival from our vantage point outside the Dog and Duck. She'd been inside for ten minutes before Lady Hardcastle said, 'Actually, do you know what? I do care. Come on, let's go and see if we can find out what it was all about.'

We breezed into the police station with the confident air of friends of the force, to find Porter and Templeman standing guard on either side of the book, Westbury sitting dejectedly on a folding chair, and Cordelia leaning on the counter, filling in a form.

She looked up as we entered.

'We're busy here,' she said. 'Your lost dog, or your missing spectacles, or whatever it is will have to wait. This is important.'

'Actually, miss,' said Sergeant Dobson, 'it's them you 'as to thank for your current good fortune. It was Lady 'Ardcastle and Miss Armstrong as found your missin' book.'

Cordelia stopped writing and looked round.

'I don't think so,' she said. 'I was on my way here to get it myself, actually. I worked it out last week.'

'I say,' said Lady Hardcastle, 'well done you. Presumably you were bamboozled, just as we were, by the conundrum of getting such a large and unwieldy object out of the building. I mean, how does one even begin to contemplate such an undertaking? And with all that to think about, why would the thieves break off from their carefully orchestrated plan to speculatively nab some other trinkets on the way? These were professional art thieves, not opportunistic magpies.'

Cordelia was paying attention, but saying nothing.

'One imagines it all fell into place,' continued Lady Hardcastle, 'when you realized that Sir Hector's pieces hadn't been a nice little bonus for the thieves, but had been their intended target all along. And if that's what they wanted, why would they bother with the cumbersome book? The book must have been taken by someone else, surely? But once you had that lodged in your mind, the idea of an entirely different gang of thieves being in the right place at the right time to take advantage of the chaos caused by the first gang just seemed preposterous.'

Cordelia put down her pen. She was engrossed now.

'Once you came to that conclusion,' said Lady Hardcastle, 'the idea that the book never left the hall at all must have seemed much more appealing. You would have wondered, as we did, whether your security guards had spirited it away in the confusion. Mr Westbury would get the insurance, and they'd have a valuable book to sell. But it wouldn't actually be all that easy to sell, would it? Something that famous, that valuable? Who would buy such a thing? It wouldn't be like flogging a stolen ham down the local pub. It would require expertise and circumspection. I have every respect for Messrs Porter and Templeman, but I think that sort of endeavour is beyond them.'

The security guards didn't seem at all distressed that Lady Hardcastle had thought them the sort of men to contemplate the theft in the first place, nor by her assessment that they were too stupid to be able to dispose of the proceeds if they tried it. They probably weren't listening.

'So that would never do,' said Lady Hardcastle. 'And then you must have thought about Mr Westbury. He's an honest man. A likeable man. A successful man. He's a man passionate about his interests – his engineering firm and his beloved Shakespeare. He's prepared to invest great amounts of energy and money in his passions. But he's not a stupid man. And in the fire and the panic on that Saturday morning, an opportunity had presented itself. An opportunity of the sort that was too good to miss. If he could make the book temporarily disappear, he could make a claim against the insurance. It was Moberley, Burgess and Vincent's fault it had been stolen, after all – they were the ones who had provided the excellent security guards and charged him for the privilege. When the claim was well under way, he could retrieve the book. He would have to keep it secret for the rest of his days, but he could not only own the most beautiful copy of the complete works of William Shakespeare ever made – I take back every negative word I have ever said about it, by the way; it's exquisite – but he could also put the full purchase price back in his bank account to fund his future Shakespearean acquisitions. Is that what you thought?'

'Of course it is,' said Cordelia. 'It's obvious.'

'It is, isn't it? What a shame for Mr Westbury that Moberley, Burgess and Vincent employs such an excellent investigator. The poor chap never stood a chance with you on the case, did he? Oh, but there is one thing you probably haven't fathomed out. Mr Westbury, why did you hide the book in the wall and not the plinth? And how did you know those wall panels came off so easily?'

Westbury looked sullenly up from his inspection of the police station floor.

'What?' he said, dejectedly.

Lady Hardcastle repeated her question.

'I spoke to Hill about making the plinth. Asked him to put a storage compartment inside – I had it in mind it might be useful for transporting the book, or for keeping it safe when it wasn't on display. I asked him if he could conceal the latch so it wasn't obvious, and he said he'd already devised just the thing. He showed me the removable panels in the hall.'

'That was possibly the only properly clever thing you did. Cordelia was absolutely convinced you'd hidden it in the plinth.'

'If you've quite finished,' said Cordelia, 'some of us have work to do. I know you love the sound of your own voice – you always have – but I have things to be getting on with. I have a bonus to collect for retrieving the Westbury Shakespeare, for a start.' A gloating smile played on her lips.

'Of course you do, dear,' said Lady Hardcastle. 'And it's well deserved. You worked terribly hard to crack this case. Only you could possibly have solved it.'

Cordelia's smile disappeared and she turned back to her form. 'Good day to you,' she said.

We left her to it.

◆　◆　◆

Back at the house, Lady Hardcastle and I were in the drawing room enjoying a well-earned cup of celebratory tea.

'What do you think will happen to Westbury?' I said as I munched on one of the McVitie's digestive biscuits I had sneaked from Miss Jones's tin in the kitchen.

'I'm not at all certain,' said Lady Hardcastle. 'He attempted to defraud Moberley, Burgess and Vincent, but although I'm sure he made the claim, it's not clear they paid out, or even made any commitment to do so. Cordelia was still investigating, though, so I shouldn't imagine any money had changed hands. I have no idea how the law treats such matters.'

'Perhaps it depends on how Mumbly, Bumbly and Fribble feel about it,' I suggested.

She grinned at me.

'You see?' I said. 'There's no trick to it – anyone can mangle names for comic effect. You're not as clever as you like to imagine, you know.'

'I feel suitably chastened.'

'As you should,' I said. 'But Messrs Moberley, Burgess and Vincent might want to send a message that they're not to be trifled with, in which case they'll press for a trial and conviction. Or they 'might want to conceal the fact that one of their top investigators was taken for a fool for more than two weeks, in which case they'll just quietly cancel his policy and refuse ever to deal with him again.'

'While making sure that Cordelia gets her bonus, to keep her quiet, too.'

'She wouldn't come out of it well if the full story became known, though, so I doubt she'll make much fuss. You could set the cat among the pigeons by telling your side of the story, mind you.'

'To what end, though, dear? It's not as though I need the money, and one likes to imagine one is above petty point-scoring.'

'Apart from all the petty points you just scored while you schooled her at the police station.'

'Oh, that was just some light-hearted joshing about. A bit of fun between old college friends.'

'As you wish,' I said. 'I hope nothing too bad happens to Westbury, though.'

'Even though he's greedy and vain?'

'Everyone's greedy and vain. It's just that most of us don't take it to quite that level of excess.'

'Or if we do, we're more careful not to get caught. Honestly, his improvised plan was as shaky as anything.'

'He nearly fooled you.'

'I had the gist of it, just the wrong hiding place. I'd have found it in the end.'

'Actually, we should both have thought of it sooner. Do you remember the stolen rugby trophy in '09?'

'Oh, my goodness, you're right. How foolish of us both. Still, all's well that ends well and all that.'

'It hasn't quite ended,' I said. 'We still need to find the Summerhays.'

'We do. I have some ideas now, but none I'm prepared to share.'

'As always.'

She grinned again, but before I could ask anything further, the telephone rang.

'You'd better answer that,' said Lady Hardcastle, 'someone might want to talk to us.'

I went out into the hall and picked up the earpiece.

'Ahoy,' I said.

'A what, dear?' It was Lady Farley-Stroud.

'Hello, my lady,' I said. 'It's Florence. Do you want to speak to Lady Hardcastle?'

'No, dear. I mean, yes. Can you both come to The Grange at once? We've been burgled.'

'Burgled?' I said. 'When?'

'Overnight.'

'Have you telephoned the police?'

'Yes, m'dear. But Dobson said that since nothin's been taken, there isn't much he can do. That's why we need you. I've been trying to call you all mornin' but there was no answer.'

'I'm sorry, my lady – Edna doesn't like answering the telephone. It frightens her.'

'I know how she feels, m'dear. Can you come, though? We need to find out what's going on.'

'Don't worry, my lady, we'll be there in a few minutes. Please don't touch anything if you can manage not to – it will help us build a picture of events if we can see things exactly as they were.'

'The maid's already tidied up most of it, m'dear.'

I was glad we were on the telephone so that she couldn't see me rolling my eyes.

'Not to worry, then,' I said. 'We're on our way.'

By way of underlining how seriously we took the Farley-Strouds' bad news, Lady Hardcastle sped up the drive at The Grange and stopped outside the door, sliding sideways in a spray of gravel. I confess I laughed at the exuberant absurdity of it.

'That was fun, wasn't it?' said Lady Hardcastle as we alighted.

'You're a very silly lady,' I said. 'But, yes, it was fun.'

Sir Hector was already at the door.

'No need for all the hurry, m'dear,' he said. 'No one's hurt, nothin's missin'.'

'Lady Farley-Stroud sounded very upset on the telephone,' I said.

'So naturally we came as fast as we could,' said Lady Hardcastle.

'Thank you, m'dear,' he said. 'Come in, won't you? And you're right, young Florence, Gertie's in a terrible state. Perhaps seein' the two of you might settle her a little.'

He ushered us inside and led the way, not to the drawing room as usual, but to the study. I remembered it from the first time we visited The Grange, but I'd not been in there since and I couldn't imagine why we might be going there now.

Sir Hector noticed my puzzlement.

'You'll see when we get inside,' he said.

Lady Farley-Stroud was looking out through the window at the front lawn and the drive. She turned as we entered and it was obvious that she'd been crying.

'Hello, m'dears,' she said. 'Thank you for comin'.'

'We're just sorry we couldn't get here sooner,' said Lady Hardcastle. 'We were out finding the Westbury Shakespeare.'

'Good heavens,' said Lady Farley-Stroud. 'You found it? Where? How?'

Lady Hardcastle told the story, complete with the full explanation, leaving out only her lengthy mocking of Cordelia.

When she was done, Lady Farley-Stroud sighed.

'Well, at least one mystery has been solved,' she said. 'You're sure he had nothing to do with stealing our painting?'

'As sure as we can be, yes. But on to more pressing matters. What happened here?'

'The maid found the library window open first thing this mornin',' said Sir Hector. 'Whole place had been searched.'

'How could she tell?' I asked. 'Did they leave a mess?'

'Not a mess as such, but nothin' was in its right place. Books not lined up on the shelves, ornaments moved – you know the sort of thing.'

I did know the sort of thing – it was the sort of thing we worked hard to avoid in our line of business. If Lady Hardcastle and I broke in somewhere to search it, we made sure to leave no trace of our presence.

'Not professionals, then,' said Lady Hardcastle.

'Thought you'd know the difference,' said Sir Hector with a satisfied nod. 'Jenkins and I walked round the ground floor and every room was the same. Nothin' taken, nothin' damaged, but everythin' slightly out of place. The big shock was when we came in here, though. Door was open like all the others, and then we saw that.'

He pointed to the space above the mantelpiece. From the way the wallpaper had faded, it seemed there had once been two paintings there, and I remembered him telling us that he had kept the two Summerhays landscapes in the study.

Lady Hardcastle clearly remembered, too.

'Good heavens,' she said. 'They took the other one?'

'Thankfully no, dear,' said Lady Farley-Stroud, pointing to the desk. 'They just took it down and put it there.'

Lady Hardcastle walked round the desk and examined the painting.

'It doesn't look as though they did anything to it,' she said.

'That's what I thought,' said Sir Hector.

Lady Hardcastle suddenly ducked down and fussed about on the floor. She emerged a few seconds later with something in her cupped left hand.

'I think I know what happened,' she said, and showed us a handful of pencil shavings.

'Beggared if I have the first idea,' said Sir Hector.

'I've had my suspicions for a week or more, but I've not wanted to say anything until I was certain.'

'But you're certain now?' asked Lady Farley-Stroud. 'What's going on?'

'Not certainly certain – there's something I want to check first – but almost certain. We've almost run out of suspects, after all, so I think it's obvious to us all who's behind it, but I shall be able to tell you more in a little while.'

Lady Farley-Stroud was clearly not satisfied with this answer, but had come to know Lady Hardcastle well enough over the past four years to be sure that there would be nothing she could do to persuade her to elaborate. She would tell us in her own good time.

'Hector, dear, do you know roughly when the elm was planted over by the eastern border of the estate?'

'I know precisely,' said Sir Hector. 'Second of October, 1880. Had it planted the day Clarissa was born. It's Clarissa's tree.'

'Thank you – that's most helpful. Do you have your picklocks, Flo dear?' asked Lady Hardcastle.

I touched my brooch. From long habit I always carried a set of picklocks, either in my bag or there, in the special brooch she had given me for my birthday a few years before.

'Always,' I said.

'And Hector – do you have a lantern I can borrow?'

'There's one in a cabinet by the front door with some matches. Keep it there in case one of us has to go outside in the night.'

She took another careful look at the painting on the desk before nodding.

'Thank you,' she said. 'We need to go outside and check something.'

'Want me to come with?' asked Sir Hector.

'Would you mind awfully if we went alone? If I'm right it might be a little cramped for three of us.'

'Not at all, m'dear. If it involves clamberin', crawlin' or general rootlin', it's probably best left to you youngsters.'

'Thank you. We'll be back in the jiffiest of jiffies. Is there any chance of a cup of tea for when we get back, Gertie dear?'

Lady Farley-Stroud stepped over to the fireplace and rang the bell.

'I'll have tea and sandwiches waiting for your return,' she said.

'Lovely. Thank you,' said Lady Hardcastle. 'Come then, Flo, let's see if we can settle all this once and for all.'

She led me out of the study, through the front hall, and out the door.

Chapter Seventeen

We walked across the front of the house to the west side. Lady Hardcastle was in the lead, walking with definite purpose.

'Where are we off to?' I asked as I trailed along behind her.

'To find the treasure,' she said.

'The treasure that's been hidden here for nearly a hundred years.'

'The very same.'

'The treasure that has eluded two owners of the house and two expert treasure hunters.'

'I think "expert" might be overstating it a bit, but yes, that treasure.'

'And what makes you think you can find it when all those others couldn't?'

'Because I know what I'm looking for.'

I caught up with her.

'Because . . . ?' I said.

'Perhaps that's not entirely fair,' she said, without lessening her pace. 'Neither Hector nor the tobacco merchant before him knew they were looking for anything at all, so of course they found nothing. Tobacco Man built his delightful neo-Gothic wing and Hector just lived here – they weren't trying to find a secret vault.

And the Freers are a couple of sinister idiots who accidentally murder cyclists and look in the wrong place.'

'It was them, then?'

'Surely you've suspected them for a while. I know I have.'

'Well, yes,' I said. 'But without a coherent story behind it, I didn't want to say anything in case it sent us off in the wrong direction.'

'Luckily, it was their insistence on heading off in the wrong direction that settled things for me. Here we are.'

Where were we, though? As far as I could see we were facing a blank Victorian wall where it joined a blank Regency wall. There was a flowerbed planted with . . . something green and leafy.

'The reason the Freers stole Hector's painting,' said Lady Hardcastle, 'was that it showed what The Grange looked like before Tobacco Man made his changes. We really do need to find out his name, by the way – we can't keep calling him Tobacco Man. What they didn't know was that they were looking at the wrong side of the house. We may never know why they didn't just look on this side as well, but once they became obsessed with that silly poem they weren't interested in the house any more, anyway.'

'They concentrated on the elm tree instead,' I said. 'The one that wasn't planted until twenty-nine years after Elderkin died.'

'That elm tree, yes. The pace of life and the setting sun. What a lot of old bilge.'

'If we know they're on the wrong track, though, why the hurry?'

'Because they might be on the right track now. They must have overheard us in the pub on Sunday night when we were talking to Daisy about the *two* paintings of The Grange. I'd lay good odds they broke in here last night, and that dear little Hephzibah made a sketch copy of the second painting.'

'Those were her pencil shavings on the floor, you think?' I said.

'Well, they could be anyone's, but Gertie runs a tight household and I doubt she'd have allowed pencil shavings to remain on the study floor for more than half a day. I'm going to say they were Miss Freer's.'

'She's no artist.'

'Thoroughly useless,' agreed Lady Hardcastle. 'But the image will be fresh in their minds nevertheless. So if they have a new sketch of the old shape of the house – even one as ineptly drawn as I'm certain it will be if Zibbie produced it – they'll eventually see, as I just did, a statue of Winged Victory on a plinth inscribed *XXI Junii MDCCCXIII* – the date of the Battle of Vitoria – against the western wall. Summerhays was very detailed in his work – it's very easy to see. Do you know, I do wonder if that's why he's enjoying a revival of interest in these photographic days – we're coming to expect realism in our images. But anyway, in his obsession with realism, he included every detail, even down to the drain inspection cover beside the statue. A drain cover that doesn't make any sense – it doesn't fit in with any of the old gutters and drainpipes as far as I can see.'

There didn't seem any point in interrupting, or protesting that I was struggling to see her point, so I just smiled.

'Now, the drain cover would have been buried by the new wing' – she pointed to the yellowish Victorian stone – 'but I'm hoping the builders didn't think about it too much and just extended the whole thing to . . . here.' She pointed again, and dabbed the soft earth with the toe of her boot. 'And as soon as the Freers figure that out, they'll be over here with a shovel. Do you have a shovel?'

I patted my pockets.

'I must have left it in my other jacket,' I said.

'Well, this will never do. See if you can find one, would you?'

It took me ten minutes, but I eventually returned with the requested shovel.

'I'd start there if I were you,' she said, pointing to the dent she'd made earlier with her boot. 'It'll be under there if it's anywhere.'

Mine is not to reason why, and all that. I dug.

The earth was soft and the digging easy. I'd soon cleared an area about a yard square and two feet deep. There was a metallic clonk as my shovel went in again.

'There,' said Lady Hardcastle. 'That wasn't so difficult to find after all.'

'Not for you,' I said. 'You just stood there tutting.'

'It's an important part of the job. Is it a drain cover?'

I scraped away a little more earth.

'It does seem to be,' I said. 'Should I clear it completely?'

'Yes, please, dear. We need to be able to lift it.'

I carried on digging.

A few minutes later we were standing beside a shallow hole with a cast-iron drain cover at the bottom. It had a recessed handle, so I tried to lift it.

Nothing happened.

I tried again.

Still nothing.

'This might be the time to switch from tutting to helping,' I said.

With a tut and a sigh, Lady Hardcastle crouched beside me. It took us a few moments to work out how we might both get a grip on the handle but we managed it in the end.

'After three,' I said.

'One-two-three-heave?' she said.

'That's what "after three" means, yes.'

'You might have meant that we pull on "three".'

'In which case I'd have said, "On three," not "After three."'

'Yes, but—'

'You're just trying to delay the moment when you have to actually do something, aren't you?'

'It's as though you can read my mind, dear. After three?'

'One . . . two . . . three.'

With two of us lifting, there were finally signs of movement.

'Another go,' I said.

'After three?'

'After three.'

'Not on thr—'

'One . . . two . . . three.'

The cover lifted. It was hinged on the wall side, and the hinges were rusted and stiff, but it definitely lifted. We shifted our grip and heaved together till the lid was standing upright and the opening revealed.

We peered in and saw a cast-iron ladder leading down into the darkness.

'Do we go down there?' I asked.

'We do,' said Lady Hardcastle. 'You first.'

I started down the ladder while Lady Hardcastle lit the lantern.

She passed it to me and I held it low to try to see what lay below me. The answer, almost disappointingly, was a stone floor.

'It doesn't go very far down,' I said. 'No more than six feet, I'd say.'

'Excellent,' said Lady Hardcastle. 'Just as I expected. When you get to the bottom you should find a tunnel. It won't be large, but it should be big enough to get through without too much difficulty.'

I climbed carefully down and stood on the damp flagstones. Sure enough, there was an arched, brick-lined tunnel, about four feet high.

'You're right,' I called.

'Go down it,' she said. 'I'll be right behind you.'

Holding the lantern in front of me, I crouched and waddled along what turned out to be a passage only a few feet long. It opened into another chamber, similar to the one I had just left, though this one had another inspection cover in the floor. I turned so that the lantern would light the way for Lady Hardcastle, who was, as promised, coming along behind me.

Lady Hardcastle's height made her elegant, no matter the occasion. If she chose, it could also make her appear commanding, or even intimidating. But it was no help in getting through tight spaces, and she emerged a good deal less gracefully than I had.

'Do we lift this one, too?' I asked, pointing at the drain cover beneath our feet.

'No, that one leads to the drains. Unless you have a particular fondness for drains?'

'No, that time we escaped through the sewers in Salzburg cured me of any romantic notions I might have had about drain exploration. But if not that, then what are we doing here?'

'We're looking for the entrance to Teddy Elderkin's treasure vault, of course.'

'And how do we know it's here? How do we know this isn't just the access to the drains?'

'Well, we don't *know*, as such, but we have a pretty good idea. If you look at the way all the gutters and downpipes are arranged around the building, this isn't at all an obvious place to put the access point. The internal drainage from the house almost certainly converges at the rear of the house, near the kitchens. There's a manhole cover next to the terrace – you must have noticed it.'

'I had not.'

'Well, it's there. It's quite decorative but it usually has a planter on it.'

'Another one of those giant's goblet things that the Freers were so disappointed by the other day?' I said.

'Yes – they clearly come as a set. Anyway, that's where the main drain runs and that's where you'd want an inspection whatnot. So this inspection whatnot must be here for another reason.'

'Not inspecting the whatnots.'

'Indeed not. Though to make it effective as a disguise for the vault entrance, it had to actually have the facility for inspecting them, no matter how inconvenient or pointless that might be. So he built his vault and put a drain cover down here to disguise it. With that done, he put a statue commemorating the Battle of Vitoria next to the entrance as a reminder of where his wealth had come from. Or possibly as a joke. Either way, he died without making much more use of the treasure, and the house was bought by Tobacco Man. He was vain and proud, and wanted to mark his territory by adding new elements to the building.'

'You read all this somewhere?'

'No, dear, pure conjecture. But all businessmen are vain and proud – it's not a massive leap. Anyway, his architect drew up his plans, but as I said on the way here, the builder was a conscientious fellow and realized the new additions would compromise the access to the drains. And so he built the little extension tunnel we just crawled through so that future drain inspectors could continue to have access to their precious sewage system.'

'And so somewhere in this cramped little . . . what are we calling it? Antechamber? Vestibule?'

'Ooh, vestibule – I like that.'

'Somewhere in this cramped little vestibule, then, is a hidden door to the vault wherein lies the lost treasure of Sir Theodore Elderkin?'

'That's certainly my working hypothesis, yes. I imagine there's a concealed latch or lever somewhere. It will operate a sophisticated mechanism that will move some of these stone blocks to reveal the vault.'

'And why do you imagine that?'

'Because it would be utterly delightful if there were. I really, really want there to be latches and mechanisms and sliding stone blocks. Help me search.'

The 'vestibule' was about six foot square with a flagstone floor. One wall was dominated by the small tunnel entrance, above which was what was left of the original iron access ladder. It had been cut off at the bottom to make way for the new tunnel, and at the top, where a heavy-looking stone slab formed the roof of the chamber and was, presumably, braced on the foundations of the new wing. The other three walls were of plain, dressed stone blocks of varying sizes, from smaller than half a brick to larger than a couple of loaves of bread, but all smooth and very precisely joined.

We took a wall each and began exploring with our fingertips. I could find no purchase between the blocks so it didn't seem as though any of them could be pulled out to reveal Lady Hardcastle's putative lever. Instead I pressed them, hoping they might move inwards instead. Nothing.

'Any luck?' I asked when I had exhausted all the possibilities of my chosen wall.

'Nothing,' said Lady Hardcastle. 'I'll do the third wall, you look for something else. There must be something here.'

She started pushing and poking at the third wall while I looked around in the lantern-light.

The tunnel and its surrounds were of Victorian red brick, which would be ideal for hiding secret mechanisms, but they were later additions and could be discounted without further examination.

What remained of the ladder could be discounted, too. No matter how strong the temptation to make use of the fact that ladders already look like secret mechanisms, it seemed foolish to hide such a thing where it might be activated by accident. The two manhole-cover hooks hanging from the ladder were interesting but irrelevant.

The ceiling was a solid slab of what I presumed to be very thick stone. There was clearly nothing there.

Then there was the floor. Ordinary flagstones. Not too worn – the place wouldn't have had many visitors over the years – and still with reasonably crisp edges. Any of them might conceal something useful, but they were all too large to be easily lifted.

And that just left the drain cover. Like the one Lady Hardcastle remembered from the rear of the house, it was made of cast iron. It was ornate and decorative, with what I presumed was the Elderkin family shield at its centre, bordered by an elaborate design of inter-woven vines and roses. There were two holes to accept the hooks hanging on the ladder.

I knelt to examine it more closely. The vines of the ivy were depicted in relief, while the leaves, and the roses – which were the stylized heraldic type – all sat well proud of the surface. Having nothing better to do, I began trying to twist the roses as though they were doorknobs.

They all moved.

Each of them rotated easily about its centre, and all but one spun freely. The last one gave a little more resistance and stopped after a quarter turn, as one of ivy leaves flipped up with a loud click.

Lady Hardcastle stopped her poking and turned round.

'What have you found?' she asked.

'A keyhole,' I said, and took off my brooch.

The lock was old and slightly stiff, but it wasn't too badly cor-roded and it took only a few minutes' work to carefully tease it open with my trusty picklocks.

There was another click, louder and deeper in pitch, then a grating noise as, in full accordance with Lady Hardcastle's wishes, some sort of counterweighted mechanism rumbled into action.

A section of wall of a similar size to the Victorian tunnel slowly slid outwards to reveal a flight of stone steps leading downwards.

'Would you like to go first this time?' I said.

'A kind offer, dear, but I think you should. That way, if I lose my footing I'll have something soft to land on.'

I took the lantern and set off down the steps.

At the bottom of the steps we found ourselves in what might best be described as a grotto. To one side was a tailor's dummy wearing an officer's uniform of the 8th Dragoon Guards. A crested helmet of black leather and brass topped with a black plume sat on a hat block in a recess. A viciously heavy cavalry sword was mounted on a wooden stand, with its scabbard in another recess. There was a portrait of a handsome young officer hanging on the wall. He was dressed in the same uniform, wearing the same sword. Other mementoes of the Peninsular War filled more niches and alcoves around the walls.

In the centre of the room was a very large chest. Made of some dark, heavy wood, it had an arched top and was bound with thick iron bands. It was locked.

'Well, if this isn't the treasure of the Battle of Vitoria,' said Lady Hardcastle, 'then this is certainly where it used to be kept. This is quite the museum.'

'I like Elderkin a little more for it,' I said. 'If the Freers' account is accurate, he was a hero. But he chose to keep it all private. He wanted to commemorate his part in the war, but down here, where only he could see it. Other men – usually men who did far less – would have had all this on display in the entrance hall.'

'You're quite right – I've been to many houses exactly like that.'

'Do we think the chest contains the treasure?'

'It's either that or some old curtains he put down here for safe-keeping,' said Lady Hardcastle. 'Work your magic, tiny lock-picker. Let's have a look and see.'

I crouched in front of the chest, directing Lady Hardcastle to hold the lantern to best illuminate the lock, and began work.

It was a particularly well-made lock, and it didn't yield immediately to my charms. But I knew I would best it soon enough – all that was needed was patience and concentration.

I didn't hear the footsteps in the chamber above us, and the first I knew that there was anything amiss was when Lady Hardcastle swung the lantern away from me and turned towards the stone stairs.

'We should have known you'd be here,' said Zeke Freer.

'But we'll take over now,' said Zibbie.

'Oh, do grow up, you silly children,' said Lady Hardcastle. 'If this does turn out to be the treasure, you'll have no claim to it. For one thing, you didn't find it. You didn't dig it up in a field, buried seventy paces west of a tree planted long after the treasure's original owner had died – it's here, in a room that's very much part of the house. If you're nice to the Farley-Strouds you might be able to negotiate a small finder's fee for alerting them to its existence in the first place, but your work here is done. Off you pop.'

'I very much think you should take us more seriously, Lady Hardcastle,' said Zeke. 'Zibbie?'

There was a familiar click.

I sighed.

'More terrifying people than you have pointed guns at us, poppet,' I said without looking up from my work. 'Put it away before you hurt yourself.'

'I don't think you understand the danger of your situation,' said Zibbie, in what she clearly imagined was a menacing voice.

I sighed again, and then stood up slowly, turning to face them.

Zeke was standing just inside the small room, with Zibbie behind him, holding a far-too-heavy pistol in her right hand and pointing it over his shoulder. If she fired and actually managed to hit someone or something, she could do some serious damage with a gun like that. But even if she missed, Zeke would probably lose the hearing in his right ear.

It would probably be best if we could prevent her from shooting.

Her hand was shaking under the weight of the pistol, but so far she was aiming somewhere in the vague direction of Sir Theodore's old uniform so I wasn't too worried. Yet. Things could turn ugly very quickly in such a small space, though, so it was no time for complacency.

'How did you get in without the key?' asked Zeke.

'How do you know we don't have the key?' said Lady Hardcastle.

'Because we have the key,' said Zibbie, holding it up in her free hand. 'It was in the base of that disgusting bust of Sir Teddy.'

'Aha,' said Lady Hardcastle. 'We'd been wondering why you smashed the bust. Thank you, dear, I think I understand everything now.'

The Freers frowned in unison, but didn't move. They seemed slightly less sure of themselves, but they weren't ready to give up just yet.

'What do you say we put the gun down and go back upstairs to see the Farley-Strouds?' said Lady Hardcastle. 'You'll have to face the consequences for killing poor Blackmore, but I'm reasonably sure you didn't actually intend to. We'd be prepared to speak up for you in mitigation.'

'Have you honestly not noticed that we have a gun?' asked Zeke. 'There'll be no facing of consequences.'

'You'll step aside,' said Zibbie.

'We'll take the treasure,' said Zeke.

'And then we'll be on our way,' said Zibbie.

'Far, far away,' said Zeke.

'Living comfortably on the proceeds of our patient and diligent work,' said Zibbie.

'Oh,' said Lady Hardcastle as she took a step to the side. 'I'm so sorry. I completely misunderstood the situation.' She gestured towards the chest. 'Please – go ahead. I presume your key will open the chest as well as the secret door.'

One of the few advantages we had in our line of work was that men, almost without exception, entirely failed to see us as any sort of threat. Just another well-to-do lady and her diminutive lady's maid, they thought. Nothing to worry about there. It should have been annoying, but it was so fantastically useful that we were actually rather pleased about it.

Dear Zeke didn't let us down.

Grinning, he stepped further into the room with his attention entirely upon the chest. No need to pay any heed to the well-dressed lady with the ready smile and chirpy manner standing to his left. What could she possibly do? She didn't even warrant a second glance.

Which was a shame. For him, at least.

If he'd been looking at Lady Hardcastle he would have noticed the slight change in her balance as she readied herself to swivel her body towards him. He'd have seen her right elbow as it hurtled at his face. He might even have had time to get out of the way before it struck him forcefully on the bridge of his nose.

I was fully prepared for the sickening crack as his nose broke, having been the one who taught her the move in the first place, but Zibbie wasn't at all ready to see her brother so abused. She yelped in shock and surprise at the sudden violence and her gun arm waved about erratically.

I was reasonably confident that she had no real intention of shooting either of us, but a frightened girl and a gun she doesn't properly understand is never a good combination. While Zeke was grunting, swearing, and trying to stem the sudden and explosive flow of blood from his shattered nose, I quickly stepped in front of her.

This focused her attention back on me, and I once more found myself in a dismayingly familiar position: someone who didn't like me very much was pointing a gun at me.

I kept my hands low and my voice quiet and steady.

'Stay calm, Zibbie,' I said. 'We can sort this out. There's no need for anyone else to get hurt.'

'She broke his nose,' she said.

'She did. And isn't that enough? Put the gun down.'

'I've got a better idea,' she said, suddenly fierce. 'You put your hands up.'

I don't like giving away trade secrets, but this was exactly the invitation I was hoping for – it gave me an excuse to move my arms.

I began to slowly raise my hands. All was well. She was expecting movement. She was still in control.

She wasn't expecting the suddenness and force of my next move, though.

I quickly ducked my body to the right. As I turned, I continued raising my arms and began to cross them, bringing the back of my right hand up against her right wrist and grabbing the barrel of the pistol in my left. Using my right hand as a pivot I was able to bend her wrist backwards, pointing the pistol even further away from us all and twisting it from her grip.

It's an effective technique, but not without risk. As we all immediately discovered.

Like all amateurs, Zibbie had her finger on the trigger so that, as I twisted the gun away, she inadvertently squeezed it.

The report wasn't anywhere near as loud as I had feared, but it was still a shock in the tiny room.

Zibbie shrieked, Zeke yelped, Lady Hardcastle tutted, and I was struck on the arm by a flake of stone from the wall, where the bullet had made a significant crater.

I handed the revolver to Lady Hardcastle, who broke it open and emptied the five remaining rounds and one spent cartridge into her hand. She put the gun on one of the stone shelves and the ammunition in the pocket of her jacket.

'There,' she said, 'that's better. I'm afraid it always ends this way when people point those things at us.' She looked at Zeke, who was still groaning. 'Oh, do stop making such a fuss, dear. Dr Fitzsimmons will set that for you in a jiffy and you'll be right as ninepence.'

Zeke said something colourfully uncomplimentary about Lady Hardcastle, who just tutted again and shook her head.

'Now,' she said, 'I'm going to go and fetch Sir Hector, and you're going to be good boys and girls for Aunt Florence. And don't be deceived by her size and her easy-going demeanour. Any nonsense from either of you and a broken nose will be the least of your worries.'

She went to push past Zibbie, but stopped at the sound of a shout from above.

'Are you down there, m'lady?'

It was Constable Hancock.

'Yes, Constable,' called Lady Hardcastle.

'Are you all right?'

'Quite all right, thank you, dear. But we have a couple of new guests for your cell if you wouldn't mind. If you start making your way back out again, we'll send them up to you.'

'Right you are, m'lady.'

There was a minor amount of sullen grumbling from the Freers, but the fight had gone out of them. We gave Constable Hancock time to get back through the tunnel and then ushered them up the steps.

◆ ◆ ◆

I followed Lady Hardcastle up the final ladder and into the Monday afternoon light to find quite the gathering. Constable Hancock and Sergeant Dobson were holding Zeke and Zibbie Freer, though they didn't seem to need much holding. Sir Hector and Lady Farley-Stroud looked anxiously on.

'Oh, Emily,' said Lady Farley-Stroud. 'Thank goodness you're safe.'

'Of course we are, dear,' said Lady Hardcastle. 'Why wouldn't we be?'

'We saw these two scoundrels arrive on their bicycles. Hector was going to go out and give them a piece of his mind but we saw that she' – she pointed at Zibbie – 'was carrying a gun. They were heading in the same direction you'd gone. We telephoned the police station at once.'

'All's well as ends well,' said Sergeant Dobson. 'I'm goin' to arrest these two on suspicion of breakin' and enterin' last night here at The Grange. Is there anythin' else I should be addin'?'

'One or two things, Sergeant, yes,' said Lady Hardcastle. 'There's the theft of a landscape by Edgar Summerhays from the Littleton Cotterell Art Exhibition. The theft and destruction of a bust of Sir Theodore Elderkin from the same show. The theft – and, to be fair, the subsequent return – of Felix Ulysses Nisbet's bicycle from outside the village hall. Pointing this awful thing at Flo and me' – she handed the sergeant the revolver – 'and the killing of Russell Blackmore during the inaugural Woodworthy and Littleton

Cotterell Cycling Club's Annual Race and Convivial Ride.' She took the pistol ammunition from her pocket and dropped it in Constable Hancock's open hand.

'Ezekiel and Hephzibah Freer,' said Sergeant Dobson, 'I am arrestin' you for . . . for all them things what Lady Hardcastle just said.'

While he and the constable handcuffed the Freers, Sir Hector came over to us.

'Well, m'dear?' he said. 'Did you find it?'

'I'm not entirely sure,' said Lady Hardcastle. 'We certainly found something. Hold on a moment.' She turned to Constable Hancock. 'Miss Freer has a fancy key in her jacket pocket, Constable. Would you fish it out and pass it to Sir Hector for me, please?'

Hancock did as he was asked and Sir Hector held the key in the flat of his hand, looking at it as though it might be about to speak. Lady Hardcastle handed him the lantern and pointed to the open drain cover.

'If you go down the ladder there, you'll find a small chamber with an even smaller tunnel leading from it. Follow the tunnel – it's only a few feet long – to another chamber and a flight of stone steps. Go down the steps and you'll find . . . well, you'll find what you find.'

'You'll come with me, though?' he said.

'Would you mind if Flo accompanied you, dear? I confess I found the whole thing a little cramped.'

'Always said a chap should have Florence with him if he's goin' on an adventure,' said Sir Hector with a grin.

'You lead the way, though,' I said. 'You should see it all for yourself without someone blocking the view. I'll be right behind you.'

Sir Hector Farley-Stroud was not a young man. I was still unsure exactly how not-young he was, but I was prepared to guess at about seventy. He was, though, surprisingly sprightly and agile, and made a much better job of clambering and crouching his way to the treasure chamber than I had been expecting.

It wasn't long before we were standing in Sir Teddy's private museum, and Sir Hector was visibly moved.

'I had no idea,' he said, quietly. 'No idea at all. Look at all this.'

He spent a few minutes walking around the room, inspecting every item in detail. He touched the uniform jacket and held up the left sleeve, showing where it had been cut off in battle and sewn up for subsequent wear by the one-armed hero. Finally he came back to the huge chest, which he regarded with a mix of anticipation and trepidation.

'Don't know whether to open it now,' he said. 'Might be the solution to all m'problems. But it might contain an old dinner service and a canteen of cutlery.'

'We thought old curtains,' I said.

He laughed.

'Yes,' he said, 'that would be more my sort of luck.'

'There's only one way to find out for certain,' I said.

'There is, m'dear. There is.'

He crouched down and fitted the key into the keyhole on the front of the chest. It turned easily with the reassuring sound of a well-made and substantial lock. Reaching his arms wide, he grasped the sides of the arched lid and lifted it. We looked inside – the first people to see the contents of the chest for more than sixty years.

'Bugger me,' said Sir Hector, quietly.

Chapter Eighteen

We were still with a shocked Sir Hector and Lady Farley-Stroud an hour later, when Inspector Sunderland arrived at The Grange – Sergeant Dobson had telephoned him as soon as he received Sir Hector's call.

Jenkins showed him in to the drawing room, where we were all sitting in armchairs drinking tea.

'Good afternoon, sir. Good afternoon, my lady,' said the inspector. He seemed to notice Lady Hardcastle and me for the first time. 'Oh, and good afternoon, my lady. Good afternoon, miss. I wasn't certain you'd be here, though I confess I hoped you might be.'

We acknowledged him with raised-teacup salutes.

'I came straight here,' he continued. 'I presumed this was where the action would be. But I take it from the absence of Dobson and Hancock that the Freers have been arrested?'

'Banged up in chokey by our trusty local rozzers,' I said.

'Good show. Is everyone here all right?'

'We're all fine, thank you, Inspector,' said Lady Farley-Stroud. 'Emily and Florence took care of things magnificently.'

The inspector smiled.

'Yes,' he said. 'They tend to do that.'

We raised our teacups in salute once more.

'The reason I'm glad you two are here is that I was hoping you might be able to provide me with a decent picture of what's been going on before I interview the Freers. Why were they here? Why did they have a pistol? Dobson was light on the detail – he just said I should hurry to The Grange.'

'Well, I was here,' said Sir Hector, 'and I don't have the first idea what's goin' on. I'd welcome a proper explanation m'self.'

'As would I,' said Lady Farley-Stroud.

'Well . . .' said Lady Hardcastle with undisguised relish. She took a sip of her tea while she composed her thoughts.

'You'd better sit down, Inspector,' said Sir Hector. 'Looks like it's goin' to take a while. Cup of tea?'

'Thank you, sir,' said the inspector. He helped himself to tea and settled into an armchair with his notebook and pencil.

'A quick précis of the Sir Theodore Elderkin story for the inspector first, I think,' said Lady Hardcastle. 'The short version is that he was a hero of the Peninsular War and he bought The Grange in 1814, after losing his arm at the Battle of Vitoria and being sent home on a full pension. The rumour was that he bought the house with treasure looted from the French baggage train after the battle. He and his wife died in 1851. A tobacco merchant bought The Grange and built the neo-Gothic additions. He sold it to Hector in 1876.'

'Just got back from India, d'you see?' said Sir Hector. 'Suited us perfectly.'

'I couldn't imagine you both anywhere else, dear,' said Lady Hardcastle. 'But years pass and the story of Teddy Elderkin's treasure is forgotten, until two self-styled treasure hunters from Yorkshire – the brother and sister Ezekiel and Hephzibah Freer – see a reference to it in . . . actually, I can't quite remember what they said about that. They learned of the treasure, anyway, and followed the trail of clues to Chipping Bevington. You'll be able to persuade them to tell you the precise nature of their discoveries, I'm sure, but at some point they decided that they needed to know what The Grange looked like in Elderkin's day. before Tobacco Man – what *was* his name, Hector dear?'

'James Tazewell,' said Sir Hector.

'Of Tazewell's Fine Snuff? I had a great uncle who swore by it.'

'Among other things, yes,' said Sir Hector. 'Owned a snuff mill north of the city. Sold pipe tobacco mostly, though. Very wealthy fella.'

'Well I never. So the Freers wanted to know what The Grange looked like before Tazewell added his delightful pointy bits to the house, and they heard that a painting depicting exactly that would be on display at the Littleton Cotterell Art Exhibition. They devised a horribly amateurish plan – but a dismayingly successful one, as it turned out – to steal the painting on opening day. They came in through the rear door of the hall – you really must persuade your ladies to lock that, by the way, Gertie dear. They brought a bucket of smelly flammables in with them, set a fire in an unlocked office, and made off with the painting in the confusion. They also took the bust of Sir Theodore, which they somehow knew contained the key to the vault. You'll have to ask them about that, I'm afraid – I have no idea how they knew it would be there.'

'I shall, don't worry,' said the inspector, who was making copious notes as Lady Hardcastle spoke.

'Once back outside the hall, they carefully – and from what we saw of the remains of the stretcher, Hector, they were *very* careful – they carefully took the painting from its frame and smashed the bust to retrieve the key. I presume it was in the base. Do you remember? Gertie insisted the base was alabaster like the bust itself, but I rather think it had been replaced with something altogether more frangible with the key inside it. That would be why we found all those tiny bits, I'd say. But anyway. This next part is just speculation on my part, but it's the only thing that explains all the subsequent events, so I'm happy to put it forward as a hypothesis. I believe they removed the saddle from a very distinctive BSA Road Racer bicycle that they'd seen parked regularly outside the hall. They rolled up the painting and put it in the . . . what's the tube where the seat goes called, Flo dear?'

'It's the seat tube, my lady,' I said.

'How boringly literal. I was hoping it might be the descending linear barge tube or something equally unfathomable. But they rolled up the painting, hid it in the bicycle, replaced the saddle and joined the crowd of panicked art lovers outside the hall, knowing that the bicycle would be there when they returned next day to retrieve the painting.'

'How could they be certain of that?' asked the inspector.

'Well, they couldn't, could they?' said Lady Hardcastle. 'But they couldn't be sure they wouldn't be spotted setting their fire, or crossing the hall in the wrong direction with a painting under their arms. The whole thing was a shambles of inept planning, a failure waiting to happen, but they thought themselves so clever. And they got away with it up to that point. They'd seen the distinctive bicycle at the same place every day for a few days so they reasoned that it would still be there – or would have returned from wherever its owner took it when it wasn't there. So they came back the next day and stole the bicycle. We overheard its owner, a Mr Felix Nisbet, complaining of the theft to Constable Hancock.'

'I remember hearing of it,' said the inspector. 'I had no idea it might be connected.'

'No, it took me a while to work that one out. I presume the Freers casually rode it to some safe spot where they wouldn't be overlooked as they took off the saddle and removed the stolen painting. And that was when their plan started to unravel. It turns out that, though distinctive, the BSA Road Racer isn't rare – at least not here in Littleton Cotterell, where there are so many keen cyclists. They had stashed their loot not in the bicycle they saw there regularly, but in another machine that was only there for the day. This was not at all how it was supposed to work. They had to trace the owner of the other Road Racer, and I imagine they had no idea how to proceed. But then fortune swung back in their direction and their chance came in the form of the inaugural Woodworthy and Littleton Cotterell Cycling Club's Annual Race and Convivial Ride. With all the local bicycles assembled in the same place, they were able to find the one holding their vital clue to the treasure.'

'Why bother, though?' asked the inspector. 'What was so important about the painting?'

'In reality, nothing at all,' said Lady Hardcastle. 'It's valuable in its own right – more so as part of a pair – but to them it represented the most vital clue in their search for the treasure of Teddy Elderkin. It was no such thing, of course, but in their inexperience they'd built it up in their minds as the most important thing, and they knew they absolutely had to have it. It would show them, they believed, some clue to the entrance to the secret treasure vault.'

'But it didn't?'

'As it turned out, no, it didn't. Nevertheless, they pursued it. They identified the bicycle as being the one belonging to Russell Blackmore. They saw it up close when he stopped to speak to us in the queue for registration before the race. The next part of their plan could now begin.'

'You're about to tell us they murdered Blackmore?' said the inspector.

'I can't prove it, but again it's the only thing that makes sense. I suggest they'd scouted the route and found a suitable location for their bizarrely impractical new scheme. They either moved one of the direction signs or made their own—'

'One moment,' said the inspector as he flicked back a few pages in his notebook. 'I asked Dobson to check with the committee . . . ah, here we are. All their signs were accounted for when they went round to collect them back up.'

'So they made their own, then. That might give you some proof if you can find evidence of sign-making in their rooms at the Dog and Duck. They broke off from the main pack – easy enough to do in the cheerful chaos of the ride – and cut across to the other side of the loop where they'd hidden their sign. It's possible to see riders coming from a decent distance along that stretch of road by the blasted tree, so I imagine one of them just waited until they saw Blackmore coming, and set up the sign to point him down the lane. The other would be waiting to stop him once he was out of sight of the road, and then the sign carrier would arrive. An altercation ensued, during which one of the Freers struck Blackmore on the head with the signpost, rendering him unconscious. They removed the saddle from his Road Racer, retrieved the painting, then hid Blackmore, bicycle and saddle in the copse and headed for home.'

'How did they know Blackmore would be alone? Why did they imagine he wouldn't tell the police what had happened the moment he was conscious again?' said the inspector.

'All valid questions, but again I point to the general air of amateurishness that colours the whole venture. It's as though they had read of such things in children's adventure stories and thought it would all be simple. But now they had the Summerhays and could finally see where the loot might be. They planned their survey, and arranged to visit The Grange while Gertie and Hector were in Gloucester for the day. Flo and I witnessed their frustration as they failed to find anything helpful – although, entirely by chance, they did come close to a clue when they lifted one of those goblet planters to see what was underneath.'

'Bought them in '96 from a fella in Birmingham,' said Sir Hector. 'Just wanted one to hide the drain cover by the terrace, but he would only sell 'em as a pair.'

'And it was drains and drain covers that were the key to it all, if only they had known. Anyway, that approach failed, so they went back to their books and stories and fixated instead on a poem they found about an elm tree.'

'Is that why you wanted to know when it was planted?' asked Sir Hector.

'Yes, dear. They were convinced they'd found the solution and dug a decent-sized hole in the grounds in search of the treasure.'

'Mogg found that. Made a joke about ambitious badgers, or giant moles.'

'That was when we learned that they were planning to keep all the treasure, so we told them to get lost and never come back. Meanwhile, we had a conversation with Daisy in the pub where I mentioned that the painting had a brother. They must have overheard me, which is why they broke in here last night to look at it. And the rest you know.'

'I don't know it,' said Inspector Sunderland.

'Oh, sorry, Inspector dear. View of the house from the west, monument to the Battle of Vitoria, drain cover, exploration, miniature museum, big chest full of treasure. Fight with the Freers – disappointingly uneventful – arrests, arrival of Bristol CID, and a big pot of tea.'

'There actually is treasure?' said the inspector. 'Real treasure?'

'More than Jenkins and Dewi could carry,' said Sir Hector. 'Gold, silver, gems, pearls – proper loot. Chap must have brought it back in smaller chests – no one could lift the big 'un.'

'Well I never. I thought it was all going to turn out to be some fantasy the Freers got wrapped up in.'

317

'No,' I said. 'It's all very real. What happens to it now?'

'Beyond my experience, I'm afraid,' said the inspector. 'I just deal with petty villains. Speaking of which, I'd best get down to the village and see the Freers, if you'll excuse me. I'll need formal statements from you all, as always, but that can wait.'

'Of course, of course,' said Sir Hector. 'Thank you for comin' straight here – we appreciate it. Things might have been very different if Em'ly and Florence hadn't been here – we'd have been in dire need of more policemen then.'

'Always happy to help,' said the inspector, standing and shaking Sir Hector's hand. 'Thank you for the tea. I'll see myself out.'

A little over two weeks later, Lady Hardcastle and I were in the morning room enjoying a leisurely breakfast.

'I do love having a mystery to solve,' said Lady Hardcastle as she sliced another sausage in half lengthways, to add to the elaborate sandwich she was building, 'but it does throw the rest of one's life into sharp contrast, wouldn't you say?'

'We could invite our friends round for dinner again – that was fun.'

Angelina Goodacre had joined us for the long-promised dinner with Miss Caudle, Dr Gosling, and the Sunderlands. I had been delighted by how well Angelina had got on with everyone, and the evening had been a great success.

'It was enormous fun, and we definitely should do that sort of thing more often. But—'

'And you were "specially commended" for your Shanghai picture at the exhibition.'

'Indeed. That was very flattering. But—'

'But all that – good friends, a warm home, tales of sub-aquatic vole civilizations and correspondence with the great minds of the age – aren't enough for you?' I asked.

'When you put it like that, I seem monstrously ungrateful for my wonderful life. But no, that's not what I meant. I was thinking that no matter how satisfying the everyday might be, it lacks a certain urgency and excitement.'

'I actually rather like it when no one's pointing a gun at me.'

'She was pointing it at the wall for the most part, dear – don't exaggerate.'

'But she wasn't the first, was she?'

'She was not, no. And I doubt she shall be the last. Harry is still blathering on about some Serbian nationalists he's been keeping an eye on. I get the distinct impression we'll be summoned for SSB duties before the end of the year.'

Lady Hardcastle's brother, Harry, had tempted us out of our well-earned retirement from the dangerous world of international espionage nearly two years earlier. We had joined him as officers in the newly formed Secret Service Bureau but had been called upon very little. The political situation in Europe was growing more fractious by the week, though, and Lady Hardcastle was right: even if his suspicions of the Serbian nationalists came to nothing, there was enough cooking up elsewhere that we would soon be longing for the mundanity of village life.

I was about to ask for some more details on the Serbs when the telephone rang.

'I'd better get that,' I said. 'It might be for you.'

'That's the spirit,' she said. 'If it's Harry, tell him to find someone else to do his dirty work.'

It wasn't Harry; it was an invitation to lunch at The Grange.

319

The spaniels – Clotho, Lachesis and Atropos – greeted us on the drive with wagging tails and excited barks; Sir Hector and Lady Farley-Stroud greeted us on the terrace with kisses on the cheek and chilled champagne.

'Oh, I say, how marvellous,' said Lady Hardcastle as she accepted her glass. 'Do I take it we're celebrating?'

'We most certainly are,' said Lady Farley-Stroud. 'Hector received a letter from the coroner this morning, didn't you, dear?'

'I did indeed, my little brandy snap. Didn't want there to be any shadow hangin' over the treasure, so we did everythin' above board. Reported the find to the coroner, spellin' out exactly where it was found and explainin' as much of the story as Sunderland was able to get from the Freer creatures. Seems that because the identity of the original owner was known, they had to trace his heirs. But he didn't have any. No long-lost nieces or nephews, neither. The fact that it wasn't actually Elderkin's treasure in the first place didn't seem to feature – spoils of war and all that.'

'So you own the treasure?' said Lady Hardcastle. 'How wonderful.'

'Actually, m'dear,' said Lady Farley-Stroud, 'it belongs to the person who found it. Which would be you.'

'Or it would,' said Sir Hector, 'were it not for the letter the coroner received from one Emily, Lady Hardcastle of Badger Lane, Littleton Cotterell. Apparently she renounced any claim on it. She explained how the treasure was found in a room that was clearly part of the original fabric of The Grange and should properly belong to the house's current owners.'

'We can't thank you enough,' said Lady Farley-Stroud as she leapt up from her chair and hugged us both.

'The Grange is saved,' said Sir Hector, 'and we shall be forever in your debt.'

'Oh, don't be silly,' said Lady Hardcastle. 'Anyone else would have done the same.'

'They absolutely would not,' said Lady Farley-Stroud. 'And we shall see to it that you both receive embarrassingly expensive gifts for birthdays and Christmases for the rest of time.'

'Now that really is being silly,' I said. 'But it's a kind thought.'

'What will you do with Sir Teddy's war things?' asked Lady Hardcastle.

'Already workin' with the museum at Chippin' Bevington to set up a special exhibit commemoratin' the man and his story.'

'That's perfect,' said Lady Hardcastle. She raised her glass. 'To Sir Theodore Elderkin,' she said, 'saviour of The Grange.'

Author's Note

May Day celebrations had been an important part of English life for centuries, but were in something of a decline until they were revived by the Victorians. While they still retained vestiges of their pagan origins, they were, by the beginning of the twentieth century, much more genteel affairs of the sort of which Lady Farley-Stroud would approve.

The expensively bound *Complete Works of Shakespeare* was inspired by the true story of a copy of the *Rubáiyát of Omar Khayyám*, bound by Francis Sangorski between 1909 and 1911. It was initially valued at £1,000 (equivalent to around £146,000 in 2023), but it proved difficult to find a buyer for it. It eventually sold at auction for £405 (£59,000 in 2023) and was packaged up to be sent to its purchaser, Gabriel Wells, a book dealer from New York. It was due to sail on 6 April 1912 but its delivery to the port was delayed and the ship left without it. Instead it was booked on the next available ship, due to leave on Wednesday, 10 April 1912. The ship was the RMS *Titanic* and the book now lies at the bottom of the Atlantic.

Edgar Summerhays is not a famous Georgian artist.

The Dragoon Guards were British heavy cavalry regiments from the eighteenth century onwards. At the time of the Peninsular War there were seven Dragoon Guards regiments, which is why the fictitious Sir Theodore Elderkin served in the equally fictitious 8th regiment. It was actually the 3rd, 4th and 5th Dragoon Guards who fought at Vitoria.

There are many stories about the Rolls-Royce company and its refusal to admit that its cars broke down, and most of them are almost certainly apocryphal. Nevertheless, the official terminology for a Rolls-Royce breakdown does seem to be 'failure to proceed'.

Debrett's is a British company founded in 1769. It now offers coaching on social skills for individuals and businesses, but its most famous publications are its directory of the British peerage and its guide to etiquette. The sections mentioned by Lady Hardcastle and Flo are, of course, fictitious.

I promise I will rewrite the circus story one day.

BSA originally sold parts – or fittings – from which bicycle builders would construct the finished machine, and in 1910 the company also began selling complete bicycles. The Road Racer was one of their more popular models and was available both as a set of fittings and a complete bicycle. By 1912 it was not, perhaps, the elite racing machine I've made it out to be, but it appealed because of its ubiquity – it's easy for you to find pictures and say, 'Ohh, so that's what he's on about.' Apart from the Goodacre bikes, the other makes and models mentioned are also real 1912 machines.

Non-British readers have asked me about pronunciation in the past, so a quick reminder might be in order. Gloucestershire is pronounced GLOS-ter-sher. Berkeley is pronounced BARK-lee. Leicestershire is LESS-ter-sher. Wolseley is WOOLS-lee. Featherstonhaugh is FAN-shaw. No one knows why.

Bradford City won the FA Cup final in the replay on 26 April 1911, beating Newcastle United 1–0 at Old Trafford in Manchester.

Lady Hardcastle observes the cognitive bias now known as the 'frequency illusion' (named by linguistics professor Arnold Zwicky in 2005) where we sometimes find that soon after we notice something for the first time we seem to see it everywhere. The phenomenon is also known as the 'Baader–Meinhof phenomenon', a term coined around 1994 after Terry Mullen wrote a letter to a newspaper asking why he was suddenly seeing references to the German political terrorists everywhere after seeing their name for the first time only recently. It explains why it seems that everyone is driving the same make of car as us when we get a new one, or why pregnant women suddenly notice that every woman in the world is currently pregnant. I couldn't imagine that no one had observed the phenomenon before, but if they hadn't, I'm happy for Lady Hardcastle to be a pioneer again.

Lady Hardcastle and Flo also talk about semantic satiation. Although the concept – where repeated words begin to sound odd or lose their meaning – was described by E. Severance and M. F. Washburn in *The American Journal of Psychology* in 1907, the term 'semantic satiation' (sometimes also 'semantic saturation' or 'verbal satiation') wasn't coined until 1961, when it appeared in the *Journal of Experimental Psychology* in an article by Leon James and Wallace E. Lambert entitled 'Semantic Satiation Among Bilinguals'. This is why Lady Hardcastle knows what it is but doesn't know what to call it.

Berkeley Castle in Berkeley, Gloucestershire is still owned by the Berkeley family. It is known for many things, most famously for the gruesome murder of King Edward II in 1327. It has only been open to the public since 1956, which is why the cyclists in 1912 can look but not visit.

Slang terms for money can be fascinating. A tenner (£10) is obvious, though finnup (£5) is less obvious and has fallen from use (it's said to be a Yiddish pronunciation of the German *fünf* – five). You may be aware of pony (£25) or monkey (£500). But cow (£1,000), plum (£100,000), and marigold (£1,000,000) have also, sadly, disappeared from our daily lexicon.

Puckfist, as well as being archaic slang for a braggart, is an old West Midlands word for the puffball fungus. It's also, in case you're interested, an obsolete seventeenth-century word for a miser.

It was Louis Rustin, a French cyclist, who introduced the pre-glued inner tube patch in 1922. The chemist Paul Doumenjou came up with the special glue that Lady Hardcastle envisaged.

The common law relating to treasure trove in England and Wales was finally codified in the Treasure Act 1996. Before then, the situation was roughly as outlined by Lady Hardcastle and the Freers. Like everything, it was a lot more complicated than that, but none of them is a legal expert so their vague understanding will suffice.

About the Author

T E Kinsey grew up in London and read history at Bristol University. *A Fire at the Exhibition* is the tenth story in the Lady Hardcastle Mystery series, and he is also the author of the Dizzy Heights Mystery series. His website is at tekinsey.uk and you can follow him on Twitter @tekinsey as well as on Facebook: www.facebook.com/tekinsey.

Photo © 2018 Clifton Photographic Company

Follow the Author on Amazon

If you enjoyed this book, follow T E Kinsey on Amazon to be notified when the author releases a new book!

To do this, please follow these instructions:

Desktop:

1) Search for the author's name on Amazon or in the Amazon App.
2) Click on the author's name to arrive on their Amazon page.
3) Click the 'Follow' button.

Mobile and Tablet:

1) Search for the author's name on Amazon or in the Amazon App.
2) Click on one of the author's books.
3) Click on the author's name to arrive on their Amazon page.
4) Click the 'Follow' button.

Kindle eReader and Kindle App:

If you enjoyed this book on a Kindle eReader or in the Kindle App, you will find the author 'Follow' button after the last page.